BOOKS WITH HEART

VOLUME 1

C.D. GORRI

BOOKS WITH HEART

VOLUME 1

A Limited Edition Paperback Anthology
by C.D. Gorri
Edited by BookNookNuts

For those of you who love to read books with heart,

I hope you find something you like within the pages of this anthology. Especially those of you who came to Literary Love Savannah 2023 to meet me! Thank you from the bottom of my heart.

del mare alla stella,
C.D. Gorri

Be sure to sign up for my newsletter:
https://www.cdgorri.com/newsletter

MARKED BY THE DEVIL

A PURELY PARANORMAL ROMANCE BOOK

BLURB

Stephanie Decatur is a good girl. She goes to Church, volunteers to help the elderly, and works as a preservation activist. So, what is she to do when a Devil marks her for his own?

Tall, dark, and handsome, Avail Leeds is just your average little Jersey Devil! The millionaire playboy is determined to keep his true nature secret from the prying eyes of the public. Insta-famous for his scandalous lifestyle, one nefarious accusation has him hiding in his tower! Hardly the image for a devil like him, but what's a guy to do when the family lawyers order him to stay put?

Stephanie Decatur has no idea what she's setting herself up for when she comes knocking on the door of the infamous Avail Leeds. The sassy female works for a committee that is trying to stop a development company from tearing down acres of the Pine Barrens for a new strip mall. Short the funds needed to keep the land a sanctuary for local wildlife; she is determined to try her best to secure them. Surely, the wealthy Leeds family can spare some cash for a good cause.

It's the last quarter moon, Avail's Devil is bursting to be let out when he spies the curvy young woman encroaching on his land! It's too late for her to run away once he sets eyes on her. Beast and man agree, this female has been marked by the devil!

PROLOGUE

S nap! Flash! Snap! Bang!

"Over here! The Dark Prince is by the window!"

Click! Bang! Snap!

"Oh, for fuck's sake," Avail growled. He could feel that secret part of him pushing to be released. Power pulsed through his veins, his beast demanding to be set free, but he fought the temptation.

Snap! Flash! The horde of paparazzi swarmed outside the entrance to the Leeds Foundation, snapping pictures and banging on the polished reinforced glass doors in hopes of catching a glimpse of him. *Their prey.*

If they only knew. He growled aloud, eyes flashing at the throng below. The man they hunted was not the useless, spoiled playboy they took him for. Avail

Leeds was something more. A predator. Not like those uncouth vultures circling with their cameras and cheap shots.

He was the real thing. A creature humankind built into legend with stories of midnight encounters. He snorted a harsh laugh. *If only I could show them. Grrrr.*

They'd been there since daybreak hoping to get a statement or a picture of him, but Avail had managed to dodge them. He was no stranger to this kind of game. *Unfortunately for him. Sigh.* They'd dubbed him the "Naughty Dark Prince" years ago, recording his exploits and reporting them with more than a touch of exaggeration, as a constant source of entertainment for *normals* the world over.

As heir to the Leeds fortune, Avail had been in the spotlight since birth. Especially after his parent's tragic death when he was an infant. His grandparents had brought him up with the finest education and surroundings a boy could have. So, yes, he was known to indulge in a bit of luxury and sport in between his family's foundation and other philanthropic works.

The Leeds family was enormously wealthy. The money had come to the family at first from the land itself. Natural resources like coal and oil had started the family's legacy. Later on, they'd dabbled in manufacturing, then real estate and development. Now the family was known for their charity.

Avail himself had increased their holdings by playing the stock market and investing in several internet start-ups. He certainly had a marvelous head for figures. The mathematical and the female kind.

He gritted his teeth at the reminder. The latter had, once again, caused him this current headache. Women would surely be the death of him, or so his grandmother promised. Often. *Oh dear. Grandmother is certain to be angry this time.*

"Denise!" Avail groaned his secretary's name as he looked out his office window.

So many of them are here this time. Ugh. He slumped back in his Perigold executive chair. The exotic French walnut was highly polished and smelled of lemons. The seat was made from the leather of a sixteen-point stag that his great-grandfather had taken down himself. He remembered that day.

Hunting with Grandfather was often the best time of his life. After all, he'd taught Avail everything he knew about controlling his inner demons, so to speak. He sure missed the old man.

His darling grandmother ordered the leather made from the buck's skin to be turned into this bit of posh office furniture for Avail when he took over as president of the Leeds Foundation. Conditioned with only the best mixtures of Mink and Neatsfoot oils, the chair was fucking amazing, if he did say so himself. Soft and strong, perfect for his six-foot four-inch, two-hundred and forty-pound frame.

He was certainly grateful for it as he slunk down into the buttery depths and cradled his head in his hands. It was only seven o'clock in the morning. How did those vultures find him so quickly?

"What have you done now?" *Why does her voice have to reach that pitch?* He cringed.

"Just the usual, Denise," he answered with a grin.

His silk shirt of the night before hung open revealing a large expanse of his muscled chest, evenly covered in a dusting of black hair. It matched the midnight dark strands atop his head that earned him the hated moniker *"Naughty Dark Prince".*

Of course, if he'd bothered to stay out of the public eye the name would probably be forgotten. *Fat chance.* Avail couldn't help himself. He simply loved life, women, and parties. Usually, in that order.

He didn't bother to button his shirt or his pants as Denise stomped across the floor in those ridiculous heels she wore. The older woman had seen him in far worse shape. He could use a shower and shave, ooh, and some breakfast.

A bloody steak and half a dozen eggs should do it, but even as he thought it his stomach revolted. *Ugh. See what happens when we mix whiskey and magic!* His Devil growled inside of him and Avail groaned aloud. The magic had been a bit much, but the little Witch deserved it. Taunting him for not being interested in her obvious wiles.

The glare coming from Denise had him refocusing his attention on the motherly woman. *Ouch.* She could singe toast with that look! *So loving*, he thought. His secretary of seven years cared about him. That was nice.

"Well, Denise, I suppose you want to know what happened-"

"Oh, a night of wining and dining the little trust fund baby? What's to know? Did *little pookie* not like getting kicked out of bed at 3AM?"

Denise Reynolds stood over Avail with a large, steaming mug of his favorite French roast, served black, in one hand. In the other was a large cup of tomato juice and six aspirin. Otherwise, he might have growled at her insolence. *As if.* He loved the crotchety older woman.

Her white hair was sprayed straight up like spindles guarding a castle. The sight was a bit harsh on his poor bloodshot eyes. *Yes*, he'd had far too good a time last night, but it wasn't with *little pookie* as much as it was with the whiskey he'd imbibed. *And the magic he'd wielded.*

It was nearing the last quarter moon and Avail's beastie had been up for some good old-fashioned debauchery. As was the little Witch he'd brought along for the ride. Bambi was a trust fund baby and a Witch. He'd met her at *The Thirsty Dog* where he'd gone to partake in some booze and dancing, perhaps a little nookie with a stranger.

He thought he'd found the perfect partner for the evening in the wicked Bambi. The woman had been down for just about anything. Including skinny dipping in the frigid Blue Hole which was just a few miles from his home.

He'd used a few tricks with some ancient runes and conjured a little light show while they swam. He'd even allowed his Devil to play a little bit as well. Hoping for a little suck and blow afterwards. *Not the card game.*

And then it had all gone wrong. Bambi had wanted promises with her sex. That was a serious no in his book. Then the taunting came and out she went. *Like a light.*

"Well?"

"Oh Denise, what can I say? She wanted more than an evening's entertainment. I simply didn't see us headed that way."

"Well, normally I'd say the girl had standards, but uh, I don't think so."

He stretched as he swallowed his aspirin and downed the tomato juice. Avail held his hot coffee carefully. Denise had a sadistic side and he'd caught her trying to burn his Devil once or twice over the years.

"Humph. How is *that* too hot for you?" She rolled her eyes and gathered the empty glass as he continued to wait for his coffee to cool down.

"I told you before, I'm not that kind of Devil, Denise," he murmured and sipped the brew as it reached the perfect temperature. *Heaven.* He continued to sip with his eyes closed ignoring every-thing but the smooth warm liquid as it slid down his throat.

"Really, Avail? You took *that* silicone doll to the Blue Hole! Your grandmother is going to be furious with you."

"Yes, yes, I know. Wait, how did you know?" He frowned.

The swimming spot had been shunned by locals for decades, but the Leeds family still enjoyed the crystal-clear waters. They were fed by an underground glacier though some still claim to be baffled by its existence. *Whatever.*

Still, he knew better than to take a normal to one of his family's private haunts. He also knew better than to use magic in front of anyone. But he'd figured it was alright since Bambi was in fact a Witch. Even better, she had her own money. So, he didn't need to worry about her motives. Ideally, she'd been looking for a little light fun on a Friday night. That was all! *How wrong he'd been.*

"Avail, you need to see this."

"hmm? What?" He turned and looked at the older woman who was staring at the television with her mouth hanging open.

"Pookie took pictures! *Ha!* Looks like you've finally did it this time. And look, an interview too-"

"Oh fuck! Turn it up!"

"Leedsy is a very naughty boy! Mmm hmm. He fed me whiskey and oysters on a silk sheet by the pool...I tell you the truth I didn't mind spanking him, but the ball and gag was where I drew the line. I like it when my men talk

dirty, you know?...Of course, that's true!...Well, he insisted on wearing my thong as a choker...Yes, I'd be willing to go out with him again. He is a big boy after all, and his endurance is divine... I found his size to be more than adequate though his oral skills were slightly exaggerated... but that is nothing compared to what happened afterwards...yeah we both saw him...the actual Jersey Devil..."

For fucks sake! On and on, the insipid woman spewed lie after lie for the next twenty minutes while displaying scenes of Avail swimming while imbibing of the locally distilled artisan whiskey, *Devil's Bite,* straight from the bottle.

How he loved that fiery smooth alcohol! Mason Lane, his friend and the owner of the distillery, created the label specially for Avail.

The perfect blend of *piri piri,* or African devil peppers, and burnt sugar, *Devil's Bite* is distilled and aged for five years in casks created from local oak trees.

Avail had cases of the stuff back at Leeds Mansion. His childhood and now permanent home, as his grandmother was determined to globetrot for the rest of her days. Especially since grandfather was dead and buried.

He hoped this story wouldn't carry to Egypt, where his grandmother was currently spending her time. She deserved a real vacation, and not this nonsense. The shrill ring of the telephone snapped him out of his musings.

"Avail here."

"Mr. Leeds, this is Mr. Henries, your grand-mother demanded I find you."

"Hello, Henries. Well, I'm at work. So I guess you found me."

"Yes. I figured as much, and I don't need to remind you that the launch of our newest campaign for Leeds Foundation, *the one you initiated*, to raise funds for at risk youth, begins *today*."

"You don't need to remind me. Our campaign, *Leeds Foundation, Believe in the Future*, was *my idea* as you said, Henries."

"Yes, well, Mrs. Leeds was not a fan of this campaign. Coupled with your latest *adventures*, I am tasked to advise you that your grandmother is seri-ously displeased. She suggests you go home, Avail."

"What? But there is a lot to do-"

"Denise will handle it. You are to go back to Leeds Mansion and '*wait out the storm'*. Those are her exact words."

"Tell my grandmother that she knows what happens at the end of the week-"

"She is aware." Avail could practically see the

blank expression on the lawyer's face through the phone. He'd never quite pinpointed what sort of supernatural the man was, but his loyalty and devotion to the Leeds family had spanned decades, *twelve or so to be exact.*

"It's almost the last quarter moon, Henries, and I have no intention of staying-"

"*Mr. Leeds,*" his voice deepened, "your grandmother has told me that if you refuse, she shall be forced to defer back to your grandfather's original will. The one where you do not inherit until you have achieved thirty-eight years unless you marry before then. Do you recall the terms?"

"Yes," Avail growled into the receiver, "I recall the terms. Tell Grandmother, not to worry. I am on my way home."

CHAPTER 1

"No, no, no," Stephanie slammed her hands down on the steering wheel of her tiny car. The tiny Smart car was cute as pie to look at. Totally worth it too. Well, when she'd lived in the city it had been worth it.

But out in the boonies, also known as the beach town of Maccon City, New Jersey, the damn automobile was more trouble than it was worth.

The thing could hardly make it up the sandy dirt covered private road that would soon lead to the beautifully preserved cobblestone driveway of the illustrious Leeds family.

According to her research, the Leeds were one of the original founding families of the Pine Barrens of

New Jersey. Like her own family tree, theirs dated all the way back to revolutionary times. *What an interesting coincidence!*

Not that she knew all that much about the state or her ancestors having grown up in western Pennsylvania. Stephanie had recently moved to Maccon City to be closer to her new job. A job she landed with the help of her two BFF's.

She missed Cora and Leandra every day. The three of them did everything together! Had since they were teens at the exclusive, another word for stuck-up, *Mrs. Parker's School for Girls*. Tucked away from normal teenagers in the wilds of Pennsylvania, the three of them had formed a little sisterhood. Vowing to always be there for each other.

They attended college together at the Brandywine campus of Penn State, opting to rent an apartment over dorm life. They even stayed, continuing to live together, after graduation. All working jobs in nearby Philadelphia.

Everything was fine until Cora got a job at a bank overseas. Stephanie was happy for her brilliant mathematician friend. *You bet she was.* Only, her heart squeezed at seeing her go.

That shocking announcement was soon followed

by another from Leandra. Her other roommate having decided to move to New York City to pursue her dreams of becoming a stage performer.

Another devastating blow to the rather introverted Stephanie. Her feelings of abandonment aside, she managed to be happy for them both. Besides, they had helped her find the perfect job and town to move to before they left. *In true BFF fashion.*

I miss those two, she thought as she curved around the long, winding road. Too much time had passed between visits. Sure, they still sent her emails and texts. *Especially Cora.*

Stephanie was almost overwhelmed by her constant barrage of the latest dating apps and trends for her perpetually single friend. *Sigh.* They knew her too well. *Fact check:* She was way too shy to go to bars or clubs without her two BFFs there to bolster her.

Her experience with the opposite sex wasn't all that satisfying. Still, she'd had to promise her two besties that she would start dating after she got the hang of being on her own. *In a year or two or three.*

Back in Brandywine, she'd had a sort of *friends with benefits* thing going on with a guy from work. It had ended before she left, and where she didn't miss

Mark, she missed sex. Just the thought of no sex for months made her want to cry. For a shy girl, Stephanie openly enjoyed sex, though she'd only ever engaged with someone she'd known on a friendly basis first.

Maybe I should Tinder? She scrunched up her nose. She doubted she could go through with it. If only life were a romance novel and she'd get swept away by some gorgeous man who'd keep her captive for a weekend and have his wicked way with her. That led to a smirk and a snort.

Sexy rakes weren't exactly thick on the ground in New Jersey these days. Or anywhere for that matter. And if they were, chubby blondes would probably not be on their top ten women to seduce. Oh well, so much for fantasies. Back to work.

As the official *Director of Charitable Donations* for the Committee to Preserve the New Jersey Pine Barrens, Stephanie was finally putting her degree in environmental sciences, *minor in finance*, to good use. Maccon City might not have been on her radar before, but the small beach town was close to perfect. And it was as close as she could get to the somewhat protected area she was trying to save.

Somewhat protected. A silly, yet real description of

the lands that the committee sought to protect. The fact was, the Pine Barrens were in danger!

Many would question why anyone would want to save what was basically, a harsh environment not suited for much, but to Stephanie the place was so much more. There was history there. *Hers.* Sure, the soil was too sandy and acidic for farming, but local wildlife depended on it to survive.

It was true that large predators like wolves, cougars, and bears had been hunted out of existence in the area some time ago. But some, like black bears, were slowly coming back to the pinelands to live and breed.

Other creatures like the gray fox, beavers, river otters, white deer, and various species of frogs and reptiles thrived there. Recently, she'd heard rumors of gray wolves in the area! Wouldn't that be something?

It was also important for hundreds of migrating birds as a place to stop, find nourishment, and even nest. Nature lovers everywhere came to hike through the many trails and kayak down the rivers and lakes in the barrens.

Stephanie was all for saving species and keeping the lands and forests a safe haven for nature to thrive. Though what she especially loved was going on hikes through the *ghost towns* of the barrens. To her surprise, she'd discovered quite a few hidden treasures among the shrubby forest. Abandoned cranberry farms, crumbling brick, iron, and glass factories, and the ruins paper mills dotted the landscape.

The remnants of these eighteenth and nineteenth century establishments still stood almost perfectly intact in some places, though the barrens had already begun slowly reclaiming the land from the decaying buildings.

Roads and trails nearly unrecognizable, she'd already gone on more than one guided tour of the ghost towns. Hooked on the local lore and legends, such as the Black Dog, the Hag of the Barrens, and of course, the Jersey Devil himself.

Imagine her astonishment when a big development firm, *Viridi Lux Real Estate*, started the paperwork necessary to develop huge tracts of land in the barrens themselves!

She'd immediately started investigating, putting all the clout of her new position to use. Still, she was unable to garner a single tidbit of information about their plan. It was all very hush hush.

Rumors of strip malls and shopping centers floated around town. *Yuck. Gag. The horror.* As were the rumors that *Viridi Lux* had greased some very influential palms. *Ah ha! Dirty evildoers!* She knew the firm was not to be trusted.

The entire thing stunk to Stephanie Decatur. She was a good girl at heart, despite the fact that she was left at Mrs. Parker's at the behest of her mother and father who enjoyed parties and travelling more than they did their daughter.

Aware that she cramped their lifestyle, she preferred to find joy in simple things like nature and her studies. Her old alma mater encouraged charitable work, and she found herself giving back to the community as a volunteer at senior centers and animal shelters back in PA. *She'd have to find some here*, she thought to herself.

And she would do all those things again, after she settled into her new home and her job. She grinned just thinking about her new job. What a wonderful feeling to be part of something as important as the preservation of an entire ecosystem! She would do everything she could to help keep the Pine Barrens wild and undeveloped.

She had more than just her job at stake. Her own family hailed from South Jersey hundreds of years ago, dating all the way back to the Revolution. In fact, her great-great-great- grand something was a naval commodore.

She'd found his information in an old family Bible that she'd inherited after her jet setting parents had died in a plane crash before her twenty-first birthday. There'd been little money left, enough to pay off her loans and get her the little Smart car. *Ugh.*

With Cora and Leandra gone, Stephanie was lonelier than ever. As the last Decatur around, she was determined to keep as much of her original home state preserved as possible! *It was her duty.* Which was why she was on this godforsaken drive to seek out one Mrs. Margot Leeds and to ask, *no*, beg if necessary, for the funds to buy the land out from *Viridi Lux!*

Thunder rumbled across the sky and she peeked out her window at the ominous looking clouds. Why were Spring storms always the worst? She sighed and rolled up the glass hoping to keep the spray off her should it start falling.

"Come on, one more mile, dammit," she swore as smoke started pouring from the hood of her lemon-yellow car.

It was after five o'clock on Friday. This was her last stop of what had been a very, very long week.

The sky was darkening. The huge clouds rolling along quickly, weighing heavily in the air. She cursed as her car stalled one final time.

"Dammit!" Stephanie grabbed her purse and slammed the door shut as she struggled to get out of her seat. *Stupid tiny car.* Good for environment. Bad for fluffy girls like her.

Might as well head to Mrs. Leeds' house and call a tow truck from there, she figured. The woman had been gracious and inviting on the phone. Finally returning Stephanie's call after she'd tracked down the estate attorney, a *Mr. Henries.* It would take her fifteen minutes to get to the house, but she was sure the kind older woman wouldn't mind.

Besides, heaven knew Stephanie could use the exercise. Her cell phone was probably still sitting on her kitchen counter next to her barely touched coffee. *Of course, it was.*

Two minutes into her trek along the sandy, dirt road and lightning erupted across the sky followed by a roaring clap that made her jump. *Of course, it did.* If Cora and Leandra could just see her now. *SMH.* She'd never live it down.

She could almost hear their simultaneous cries. *You've got the worst luck, Steph!* It was true. She did. Anytime they'd planned a day trip, it either rained or snowed the second she got in her car.

She'd ruined more picnics, beach days, and weekend camping trips with her friends than she could even count. Not that they minded. True BFFs they simply packed the ponchos and rainboots. If only she'd remembered them now. *Sigh.*

"Crap. Crap. Crap!" She groaned as the first few drops fell on her head. *Okay*, it was not so bad. A drizzle really.

The following *splat, splat, splat, splat, splatsplat-splatsplat* caused minor panic to swell in her chest. *Nope*, of course it would not simply drizzle for her. Dismay increasing as her carefully styled, wavy blonde hair quickly became plastered to her head.

With a heavy sigh, Stephanie gripped her purse and hurried along the suddenly exceedingly difficult to see path. Darkness fell quickly with the rain. The only hints of light were the bouts of lightning that flashed every few minutes. She refused to think of the animals that stayed hidden in the trees along the road. She knew far too well what lived in those woods. *Eep!*

"Ow!" Panic flaring, she stepped into a small hole, rolling her ankle and falling to her knees in the quickly gathering mud. Stephanie groaned, kicked off her high heels, and scrambled to her feet.

"OW! Dammit," she yelled as pain shot through her right ankle.

"That's just great," she hobbled forward, mumbling to herself as she heaved up the steep incline. She could have sobbed with gratitude when her bare feet came into contact with a cobblestone road. The one that would take her right to Mrs. Leeds' driveway. *So close!*

"Finally. Oh, thank God," she whimpered and limped towards the gate.

Whining wasn't really her thing, but these were extenuating circumstances. Soaked to the bone and injured! She had no choice really. Whine or break down and cry in the middle of the private drive before she even got to the begging part. *Heck no!* She would not give up now!

Aching and freezing, Stephanie stopped for a second and stared at the enormous house before her. The *Leeds Mansion* had definitely earned that title. The place was huge! There was so much to take in. The marvel of the construction itself, the setting with the barrens as a backdrop, it was simply over-whelming! She'd need days or weeks to study it all. *If only.*

The private cobblestone road stopped at a wrought iron gate. A locked gate. *Of course.* But beyond that was an absolute wonderland. The gorgeous cobblestone drive continued, leading the way to a huge castle-like abode at the very edge of the barrens she wanted to preserve! Like something out of a fairytale. *The Beast's castle*, she mused.

Excitement and awe warred within her. This place screamed old money. Would Mrs. Leeds even let her in the door? She had been invited, though perhaps arriving soaked and muddy wasn't the best way to meet the person you were hitting up for some funds.

Oh well, she'd come too far not to try! Rain and mud be damned! She looked for a bell or intercom only to find an "out of service" note taped to it. *More of my wonderful luck.*

"Oh no," she growled. A deep growl sounded from off to the side and Stephanie paused. *Oh crap! Bear? Fox? Wolf?* Like it mattered. Any of them would do some serious harm. Panicked and more than a little worried, Stephanie shook the huge gate. She pounded the iron bars and rattled the door on its hinges, but the thing did not budge.

There was no way in hell she was hobbling back down to her car. Especially not with the possibility of big-toothed predators lurking nearby. Besides, the stupid thing wouldn't start anyway, and she had no phone.

Lightning crack and thunder shook the skies overhead. Shivers ran down her spine, were it not for the rain she'd probably break out in a nervous sweat. The linen dress that was so comfortable in the warm afternoon sun, was itchy and completely see-through now that it was drenched and plastered to her many curves.

As a plump, or as she preferred to be called, *fluffy* chick, she didn't normally do dresses. But today had been special. She'd had a lunch date with Tommy from work. Or, that is, she thought she had when she'd gotten up that morning.

After waiting twenty minutes for Tommy, the rat, at *Roll Over*, a local sushi joint, she'd finally decided she'd had enough and left. Unfortunately, being stood up was not uncommon for her. It had happened before and according to her friends was because she chose the wrong men. Or as they called them, *guys with sticks up their asses and small dicks they don't know how to use.*

Taste in men aside, she was stuck wearing a stupid linen dress in the stupid rain! Also, now that she thought about it, she was hungry and cranky from her missed lunch. Worst of all, she was soaking wet and her car, *her poor, tiny car*, had broken down. *Again.*

If these people thought they were going to lock her out of the one place that promised sanctuary in a five-mile radius, they were crazy! Stephanie simply wasn't going down like that! Straightening her spine, she walked past the broken intercom, wiped the rain from her eyes, thanked God she chose waterproof mascara, and looked for the lowest side of the gate.

"Found you, you bastard," she growled and swung her purse over the black wrought iron.

Only grimacing slightly when the once butter soft, ivory leather bag landed upside down in a muddy puddle on the cobblestoned ground.

"Okay, now me."

Cue the ominous music. *Key word: fluffy.* Stephanie might enjoy hiking and swimming, even some light tae kwon do. But climbing a fence while injured and hoisting herself onto said seven-foot-tall fence was something else entirely.

"No choice," she growled, a fierce determination shining from her blue eyes.

Thunder boomed and her foot slipped off the rung the first time she tried. The second time, she stepped onto the rung and quickly found she wasn't going to be able to lift her legs in the tight confines of her linen dress.

Groaning, she dropped to the ground once again, avoiding landing on her hurt ankle. Stephanie swore aloud for the tenth time in a row. Unable to rip the surprisingly sturdy fabric, she had no other choice but to peel it off her wet body.

"Okay, third time's the charm, Stephie-girl," she grunted as she climbed and heaved herself up onto the top of the fence. Thankfully, the spikes were only every couple of feet. The space she now occupied was flat if a little bit high.

It was the getting down that concerned her. *Crap on a cracker.* She hadn't thought through to that part. Nor did she remember to toss her dress over to the other side of the fence. *Uh oh.*

"What the hell are you doing?"

The sound of a deeply masculine voice reached her ears. Startled and shocked, the rich timbre of the question not only brought her focus to the man, *the naked man,* standing in the rain below her, but made certain slumbering parts of her stand up and take notice as well.

Hot damn! Through the falling droplets of rain, Stephanie looked down into the darkest pair of eyes she'd ever seen. She had time to think one word before she felt herself slipping. *Gorgeous...*

"Ah!" Losing her balance, she fell forward and almost crashed down onto the undoubtedly hard, though rain-soaked cobblestone. *Almost.* If not for the sudden expanse of man that now cushioned her curvy body. *Eep!*

CHAPTER 2

A loud sigh escaped Avail. He was going to lose his mind. *A week.* He'd been cooped up inside the house for a full week. Like a child who'd been punished.

His beast was riding him hard as he always did during the last quarter phase of the moon. Most Shifters suffered from FBB, or *full moon blues,* as he liked to call it. But not him.

Typical *animal-to-man Shifters or Weres* were bound by rules that didn't exactly apply to supernatural creatures like him. He was the very stuff of legend and lore. A true New Jersey legacy. *Growl.*

Avail, my boy, do not leave the grounds until after the moon passes. Keep your little Devil on a leash. I will not forbid it, as I know that would merely tempt you to flout my will, but I strongly suggest you heed me. Love, Grandmother.

The text message he'd received from his Grandmother had come with a series of emojis that he could not even begin to decipher. He'd have to chat with Henries about providing his dear old Grandmother with such a device. And for plugging his private cell number into it.

He shook his head. The woman was infuriating and humiliating. Demanding he obey or allow her to set him up like some simpering idiot who could not find his own mate. As if! He could certainly locate a woman to wed without any help!

Find her. He ignored the pesky little voice inside of him that seemed more than on board with the idea of finding his mate. *Shut it. I am too young to settle down.*

Now that the idea had settled in his brain, Avail found himself outside in the rain instead of in his warm, dry rooms. He stretched his shoulders, rolling the taut muscles under the hammering downpour. It wasn't anger that drove him. He was simply annoyed. And restless.

He'd Changed earlier and had a short run through the barrens to relive some of his energy. Avail wasn't worried about anyone seeing him. The grounds around his home were large and sprawling. *And private.* An enormous bonus for him.

A huge, wrought iron fence kept the outside world from drawing too close. He'd recently had a top security system installed by *Draco Fortis.* The best in supernatural protection and surveillance. He certainly hoped so, fucking thing had cost a fortune.

Lightning flashed overhead and he waited for the resounding boom that followed. *Yes!* He enjoyed walking in the storm in nothing but his skin. The entire experience was freeing in ways normals could only imagine.

The need to expel energy, *to hunt, to find, to fuck* had been driving him nuts inside. Sure, he had to obey his grandmother, lest she force him to get mated and shackled for the rest of his life in order to run the company and enjoy his rightful position. But he hadn't gone far. Hadn't allowed his Devil to roam as freely as the beast craved.

Grandmother Leeds wouldn't like it if another sighting occurred so close to last time. *Fuck.* All he wanted to do was run, maybe even go for a little flight. Damn that Bambi and her stupid lying rumors! He hadn't even shown her his Devil!

Still, if he risked a Change outside his grand-mother might find out. If she found out, she'd retaliate. Matchmaking being her favorite form of torture, he'd have to endure endless set-ups with whatever horrible relatives of friends that she could find. *The horror!*

He could not go through that again. No matter how hard his Devil rode him. The last time she brought home a girl for him to meet he was eighteen. The woman was a *dear* granddaughter of a business associate.

Clingy and simpering, the creature was practically drooling with the possibility of an early marriage proposal. *Shudder.* Oh yes, his Grandmother was wily and sometimes cruel, but he loved her anyway.

He knew she loved him back. Despite her claims that family duty was the only reason she'd taken him in. She wasn't fooling anyone. Both his grandparents loved him, and he returned their affection. He just didn't want to be forced to find a mate. Not until his *promised* was revealed to him.

Avail had had a happy childhood far as he could tell. Okay, so he was a tad spoiled, but was he really to blame? Grandfather had taught him all about his supernatural side, where Grandmother had made sure he was clothed, fed, and did his studies.

The legend of a Devil's *promised* was something

Grandfather had regaled him with in his youth. Of course, it was a myth. *Kind of like him.* And yet, Grandfather had told him he knew the second he laid eyes on his wily wife that she was his.

His inner Devil roared and raged inside of him with a ferocity he hadn't yet felt. *It will get worse, Avail.* His Grandmother had assured him of this. The Beast would continue chomping at the bit until he found a mate to temper that savage side of him. At thirty-one years old and a confirmed bachelor to boot, he had no intention of settling. *Grrrrr. Snarl.*

"I like being single," he told himself firmly.

His Devil growled louder. A bit insistent really, but Avail shook his head. *No.* He loved his life. Who in their right mind would give up the freedom to sample a different woman anytime he chose? Not this Devil!

Thunder crashed above, echoing his alter ego's state of mind. *A brisk run then,* he thought. He took off on his two legs and tried to settle his beast. As an expert in the art of seduction, he had years before he'd get his fill of the opposite sex.

Come now, there are too many women we've yet to try, he cajoled his inner Devil. *Be honest, we are bored with them.* He vaulted over a fallen branch as he wrestled with himself over the issue.

It was true. He was tired of the same simpering smiles and vacant expressions. Even worse, the ones who looked at him with dollar signs in their eyes. They were all so boring.

He barely had any interest in the little Witch he'd picked up the other night. And boy did Bambi get her revenge. Grounded like a schoolboy! Ha!

Before Bambi, there was that stacked redhead. She was fun. But even then, he'd had to work to rise to the occasion. *The shame.* Okay, if he were being totally honest, he had no desire to partake in another shallow meeting. Those encounters were just not satisfying. As impersonal as a handshake.

Even with Bambi he'd been insistent. Stopping her attempts to arouse him before they'd done more than strip and swim. And no, he hadn't felt the need to perform for her in the least. She was just so, so *not right.*

Fuck. What was he going to do now? *Find our mate! Grrr.* Blasted Devil and his one-track mind. This was serious. He doubted his mate was going to fall from the sky and with the rising last quarter moon he found himself to be truly volatile for maybe the first time in his life. *Fuck.*

A horny Devil is an angry Devil, best get some pussy while you can. Of course, he'd recall his grandfather's crude saying when he was stuck with no chance of finding relief for his pent-up state.

He pushed himself harder along the rocky paths. Cock at half-mast, he turned his face to the skies, allowing the rain to cool him. *He could always engage in a little mano e mano. Ugh. Unappealing.* He circled back to the house, growling and grumbling along with the thunder.

Stomping his bare feet across the uneven earth until he reached the cobblestone towards the South entrance of his house. He'd much rather be walking across the wet, sandy earth of the barrens, which served as his backyard, to the hard, cold stone. But *something* was calling him to walk in that direction.

An unearthly pull. Uncertain of its source, he paused for a moment. A faint scent danced along his nostrils, teasing him underneath the smells of rain, mud, and ozone hanging in the air. His desire to find the source of that scent was almost overwhelming.

Ilis feet hurried along the uneven cobblestone, unburdened by both the unpleasant hardness and the incessant weather. He had one driving force, find the source of that delectable fragrance.

His Devil nudged him, urging him to move faster in that direction. The scent grew stronger the closer he got to, well, *whatever* it was that he was racing towards. He simply couldn't resist whatever magic or fate was drawing him towards *it*.

Like a child at Christmas, he raced towards whatever wonder awaited him. His heartrate sped up. Something life changing was waiting for him, he felt it. The owner of that scent was near, just around the corner, *or* down the driveway as it were. Then he heard it.

Over the howling of the winds, a noise coming from the South gate reached his sensitive ears. Avail picked up his pace. Racing towards his destiny, he shook his head, chasing the rain off his thick waves of hair.

Must find. His Devil pushed to be let off his leash, but Avail quieted the beast who lived inside him. *Not yet.* It wouldn't do him any good to expose his family secret. Not until he knew who or what it was that he sought.

Of course, he reserved the right to change his mind after he set his gaze on whomever thought to trespass on his property. The Leeds family name was old and feared by those who'd been in the vicinity long enough to know better. *A newcomer then or some local daring to test his patience.*

There was always that one normal who thought to get a closer look at the place where a legend was born. They sometimes came, knocking on the door during a dark, stormy night then running away before anyone could answer.

How disappointing if that were now the case! Or not. *Someone to scare. Someone to toy with. Yes please,* his Devil growled.

The idea held merit. *Hunt.* Yes, they were on the hunt already. *Scare?* Maybe. *Kill?* Not likely. *Lick?* Perhaps. *Chase?* Yes, definitely. He could chase down the source of his temptation without giving away anything. *Grrr.*

A good hunt. That was one way to sate his baser urges. Those cravings that came stronger each month. He'd refused to acknowledge it for what it was for so long, it was strange to admit it. His Devil's need to search for his *promised mate* was growing stronger. The idea that there was one woman in the universe who could calm his beast was something of a revelation.

Did he dare believe in such a thing? *No. I'm not ready to be mated yet. Grrr. Okay, that's a lie. But what if I can't find someone meant for me? What if she does not exist?* Terror gripped him for a nanosecond, but it was enough to stop him in his tracks.

The storm raged all around him. Wind whistled through the trees, the entire grounds would have been engulfed in darkness were it not for the strategically placed security lights and the flash of lightning every now and then. But none of that mattered as he turned his head towards the source of that delectable aroma.

Avail growled as his prey came into view. Was this why he'd practically run from the woods back to the house when he'd been trying to drive back his Devil's baser urges? Was this the magnetic force that had beckoned him forward in the stormy night?

Beautiful, was his first thought. The blonde woman, clad only in scraps of black lace straddling his fence, was simply breathtaking. Bountiful curves, soft and womanly, she was enough to tempt the Devil himself. *This Devil, for sure.*

How the hell did she get up there? She didn't look particularly athletic. No, she looked just as a woman should. Curvy and plump, all pale skin and long, golden hair. He inhaled and his Devil growled deep and long.

That hypnotizing scent. It's her! Avail breathed deeply, tasting her sublime fragrance on his tongue. He faltered as one glaring thing registered in his barely human brain. *She's a normal!* Well, fuck him. Could this be a mistake?

How could this woman whose scent tempted him

from a mile away be a normal? *The Fates must hate me.* Well, that was one answer. Perhaps his beast was simply too overcome by the last quarter phase of the moon to differentiate scents correctly?

Grrr. It seemed his Devil took exception to that supposition. *Okay. Fine. I admit her scent speaks to me, but what the heck is she doing here?*

He was a big enough devil to admit when he was attracted. But that couldn't explain her presence on his land. Was this delectable morsel just another groupie? Anger furrowed his brows. *Of course.* That damned Bambi and her ridiculous interview was bound to produce some unhinged weirdos. Even gorgeous ones.

Sometimes they got a tad aggressive, taking matters into their own hands, thinking it within their rights to stalk him. To these unhinged individuals, the *Naughty Dark Prince* was free game. Every time those paparazzi vultures found one of his affairs or evenings out newsworthy, they filled their tabloids and blogs with images of him, usually in various stages of undress, for the whole damn world to see! Sometimes to dire consequences.

He hated to admit it. *Oh, the shame.* A healthy Devil like himself brought so low by women! If

Denise and Grandmother could see him now. *Shudder.*

They'd told him time and again that he needed to choose more discerningly if he was going to fool around. But was he to blame, really? How could he know that some of his dates would snap pictures of him and later sell them when he was unawares?

Okay. He should have suspected, after all, he was filthy rich, devilishly handsome, and powerful to boot. A triple threat if ever there was one. And that was in all modesty, just plain speaking.

Avail didn't believe in beating around the bush. It was why he was so damn good at playing the market and earning millions upon millions for the family. If only Grandfather hadn't put that stupid clause in his will giving his Grandmother a way to tighten the noose.

Ugh. He could hear her now. *"Avail, haven't I told you to settle down. Stop fooling around with all this insta-fame nonsense. Your grandfather would not approve of your behavior. For Devil's sake, boy, stop acting like a peacock and find your promised."*

Every time he heard his grandmother's words in his ear, he grimaced. How disappointed she sounded, even if only in his head. It was not his fault the *Naughty Dark Prince* had a surprisingly large number of followers on Twitter and Instagram. Don't even get him started on his Facebook page. Of course, he didn't actually run any of those social media pages.

No, that was up to his somewhat deranged fans. And here he was stuck with another one who thought to trespass during a thunderstorm in nothing but her panties. And what nice panties they were. *They'd look better on my floor. Growl.*

Still, he had to exercise caution. No matter how hard his devil was pushing him to go to her. Maybe this would be fun after all. Besides, he didn't see any hidden cameras on her person. *Where would she put it?* She slipped precariously on the wrought iron, swinging one plump thigh around the top and gripping it with all her might. He could hear the increase in her heartrate from where he stood. *Damn.* He needed to stop this before she got hurt and tried to sue him.

"What the hell are you doing?" He bellowed. Looking to startle the Venus into telling him the truth, angered as he was by the idea that she'd come to tempt him with her wiles only to use him for her own bit of insta-fame.

Her surprised gasp and consequential fall towards the ground were not what he had intended.

Still, the danger was evident. Avail moved quickly. Using his supernatural speed and strength, he raced over the slippery cobblestone to catch the tumbling female in the nick of time.

His hands touched her wet skin and, *zap*, he felt as if he'd grabbed hold of a live wire. Heat spread through his body from that one point of contact. He hardly felt the rain for the woman burning in his arms.

An insatiable desire to kiss the woman, taste her lips, and elsewhere filled him. Lust addled he pulled her tighter against him. The need to carry the stranger home pounded in time with his thunderous heartbeat. *What is happening to me?* Never before had he felt this way, still, deep down, *way down*, he knew. *Mine,* growled his Devil.

"You're naked!" The trembling blonde beauty screeched over the storm.

Well, that's surprising. He hadn't taken her for a prude. Especially in her current state of undress.

"So are you, pet," he countered.

Ignoring her meager struggles to be put down, Avail turned with the near naked beauty in his arms. *A sassy little thing for certain,* he mused.

Determined to find out if his initial reaction was a fluke, he started his trek back towards his home.

The little blonde squirmed in his arms, this way and that. She pummeled his chest, as if her tiny little fists could hurt him.

He smiled. Didn't she know it was futile to resist him? Besides. He was Avail Leeds, women clamored to gain his attention? The little groupie should be happy.

Finally, she gave up her struggles with a harrumph. She crossed her arms, pushing her plump bosoms up further. *Mmm. Berries.* He wondered for a second if they'd be dark and dusky, or pink and tip tilted? Either way, he couldn't wait to taste.

The rain continued to pelt them. The cold apparent despite it being spring. The woman shivered and he held her closer, using his body to heat her. The woman turned her head refusing to look at him. *Well, that won't do.*

Missing the feel of her fingers, he jostled her a bit, approving the way she gripped his arms. Her tiny squeak of surprise was adorable. Even better was the way she squirmed closer to him. Her soft breasts pressed against his chest had his Devil, and other parts of him, perking up.

She seeks warmth. Is drawn to our heat. As it should be. A feeling of rightness settled into his body. Perhaps Grandmother was correct, and he'd been missing *this* in his life? But did mates generally fall off fences into the arms of waiting Devils? He'd never heard of such a thing.

"Where are you taking me?" Her voice was husky from the ravages of the storm.

He'd see to it she got some tea once they were inside. The need to comfort and protect paramount. Well, right after the need to do *other things*. His cock hardened, bobbing just under her plump bottom as he carried her across the paved patio, despite the cold rain pelting them.

"Inside," he inhaled her light, delicate fragrance and almost groaned at the sweetness.

His Devil tensed. *So sweet. So special. So mine.* He started across the slip free tiles surrounding the covered up inground pool.

It would be another month before they opened it for the summer. He wondered briefly if she liked swimming. Pictured her in the cool depths with him and nothing else between them. *Yes.*

With each step his Devil pushed forward. The feel of her soft skin, the delicate perfume that surrounded her, the timbre of her sweet voice, all of it, all of *her,* made his heart hammer inside of his chest and his cock pulse with need.

"You should put me down now! Really, I'm too

heavy for you to carry like this," she leaned into him, cupping his ear before speaking.

Oh fuck. He knew he should answer her, but he couldn't speak. Electricity danced down his spine, zapping him with awareness as her heated hands reached for him of her own volition. Warm breath tickled his earlobe, the heat assaulting his senses. *And what a sweet assault it was!*

Avail breathed through his nose. *In and out.* Sucking in the fresh, damp air that with it, brought her own sweet scent into his body. *Hell*, into his very blood. *Want to taste.* His heart thudded. Head pounded. His Devil scratched at his skin.

He couldn't let him out. Not now. Not when he held her in his arms. She was delicate and fragile. *A normal.* He'd hurt her if he Changed. It was too dangerous. *Never hurt her*, snarled his inner Devil. *She is ours. Mine. My promised.*

"I said you can let me go!" The luscious creature yelled over the booming rain yet again, but he found words were a little hard to form now while his Devil raged inside.

What? She wants to leave me. NEVER! An over-whelming surge of possessiveness nearly sent Avail to his knees. He did not know this woman from Eve, but she was *his. His.* And she wasn't going anywhere.

"No," he grunted the word forcing one leg to move in front of the other. It was getting more and more difficult to hold on. The clouds and rain hid the moon, but he still felt it pull at him. His Devil begging for release with each step.

"But-" she sputtered, her blonde hair sticking to her gorgeous cheeks as she tried again to persuade him to drop her.

"You. Are. Mine," he stared into her bright blue eyes as he spoke. *The exact color of the heavens,* he thought.

"Who the hell do you think you are?" The woman who was his yelled, batting her tiny fists against his chest. *So freaking adorable.*

"Oh pet, you have no idea, do you?"

"You can't just pick people up and say they're yours!"

"Can't I?"

Her stunned expression was not a denial. At least, Avail didn't think so. He couldn't help himself. Needed to get closer. Grinning like a madman, he leaned down anticipating what she'd do once he captured her plump lips in a short, searing kiss.

Or, *that was the plan.* Until his lips actually met hers. In that one moment, when his mouth touched upon the silky perfection of hers, all thoughts of a quick peck evaporated.

Avail groaned and deepened the connection. Her shocked gasp allowed him entrance to the hot, seductive cavern of her mouth. And did she respond to him? *Hell yes!* His little pet was right there in the moment. Lips pressing, tongue twisting, earth-shattering as any kiss ever was in the history of kissing.

Holy hell! A rumbling growl built up from his soul, threatening to erupt like a dormant volcano from his mouth. *Grrrrrrrowwwwlllll.* His Devil side wanted out. Last quarter moon or not, his beast wanted to mark this woman. Here. Now.

Well, fuck me. This is really happening. He couldn't have known that the entire world as he knew it was going to turn upside fucking down and inside out the very moment, he'd tasted her, could he? *Hello, Universe, not even a warning?*

Okay. He'd been kind of certain this delicate female was his when he saw her straddling the fence in her decadent underthings. *Black lace. His favorite.*

Kinda certain. With a hint of skepticism. But not now. Not after he'd laid his mouth upon her sweet lips and sampled her heady flavors. Certainty took on a whole new meaning in that one single touch.

Without any sense of self-preservation, Avail

dove head-first into that passionate kiss. And he knew without a doubt. *She. Is. Mine. My mate. My promised.*

Speaking of which, his soon-to-be mate whimpered as he raised his head. Blue eyes glazed with lust met his. Shock and something akin to awe evident in their depths. Rain still poured from the skies, he knew he should hurry and get her indoors, but he couldn't move. Not yet.

"I, uh, guess you proved me wrong," she said.

"Yes."

"Seriously though, who are you?"

"What is your name?"

"Stephanie Decatur."

"Why did you come here?"

"I came to see the Leeds'," her guileless baby blues blinked up at him and his heart skipped a beat or two. *Damn*, but she was lovely.

"Well, you found one." Not a lie. *Kudos to me!*

"But *who* are you?" *A curious little one*, he grinned.

"I'm all yours, pet," he winked.

"Tell me who you are!" She shouted over the weather.

"How about I show you?"

Blue eyes flashed, her temper really starting to show as he smiled again. At least she would never bore him! *Stephanie Decatur,* he liked the sound of it. Liked Stephanie Leeds even better.

She wanted to know him, did she? *Well then, here goes,* he thought and did the one thing he swore he would never do as long as he lived.

Avail tipped his head back, reveling in the rain as it turned to steam once it made contact with his burning hot skin. Savored the flavors of his tiny mate on his tongue. *Yes. So good.* He reached inside himself and called to his other half. That part of him so deeply embedded he sometimes wondered if there was a difference. *Come, our mate wants to know us,* he crooned to the beast. *Yes,* was the ready answer.

The tiny woman *eeped* as he began his Shift with her still balanced in the cradle of his steel arms. Magic hummed over his body, the power warming them both. Stephanie's eyes flashed with fear, but he knew it would be over soon.

Human skin gave way to thick, reddened flesh. Face elongated taking on the wyvern-shape of his other half. His nostrils grew and with that his senses increased. The woman in his arms smelled fucking delicious.

Arms and chest both thickened, covered in smooth, oval shaped scales the same dark red of his skin. They glistened in the rain and flashes of lightning that shone overhead. *Yessss,* his Devil hissed the word as he emerged.

Claws, four inches long and black as night, grew from the tips of his fingers. Avail was careful to keep them tucked away from his soft-skinned mate. He would not hurt her for all the world. *Mine.*

Electricity and something *more* zipped along his spine. He welcomed the magic, feeling the Change wash over him was nothing new. In fact, he reveled in the fierce strength and heightened awareness that accompanied it.

Muscles bulged and grew. His feet transformed into huge, cloven hooves. Thick, black fur sprouted along his long, powerful legs. Enormous black wings unfurled from his back at the same time a great rack of antlers protruded from his forehead.

"Oh my God!" Stephanie shouted.

"Not quite. You wanted to know who am I, pet? *This* is who I am," his voice emerged as a seductive growl over the rain and thunder that continued to boom in the distance.

His forked tail whipped to and fro behind him as he pressed the woman closer to his chest. *Smells good. Want her. Mark her. My promised.*

Desire thrummed inside of him. Her eyes, the

color of a summer sky, widened as they took in his massive, reddened form. Impressive, he knew.

Avail wondered if it was his tail that came a little too close to her face before tucking behind him that was the final straw. Those perfect eyes of hers met his once more before rolling up in the back of her head.

His mate had passed out! Hardly flattering considering he'd never revealed his Devil to anyone besides family before. Maybe he should have waited? Tried harder to deny his Shift. But how could he?

Everything in his blood told him the female was his. His mate, his other half, the one being in the world to temper his beast. A beast that had wanted to meet her. *Mate her. Mark her.*

Lightning sounded and he looked down at the now unconscious female. He had to take care of her first. Then he'd explain. All of it.

"Come, mate, let's get you inside."

A direct descendant of the first *Jersey Devil* born by his ancestor, a White Witch lovingly referred to as Mother Leeds by his family, in the early eighteenth century, Avail was perhaps the closest, truest thing to the original Jersey Devil alive today.

Rumor had it that his ancestor had had an affair with the actual Devil himself, resulting in one small, *gifted* offspring who turned out to be Avail's grandfather's grandfather. Of course, the *Devil* she'd had the affair with was a lesser Demon, name of Rosier, but most didn't know that.

A prince of Hell, his powers were extremely strong. Still are for that matter, tough he had not come back to the surface as far as Avail knew. His son, Avail's ancestor, being half-Witch and half-Demon, took on the shape of a hybrid Wyvern Shifter and was even gifted with some magic of his own.

True, there were other half-Witch half-Demon beings running about, but none had the reputation of the Jersey Devil. Thanks to his uncles and cousins, sightings have kept them in the limelight over the centuries. The *gift,* as it were, being passed down to the men in the family only, was still passed through the women.

There were a few dozen Jersey Devil descendants running around the north east, but Avail Leeds was the one and only *direct heir.*

Dark Prince, indeed. And now he'd found her, his *promised,* the princess of his heart. The one woman in the whole world born to tempt and tame the Devil himself.

His blood sang with the heat of her nearness. Her

light heady fragrance assailing his sensitive nose as he cradled her against him. He wrapped his large wings around them, keeping her safe from the battering winds and rain of the storm.

"Mine," he growled.

Avail stomped towards the front entrance of Leeds Mansion. Usually, his Devil was out for blood or sex during the last quarter moon. Not that he'd deny wanting the nearly nude beauty in his arms, but, to his immediate surprise, his first instinct was to care for her.

Strange. He'd never felt such a compulsion before. And to think, had his grandmother and Mr. Henries not forbidden him to go out that evening he might not have been there to receive his beautiful *promised*. He'd have to send them a gift basket. One of those fruit flower thingies should do nicely.

He'd store that thought away for later. Right now, he had better things to do.

Mine.

CHAPTER 3

Stephanie sighed and snuggled deeper into the luxurious softness of her bed. She didn't remember where she got the enormous comforter or the silky sheets, but she sure as hell was glad.

Smooth and soft against her skin, she sighed again, rolling onto her side. She was flush against something warm and hard. Not her mattress. Sleep kept her eyes shut as large arms wrapped around her, stroking her back as soft lips nuzzled her ear and neck. *Mmm.* She liked that. *A lot.*

The clean scent of rain mixed with a fiery spice reached her nose. *Mmm. Smells good,* she thought and pressed herself even closer to the source. A low rumbling growl vibrated through her body.

What was that? Earthquake? Slowly, she opened

her eyes. Stretching her body in an effort to try and shake the sleep from her absolutely exhausted frame. What a pleasure to catch up on a few hours! She hadn't slept that securely since her roommates had left. *Sigh. Stretch. Wiggle.*

"If you keep moving like that, pet, proper introductions are going to have wait till *after*," a low voice murmured while soft lips and a warm tongue teased her ear.

Stephanie froze. Her entire body stilled. Hell. She didn't even breathe.

What the-? Okay. *Fact check:* She did not own silk sheets or goose down comforters. She did not currently have a boyfriend or lover. She did not drink last night or go home with anyone. And she certainly did not remove all her clothing.

Did she take off her dress? A vague memory of her car stalling out, the rain plastering the linen dress to her body, a fence- Crap. But she knew she did not remove her underwear and bra. Ha!

"Um, who are you," she pushed against the enormous, and yes, naked, chest of the man who was cradling her against him as if she belonged there. No, she was not about to admit to herself that she wanted to whine the second he released her.

"I should be asking you that. It was *you* who trespassed onto *my* property."

Then it all came rushing back. The car, the storm, her ankle, her dress, the fence, and the, *the huge, red guy with horns and a tail? Oh. OH.* For the first time in her life, she was fucked. *Yes, please. I mean, uh, no. Eep!*

Uneasy by the turn of her thoughts, she stared at the gorgeous stranger and tried to come to grips with what the heck was happening to her. *Okay. I am okay.* Not hurt. Not molested. Just naked. *Okay then.*

So, sue her if she was a tad bit disappointed. It wasn't everyday a gorgeous hunk of man strode up to her naked and plucked her out of the rain to, well, to take care of her and cuddle? *Well, damn. Maybe he's just a nice guy who would've done that for anyone.* She couldn't help but feel disappointed at the thought.

"What's going on in that beautiful head of yours, pet?" His fingers danced up and down her arms, teasing her skin, tempting her to snuggle back against him. *No. Bad.*

"Stop that," she snapped. *Hmph.* Once again, she was not going to admit disappointment when he readily complied with her request to be left alone.

"Okay, I am naked in your bed. I guess I can tell you more than my name. As I said before, it's

Stephanie, I work for the Committee to Preserve the New Jersey Pine Barrens."

"*Stephanie,*" he purred, "Beautiful name for a beautiful woman.

He purred. *The man purred.* And damn if it didn't get her all achy in her girlie parts. True, his line was corny, and yet, she hoped he meant it. *Sigh.*

"I'm Avail Leeds," he lifted his hand, and she did the same, dropping the sheet in the process. *Pervert.* He had the audacity to laugh as she scrambled for it.

"Shame on you, mister!"

"Don't panic, sweet Stephanie. You were soaked to the bone. I undressed you and got you under the covers then crawled in with you to keep you from freezing."

The fact that it was still storming outside stopped her from yelling some more. That and her hair was damp. So, maybe he wasn't lying. *Right now, anyway.* But what about everything else?

"Okay. Even if I buy all that, what was the kissing and touching about?"

"I couldn't not touch you if I tried, *my promised,*" he sat up, the sheet dipping low on his waist. She knew he was as naked as she was, but the reality of *seeing* such a perfect specimen of man in the buff was simply out of her experience. Okay, she drooled a bit.

"Wait! You were already naked in the rain when you saw me outside by the fence," she realized.

"Yes."

"Why?"

"There I was just taking a walk, hoping to release a little energy, when I found you. I guess Fate had other ideas for me this evening," his growly voice made her shiver. Or maybe it was his fingers that were causing such a reaction. There he was, teasing her wrist with light touches. Small, soft strokes that were driving her insane.

"In the rain?" She cleared her throat.

"Yes."

"Without clothes?"

"Yes." *Oh, great. Another one-word answer.*

"Um. Maybe we should get out of bed and talk?"

"We could do that," he grinned and moved to stand.

"Wait! Um, I'll close my eyes," she slapped her palm over her face and ignored the sound of his rumbling laughter.

"You can look *now.*"

One perfectly arched eyebrow raised lifted to the top of his forehead. *Eep.* Caught in the act! The tall, dark, and sinfully handsome Avail Leeds had turned around to find her hand had slipped down to her chin.

What he didn't know was that Stephanie had dropped said hand as soon as he'd gotten up from the bed. *How could she not?* He knew she'd been watching as he stood and flexed his delicious looking ass into a pair of jeans on his lower body. *What a shame to hide that body. Tsk.*

Heat suffused her cheeks, but she refused to look away. So, she peeked. *BFD.* He was too good-looking to not be aware of the effect he had on women. And she was only human.

"Sorry," she squeaked.

Stephanie bit her lower lip and looked down at her hands as they fisted the silk sheet tucked over her front. *Okay. I am naked. In a stranger's bed. A stranger who I am sure turned into some kind of red-dragony-monster-thingy. Oh damn.*

"Here, pet. Put this on," he handed her a fluffy white half-robe.

"Aren't you going to turn around?"

"Nope," he grinned.

She wanted to scream at him, but why bother? The truth was, she wanted him to look. Never wanted that before. As a fluffy chick, she tended to prefer the lights out. That way she could ignore the not-so-subtle suggestions of her lovers to seek a healthy lifestyle.

As if I have all day to cook healthy meals and work out for hours at a time! Hello, bills to pay! Besides, she liked her lifestyle. Her job was interesting, her co-workers were nice. Maccon City was turning out to be a pretty exciting place to live all in all. *Especially since she ran into him.*

So, he thought he was going to make her blush? Ha! The imp in her had her biting her lip seductively as she donned the terrycloth robe over her sheet. She smiled coyly while tying it before standing up and yanking the sheet out from under the thick fabric, revealing nothing more than her bare legs from her knees down.

"Ooh, that was naughty," he smirked, "You know, I'd rather you were naked, but if you have to wear something, I like you in my clothes."

"Really? You know that's creepy right?"

"Is it? Just being honest. I wouldn't want our relationship to begin any other way."

Stephanie stopped. *Relationship?* What was that supposed to mean? Surely, he wasn't going to try and make her think he was into anything more than a bit of sexy times with a stranger? Just look at him. The guy couldn't be hurting for dates. And yet he seemed to find her attractive.

So why not go for it? Stephanie straightened her back. That little devil on her shoulder was at it again! *You haven't had sex in forever, Steph. Why not indulge a little?* Okay, now that devil sounded just like Cora. Her BFF was the free loving sort. Never really Stephanie's style, but it had been a long dry spell.

"Pet?" Avail extended a long-fingered hand which she took cautiously. Heat flooded her from the innocent touch. *Almost like I'm touching fire.* What a way to burn! *Sizzle.*

Always the practical one, she'd never really been wined and dined, preferring to let her potential bedmates know the deal from the get-go. *Why not start now?*

Just the idea of abandoning all sense of reality and falling into his arms filled her with all sorts of lovely little decadent tingles. *Hang on. He hasn't even tried anything yet. Not really anyway.* She stepped across the cool marble floors and wondered at the predicament she found herself in.

"Thought you might be a little puckish after your ordeal. Please sit." He led her to an intimate little side table near the roaring fire that blazed from the far side of what she assumed was his bedroom.

An array of tasty small plates covered the surface, along with an antique looking ceramic tea pot that rested on a shiny silver warmer. It was so cozy and elegant, she smiled as she sat down. Noting the beautifully painted dishes and the delicately etched silverware. Everything sat on a spotless tablecloth that was embroidered with a fancy *L* monogram in each corner.

She bit her lip, stifling a sigh at the beautiful and romantic scene before her. Why would a man she just met create such a seductive stage for her? She wasn't sure but didn't think it wise to give anything away. *Let him work for it.* Cora's voice again.

Stephanie was just your average plump blonde thirty-something. Hardly someone men wanted to pamper and wow with their fancy good manners. At least, not the men she knew.

The heck with them. She might be bigger than what the fashion magazines claimed was acceptable, but she was a good person. She was honest, trustworthy, and hardworking. Even chubby girls deserved a little TLC. *So why not take what he was offering?*

Maybe because it came with a secret attached...

Where Stephanie was interested in a little footsie with the gorgeous man who claimed to be Avail Leeds, she wasn't so interested in being eaten by the red-scaled monster she could have sworn he turned into just outside. *Maybe I imagined all that?*

"I've prepared a little charcuterie board for us. Now, what has you thinking so hard, pet?" Avail leaned over and started putting little bits of cheese and toasted bread on her plate. Followed by some roasted grapes and what she thought was sliced prosciutto.

"Uh, thank you. I have to ask you, was that real?"

"Was what real?"

"Did I really see you turn into that, uh, I'm not sure what it's called?" Eyes down, she had no desire to insult the man who sat across from her.

"Devil," his handsome face remained trained on her. The rugged jaw at odds with the suave sensitivity she saw in his dark eyes. *Dayum*, he was so good to look at.

"What did you say?" Distracted by her preoccupation with his face, Stephanie felt her cheeks flame again.

"I said, people call my kind *Jersey Devils*. Fruit?" He asked as he scooped up sliced melon and dried apricots and set them on her plate.

"Would you like sugar or honey in your tea?"

"Sure," Stephanie replied.

She was almost afraid to look away. Afraid he'd

laugh or smile or hint at this being a joke of some kind. Maybe a weird rich people thing? But nope. He just answered.

"Which is it? Sugar *or honey?*"

"Oh. Um, honey, please." *Swallow.* She hadn't expected him to just admit it. *Now what?*

Stephanie shivered despite the borrowed robe and roaring fire. Maybe she caught a chill in the rain? *Nah.* She hadn't been cold when she'd woken up. How could she be with six feet plus of sexy man wrapped around her?

It'd been a long while since she'd been roused from sleep by such a promising specimen of man. Her pink bits had been working in some serious overtime ever since. She licked her lips, eliciting a growl from her host. Was it bad she thought it sexy? *OMG. Is this Stockholm Syndrome?*

Should she be finding her kidnapper sexy? Well, he didn't exactly kidnap her. Just kind of stated his claim and brought her back to his lair. His awfully expensive, elegantly decorated lair. Perhaps she should've feigned sleep a while longer to get her bearings? Or just to enjoy his attentions? *No. Bad girl!*

"Try the grilled eggplant," he brought a morsel to her mouth and she opened obediently.

Stephanie loved vegetables despite her fluffier stature.

"S'good," she wiped her mouth on her napkin and swallowed, keenly aware of his attention.

Between nibbles of decadent goodies and sips of the caffeine rich tea, Stephanie started to feel almost normal. Okay. *Fact check*: She was drawn to the man sitting across from her. *Like seriously drawn.* Stephanie was an adult. A single woman. She was totally capable of making her own choices about sex. More to the point, about whom she was going to have sex with. *Why not him?* Her body tingled with anticipation at his nearness. He was handsome. Smart. Kind. *And he sometimes had a tail. Swallow.*

She definitely recognized him now. Avail Leeds, the rich bad boy dubbed the *Naughty Dark Prince* by the tabloids. He was undoubtedly related to the woman she'd intended to meet with. A woman who did not seem to be here.

"Is there anything else I can get you?"

"Oh, no I couldn't eat another bite." She sipped her tea, wondering if she imagined his whispered *I sure could.*

"You seem to be taking this well," he mused.

"Well, do I have a choice?"

"I suppose you could freak out," he said.

"But that doesn't seem like you. Anything else I can do for you right now, pet?" His voice deepened with unspoken promises. Stephanie wanted to scream heck yeah, but she was tougher than that. *For now.*

"Yes, can you tell me where Margot Leeds is?"

"Grandmother? What for?" Shocked eyes, darker than any human eyes she'd ever seen, met hers.

"Is she here?" Refusing to be cowed by the severity of his glare, Stephanie met his gaze steadily.

"No, she's in Egypt. Will be until the end of the season, why?"

"She's the reason I'm here."

CHAPTER 4

"What was that?" Avail cocked his head to the side.

"I made an appointment with her to discuss her donation to the committee. She told me to come here today-"

Avail gripped the arms to his seat. His meddling grandmother couldn't have known what Stephanie was to him! Could she? He needed more information. Inhaling a deep breath, one that brought the subtle flavors of his future mate to his nostrils, Avail opened both eyes and focused entirely on her.

"*When* did you make this appointment with my grandmother?"

"Last week."

Last week. After his unfortunate date and the

headlines that had followed. *Fuck.* The blasted woman had been manipulating him since he was a child, of course, she'd manipulated this situation. *She's probably been scrying for my mate for ages unbeknownst to me.* A *gift* given to her upon mating with his grandfather, Margot Leeds was something of a prognosticator.

He never could get away with a damn thing as a child. She always knew what was going on despite his attempts to bribe the servants or hide his deeds in the woods. And now she'd manipulated this. He didn't know if he wanted to scream or sed her a bouquet of flowers to thank her. *Hmm. Perhaps both.*

Avail took one look at Stephanie, honey blonde hair curling softly around her shoulders as it dried, bright blue-eyes wide and waiting, plump lips slightly open. She was suddenly everything he'd ever wanted and hadn't known he was looking for. *But she was my discovery, dammit all, not Grandmother's!*

"Avail?" His name whispered on her lips snapped him out of his inner debate.

"Do you know who I am, pet?"

"You told me yourself, you're Avail Leeds."

"Yes, but do you follow the news?"

"I'd have to be living under a rock not to know about the *Naughty Dark Prince* though it took me a second to place you," ducking her head she shrugged her shoulders, and he couldn't help his body's natural reaction to the innocent movement.

"And do you believe me when I say I am the Jersey Devil? Or one of them at any rate."

"I admit I am having a difficult time accepting that, though I know what I saw," her whisper held a mix of awe and fear. She was so brave, his promised one. He nodded encouragingly and smiled at her, oddly proud of her honest and forthright answers.

"My grandmother has been after me to settle down for some time. It seems, she found you for me, pet," he shook his head in exasperation with the older woman.

"Excuse me?" Stephanie's eyebrows shot up.

"Lucky for me, Grandmother is always right. You are *my promised*, Stephanie Decatur."

"Um, we just met," she stood up, backing away from him.

No, no, no. This wouldn't do at all. Avail stalked his mate. One step at a time. Careful not to send her running. Lightning crashed, thunder boomed, and the lights flickered. The perfect setting indeed! *What woman could resist a big, strong man during a thunderstorm?*

Living out in the boonies often meant a loss of

power when storms proved incredibly strong. The manse had back-up generators of course, but they were typically used for kitchen appliances and such. The dark didn't bother him. In fact, his Devil had a natural affinity for it.

His little mate, however, proved just a tad skittish. She jumped when the lights flicked one final time before turning off completely. He wanted to go to her, to hold her in his arms and assure her of her safety. He'd never allow anything to harm her. *Never!*

"Stay back, please, I need to think," hands held out in front of her as if warding him off, Avail stilled. *So cute. She means to keep me at bay.*

"Now, pet, why think when you can feel?" He moved quickly, closing in on her tempting frame.

Her legs bumped the back of the bed as his hands settled around her waist. He tugged gently, bringing her body flush against his.

"Um, things like this don't normally happen to me-"

"Things like what, pet?" He brushed his lips across her cheek, moving slowly down the silky skin of her chin and neck. He couldn't get enough of her. *Want to taste every inch.*

"I don't know what to do," she whimpered as his lips settled on the pulse at the base of her neck.

"What do you mean?"

"You're trying to seduce me."

"I am seducing you, pet."

"That hasn't really happened to me before. *Oh, oh my,*" she moaned as his teeth nipped, tongue laved, and lips soothed the skin between her neck and shoulder. His gums ached with the need to loose his fangs. *Fuck.* He wanted to mark her. Now.

"Good. Then I don't have anyone to hunt down and kill," he said capturing her lips in a lingering kiss.

The taste of her was absolutely delicious. And he didn't mean the caramelized pecans she'd nibbled along with a piece of soft, sweet cheese drizzled in honey. Avail meant *her.*

His promised one's flavor was a heady mix of the sweet, golden liquid he preferred to sugar. A hint of spring flowers, but with a subtle bite to her too. Like the *piri piri* peppers he loved so much. He nibbled and teased, growling his disappointment when she pulled away. *Whine.*

"Hunt down and kill?" He smelled her dimming arousal and was determined to fan the flame. As soon as he answered her question. *Blast! Ixnay on the illskay!*

"Or maim if killing bothers, you," he licked her earlobe, taking the soft flesh between his lips.

He would only ever speak the truth to his mate. Lying didn't sit well with him. He figured she should know about his slightly possessive Devil when it came to her. In other words, if any other person, man, woman, beast, or both dared touch her, his Devil was sure to come out and play. *Mine.*

"Um, that seems a little much, no?"

"When it comes to you, pet? Nothing is too much."

"Look, it was, um, nice meeting you, but I think I have to go-"

Panic had him still as a statue. She could not leave. Not yet. His devil pushed at his skin, the pull of the moon making his beast harder to control. Especially with the temptation of his mate right in front of him.

"Do you really want that?" He asked. His voice a purr in the dark room.

"Yes. No. I, I don't know-"

Avail knelt at the foot of his mate. She was a normal. A human. He knew he should move slowly. Tread with care. Do all the things for her that his Grandmother had instilled upon him when he was a boy.

Treat your mate lovingly, Avail. Don't just bash her over the head and bring her back to your lair caveman style! Behave with some tact.

But what was wrong with the whole caveman thing? He'd found his mate! His entire body was on fire with wanting her. Why couldn't he just take the choice away? Kiss her until she was writhing beneath him, mindless and needy. But no. That wouldn't do. He wanted her willing. He wanted to be the one she chose. *An hour in her presence and I'm completely pussy-whipped. Sigh.*

Even his Devil shied away from such a thought. *Fuck.* He knew better than to act on his desires, but it was difficult when she was standing there in his robe. Like a present begging to be unwrapped. *Slow down.* He had to pace himself. Even if doing so was going to give him the bluest balls he'd ever had.

"I don't know what I want," her small whisper turned into a giggle of embarrassment. Her light laughter teased his senses, bringing forth a smile when he wanted to howl in pain.

His promised was beautiful when she smiled. A knockout. She covered her face with her hands, and he wanted to rip them away so he could look at her. He thought better of it and stood next to her, willing himself to retreat until she was sure of what she wanted. *Me. Pick me.*

"How about a tour of the house then? We can talk." *And kiss. And maybe a little groping.* His dick throbbed and he swatted it when she turned away, demanding the blasted muscle behave itself.

"Really?"

"Anything for you, pet," he took her hand and kissed her fingertips. He was happy to see a look of disappointment cross her face when he let go. Avail went to his dresser to retrieve a pair of soft, thick socks.

"What are you doing?'

"For your feet," he said. Kneeling down, he gently lifted one foot, then the other. Carefully unrolling each thick, grey sock and smoothing them on her dainty little feet until he was satisfied, she was warm and protected from the hard tile.

"Thank you. That's really thoughtful. I hate walking around in my bare feet."

"My pleasure, Stephanie. Shall we?"

Hand in hand they left the comfort of his room and he showed her the east wing of Leeds Mansion. The home of his ancestors had started with a one room cabin. Knocked down and rebuilt over the years until it was the sprawling home he now lived in and shared with his globetrotting grandmother.

"So, you live with your grandmother?"

"Yes. She raised me. But she is rarely home these days," he smiled thinking of his robust grandmother. She was a pip. A horror to live with, but he loved the blasted woman.

"She just travels all the time?"

"Yes. Ever since Grandfather passed."

"I am so sorry," she squeezed his hand, sympathy softened her gaze.

"It's alright, pet, he always was a daredevil. Pun intended."

The mention of his alter ego brought a frown to her face. He needed to move even slower on that front. Stephanie still did not seem sure about that side of him. Even after she'd seen him tail and all.

They walked through the main hallway into one of the entertaining rooms. A healthy blend of modern and antique furniture graced the mansion. Avail was a firm believer that comfort should come first, but his grandmother refused to part with their history.

The result was a somewhat eclectic, yet beautiful home. At least he thought so. *What if she doesn't like it?* He'd certainly be willing to compromise on some changes for her. Worried, he stole a glance as she ran her hand the soft leather couch in the east parlor.

"What do you think of Leeds House?" he asked trying not to let his nervousness show.

"I've never seen anything like it. It's beautiful," she smiled. Relief poured through him. *You have got it bad, my boy.*

"Can I ask you about the whole Jersey Devil thing?"

"Of course. What do you want to know?" He tensed. For the first time in his life, it mattered whether someone approved of him. Of what he *was*.

"Were you cursed?"

"Hardly!" Affronted he recoiled as if she'd slapped him.

"I'm sorry. I am just trying to get a handle on this. It's not every day you meet a legendary creature," she mumbled.

"Sorry. I guess I am closest to a Shifter-"

"You mean like a Werewolf?"

"I am hardly a dog, but yes, I suppose."

"OMG! They're real?!"

"Of course, they are, pet."

"No shit?"

"No shit," he laughed at the crude word.

"And you are like that? Like you turn into the Jersey Devil on full moons?"

"Not exactly. I can Change at will though the call is stronger at times."

"What does that mean? Oof!" She tripped over the leg of a side table and would have went sprawling had Avail not caught her in time.

Awareness pulsed through him as he held the soft form of his mate in his arms. Her heart was pounding, he could hear it. The scent of her arousal musky and strong, he breathed in, savoring it.

"Let's head back. The lack of light will make it difficult for you to see where you're going and it will be chilly in the other rooms," he whispered.

"Um. Okay," she straightened. Avail mourned the loss of her touch. *Soon.*

"I have so many questions."

"Yes, well, before you begin, you need to understand that I am not really supposed to discuss this with you. You are, after all, *a normal.*"

"A what?"

"Normal. It is our word for human."

"Oh, but I saw *you*," disappointment marred her voice.

"Look, the only reason I revealed myself is because I couldn't help it."

"What? Why not?"

"Because you're my mate, pet. My Devil knew it the second he scented you on the night air."

"What does that mean?"

"You. Are. Mine." Possession filled him and he noted her scent.

Yes. She liked that. Despite being a thoroughly modern woman, his pet enjoyed it when he stated his claim. Good to know. He would state it loudly and often. *Mine.*

"But we just met-"

"That has nothing to do with it. You see, well, I suppose I should go back to the beginning. You see my ancestor, the first Mother Leeds, was a Witch."

"They're real too?"

"Yes. I guess it will go faster if you just assume most things you have heard about are in fact real."

"Okay."

"Okay. *Good,*" he was pleased she trusted him. He continued his tale, as he led the way back to his rooms.

"She dabbled in the usual fortune-telling, healing, glamours, and the like. Then she moved on to some *forbidden magic.* Her pursual of those *dark arts* led to a meeting with a demon that many mistook as the actual Devil. *Yes, he exists.* Anyway, this one was a prince of Hell, a powerful Demon named Rosier."

"Whoa."

'Exactly. Well, experiencing an instant attraction, it would seem the two of them had a wild affair resulting in the birth of the very first Jersey Devil right here in the Pine Barrens almost three hundred years ago."

"I always thought it was just a legend."

"Aren't most legends just truths that people no longer believe?"

"I suppose so."

"So, what *I am* is a direct descendant of that first Witch-Devil hybrid. A Shifter and not. A Witch and not. I am something *else*."

"Are you dangerous?"

"Yes. But not to you. I would never hurt you, Stephanie. You are my mate."

"Why do you think I am your mate?"

"I don't think it, I know it. My Devil knew it the second we scented you on the night air. You are my *promised*. The only being in the entire universe created for me."

"That's unbelievable," she whispered.

"Can't you feel, Stephanie? I can. Right here," with his larger hand wrapped around hers he tugged until her palm covered that part of his chest where his heart resided. It thudded heavily under her touch.

"Wow," she gasped. Her musk grew thicker. The Devil inside of him reveled in her heightened state. *She wants us. Mark her.*

"I know you have questions, pet, and we will get to them, but not right now. Having you this close, all I can think about is touching you. Kissing you. Here and here," his fingers ran over her lips and neck, caressing his way down her lush body.

"Avail," she moaned his name and swayed towards him. Her body responding to his already. *Yes.* It was good that she recognized him as her mate even if only on a physical level.

"Stephanie," he said her name softly and bent to lift her princess-style as they entered the darkness of his bedroom.

His Devil roared inside of him. The beast overcome with pleasure and anticipation as he made his way through his childhood home back to his lair. The temperature was warm with the fire still glowing in its grate. The orange and yellow flames reflected off the black marble mantle, giving the room an unearthly glow.

"I shouldn't feel like this," she whispered, arms wrapping around his neck.

"Like what?"

"So, attracted to you." Her confession spread warmth through his body, made him want to pound his chest.

Why shouldn't it make him proud? She wanted him. His woman desired him, and he would give her everything she wanted. *Anything. All of it. Here. Now.*

And if he was a very lucky Devil, she'd be wearing his mark soon! *Grrrr.*

CHAPTER 5

Stephanie could hardly believe what was happening. The halls of super-slutdom were seriously going to ask for her photograph if she continued on this path! Not that she cared. Some things were simply worth it.

At least, that's what Cora always said! As for herself and Leandra, they were a little more cautious in their sexual escapades. But if she were being honest, she'd always wondered how it would feel to act on her desires. *To give in to lust without fear of judgement. The possibilities were endless.*

Liaisons of the pounce first, ask questions later variety were fairly unknown to Stephanie. But hey, what the heck? You only live once, right? To think she made fun of all those folks who tweeted

#YOLO every chance they got! *If you can't beat 'em, join 'em!*

She always left that kind of carefree, wild existence to others. Like her BFFs Cora and Leandra. True, the later was a tad bit tamer than the first, but both women outshone her in the field of sexual experience. *To her utter consternation.*

Couldn't be helped though, right? Stephanie's own shy nature and curvaceous body kept her from engaging in wild encounters with the opposite sex. Always too damned embarrassed to just let herself go. She felt her face heat, imagining her flush at her private thoughts.

Couldn't be helped with her coloring. Baby soft blonde hair, pale ivory skin, and blue-eyed, you'd think she'd have them lining up! Not that she was ugly, she certainly didn't think so. In the 1950s, she'd have been ideal with her extra curves. But nowadays, with tall, waifish models on every cover and thigh gap a thing of pride, well, she was hardly anyone's ideal woman.

Certainly not the men she'd been interacting with. Hence the guy who stood her up at lunch today. Okay. *Fact check:* Stephanie was used to awkward interludes and coffee dates that ended with a mutually agreed upon appointment for sex or not. A girl had needs and a modern one could see about getting those needs filled by something other than a battery-operated toy.

She fully understood the physical side of intercourse, the necessity of it, having engaged infrequently herself. Flushing again she surprised herself with thoughts of a wild interlude with Avail. Would he fulfill the promise those dark eyes made every time he looked at her? Would he make her wild with longing or would he disappoint her? *Doubt that's even possible. Look at him for god's sake.*

Perhaps it was the blandness of her past experiences that had her reacting so uncharacteristically to Avail? Maybe it had been too long since she last indulged? Either way, Stephanie was almost ready to admit the man had her panting in anticipation.

He was sex on legs. A six-foot something, dark haired, dark eyed, full-lipped boy toy that she was dying to get her hands, maybe lips, *okay*, both on! Jersey Devil or not, he was freaking hot. Like *super-fuck-me-now-please-yes-I-will-call-you-daddy-hawt!*

In that light, she could be forgiven for currently jumping his bones. So, what if the man was the grandson of the woman she was supposed to hit up for a large sum of money for her job? That was the least of her concerns. The foremost being, how to get him to never stop what he was doing to her.

"You're thinking too hard, pet. Let me fix that for you," he growled against her skin. And damn if she didn't feel moisture dripping from her slit at his words. *Freaking sexy-ass Devil!*

She moaned when his hands brushed past her nipples, then moved on to squeeze her ass. *Mmm.* He was everywhere at once. Touching, groping, kneading her ripe flesh. *Oh lord,* that felt fantastic!

Stephanie couldn't not reciprocate if she tried. Fingers greedy to explore more of him, she ran her nails down his muscle carved torso and further still until she caressed the thin denim that covered his long, thick, decidedly impressive evidence of his imminent need for her.

He wants me. Giddy with the knowledge, she squeezed and explored him over his jeans, dragging a low groan from his lips. *Okay.* She was a super-duper slut. But who cared?

Things like this never happened to her, and she planned to take full advantage. Who would even believe it? The *Naughty Dark Prince* himself, the very one her coworkers drooled over, had his tongue in her mouth as his hands worked the tie of her robe. *His robe actually.*

She could hardly think. Didn't want to anyway. Her body was on fire for him. No one had ever brought her to such a fever pitch before. She needed more, wanted to see and feel all of him as he teased her body to new unexplored heights. *Oh, did he just put his tongue in my ear? Who knew that would make my toes curl?*

Pressing her body against his strong, muscular frame, she lifted on her tip toes to plunder his mouth. She felt unusually aggressive. Every cell in her body screaming for her to mount this man. Make him hers. In. Every. Way. Possible.

Tugging his head down, she sucked and nibbled, kissing him with everything she had in her. *Need to get closer.* She moaned and shrugged her shoulders, allowing the robe to dip further down her back. His approving growl was like a tug directly to her clit. Her body never responded like this to men.

Eager and hungry for him, Stephanie refused to think about any of her old hang-ups. She unzipped his jeans and shoved down the material, wanting more of him.

Avail did the same with her robe, just as eager. With a seductive little wiggle, she was freed of the offending garment. *Finally.*

"Mine," she heard him, though he spoke in a deep whisper.

He held her apart from him for a full minute, simply looking at her. So, she did the same. Taking in every inch of his corded frame. *Yes,* she thought. Now, they could look and touch and taste to their hearts' content.

This was so much more than attraction, she thought wildly. She could almost fall in love with him, the way he looked at her so profound. No one had ever made her feel like that. Like she was perfect and beautiful.

Panic made her heart pound, or was that him? She swayed on her feet, and he was here to catch her. His mouth sealed over hers. Taking control of the kiss, he walked her backwards until she felt the bed underneath her.

His skin was hot against hers. *So good.* His whispered words making her want to come so badly. No one had ever touched her in so many ways. With words, and lips, and hands. She was practically desperate for him to sink into her. *To unite them. Make them one. Yes. God, yes.*

Sanity crept back in for a moment as his tongue slid out of her mouth. Hands framing her face he slowed their kiss to just lips. A smooth, soft meeting that made her want to weep.

"Stephanie," he whispered her name with such tenderness once again her heart squeezed.

I could love this man, she thought. Panic flared and had her stiffening under his mouth. *Don't you dare ruin this, Stephanie. It's just a moment out of time. You can handle a sexy as sin man for one night.*

"Pet? You alright?"

Shaking herself out of the stupid argument she was having in her mind, Stephanie willed herself to focus on the now. On the pleasure.

"Yes, I am. Avail, will you make love to me?" She asked boldly. No more playing. She was going to take him for herself. Even if they only had this one night.

"I intend to, but only if you're certain. Are you?"

"I am. I want you."

"I want you too, pet," he growled capturing her mouth in a hard, aggressive move that made her want to open for him. To deny him nothing. His head lifted. Dark eyes glowing with a reddish light. *Was that his Devil?* She knew it in her heart that his beast came to the surface to see her. That fact turned her on even more. *I make him lose control.*

She felt powerful and sexy under his heated gaze.

Her nipples pebbled into hard points and her channel squeezed on air, waiting to be filled. *Never like this.* There was some unknown chemistry between them. She could feel it. A living thing, almost, this fierce desire in her, this incredibly wanting. More than anything she wanted him to fill her, to possess her. Craved it, with every fiber of her being.

"No more games, pet. This is about to get very real."

There was only one thing she could say in reply. One word that would bring with it the release she'd been on the verge of since she woke up in his bed earlier that evening. She licked her lips, moistening them with her tongue, acutely aware of his focus on the small pink muscle.

"*Yes.*"

CHAPTER 6

Avail held on to his humanity by a thread. The Devil inside of him pushed at his skin, wanting to be a part of the mating as much as his human half. He drove the beast back down, just barely. Allowing his alter ego to peek through his eyes at the wondrous creature he meant to mark as his own. *Yessss.*

"Ah, pet, you're killing me," he groaned and swiveled his hips, enjoying the friction their bodies created. He couldn't wait until he was inside of her, doing all the naughty little things he'd been thinking since he saw her straddling his fence.

Her musky, sweet fragrance filled his nostrils. The scent of her arousal was growing stronger.

Enough to tempt the very Devil. Delicious. But where should he begin?

Such a blatant invitation to be seduced. An abundance of flesh for him to explore. He could get drunk on her. Gorge himself on her sweet, spicy taste. Spend hours learning every perfect inch of her. And still he'd want more. *As it should be,* his Devil growled.

He could hardly contain himself. She squirmed beneath him as he kissed and touched. A tease here. A nibble there. On an on he went torturously slow, until he drew a sharp, satisfying hiss from her plump lips. His little mate was as needy for him as he was for her.

Grrrr. The soul deep grumble built up from his stomach, sounding loudly through his chest to his throat. Never had he felt so many conflicting emotions. Desire, passion, possessiveness, and pride in his woman, but also uncertainty, the need to go slow, to care for her. *Shit. I sound like a fucking idiot.*

Or did he? He'd never met his mate before. These new emotions were bound to calm down once he had her a few dozen times. *Yes. Good plan. Mark her as mine. No one else can have her.*

The very thought sent his Devil in a rage. But no, anger had no place here. Not when she was in his arms. Avail wanted her so bad. To touch, feel, experience all of *it*. All of *this mating*.

He wanted to melt into her. Couldn't pull away if he tried. Not that he wanted to try. His whole body burned from need. He ran his hands over her gorgeous curves, loving every dip and swell. *Perfect.* She was fucking perfect for him.

So soft and warm. Like a woman, *his woman*, should be. He flicked the hard nubs of her nipples with his fingers before he gently cupped her heavy breasts. Lifting and kneading them with a tender touch before adding just a hint of pain to the hard nubs. Making it all the better for his lovely little mate.

Her mewls of pleasure told him she approved of his careful ministrations. The sounds of her heavy breathing and gasps drove him wild. Avail wanted more from her, he wanted it all.

He lowered his skilled fingers to the rounded globes of her ass while he attended her breasts with lips, teeth, and tongue. Loving how small she was beneath him, and not. Her ample curves touching him, cradling him as she'd been born to do. *Yesss.*

He tugged her closer to him. Not satisfied until he was touching every inch of her against his own flesh. His Devil was right there, in the moment with him. The two halves of his soul working together to mark his mate with his scent, his touch, his claim.

"So beautiful, so mine," he touched her face with his fingertips. Tracing her soft features, eyes mesmerized by her beauty. And she was beautiful like this. All flustered and bare to him, her desire an open book for him to read.

With great reverence he bent and kissed her soft skin. Never like this before. It was as if his need for this one woman was hot enough to start fires on its own. Maybe it was.

He knew the stories. Had heard them as a child. Despite the legends, a Jersey Devil only breathed fire after he'd mated with his promised one. Perhaps that was why his chest felt aflame? Whatever the reason, he was going to see it through. There was no turning back now.

"I want to give you tenderness, pet. I want to worship you," he whispered.

His desire to treasure every sweet inch of his promised pulsed through his blood. Then he smiled. Realizing nothing was stopping him, Avail scooted down to the edge of the bed.

"Mine," he growled once more. Unable to stop himself from repeating the words.

His tongue laved at her rounded belly, covering

the closely cropped curls of her mound with soft kisses as he pried her thighs gently open. He could only stare for a moment at her glistening pink perfection. *Fuck.* She was gorgeous.

He could wait no longer. Dipping his head, he swiped his tongue across her plump folds. Reveling in her flavors.

Mouth latching onto her clit, he tugged on the sensitive flesh, satisfied when she cried out and bucked wildly against him. *So responsive.* He couldn't wait to hear what other sounds she made as he continued to pleasure her.

Hands skimmed up her shapely calves to her thick thighs, his mate moaned as he slid a single finger into her sex. Her tight channel clenched him as he licked at her nub. Tension spiraled throughout her body as he brought her nearer to her climax.

He felt invincible holding her like that, loving her like that, bringing her pleasure. Like he could do anything as long as he held on to this one woman. And he intended to hold on for a very long time. After all, he was only starting to convince her she was his and his alone.

"Avail!" She crowed his name. Back arched as she found yet another climax on his tongue. Her flavors

burst on his taste buds, spicy and sweet. All her. *All mine.*

"Please," she begged, pulling on his hair until he slid up her body.

She gripped his face, kissing his mouth. *So fucking hot.* His Stephanie was passionate and unafraid. She wiggled against him, sliding her sex along the hard length of his cock. *Fuck me. Yes.* He needed to be inside of her. *Now.*

The warm honey of her arousal allowed him to spread her slick sex open. He tested her with his fingers, dipping one and then two into her undulating heat.

Avail lifted up, aligning his swollen head at her entrance. His mouth feasting on hers, he pushed himself slowly inside of her welcoming channel. *So tight. So fucking hot.*

"I'm going to mark you, pet, take you, make you mine," he growled the words, but did not move until she nodded her assent.

"Say the words, love. Tell me you want me to do this," he commanded. Avail wanted no misunderstandings. Once he marked her, she was never getting away from him. *Mine.*

"Yes, Avail, yes. Please," she moaned tugging him closer with her small hands wrapped in his hair.

Her channel clutched at him as she ground herself against his pelvis, striving towards the ultimate goal. She felt so good. Like coming home. He swiveled his hips, a slow, deep swirl that had his dick sliding even further down into her molten core.

Heaven. He was in Heaven. The irony was not lost on him, descendant of a Demon and all. If this was as close to the actual pearly gates as he'd get, he'd die a happy man. He pressed her down into the mattress.

Luxuriating in her warmth. Only a tiny shred of sanity kept him for rutting on her like an animal. His promised deserved better, she deserved so much more. *Roses, champagne, diamonds, sunsets, long trips to tropical islands. Anything. Everything.* He wanted to give it all to her.

Thick legs wrapped around his waist, she pulled him closer. Avail increased his pace. Something was pushing him on. His Devil? The urge to mark her? *Yes. Mark. Mine.* He pumped his hips, glorying in how perfectly they fit together. So tight.

"Stephanie," he said her name, looking into her glazed blue eyes. He wanted her to fall with him, wanted to make this moment perfect.

He found her clit with his thumb. Circling the small nub as his cock rocked deeper inside of her. *Tap, tap, tap,* he kept rhythm, steadily increasing as

she began to tense. Back arched, mouth opened in a soundless scream she scratched at his shoulders wildly. His promised was passionate.

Raking her nails down his back, Avail threw back his head and roared. Cock pulsing, semen coating her walls, he came, and came, until he was hoarse.

"Mine," he growled.

Cock still swollen. He pumped slowly. Swivel, swivel, swirl. Holding her against him, Stephanie's eyes widened.

"But? Oh!" She gasped as he touched just that right spot inside. Urging her legs to spread wider, he ground his pubic bone against her swollen nub.

Loving her cries of pleasure, he repeated the move again and again. Nipping her once below her ear, and twice on her neck he used his tongue to soothe her skin. The beats in him reveling in his mate. Then he found the spot where he'd leave his mark, just above her left breast.

Cock throbbing with the need to come again, Avail didn't rush it. *No.* This was for her. All for her. He needed her to come with him. Using everything he had, his body, hands, and mouth, he brought her to new heights.

Slowing down to an almost painful pace, he steadily increased. Her ultra-sensitive body tensing with awaited ecstasy. He felt her vaginal walls clench around his dick. Milking him, sucking him in deeper. *So good.* Pleasure began to spiral, the beginning of ecstasy. *Oh fuck. Yesssss.* And then, he struck.

Swallowing down the life-giving fluid of his promised, Avail felt the bonds of their mating surround him. The pulsating magic wrapped around the two of them, connecting them as nothing else in the universe could. No laws of man or beast. This was something different. A complete union of two beings made for each other.

For as surely as she was made for him, Avail knew in his soul that he was made to love her.

"Now, you're mine," he said as he slowly withdrew from her intense heat.

She gasped, a sound he readily swallowed. Kissing his mate. Soothing her. *Mine, mine, mine.* The never-ending chant repeating in his mind.

"That was incredible," she whispered. Exhaustion taking over, her features stilled in sleep as he looked on.

"Beautiful mate," he kissed her head, pulling her closer against him and covering them both with the blanket.

Before he succumbed to sleep, he had a brief moment of panic. Yes, she'd agreed to allow him to

mark her, but he hadn't explained all of it. Not really. He'd failed to tell her of the changes that she would experience. The ones involving certain magical powers that were bound to occur, perhaps even a more bestial side to his promised. Anything could happen really.

His grandmother had been given the gift of precognition upon her mating. A Witch's gift really. Most mates received something similar. Of course, there had been one that was unlike the rest.

Some long-ago ancestor, he recalled. She was given an animal of her own to Shift into, a lynx or some other woodland cat, if he wasn't mistaken. Rare for a Devil's mate to receive her own animal as a gift, but not unheard of. At any rate, he needed to prepare his promised for whatever she'd experience as a result of his marking her.

Plenty of time, he told himself as he snuggled into her heavenly body. How did he get so lucky? He breathed in her spicy feminine scent and couldn't resist dropping another kiss on her soft lips. *I'll tell her everything in the morning.*

Except there was a snag to his plan. When Avail woke up the next morning, he was alone.

Roar!

CHAPTER 7

oly crap. Stephanie yawned softly and turned over. *Mmm. Soft sheets. Wait, didn't this happen already?*

Sated and deliciously sore she turned over and stretched. Noticing more than a few sticky parts on her body. *Eep!*

She wondered if she forgot to shower before bed. That wasn't like her. She had a routine. *Bath, book, bed.* Her favorite Friday night practice.

So, why was she sticky again? Opening her eyes wide, she blinked once, then twice. *Uh oh.* She peeked at the enormous, naked man snoring softly beside her.

Oh no, I didn't! Looking at the large expanse of his

huge naked back and to her own unclothed girly parts she started to panic. *Uh oh. Yes. I did.*

Biting her lip, she slid out from the covers. Careful not to rouse her mysterious lover of the night before. *Looks so peaceful asleep. Almost like a boy.*

She smiled abashedly. He was unlike any other man she'd ever met. Naturally. The man turned into a supernatural creature, for heaven's sake. A fact he didn't exactly hide from her. On the contrary, all that talk of Devils and mates and his family history swam around in a jumble in her mixed-up brain.

She needed to think. To breathe in some fresh air that wasn't full of that spicy, manly musk of his. His scent was everywhere. On her skin, in the sheets. *Dayum.* She was about two seconds away from jumping him asleep or not.

What the heck? Eep! Stephanie never felt like this after sex. Then again, this wasn't exactly your average, every day, noncommittal sex with a guy. The kind she had experienced in the past however infrequently.

Nope. This was like *mind-blowing-touched-my-soul-and-heart-life-altering-I-will-never-be-the-same-sex. Oh shit.* She felt a full-on panic about to blow, but that couldn't happen there. No. She needed her own space.

Not thinking about anything other than getting away from Leeds House, she quietly found and donned one of Avail's button-down shirts, a clean pair of joggers, and some rubber-soled slippers. She stole one last look at him. God, he was so handsome.

And he'd been so gentle despite the naughty things he'd said and done to her. Things no one else ever tried with the fluffy blonde. Okay. *Fact check: I just had the best sex in my life with a gorgeous millionaire and I am skipping out the morning after.*

Before she chickened out and talked herself into staying. If she did that, she would wind up begging him to give their one night of sexy fun times another go. How could she live with herself if he said no?

No way. It was better to leave with a good memory, than as a bad one. Stephanie high-tailed it out of there. Remembering her dead car at the end of the long, winding road that led up to the drive-way, she cursed just thinking about the half-hour walk back to the edge of town. *Oh well.* At least she would have time to think.

Only two and a half hours after she'd left Avail's warm bed, Stephanie found herself back at the office. *Dammit.*

It seemed *Viridi Lux* was not thrilled with the injunction she'd threatened to file against their company should they proceed with the intention to purchase tracts of the Pine Barrens for development. She might have even suggested that those tracts were illegally available for purchase due to some heavy-handed methods by the elusive company.

In turn, *Viridi Lux* had contacted her boss who had been calling her all night long. A fact she had not learned until she retrieved her phone from her bag. Thank goodness for waterproof phone cases. *Or not.*

Viridi Lux demanded an emergency meeting as soon as possible. On this very bright Saturday morning, in fact. And there went her plans to soak in a hot bath and munch on potato chips and onion dip until she figured out what to do about her annoying craving for a certain gorgeous millionaire. *Grrr.*

Avail hadn't called or tracked her. *A good thing.* But for some reason she felt oddly disappointed. Lucky she'd found her purse outside of his gate where she'd dropped it. *So, I guess he couldn't find me if he tried.*

Didn't matter. She'd needed her purse. That way she didn't have to replace her license and credit cards, and she'd already called a tow to get her car. There was no reason to see the big guy again at all. Especially since he seemed uninterested.

It doesn't matter, Stephanie. You wanted the experi-

ence and you had it. Maybe it had been the weather. Some crazy attraction brought on by all the thunder and lightning. What would a man like that see in her anyway? Well. He must have seen something. He did pursue her rather ardently.

Still, doesn't matter. She was the one who left. *Snuck right out of the house doing the walk of shame. Didn't even give him a chance. Ugh.* She hated arguing with herself.

Besides what would he have said? Thanks for the sex, off you go! She simply saved herself the embarrassment of an awkward parting. Stephanie was a realist. She was simply not the type of woman to inspire happily-ever-afters. Especially not with men like him. *Focus. Work.*

She straightened her spine and winced as a slight pounding in her head made itself known. Her chest squeezed and she took a moment to breathe. Harsh cleaning liquids and someone's body spray threatened her stomach with an untimely reappearance of her meager breakfast. *Yuck. Strange. Maybe I caught something when I was out in the rain?*

It was a typical spring in New Jersey, thunderstorms one second and bright blue skies the next. But normally, she was a bit heartier than that. Sighing once more, she opened the main door to the offices the Committee rented. *Time to get ready to prepare for my meeting! Yay. Ugh.*

Wearing gray slacks and a tight yellow top, ignoring the looks she was getting from her co-workers, Stephanie stepped lightly over the tiles floor. Her low-heeled sandals clicked loudly as she made her way. Usually conservative, today she felt more alive and vivacious.

"Hey, uh, morning Steph. Wow, you look great! I want to say sorry for missing our lunch date yesterday-" Tommy, her co-worker and the rat who stood her up at *Roll Over* the day before, seemed to stumble over himself trying to get near her.

"Don't worry about it," she replied.

Oddly repulsed she stepped back. More than a little anxious to get away from the guy who only yesterday she'd have gone to lunch with. *Yuck.*

What was she thinking? She took in his prematurely receding hair line and flabby body, wondering why she would have ever said yes to the man. It wasn't so much his physical appearance that was repugnant, more the way he didn't bother trying to hide his leer. As if she was some object for his perusal.

"My eyes are up here," she snapped her fingers, and he had the grace to at least look abashed.

"Sorry, you just, uh, look so different."

"It's just clothes, Tommy, but it's not an invitation. Understand?" A growl welled in her chest.

Startled by the sound, she turned around and stepped into her office. *WTH?* She only knew one person who growled in his speech. *Guess the company I kept last night rubbed off on me.* She sighed wondering again if she'd not made a mistake by leaving so abruptly.

Yesss. The word, so clear in her head, definitely was not her. Stephanie panicked. Breathing deeply, she sat down and took out her compact. Bright blue eyes stared back at her. At least they did for a second. They were soon replaced with gold ones with oddly slitted pupils. *Oh shit.*

She had no time to think about the sudden appearance of what so closely resembled her lover of last night's eyes reflected back at her. There was a sharp knock at her door and in walked a heavily made-up woman who reeked as if she bathed in the most obnoxious brand of perfume available.

"Ms. Decatur? I'm Angie White, president of *Viridi Lux,*" her sinister smile made Stephanie want to snarl at the Witch. *Wait, Witch?* Startled her eyes opened wide as she gestured for the woman to sit. *Yessss,* answered that new part of herself, *Witch.*

"Hello Ms. White, nice to meet you in person," she lied.

"Yes. It is nice to finally meet the person giving us such a difficult time."

Stephanie tensed at the threat lingered under the stranger's smile. She smelled foul. Sour and tart despite the cloying perfume she wore. Donning her best professional smile, she replied in an even voice.

"Ah, well, it is our prime goal to protect our local wild places here in South Jersey, and I am afraid your company is after their very destruction."

Stephanie pushed back the desire to leave the room. Something inside screamed for her to get away from the woman, *no*, the *Witch*, in front of her. *Danger.* She was in danger. The urge to run strong, she dug in her heels. This was her *job*. She needed to be a professional in this place and no one, Witch or not was going to send her running.

"Nonsense. *Viridi Lux* is a forward moving company and you have been a thorn in our side these past months," Ms. White smiled.

An unfriendly smile. One that had alarm bells sounding in Stephanie's head. The hair on the back of her neck stood up. She looked around for a distraction, but there was none. Besides, the part of her warning her of danger, seemed to salivate at the idea of an altercation. Never one for violence, Stephanie practically gasped aloud. Ms. White zeroed in on the sound and smiled widely. *Falsely.*

"I have a proposition for you Ms. Decatur if you'd care to read the following documents. Then maybe you can understand what we're trying to do," she held out a manila folder which for some reason made Stephanie shy away.

"Uh, you can leave that on my desk Ms. White, and I will get back to you after I've had the time to go over everything. Thank you and goodbye."

Yes, she was blunt to the point of being rude, but something weird was happening. Stephanie didn't know what the voice inside of her was, but she trusted she was right in stating that this woman was a dangerous enemy. Disturbing news on its own, but not as bad as her happy anticipation of the upcoming violence should this meeting not end immediately. *Eep!*

"No," Ms. White said, "I insist on waiting. Here take this." She pushed the file towards Stephanie. Her aggressive stance at odds with her small stature. *We can take her. Crush her. No more Witch.* What was that? *Eep!*

"Uh, you should go," Stephanie leaned farther back. Disconcerted by the way the woman's show of force, she growled deep in her throat then disguised it by coughing.

"Excuse me, I need to get a drink," she stood and moved to go around her desk but was cut off by Ms. White.

What was this lady's problem anyway? There was something so off about her. It tickled her nose, making Stephanie want to sneeze at the same time that voice inside her growled and snarled. *Want out.*

"Take it!" Ms. White inched closer her eyes glowing a purplish color.

The air stunk like ozone around the Witch. *Yesss. Bad magic.* She didn't know how she knew it; she just did. Stephanie put her hands up defensively. Breathing raggedly, she sucked in the stifling air.

The sound of heavy footsteps reached her suddenly sensitive ears and her eyes darted to the door. There, big as life, Avail Leeds stood snarling at the Witch in her office.

"Get back," he commanded. "Stephanie, you alright?" He asked quietly. His black eyes ran over every inch of her in the span of a few seconds.

"Avail," she exhaled his name, a feeling of contentment settled over her.

"Ms. White, I believe your meeting is over. Leave the file. I will be contacting your superiors about this incident," Avail snarled at the woman who visibly paled at his presence.

"Avail, I had no idea you were acquainted with Ms. Decatur." She still withheld the document she'd been more than willing to shove at Stephanie just moments before.

"Heed my words, *Witch*, Stephanie Decatur is under my protection, as are the lands which you seek. As of twenty minutes ago, the tracts of land in question have been purchased by Leeds Foundation as a designated wildlife reserve. *Viridi Lux* cannot touch them. Now, leave the file and take yourself out of here."

"Apologies, Avail," eyes lowered the Witch fled dropping the file on the floor.

Stephanie growled at the familiar use of his name from the other woman's lips. *Who did that overly made-up hussy think she was anyway?* No looking. He was hers dammit.

"No, pet, don't touch the file. It's cursed," he mumbled a few phrases over it, ensuring the door was closed before doing so. He lifted the document and placed it on her desk before coming to stop in front of her.

Stephanie moved closer to the man, never taking her eyes off him. She felt the fear his words had instilled in Angie White. Exactly how she did that, she had no idea. She just knew it made her all hot and bothered. *Very hot.*

The anxiety that had caused her to hyperventilate moments ago subsided in the strength of his presence. He was so big, so handsome, everything she'd ever wanted in a man. *And he'd actually come for me. Why wouldn't he? We are mates.* She couldn't wait to have him alone. Maybe then she could satisfy her need for him? *Get closer. Mate.*

The sound of her breathing was unusually loud, but she didn't care. It was just the two of them closed in her office. No one could see or hear them. If she were quiet enough. *Oh hell,* she'd risk it. Stephanie bit her lip and launched herself at him. And hot damn, he caught her.

"Always," he said against her mouth, crushing her to him, "I will always catch you, pet. Didn't I make that clear last night?"

After a few passionate kisses and a little maneuvering, she sat astride her man in her office chair, praying the door was locked.

"I was confused this morning," she hid her face in the crook of his neck. Embarrassment heating her cheeks.

"You should've woken me, pet."

"I know. I'm sorry. I just didn't want to overstay my welcome."

At that he frowned. Pushing her hair back from her face with his long fingers, Avail leaned his forehead against hers.

"I know this is fast. But like I explained, though apparently not that well, you are *my Mate*. Stephanie, you are *my promised one*. The sole being in the entire universe created for me and me alone. You accepted my Mark last night, pet. We are now bound together, *for eternity*."

"That's a bit fast. Isn't it?"

"Not for me. Not about you. I knew it when I saw you stuck on the top of my fence."

"Oh, how embarrassing!"

"No, pet, you were gorgeous, *are gorgeous. Perfection*, pet. My feelings for you are stronger than I ever imagined they could be, but I understand you've been raised a *normal*, used to your *normal* ways. It will take time for you to accept, I suppose."

"Speaking of that, am I? Still a *normal?*"

That statement sparked his interests. He peered into her eyes intently, inhaling deeply.

"Your scent has changed. I don't know, pet. Tell me, how do you feel?"

"Different. Not alone. I, I can't describe it."

"When one of my kind finds his mate and gives her his Mark, a gift sometimes accompanies it," he explained.

"Like a voice inside my head?"

"Are you hearing a voice? This is extremely rare, pet. Are you sure?"

"I am very sure. It's like I've got a split personality or something all of a sudden. Kind of cool though, considering it warned me against taking the folder from Ms. White. What was that anyway?"

"Ah, yes. The owner of *Viridi Lux* is a Witch, not good or bad really, but she is power hungry. That folder was bespelled. And your *voice* warned you against touching it?"

"Yes." The second the Witch had entered her office her inner alarm system started going nuts.

She'd wanted nothing to do with the woman. When she'd addressed Avail so informally, well, Stephanie had wanted to tear into her with her claws. *Wait. Claws? Yessss.* Stephanie closed her mind to the voice inside of her and focused instead on the man in front of her.

She'd deal with the rest later. Right then she only wanted one thing. Ignoring the noises from outside her office door, she scooted closer to Avail. Nuzzling his neck with her lips, she noted with some pride his immediate reaction to her nearness.

He was so virile. *So big.* The taste she'd had of him the night before was lovely, but she needed more. Desire flared between them. Stephanie gripped his shoulders and undulated her hips against him, loving the harsh groan that escaped his lips.

"Avail?"

"Yes, my promised," he gripped her hips and flexed upwards, black eyes boring into her.

"Take me home. *Please.*"

"So demanding, pet. I like it."

"Now, Avail." She bit his lip, swallowing his snarl as they kissed once more before leaving her office.

Silently they walked to his car. Oblivious to the questions headed her way, she escaped with her hand in his. The tension between them was almost tangible.

He sped the entire way to his home. Taking shortcuts through back streets she had no idea existed. It was thrilling and scary all at the same time.

Without words he opened the door for her, lifting her out of the vehicle he slammed her into his body, joining them at the mouth while he raced with her in his arms to his bedroom.

Fuck yeah. So hot. Beyond her experience for sure, but she had a feeling it would become something of a frequent occurrence in the future. *Fact check: I can live with that. Yesss.*

She fell to the soft mattress as he struggled to free himself of his clothing. Not this time. It was her turn to play with her big, bad Devil. She stood up and pushed him onto the bed.

"Stephanie?"

"Take off your pants," she commanded.

Avail's eyes flamed with desire; he did as she bade. His long, hard cock stood out tall and proud from his nest of dark curls. Stephanie licked her lips. She couldn't wait to taste him. Moving down to her knees, she ran her hands up the thick, corded muscles of his thighs.

"Stephanie," he growled.

"It's my turn, *pet*," she used his nickname for her, giving him a saucy wink before wrapping her lips around the pulsing head of his cock.

His loud hiss egged her on. She took him fully into her warm, wet mouth. Slurping and sucking, coating him in her saliva. She wrapped her hand around his length, finding she needed both to get a firm grip. Slowly she pumped him from root to tip, keeping her tongue pressed on that throbbing vein under his head.

"Fuck, Stephanie," he fisted her hair, pushing her more firmly over his dick. Moaning she took him deeper, loving the ferocity of his actions.

She pushed him to his limits. Flexing his hips, he grunted and groaned as she swallowed down the trickle of moisture that preceded his release. Damn, he tasted good. *So good.*

Lowering her attentions, she cupped his firm balls. Cradling and kneading them each tenderly as her mouth continued to work him. He pulled on her hair, forcing her to look at him.

"No more, pet, I want to cum inside of your pretty pussy," he growled. His Devil in his eyes as he pulled her astride him, tearing her clothes off with black claws.

Stephanie moaned, running her hands over the reddish flesh of her mate. Yes, his Devil was pushing through, wanting to be part of their coming together. And she loved it.

He lifted her just a fraction, thrusting her down, impaling her on his cock. They both groaned as the sensations threatened to overwhelm them.

"Mine," he grunted, lifting and pushing her, up and down, fucking her on his cock.

"Yours," she returned panting heavily. She hardly noticed when her nails thickened and grew or when her fangs descended.

"Stephanie, come, now!"

His demand was answered by her snarl. Ripples of pleasure coursed through her from clit to core. Her walls fluttered around his thick rod. Milking and sucking him deeper and deeper. *Mark him. Mate. Now.* Without thought she raised her head and struck him with her fangs right above his heart.

The action both shocked and pleased her. Suckling his skin, she drank down his essence and felt their bond strengthen. His roaring release sent her spinning off into a second orgasm stronger than her first.

"Mine," she yelled as the pleasure threatened to overcome her.

Hours later they lay in a tangle of sheets and limbs. Deliciously sated she ran her hands over his now flesh colored skin.

"Pet?"

"Mmm?"

"You Marked me," his tone sounded satisfied to her ears.

"I guess I did," she said and kissed his chest.

"Do you know I think you received quite the gift

from our mating, pet," his fingers tickled the skin at the base of her spine.

"I think you're right, she said softly.

"Are you angry?"

"Angry? No, just a little scared."

"Listen to me, love, no matter what happens I will be by your side. Always," Avail lifted her face with a finger to her chin.

His dark eyes stared into hers so intensely she could have wept for the emotion shining in them. Her heart squeezed. *Fact check: I love him. Yes. Love.* A love he readily returned.

"I love you, my promised," he smiled, kissing her lips until she sighed against his.

From a shy fluffy chick, to a fully Marked *promised* to a Jersey Devil, Stephanie was sure she needed a moment to adjust. *Fact check: Yes.* She had to adapt to the new and strange Changes in her life, but there was nothing that said she couldn't fully enjoy herself while doing just that!

EPILOGUE

"**D**o what now?"

"Just close your eyes and talk to her. Get her to come out."

"How? And do I need to be naked for this?"

Avail grinned at his mate. His promised was wild in the bedroom, but adorably shy in the privacy of their woods. Still nippy out, he'd carried her to this spot in a blanket before divesting her of it and those naughty little lace panties she'd been wearing.

"I'd prefer you naked always, pet," he nipped her lip and soothed the abused flesh with his tongue before stepping back.

"Now, concentrate."

"Oh fine, but no sexy times for you after making

me freeze to death out here," she mumbled and closed her eyes.

No sexy times? *Sad sigh.* He'd just have to get her to change her mind. After he got her to Change.

"That's it, pet. Close your eyes. Picture an empty room. No noise, no distractions. Just you and your beast. Open your heart to her, pet. You can trust her. She is your other half. She will never hurt you. Just like I will never hurt you, love. You are safe. Protected. Strong and fierce. That's it. Give in to your Shift, pet. I'm here. I'm not going anywhere."

Avail stood in stunned silence as he watched the lush figure of his promised contort and twist. A hum of magic filled the air, a shimmery sort of essence surrounded her frame. Could it be? He'd never heard of this kind of thing happening before. Shocked he gasped aloud.

Eyes wide he took in the glorious figure of his mate. Her slitted black eyes blinked up at him as she struggled to her feet. *Or hooves.*

"Avail?" Her voice was slightly deeper, musical to his ears.

She flexed her wings. Her great red wings and stared at her deep red hands. A Devil. Like him. She was a female Jersey Devil. And so fucking lush and beautiful she made his heart stop.

"You're perfect," he breathed. He crossed the room, standing beside her. His Devil reaching for his mate together they ran and flew through the barrens.

They played like children. Exploring the grounds and each other. Carefree in the wilderness they both loved.

"This is amazing," she said, coming to grips rather quickly with her new side.

"Are you certain you are okay with all of this, pet?"

"How could I not be? This feels right."

"Because it is, pet."

As the sun set, Avail brought his mate back to Leeds House. Their home now. In their human skin once again he carried his mate, tucked her against him to protect her from the chilly night air.

He smiled as he thought about the text message he'd received from his grandmother earlier that morning. Choosing the perfect moment to tell his mate would prove interesting.

Avail, make sure your promised is well rested over the next few months. Twins are not an easy feat. Looking forward to your naming the little girl after her great-grandmother.

He exhaled. Grandmother was a pip. He only

hoped his children didn't inherit her less amiable qualities. *Shudder.*

"You alright?"

"Of course, pet. I have you."

"Yes. You do," she smiled and wrapped her arms more securely around his neck.

Ah. Yes. She was with him. His promised. Safe and sound. He reveled in the knowledge that he had finally found her. His Devil was officially caught and content that she was his. *As I am hers.*

Both of them claimed and loved.

Both of them *marked by the Devil.*

The end.

Liked this story? Read the next book Mated to the Dragon King or discover more Purely Paranormal Romance Books by C.D. Gorri by visiting http://www.cdgorri.com/series/purely-paranormal-pleasures/

BLOOD SONG

A SANGUINEM COUNCIL BOOK

BLURB

Her blood sings for him, will he answer the call?

Aleksei Delov is the owner of *Timeless Possessions*, part of a global conglomerate of corporations. The immortal Vampire Prince is renowned for his ability to acquire authentic, priceless antiques for his various private clientele. Alek's reputation is every-thing, until he meets *her*.

Carina Martin has a unique talent to find objects and to identify them by touch. She uses it for other people in order to eke out a meager living among other *normals* along the East Coast, but there is more to life than that, and she is dying for a piece of it.

When someone robs Aleksei and passes off fakes in his name, he tracks Carina down and offers his patronage in exchange for the use of her abilities.

But he is not prepared for his reaction to the beautiful normal. Can he resist the female, or will he be seduced by her blood song?

PROLOGUE
CARINA

"Have you heard of the *Sanguinem Council?*"

He spoke with a slight accent. His voice had that deep, velvety timber I loved and it seemed to tease and stroke up and down my spine like a lover's hands. I wasn't prepared for it or for my wildly inappropriate reaction considering my precarious situation.

I hated to admit it, but I hardly understood his question lost as I was in the contemplation of his voice. That coupled with the loss of too much blood had left me lightheaded and dizzy. My fingers and toes had already gone numb, and I felt as if a frozen sort of shroud was draped over my beaten body. I was dying and I knew it.

That did not change the fact that the stranger

speaking to me was positively dazzling. Breathtakingly beautiful men were not exactly my forte, and he was better looking than anything or anyone I had ever seen.

Silver eyes seemed to take me in from head to toe in an instant. If not for that movement, he could've been a statue. Tall and built under his impeccable suit. Who dressed like that around here, anyway?

Oh yeah. He was definitely better looking than anything I'd seen in the last twenty-four hours. But that was not hard to accomplish considering I was lying on an uneven cobblestone alley between poorly handled plastic bags of rotting garbage, broken bottles, drug paraphernalia, and puddles whose contents I would rather not think about.

In between them were the usual marks of the rodent population, scat from various strays and nocturnal critters, and whatever else wallowed in the dank and dark alleyway. What was it he said again? Oh yeah, something about an *Sanguinem Council?*

More supernatural business. Shit I tried to stay out of, though that was hard since I had a foot halfway into that world myself. Being a psychic kind of sucked, especially for a *normal* like me. I could hardly recall a memory where someone didn't look at me like I was crazy when I revealed what I could do. Which was probably why I had so few friends.

Normally, I didn't care for pity parties. But fuck it. I was dying. If I couldn't feel sorry for myself when I was dying, when was the appropriate time? SMH. Yeah, this really sucked. And I was feeling worse by the minute. Numbness didn't mean I couldn't still feel the pain. On the contrary, the bitter cold seeping through my blood was like a thousand needles racing through my veins. It hurt like fuck.

"Focus on my voice," the stranger said and my eyes locked on his, "We, those of us who follow the old ways of the Sanguinem Council, are a group of Vampires who provide patronage to certain humans we are interested in seeing reach their full potential. Humans like you, Carina Martin," he smiled briefly, showcasing his perfect white teeth on a way that was both predatory and somehow enticing.

The handsome man cocked his head and flared his nostrils, closing his pale silver eyes for a moment while he sucked in a deep breath. I stared as the tip of his tongue darted out, licking his lips. He growled a bit, as if he was savoring whatever scent he was picking up.

Suddenly, I understood. Here was a man who was not a man at all. He was one of *them*. A creature.

An *other*. A supernatural, like they showed on the news. But what kind? My own human senses could not tell me unless I was touching him. He could be a Shifter or a Fae. A Vampire perhaps?

A trickle of fear raced down my spine. Yes, something inside me was practically jumping up and down at the thought. Vampire. That seemed to fit the pale, powerful predator in my midst. The strongest of all the races that had only recently come to the attention of the rest of the world and this was the first one I had ever met. I had to admit I'd been shocked when all matter of paranormal creatures began to make themselves known but then again how could they not?

Technology being what it was, it was only a matter of time really. So it was fact. For the past few years or decades, whatever really, supernaturals the world over had all outed themselves in small reveals. Not unified, and not on any timeline known to humans. They worked alone and slowly. But what was slow to a being whose lifespan was inconceivable to a human? What was time to an immortal?

I remembered my first experience of the supernatural world. A Pack of heroic Werewolves appeared on a video on the internet with footage of themselves shifting and chasing a would-be rapist from Central Park. They broke the web with that footage. With it came a myriad of conspiracy theories.

Was it a deep fake? Were they even human? All sorts of activists and nut jobs had crawled out of the woodworks to nail the story. At the time, I was between foster homes and I didn't give two shits about a Wolf Pack across the Hudson.

Live and let live. That was my creed. But other normals had their panties in a bunch over the whole thing. We needed new laws they said, new jails for people like that.

Whatever. I just wanted to keep my head down and make a living. *And get my revenge.*

"Are you hurting?" the stranger crouched beside me and I tried to move, to scoot away, but my body protested.

Speech seemed beyond me. I tried to respond, but all that came out was a groan. Or something like that. My jaw had been broken by the first pair of fists that had struck when Vladek's men had finally caught up to me.

The pain I'd felt then and when another goon had knocked me into the brick wall was all slowly fading away. That wasn't a good sign. At least when I was in pain, I knew I was alive.

"Easy," the man lifted my head and placed something soft beneath it.

Was it his jacket? Oh, no. He was dressed so finely, I'd hate to think what the muck covering the alley floor was doing to the expensive-looking material.

Who was this guy? Some kind of guardian angel? No. That wasn't right. My mind kept racing back to the first supernatural word I'd thought that had made any sense.

Vampire. He was a Vampire. I don't know how I knew. I just did. That look was far too predatory to belong to some ethereal being sent to lead me to the hereafter. Wherever the fuck that would be, who knew?

I had more pressing matters to think about. Like whether the tall, gorgeous man in the black on black suit was friend or foe. Either way, right behind that initial jolt of fear, raced another emotion. Something I had to work hard to ignore. A pesky little itch that occasionally flared to life, though I'd managed to resist all manner of persuasion for the past twenty-five years.

I didn't know what to make of it really. I'd never felt like that before. Especially not under those circumstances. I guess all those foster parents were right, I really was fucked up.

Oh well. Nothing like dying to make a girl horny.

"Are you able to follow what I am saying?"

I tried to answer his questions, but I could only gurgle in response. My eyes widened. I started hyperventilating, making any number of nasty little noises in lieu of speech.

Oh, that's attractive. FML.

The fuckers who'd been tracking me down all damn day had finally caught up with me not too long ago. They did a hell of a number on my face and neck too. But what did I expect after targeting a man like *Vladek the Merciless?*

I mean, it was right there in his name. The mobster was not known for his forgiving nature. I knew that going in, but this was and had always been personal. Vladek was responsible for the death of my parents.

His goons ran the drug dealers who'd gunned down my mother and father when I was just a baby. Bouncing around the foster care system was one hell of a shitty way to grow up. Far as I was concerned, that Russian fucker deserved everything he had coming to him.

As for what I'd done to deserve such treatment,

well, I simply rerouted one of his trucks to a non-disclosed location. I'd called in a favor from a hacker friend who managed to get inside the GPS systems of the truck that was holding Vladek's merch.

Now my merch.

"Don't try to answer with words. Simply nod if you understand me," the stranger instructed.

I nodded once, to show I heard him and was still listening. Maybe the hottie would say something worthwhile. If not, he could get the fuck out of my alley and let me die in peace already.

"My name is Aleksei Delov, Miss Martin, and I would like to offer you my *patronage*."

I didn't have any idea what he was talking about, so I waited for him to continue. Not like I was going anyplace else without some serious fucking help. The cold, wet filth covering the ground was slowly seeping through my clothes. I admit I couldn't feel my toes and feet, or my hands, but my back was soaked.

Fuck. This was my favorite jacket. A little black leather number I'd picked up at a consignment shop that fit my curvier-than-I'd-like frame perfectly.

"Ms. Martin? Do I have your attention?"

I blinked once.

"Good. Blink once for yes, twice for no."

I blinked once again, and he smiled even more brilliantly than before. He could've been a model with that perfectly symmetrical face. He had glossy, thick locks that matched the smattering of hair that covered his chin. I always did like a five-o'clock shadow on a man. Still, he'd been hot before, up close he was almost too gorgeous.

"Under my patronage you would be protected, taken care of, I can start by healing your wounds."

So my little sixth sense was right. There was only one creature I knew of that could heal humans. Fear spiked through my blood, but with it came that other emotion. One that closely resembled anticipation but bordered on lust. Something inside me recognized him and wanted what he offered.

There was that sliver of dismay again, making itself known with a sharp tremble that wracked my body. And that, once more, was followed by a wicked urge to get closer to the stranger. To kiss the hard slash of his lips and bare my throat for his pleasure.

And mine, the naughty voice inside my head insisted.

"Blink for me, Miss Martin, once if you accept my offer," he said, and the deep seductive tone of his voice made me want to close my eyes and just listen to him for the rest of my life.

Only thing was, if I didn't answer him, the rest of my life was unlikely to be longer than a few minutes.

Fuck. What kind of choice was that? I've always wanted to see more of the world, but was I ready to become a Vampire? I hoped to convey my question through the look on my face. Surprised even myself when it worked. The beautiful male Vampire seemed to understand. He cocked his head to the side and his eyes burned for a moment like molten silver.

"I understand your concern, Carina. I am a Vampire, as you've no doubt ascertained by now, but I assure you, this bite will not be the one that turns you. In order for me to make a Vampire, you would have to drink from my vein as well, among other rituals that would need to be performed to seal the pact."

I gurgled once again, wanting more information, but unable to verbalize my questions. This was frustrating me, and yet as I slipped further away, I knew I was going to agree. What choice did I have?

"You do not know me, but I do not lie. I have no intention of turning you today."

I blinked. Hard. And watched his helpless reaction. The stranger's nostrils flared and his eyes glowed. I wondered if his fangs were descending even then and my fear spiked again.

Fuck it. I was too weak to argue. Too close to death to have any other options. So, yes, I waited a beat and blinked my eyes once more. Nodding my head as much as I could, I accepted the Vampire's offer.

"It will hurt at first, understand? There is nothing I can do for that here," he seemed to struggle with that part of it, and for the life of me I didn't know why he should care if he hurt me or not, but I appreciated it. Really I did.

"My offer of patronage comes at a price. My help for yours. Are we agreed?"

I blinked my response. Yes, I agreed. I would help him and he would save my life. That was only fair. His eyes blazed like molten silver, glowing even brighter in the darkness that surrounded us.

I could hardly breathe as the walls began to close in on me. This was really happening. I wasn't lost in some dime store novel or one of those b-movies I can't seem to get enough of.

No. This was real. I tried to move. Some deep-seated fight-or-flight instinct, I supposed, but my legs didn't cooperate. I was completely numb now from the waist down. Arms too. Shit. I was losing feeling in all my extremities. Except for the cold. That I still felt like ice water seeping into my blood.

He was offering me the only way out of an impossible situation. But again, if I were honest with myself, I would have to admit I was more than intrigued. I was outright curious. I wanted what he offered. And maybe something more as well.

"Blink one more time, so I know for sure," he growled the words.

I did, and the Vampire's impossibly gorgeous face seemed to hover above mine. My eyes widened as he plucked me off the floor effortlessly. Holding me in his arms as if I was light as a feather. But even half-dead, I knew better than that.

His strength was disconcerting, as was the inhuman speed with which he'd moved me to the far side of the alley. He'd looked so polished and suave from a distance, but up close he was so much more.

Every inch of his face commanded my attention. He captivated me, so much so it ravaged my heart to look at him. His lips were a hard slash across his face, his jaw and cheekbones were chiseled as if carved from marble, his nose was straight, and the smattering of five o'clock shadow gave him just a touch of roughness.

If this was any other circumstance, I might have

tried flirting with him. For now, I was simply grateful to be off the dirty, wet floor. He used one long-fingered hand to push my hair away, off my face and past my shoulder, then he tilted my face towards his.

He was still growling softly in his throat, reminding me that he was a predator and I was helpless. A willing victim. All I could do was trust his word that he was trying to help. Not because he liked me, but because he needed me.

Still, trust was a tough concept for someone like me. Someone who'd been used and abused by the system and the very people who were supposed to keep me safe. But there I was, putting my life in the hands of a stranger. A hunter. One I could not possibly defend myself from.

A Vampire, for fuck's sake.

He caressed my face with exquisite gentleness and I had to admit, it was unexpected. Unnecessary too. I would have thought he'd simply strike my skin with his fangs and drink from me regardless of my comfort, but no.

Aleksei Delov was far too sophisticated for such animalistic behavior. Unlike the goons who'd had their fun tearing at my skin with claws and snarling at me like a pack of rabid dogs. Vladek's Werewolf posse had treated me like a plaything.

Not him, though. Aleksei was nothing like those thick-necked thugs. Time slowed down and his silver gaze bore into mine. My breath caught in my chest at the heat I saw in that unwavering stare.

That smoldering look and his oh-so-tender touch caught me off guard. Tiny electric bolts of pleasure raced through my veins as he bent his head and pressed my face to his neck.

I breathed in his expensive cologne, surprised myself by catching a whiff of something spicy and altogether delicious beneath it. The fragrance was intensely masculine and somehow, it beckoned me.

"Relax, little one, I have you now," his voice was a soft whisper against the cradle of my neck.

I trembled in his arms, not from the cold, but from his warm breath. That warmth and the way his words tickled my ear surprised me. Aleksei held me close in an embrace that was positively intimate, and soon I felt his open mouth close around my bruised neck in a move that was more kiss than bite.

Then I felt it, his sharp, needle-like incisors punctured my skin. There was pain, but it was brief, followed quickly by heat. *So much heat.* After a long, drawn-out moment, I could finally move, and I moaned out loud, clutching his shoulders as pleasure raced through my body. It started with my core, then spread, filling every inch of my being.

We were both breathing heavily when he lifted his head. I stared at his red-tinted mouth first, then at his silver eyes.

"Rest now, little one. I've got you," his husky voice filled me with pleasure.

Eyes blazing, he traced a line from my eyebrow to my chin, and I swear I'd never seen anyone look at me quite like that. I wanted to say something, anything, but words were beyond me. Then it didn't matter anymore what I would or could not say.

Blackness swallowed me.

CHAPTER 1
ALEKSEI

"Vladek the Merciless is a fucking thorn in our side," Klaus grunted.

"Do you have to call him by that fucking idiotic nickname?" I replied.

Klaus snorted. Of course, when he used the idiot's moniker it was meant as more of an insult. The Vampire in question had started out as a minor competitor and something of a minor annoyance about fifty years or so ago.

He was never big enough to garner my interest or concern. Till now, it seemed the asshole had suddenly grown a set of balls. Too bad he set his sights on coming after me and mine.

"What did Princess Ana say?"

"She was pissed as hell, Klaus. She expected her

shipment and instead received a fake bearing my symbol."

"That bastard had the audacity to use your royal seal? Where the fuck did he get it?"

"A forger, I assume," I shrugged.

Vladek was going to discover sooner than later that I was not an easy mark. I was the grandson of the first Aleksei Delov. His namesake and the heir to his legacy.

"You've only just taken the throne as *Knyaz*," Klaus sputtered.

The head of my guard was obviously furious. But he was right. As the newly crowned Prince or *Knyaz* of my Clan, the last thing I needed was something or someone to jeopardize my position.

Over the past few months, I'd alternately defended my right to ascend and battled challengers to my title left and right. Those who survived a challenge by my mercy, pledged loyalty and made restitution as was the law.

The others were buried in various undisclosed locations by Ivan, my right hand, and Klaus, my blood brother. The two of them had been with me longer than anyone else, though I now ruled a Clan of over five-hundred adult Vampires and was head of a major global conglomerate with many of them in corporate positions of power.

Together we had amassed quite the fortune. My reputation in business was respected, but I had earned that with Klaus and Ivan by my side. They'd helped me work to grow my business to the best of its kind.

Now *Timeless Possessions* was under attack. Just one of many companies under *Sitio Global*, this act of aggression was personal. For this company was my first and also my favorite. The hunt, tracking down various antiquities, holding history in my hands were some of the few pleasures I still found in this world filled with so much ignorance, waste, and hatred.

"Vladek made a mistake going after me," I growled and crumpled the receipt the dockmaster faxed to me in my fist.

Stealing from a Knyaz was punishable by death without trial. I was within my rights to seek revenge. But I had to find the items he stole first.

"Did the Princess give you a deadline?" Klaus asked.

"You know Ana," I snorted.

Princess Ana de Medici was the leader of a very large Vampire Clan, living just across the river in

Manhattan. Her numbers tripled mine and war with them would be decidedly unpleasant. To say the least.

"Well, we know the artifact arrived. It was picked up. Then a group of Werewolves hit it as soon as it left Port Jersey," Klaus said, "that's when our little psychic got to it."

I couldn't help but admire the work of the female who'd caused Vladek's plans to be upended. Imagine being outmaneuvered by a normal? It would be funny if I didn't need the damn artifact to appease Ana and to redeem my reputation before the whispers got worse. To a man in my position, even a hint of doubt could cost me my life.

"I think I hear something this way," Klaus pointed, but I was not inclined to follow.

No. That way was wrong. A tingling sensation worked its way up my spine. Every extra Vampire sense was on high alert.

"Stop," I said and closed my eyes.

Close now. I was very close. Sifting through the various smells, I looked for the one I sought among the trash, defecation, and general despair that hung in the frigid air of this part of Newark. Anticipation hummed through my veins, and I could feel myself loosening the tight grip I had on my control.

So very close now.

Everything was riding on me finding this female. My Clan was small, but it was important to the *Sanguinem Council.* That particular Vampiric consortium owed most of its fortune to my business endeavors. But there were whispers in the air of deceivers, upstarts, and a general unpleasantness among the members. And it all boiled down to one name. *Vladek.*

Rumor had it he was pulling the strings of one elder seated on the Council. I should leave. Claim my independence, but the House Delov had pledged loyalty before I came in to power, and I would honor the wishes of my forebears. And yet, this was an offense I could not let go.

The stink of fear and hopelessness invaded my nostrils, and I took shallow breaths as I hunted. Klaus's booted steps echoed behind me, and I knew he would watch my back as I sought her. The one person who could help me end this.

The streets were ugly in this part of town. Thugs and gang members used it as their personal playground, but I paid no mind to the gun toting hustlers.

Normals slinging drugs were not my concern. The more violent offenders, however, the ones that raped, murdered, and hurt the innocent, their blood called out to me. I wanted to take it from them. To end their miserable little lives. But I had not been that kind of Vampire for centuries. Still, I knew they were there, and I was not the only monster roaming that night.

"Later," I told Klaus. I could feel my blood brother sensing what I did, but we had no time to play hero. Not then. We had other things to do, and I sensed I was closing in.

My chest vibrated with the force of my growl. The vicious side of my nature had been at the forefront for too long since I'd been in the company of other Vampires with little time in the normal world the past few months.

Taking over the Clan, ascending to my title of *Knyaz* as my grandfather willed, was not as easy as it sounded. Now, I had to fight to keep my position and my reputation. The looks I was getting as I rushed down the crowded streets near Newark Penn Station were wary at best.

They'd done a good job, cleaning things up in the area. The whole *Beautify New Jersey* concept seemed to be working for the good people of the city council. Of course, that didn't matter to those of us who thrived on the fringes of what was considered civilized society.

As I drew closer to my target, the streets became less polished. Trash cans overflowed and the homeless and despondent sat in cardboard boxes huddled tight against the bitter air. One look in my direction and they averted their eyes.

Even those less fortunate were aware that predators walked in their midst. That's what I was alright. Klaus too. Predators. Cunning, agile, and royally fucking pissed off.

Vladek had gone too far attacking my business and forging my seal, and there was going to be hell to pay. But first, I needed to find the artifact he'd stolen from me. And to do that, I needed to find the someone who stole it from him.

Unfortunately, that asshole's fucking thugs were busy tracking the very same someone I sought. I knew I was one step behind them and that infuriated me. The stink of unleashed Werewolf was in the air. Fucking hell. That could prove fatal for the normal we were out to locate.

The woman, a human named Carina Martin, was nothing special on paper. At least, not on the dossier my team of detectives sent. Of course, her photo was intriguing. Her Spanish heritage was evident in her golden-brown eyes, tanned skin, and thick, curly hair.

Though my blood was Russian, I had a soft spot for Whiskey, not Vodka. Her eyes reminded me of the 1950 bottle of Macallan single cask I had on reserve for special occasions back at my estate.

Carina Martin had a troublesome past. The female with the whiskey-colored eyes was orphaned as a baby and sent to live in a series of foster homes, one worse than the other. I hardly made it through the reports of abuse and neglect without wanting to kill something.

Fucking parasites claimed to want to help children who'd suffered the greatest loss, the tragedy of losing their parents, only to use them as a means to an end. A tiny monthly check from the government that was supposed to go towards caring for the tiny ones they'd promised to raise.

Unfortunately, that was rarely the case. Those who gamed the system at the expense of others deserved to be treated in kind. But that was for another day, and I pushed back my anger to focus on finding her now.

So many monsters in the world. Still, Carina was special for other reasons besides her tragic past. Based on various accounts from the streets, she was something of a psychic and a major pain in the ass for the low-lives and thugs who plagued the less fortunate.

Her most recent project proved that. Imagine a normal stealing a truck belonging to Vladimir the Merciless. Odd for a little normal, psychic or not, to attack a man rumored to be as dangerous as he.

Not to mention myself. But I doubted she was even aware of me or my connection to that shipment. If she was then her actions were even more brazen than I'd thought, and I couldn't help but admire her *hutzpah.*

Just thinking his name brought me to murderous rage. He'd stolen my shipment, was trying to ruin my reputation among not only my best clients, but the inner circles of the Council as well. Fucking rat bastard.

If someone was hitting Vladek where it hurt, I wanted in on it. Especially after what that sonofabitch was trying to pull. He had the unmitigated gall to send a fake to my most important client with my seal. Princess Ana had not been amused.

I knew I had to make things right, and that bastard had to be taken down. If this little human was going to give it a try, I was certainly Vampire enough to join her. After she led me to my artifact.

But all my thoughts stopped and my entire body froze in place like a statue. My heart pounded heavily inside my chest and breathing became a chore. A ferocious growl tore from my lips and I turned towards an alley where the stink of Werewolf was still fresh.

"What is it?" Klaus asked.

Truth was, I had no idea. Something was wrong. Terribly wrong. The stench of Wolf, fresh spilled blood, and terror filled the air, but with it was something else. I was oblivious to everything but that one elusive fragrance. It was dark and heady, tantalizingly unique. It seemed to tie me up in knots and I was incapable of movement.

"*Moy Knyaz?*" Klaus' voice had my eyes snapping to his and my lip pulled back in a snarl.

"Call for the rest of the guard and hunt the Werewolves who did this. Go now," I commanded and watched as my blood brother bowed, then turned to sniff the air.

I knew he would follow the stink of Werewolf, and I trusted him to act accordingly. I just needed him away from here. Away from her. This was it. I had found her and my control was hanging by a thread.

I turned and walked into the dark alley located

not far from the Prudential Center, and my eyes zeroed in on the still form lying on the cold floor. I was stunned. A million emotions flitted through me and all I could think was I had no idea when I began this trek that she was going to be more important to me than I could have ever imagined.

They were gone already, but I trusted Klaus to pick up their scent and hunt them down. Vladek's fucking attack dogs had done a number on her. The coppery tinge of blood filled the air. I breathed deep and suddenly my fangs descended.

Bloody fucking hell. My senses were all fucked up. My heart pounded heavily inside my chest, pulse racing as it hadn't done in a century or more, and my dick chose this moment to go hard in my pants.

What the fuck was happening to me? My nerves twitched, and I hissed and pressed myself against the cold brick wall. I could not risk going near her until I had myself under control. Cock throbbing, thunder roared in my head, and I was fucking salivating.

Moya krov' pesnya.

The words resounded in my brain, and I gasped. It was nothing more than a tale. An ancient myth among my Clan. A story Grandfather Aleksei had told me long ago.

Moya krov' pesnya. My blood song.

Could it be true? It had been a century since I last visited Saint Petersburg, and yet my Russian roots were as strong now as the day I'd turned.

Vampirism was my heritage. It was my gift to give to another. One other. *Moya krov' pesnya.* Though I never thought to meet her.

"Moya krov' pesnya," I said it aloud this time and conviction ran through me.

The old tales were true. She was mine. A human whose blood was designed specifically to seduce me, *an immortal*, into creating a *svyaz* or permanent bond between us.

These things were not to be taken lightly. I knew this, and yet I wanted her with everything I was. I longed to join with her, to turn her. It was like a burning, pulsating need within me.

The old ones, the ancient Vampires who kept the stories of our kind, believed more than anything that these myths were true. And here she was, proving them right. I'd found her. My own blood song.

She was a gift, a blessing. Or so I'd always believed, and yet, I was not ready for it. I had so many things to do. To fix my standing with the council, appease Ana, hunt Vladek, and make my Clan strong enough to protect her.

Fuck. I had no time to do any of that. She was

here. Now. I pushed aside all of my own petty thoughts and feelings. They did not matter right then. Taking the chance, I moved cautiously forward.

Her blood made a red puddle beneath her, and I trembled in my rage. But she was not dead. Not yet. Her suffering was almost too much to bear, and I struggled to breathe normally.

Bruises marred her delicate skin. Their claws and teeth had ravaged her. I wanted to roar my rage and tear down the entire city looking for the animals that hurt her. That was already in motion. Klaus would obey my command.

I knew that for the fact it was, but still I was inconsolably angry. I had been too late to save her from them. Yes, the Wolves had sealed their own fate, and maybe that would be enough, but right then I didn't think so.

My fangs refused to withdraw, and my claws elongated, at the ready to defend my female, but the bastards were gone. I closed my eyes, and that was when I heard her struggle to breathe, growing fainter and fainter still. I had no time to lose. I needed to present her with a choice.

"Have you heard of the *Sanguinem Council*?"

Whatever idiocy made me speak of that which

was more underground ideology than an actual place or group, I had no idea. But it was as honest as I could be at the moment.

I did not want to frighten her more than I had to. She'd already gotten a taste of violence from the dogs in Vladek's employ. And I meant that literally. Only wannabe mobsters used rogue Werewolves as errand boys.

Fucking coward.

I offered to heal the sweet mortal's wounds, but giving her my bite was not as easy as it sounded. Her blood called to me. Literally. I feared once it touched my lips, I'd succumb to bloodlust and consume every drop of her sweet life's essence.

The burning need to fill her with my own blood, to bond us permanently roared to life, and I had to fight to control myself. I would never harm her, never take against her will, but yes, I wanted to perform the exchange. The *svyaz* which would tie us for eternity. Only sanity stopped me, and the sound of her faint heartbeat growing stronger as the healing agents of my saliva and venom worked to close her wounds.

Cradling Carina safely in my arms, I used my supernatural speed to whisk us back towards where Klaus and I had left my black Mercedes. He would find another way home, this I knew as I placed her gently in the car.

The taste of her blood was still on my tongue and, gods forgive me, I wanted more. Thirst and desire burned inside of me, but she was weak, unconscious, and I would never ever take advantage of the situation.

I needed her whole, alive, and completely well. Her skin felt warmer now than it had when I first lifted her slight weight and I was relieved I had the ability to help her. The sound of her heartbeat returning to its former strength pressed my own to thud gratefully inside my chest. She would recover. She had to.

The drive back to my estate passed in a blur as I navigated back streets and alleys until we hit the highway. I stepped on the gas pedal of my Mercedes AMG GT, pushing it to the floor.

The female beside me moaned, and I slowed down a bit. For her sake. That was a first. I was not known for my compassion, and yet as far as she was concerned, I wanted nothing more than her absolute safety, comfort, and pleasure.

Bloody hell. This was going to be a problem. I had to get it under wraps and fast. I needed the woman to help me so I could better protect her. I had to hunt that fucker, secure my reputation, heal the rift between Ana and myself, report to the council, and confirm peace in my Clan. Then and only then would I even consider telling the sweet mortal what she was to me.

Why Vladek thought targeting my reputation was a good idea, I would never know. But I had to restore my clients' confidence in my abilities to curate and obtain rare items. But more importantly, I had to avoid a war with Ana's Clan, and I needed to make certain my Clan knew without a doubt *I* was *Knyaz*.

The gates to my home opened as I neared them. I sped to the curved driveway, stopping only when I reached the front doors.

"*Moy Knyaz?*" Ivan asked and caught the keys I tossed his way, holding the front door wide while I passed through with my burden.

He had been with me for almost two-hundred years now and was as loyal and faithful a friend as I had ever known. Of course, he was also a stickler for titles and formalities.

"It's fine," I growled and headed to my bedroom.

I'd had every intention of placing her in another room, since bringing her to the infirmary was not gonna happen. Fucking hell. My blood boiled at the very idea of placing her anywhere else. I'd thought maybe the room adjoining mine would suffice, but no, I couldn't bring myself to do it.

The thought of placing her in any other room had my fangs threatening to descend and my claws ready to tear the fuck out of anyone who came near her. Part of the reason why I'd sent Klaus after her attackers rather than allow him to enter the alley with me.

Perhaps my aggression was one of the effects of drinking her sublime blood. But no. That was not the reason. Everything inside of me told me why she was in my bedroom, my bed, and not in the medical wing of my estate where I would've taken any other normal who'd been injured and needed my care. It was because Carina Martin was not just the average little normal.

She was my *Chosen*. My blood song. And I was a second away from killing the next person who tried to enter my room with her inside it.

"Alek? Klaus had me send the others to his location. He reported back five minutes ago, he is *en route*. The Werewolves are dead-"

"I can't discuss this now."

"What's going on? Can I help?" Ivan entered my

room where I was currently removing Carina's dirty, blood-stained clothes.

I turned and snarled, shielding her with my body, fangs bared, claws out, and chest heaving with the energy it took to restrain myself.

"Apologies, *Knyaz*," Ivan stilled and averted his eyes to the floor, but even that show of submission was not enough.

"Leave us," I growled and tried to put a leash on my instinct to hunt and kill anyone who came near my as of yet unmated female.

"Sir?" he said, facing the wall, "I understand. Can I bring you something to help? A washcloth? Antibiotics? Ointments?"

Booted footsteps sounded in the hallway and another joined us. I smelled the blood he'd spilled on my order clinging to his clothes, and it offended me. I wanted to hurt the Wolves who did this, but I'd have to be content with knowing my blood brother had taken their lives on my order.

"Klaus," I turned my head to look at him, eyes flashing fire as I struggled to control myself.

"*Moy Knyaz*," he said and bowed deeply, "it is done. The female's attackers have met with a far worse fate than I am certain they had in mind for themselves," he reported.

I saw the bloodlust still visible in his eyes and used my innate powers as Knyaz to calm my guard. He exhaled slowly, and the glow receded, leaving only his native green irises behind.

"Thank you," he said, and I understood.

Being a warrior was not easy. A Vampire could fall prey to his own inner beast. Klaus battled with his demons on a daily basis. Like so many of us who were turned, we wrestled with our Vampire natures. Bending and forcing them to submit to our reason otherwise we would all be doomed and ruled by an uncontrollable desire to kill and maim and feed. That would be the ruin of our species.

"Ivan?"

"Yes, *moy Knyaz?*"

"Please, bring the antibiotics and ointments. Leave them by the door," I cleared my throat, "But do not enter. I can't let anyone near her. Especially while she is wounded."

Every muscle in my body tensed as both men cocked their heads to the side in their bids to listen to their leader. Klaus' gaze remained away from where I stood blocking Carina with my body and Ivan left to gather the supplies.

Thank fuck. I'd hate like hell to tear the men

apart. But I would. For her, I would do anything. I acknowledged that one truth with a frown.

I was the *Knyaz* of the House Delov, but for this woman, this precious female, my chosen, I was nothing more than a servant in my own house. Kneeling at her feet, begging to be recognized.

Fucking hell. This was insane, but my heart pounded whenever I was near her. She was my blood song. I would do anything to ensure her safety, her happiness. Carina Martin was my whole world.

And she did not even know it.

"You are possessive of the woman already? Is it true? Is she your *Chosen?*"

"Fuck," I struggled to control my reaction to Klaus' statement, when all I wanted to do was snarl and snap at him, "Is it that obvious?"

"I've never lied to you, brother," Klaus grunted, "I have never seen you look the way you did caring for her and in your own room too. Your expression and destination gave you away."

"*Moy Knyaz?*"

I turned to see Ivan, one of my oldest and most trusted men almost stepping into my room, but Klaus's arm shot up and stopped him. Thank fuck. I would've attacked.

Even then, I growled and hissed, and both men stared harder at the floor. Typically, I did not give in to such displays of dominance, but my body was not my own anymore.

I fought with myself, forcing my attention back to cleaning her wounds, and ignored the two of them. My men. My trusted men, I repeated.

"I am worried for you, Alek," Klaus said from the hall.

"Save your worry for her. You can bring in the supplies now, I have control of myself."

Both men were loyal, I appreciated their concern, but it was unnecessary. I was fine. It was Carina who presently suffered. She moaned and tossed her head, but I waited for the sound of the cart to stop and Ivan to retreat before I turned to move it closer to where she was lying on the bed.

I glanced at the sheet beneath her and frowned, Ivan must have placed it there earlier, but I'd been too far gone to notice. It was heavy and lined with plastic. The kind used in the infirmary. Good. That would make it easier to clean and tend her wounds before I could place her under the covers to heal.

She frowned and I knew she was in pain. Since we did not exchange blood, her healing was progressing much more slowly. I could scent her in the room, on my clothes, in my mouth. Even her blood was tinged with that caramel cocoa-butter flavor that would forever remind me of Carina.

It clung to my lips, but I pushed away my thirst for her. Would I always crave her blood? Would I even be able to feed from another? I had no idea. But it didn't matter. My needs were second to hers. Always would be.

I frowned as I removed her dirty, bloodstained clothes and drew another sheet to cover her nudity. There were long, deep scratches on her chest and neck. Large bruises to her ribs and abdomen. Her knees were scraped, and she'd broken fingernails fighting the animals who'd attacked.

How I longed for their deaths. I was mildly soothed by the fact that Klaus had executed my will with speed. Like the sword in my right hand, he struck hard and true. She was avenged. And now I could heal her.

Still, I wish I could give her my blood. But I could not. Not yet, anyway. I would not begin the process that would turn her into a Vampire without her approval. And she had most definitely had not seemed to want to be turned when last we spoke.

Perhaps in time, I calmed myself with the thought and bathed her wounds. The healing salve was an ancient remedy mixed by Witches under my employ. It would work for humans and supernaturals alike.

"Is there anything you need? To feed perhaps?" Ivan asked from the doorway.

"No."

How could I think of food when she was still so quiet and pale? I watched for any sign she was fighting the agents in my venom that would help heal her. Sometimes a Vampire's bite had residual effects on a person after he or she was used for feeding. I only hoped it would not bring her any further suffering or pain.

"Alek, I brought water for the female should she wake," Ivan held a tray by the door.

His gaze still averted, I walked over to retrieve it and growled when he did not release it immediately.

"Go."

He bowed and turned around, leaving only one pain in the ass standing in my hallway.

"Well, I'm not fucking asking," Klaus muttered and took position as guard.

The fucker always did whatever he liked, and he was an excellent soldier. I nodded once and waited for Ivan's footsteps to recede down the hall. Klaus turned to face the hallway, and I shut the heavy double-doors that led into my suite.

I'd had my private rooms enchanted to ward off any who would harm me and made a mental note to include Carina in the protection spells. They were not infallible, but they did help.

This was my home, but as the new *Knyaz*, I had many enemies. I could never let my guard down. Especially now.

I carried the tray back to the bed and left it on the nightstand. Then I continued my inspection of the delicate female's bruises. Cleaning them and applying the salve as I went, my hunger to kill the sonofabitch who'd ordered this brutal attack grew as I counted no less than five injuries that could have killed her had I not been there in time.

She was here now. Safe with me. I repeated that little fact every few minutes or so just to keep myself sane. The mansion was my home, but it also housed six of my honor guards, a handful of servants, and various visitors from within my Clan at any given time. Still, my personal wing was off limits to everyone except Ivan and Klaus.

When I was named *Knyaz*, I made my blood brother the head of my guard. Klaus was and remains the truest friend I have ever known. I trusted him even more than Ivan, who'd practically raised me.

We'd fought in the Blood Wars together, that hated battle between Vampire Clans that had raged for nearly sixty-years and across every continent. He was loyal, and an irritatingly devoted SOB.

Ivan had come into my employ as a young man. Hired by my grandfather to see to it that I had the proper education for a nobleman. True, we were poor as shite, but we were Vampire nobles all the same. Ivan stood with me while I scrounged to fill the family coffers. He'd been right there with Klaus and me through our worst struggles.

"No," Carina moaned unintelligibly, and I was jogged from my reverie.

I bent forward to listen. Anger rolled through me as I saw the bruising on her neck begin to darken. She had obviously been choked. There were scratches on her throat and face. No teeth marks, thank fuck. She would heal as a result of my bite. The Werewolves did not taint her with their venom. She would get well, but slowly.

Something inside of me pushed and snarled. It pressed me to give the sweet normal my blood, to begin the bonding process and to speed up her healing, but I pushed back. I was tempted. So fucking tempted. But if I fed her from my vein, it would start the process of changing her from human to Vampire.

That choice was not mine to make. Pissed off at myself, I refrained, but only just from biting into my wrist and giving her my blood. It would heal her more fully and so much quickly than the venom from my bite alone.

Shit. This was an impossible decision.

"Her wounds are not life-threatening," Klaus' voice broke into my train of thought.

Growling, I turned my head to make sure he was still facing out before I sliced the remainder of her ruined clothes with my claws. Using great care, I tugged them off her body. I was mindful not to cut or bruise her delicate skin, and when I'd finished undressing her, I readjusted the sheet covering her body.

I needed to protect her modesty, hide her from prying eyes. Eyes that I would personally pull from their sockets if any dared take a gander at her. She was under my patronage now. Mine to protect.

Need pulsed through me, but again I was not such a monster to gain pleasure from looking at her without consent or awareness. My efforts were perfunctory and necessary, not that my cock gave a fuck. But that I could ignore. The blood and bruising that marred her delicate skin. Not so much.

I wanted to hunt the fucking monster who

ordered this atrocity. But she came first. I had to clean her wounds. Needed to tend her myself. I tried to reason it was only to prevent infection, but then why didn't I just send her to the infirmary to be treated? No. That wasn't why. She was too important to leave in the hands of anyone else. Besides, I didn't think I could.

The bowl of water turned red and brown as I cleaned her skin. Those motherfuckers had left her in a ditch. They'd choked her and cut her with their dirty fucking paws. Left her in a cesspool that wasn't fit for an animal. The image of her clinging to life in that alley in a pool of her own blood was forever ingrained on my brain.

Fucking hell. My whole body was vibrating with pure red rage. He would pay for that. Slowly and painfully, Vladek would pay. Then she moaned and all thoughts of vengeance left me.

"It's alright, you will be alright," I whispered while I tended her.

As if my words alone could somehow will her to health. There were no life-threatening wounds left, only bruising. She would be fine. And as I dried her skin with the soft washcloth, I whispered to her, coming to the realization that she meant more to me already than anyone else I had ever met.

Longing filled me and as I listened to the steady, strong beat of her heart, I realized she was getting better. For the first time in my eternal existence, I thanked the universe, the gods, every fucking thing I could think of, offering praise, and making every conceivable bargain to ensure her health.

Anyone who knew me would tell you I was not a man, or a Vampire, of faith. Hunger and violence were a Vampire's first instincts. I had honed my urges, turning them into a lethal skill set used to further my business and my Clan.

I am Aleksei Delov, the Knyaz of my Clan, and a Vampire for over six-hundred years. Yet in all that time I had never felt anything like this strange, all-consuming urge welling up inside of me now. It was like a litany repeating over and over again in my brain. Tattooing itself into my head and making it almost impossible for me to think anything other than those three little directives.

Protect, cherish, claim.

Yes. I wanted that. Yearned for the fragile creature in my bed with everything I was made of. It felt strange, and yet, I welcomed it. Fuck, I needed it. More than air. More than blood.

"Moya krov' pesnya."

I was repeating myself, but it didn't matter. I

brushed her hair back from her face with my hands and studied the sleeping beauty while I took the muck and blood-soaked cloths and tossed them on the wheeled cart. Her smooth skin was cleaned, and I'd placed ointment on her bruises.

She was beautiful. So very lovely. Not my typical choice of female companion, but I knew now that I had been wrong. So very wrong.

I'd always gone for tall, thin, lethal-looking blondes. Carina Martin was the polar opposite. She was petite, short really, and curvy. A beautifully sculpted female with hills and valleys I was dying to explore.

Wrapped in a new, clean sheet, I lifted her and pulled the soiled infirmary sheet to the floor. Her sweet caramel scent wafted into my nostrils and I wanted to rub my nose in the crook of her neck, to breathe her in deep, place my lips there, my fangs, drink from her, and mark her as my own. Shivers ran through my body, but I managed to find the strength to deny my thirst. Then I laid her down under the covers and tucked her in.

"Soon, my love," I whispered and traced a line from the slight widow's peak on her forehead to her stubborn chin.

Lovely, indeed, I spent the next minutes memorizing every centimeter of her face. Her hair started at the roots as midnight black, but grew lighter all the way to a golden hue at the tips. I had to admit, the overall effect was very pretty. Very pretty indeed.

I especially liked her unique whiskey-colored eyes. I wanted to see them trained on me once more. But she needed sleep, and so I would wait at her side until she woke.

Gritting my teeth against the unquenchable thirst I felt just being near her roused within, I forced my fangs to withdraw, and groaned at the fact that there was nothing I could do for that hardness in my pants.

Fuck, I should not be thinking about my cock, but Vampire or not, I was still a man. And the slacks I wore were fucking uncomfortable with a hard-on.

Don't be a prick, I scolded myself. Inching the chair closer so I could breathe in the divine scent that clung to her, I contended myself with watching over her.

It would be caramel and cocoa butter dreams for me. The combination was intoxicating. I could not leave her side. She might need something during while she rested, and of course I would not entrust her care to anyone else. But even as I sat, I knew this was going to drive me fucking crazy with desire.

Calm the fuck down. I growled in my throat, but it was no use. Between my dick and my fangs, I didn't know which mindless appendage throbbed more.

Groan. Come on, I was not some psycho obsessed with this lovely creature. I could back off if I wanted. Only, as it turned out, I could not. I abso-fucking-lutely couldn't bring myself to leave the room. Shit. I had to admit, I sort of resembled a psychotic boyfriend at the moment. The kind who made relationships out of daydreams.

Oh well. I was in trouble and I knew it. A nerve twitched in my cheek and I ran a hand over my face. Scooting the chair closer still to where Carina lay tucked safely inside the covers on my bed. I couldn't risk lying next to her. It was all I could do now to keep myself from staking my claim.

Calm, I am not a monster. She would have the choice. I offered my patronage, and that was what I would give her for now.

The old Sanguinem Council special, I smiled to myself. She went after Vladek for a reason, and I would find out why. If it was revenge she wanted, I would give it to her. I would give her everything.

My Chosen. *Moya krov' pesnya.* My blood song.

CHAPTER 2
CARINA

"Timeless Possessions* will not be permanently damaged, Ivan, and neither will I."

That voice. It was familiar. I heard it coming from the other side of the room as I slowly blinked awake.

"But Alek-"

"Fuck off, Ivan, leave the boss alone," someone else spoke, a raspy, huskier sounding voice, followed by what sounded like a slap on another's shoulder.

"I am merely concerned, *moy Knyaz,*" the one named Ivan returned.

More slapping of shoulders and a hastily whispered *shh.* Funny, I knew I should be afraid, but their chatter only put me at ease. Or maybe that was the expensive, crazy, good-smelling cologne that remained in the air and clung to the pillow I was resting on.

I opened my eyes, but the room was dark. Too dark to make out colors, but I could see shapes. The figure of a man standing not too far away. For some reason, I was not afraid. I knew I was with him. The man who'd saved me from dying of my wounds in a ditch in an alley in Newark. Except he wasn't a man.

Memories of his voice and the promise he'd made me came flooding back. I licked my dry lips and tried to process what had transpired. He was a Vampire. That much had been clear to me before his eyes had started to glow with hunger. And I wasn't attacked by ordinary thugs. No, I'd been attacked by Werewolves working for Vladek the Merciless.

My hand reached up and covered the spot on the right side of my neck where the Vampire had nuzzled my flesh, then bit, transferring whatever healing agents existed in his saliva or venom to me. I wasn't sure of the exact physiological process, I only remembered how it felt. Sharp pain that had soon been replaced by white hot desire. So, good. Yeah, it felt good.

Fuck. What have you done, Carina Martin? I closed

my eyes. I was no longer dying, but my strength was not fully there yet. I knew the answer to my question even as I thought it.

I'd gone after Vladek, seeking revenge for the crimes he was responsible for against my family, and he sent his dogs after me. I was spunky for sure, but I was no match for a pair of superhuman mongrels. Werewolves who'd had fun treating me like a brand new squeaky-toy.

All I'd wanted was for Vladek to pay for my parents' murder. Simple, right? Only it wasn't. Not anymore. I'd believed the man was just another mobster fuck who deserved whatever he had coming, but now I knew differently. He was one of them. A supernatural. Probably another Vampire.

And now I'd gone and accepted the, what did he call it? Oh yeah, *patronage* of yet another creature I had no chance of escaping from. But for some reason, escape was the farthest thing from my mind.

The spicy scent that I'd begun to associate with the Vampire who saved me seemed to fill my nostrils and wrap around me like a warm blanket. I recalled his breath and the gentle caress he gave me the night before. Truth was, I should be pissing in my pants with fear, but all I could muster was curiosity. And a hefty dose of lust.

Even cloaked in shadows and across the enormous room I found myself occupying, my rescuer looked damn good. I blinked my eyes and shook my head to clear my mind. I felt okay. Tired, but good. Odd, considering I just had the shit kicked out of me.

Wincing against the lingering pain in my ribs, I sat up. *Or* I tried too. Whatever I did, it was too quickly and I felt a wave of dizziness that had me crashing back on the fluffy pillow that was so not mine. My studio apartment in downtown Jersey City had nothing on this place.

The room I was in was done in ivories and golds. There were actual paintings, not prints or posters, on the walls, heavy polished furniture, and bookshelves filled with what looked like original leather-bound books even in the darkened light.

Clearly, Mr. Hottie McVampire was loaded. This place was simply too rich for my foster care system growing up ass. I wasn't a snob or the reverse, but this was not my usual kind of digs. Don't get me wrong. Being the practical person I was, I understood how the world worked.

I liked money, understood it made things easier for the rich and beautiful, I just didn't have any. Supernaturals were in a different class than the rest of us normals mainly because of their longevity. At least, that had always been my opinion. But maybe it was the money that made all the difference. Shit. I did not belong in a place like this.

"Easy, little one," a familiar deep voice whispered from close by, "Let me assure you, Carina Martin, you are exactly where you should be."

Shocked and more than a little surprised that he'd read my mind or picked up on my feelings so accurately, I lifted my eyes to his face. Strong hands gripped my upper arms gently, leaning me forward while he placed another pillow behind my head. The lights brightened slightly as if by magic, but all I could see was him.

His silver gaze was brilliant and clear, focused on my face, which made my breath hitch and my heart skip a beat. I licked my lips, pausing when his eyes followed the movement.

His chiseled features were enhanced by the shadow on his cheeks, and I found myself staring too long. He was ruggedly handsome for someone so finely dressed. Even I could tell the black shirt and jeans he wore were designer.

"How do you feel?"

"Cou," I cleared my throat, "could I have some water?"

"Of course," he murmured.

He took a heavy-looking crystal glass filled with ice and water off the end table and lifted it to my dry lips. I was embarrassed to find I had no strength to hold it myself, so I allowed him to minister to me as if I was a child. The icy liquid soothed my damaged vocal cords as it slid down my throat. It felt good.

When I was finished, I looked down, noticing my clothes were gone. A tremor ran through my body as I took in the black robe I wore. It was huge and most definitely belonged to a man. *Or a Vampire*, I figured as it was his scent clinging to the fabric.

I closed my eyes and allowed my *other* sense, that part of me which I'd learned to use after years of denial, to roam. *Yes*, the robe was his. *No*, he was not just a man. He was so much more than that. *Vampire. Protector. Patron. Fate. Mine.*

I shivered and opened my eyes, blinking rapidly until his concerned face came into focus. I knew it had only taken a moment to connect with my abilities and get a read on the fabric, but I was not prepared for that bit at the end. Or the certainty that came with that last monosyllabic word. *Mine.*

"Are you alright? Here, allow me to adjust the light," he took a remote from the same end table and pressed a few buttons. So, it was not magic then, just technology, and I smiled with the realization as the room grew even brighter.

When I opened my eyes again, I found him looking at me with worry and concern. Touching truly, but I did not know why he should care. I didn't know him from Adam. The light allowed me to see my surroundings more clearly.

The bed I was in was enormous, bigger than any standard king size, and it had navy silk sheets and a matching duvet trimmed in gold brocade. *Rich*. Definitely rich. From a girl used to cotton and cheap microfiber it was positively luxurious. I noticed the amused expression on his face and stopped brushing my hands across the top sheet.

"Where am I?"

"My estate. You are safe here, Carina, let me assure you."

"Am I?"

I might be safe from Vladek, but who was going to protect me from him? The thought surprised me and I looked away from him, afraid he would read it in my face.

"Of course," he answered, oozing confidence, arrogance, and a blatant masculine sexuality that made my core heat and my pulse race.

His nearly black hair was combed away from his face, but his silver eyes had a hard glint to them that was more like steel as he studied me.

"You'll be disappointed if you keep looking at me like that," I shook my head and looked down at my feet as I sat up, pulling the blanket off.

"Looking at you could never be disappointing," he frowned and I could see he was fighting something.

Maybe the urge to bite me again? Hunger. Thirst. Yes. It was like I knew how he was feeling, but I had no idea why we should be connected.

"Are you going to-"

"No," he answered my unspoken question and stood up, running a hand through his hair.

But I knew he wanted to. He wanted my blood. I felt his desire for it, his need, but for some reason I was more turned on than afraid and I had no idea why.

He was breathtaking. Gorgeous. A true predator. Vampire, my mind hissed. And yet I was not afraid. Well, not too afraid. There was something about fear and anticipation though, wasn't there?

Maybe I read that somewhere. Maybe I was just losing track of reality. He crossed the space between us and took my hands, pulling me to stand in front of him. He was huge. A good foot taller than me, with shoulders twice as wide.

I knew without having to check that every inch of him was hard like iron. Muscles corded his tall frame, and I knew without a doubt he knew how to use them. This was no soft aristocrat. Supernaturals were secretive, but even they had classes and social distinctions among them.

He was a mystery then. Rich, but powerful. Strong, but suave. I didn't know his past, but he was so familiar to me somehow. Like I had been searching for him my entire life. He was deadly. I needed to remember that one irrefutable fact.

And yet, even as his face grew closer and his focus seemed intent on my lips, I was not afraid. Not until I realized I wanted his lips on mine and the smug bastard seemed to know it.

I shook my head, breaking the spell. He was gorgeous alright. A dark prince charming if ever I saw one. But I was too weak for that kind of thing. Besides, girls like me didn't do fairytales. Time for proper introductions.

"What is your name again?"

I lied. I knew his name, but I was still trying to

work out why I wanted to kiss him so desperately. Why the word *mine* seemed to flash in my brain whenever he was near.

"My name is Aleksei Delov, but you can call me Alek, Carina Martin."

"Alek," I nodded, "I suppose you want to know how I got involved in all this?"

"Yes, of course, but you can rest first."

"No, let's get this over with," I walked past him slowly, pulling my hands from his as casually as I could.

I didn't want him to see how badly his touch affected me. How much I wanted it. Fuck what was wrong with me. I didn't believe in fate and I didn't trust he was not using whatever Vampire powers he had to compel me to feel this way.

"You can freshen up first, Carina. And I swear I am here to protect you. You have my patronage now."

"You said that already, but what does it mean?"

"We can go over that after you've had the chance to shower and dress, to eat something."

My stomach rumbled, and I bit my lip in embarrassment. Trust the fat girl to be hungry at a time like this. I gasped as he crossed the room in the blink of an eye, catching me when I wobbled unsteadily on my feet.

"I'm too heavy," I said, and this time his smile was so wide it almost knocked me out.

"You are light as a feather, Carina."

"That's the first lie you've told me so far," I said.

"I would never lie to you, little one. You are not heavy for me. Your body is sublime. Perfectly curved as a woman should be."

His eyes widened as they dropped down to roam my body and I realized the robe had opened to show an indecent amount of cleavage. Instead of covering myself, I allowed him to look, appreciated the fact his eyes returned to mine almost as quickly as they'd raked over my body.

"I'd heard rumors that Vladek the Merciless hated one man above all others, but I didn't think I'd ever meet him in the flesh."

"I see," he bent down and returned me to my feet.

I missed his warmth almost immediately and was glad when his hands rested on my waist. My own hands went to his chest, and I felt his heart beat slow and steady beneath them. And I wondered, not for the first time, if Vampires were alive or dead.

"And what do you know of our dispute?" his voice interrupted my thoughts.

"Nothing really," I winced as I tried to shrug, "just that he hates you and started a campaign to go after you which is how I got on his radar of course," I offered.

It seemed pointless to lie. I'd been trying to find a way to attack Vladek for a long time. If this man could get me closer I was more than game. Besides, there was something about him that was entirely alluring. If I was being totally honest I'd admit I was attracted to him. And it was getting worse with every minute I stayed in his company.

"Here," he offered his hand, and I allowed him to help me walk.

Wobbly as a newborn kitten, I breathed heavily and took small, slow steps with Alek hovering near should I fall over.

"Where would you like to go?" he asked.

"The bathroom," I said, and raised my eyebrows in exasperation.

Sheesh. Let a girl pee now and then.

"I understand," he smiled and there was that grin again.

I managed to find the clawed foot of one of the several end tables and began to trip. Maybe it was the sheer animal magnetism radiating off him that knocked me completely off my feet. Or maybe it had something to do with getting my ass kicked. Either way, I was in his arms once more.

Only this time he was not smiling. Brows furrowed in concern and maybe a flash of anger, Alek's growl rumbled through his t-shirt and my robe. It felt delicious and tempting, altogether dangerous which is why I suppose, I leaned closer and wrapped my arms around his neck instead of demanding he put me down at once.

The Vampire's growl grew louder as his lips loomed close, and then he was pressing them against mine. Shockwaves of pure undiluted lust washed over me at the insistent pressure of his mouth on mine and soon I found myself opening for him.

He groaned and captured my lips in a kiss that was hot enough to sear my soul, but it was over far too soon. He ended the kiss, lifting his mouth and immediately I missed the warm pressure that was all him.

"Here you are," he allowed me to slide down his body till my feet touched the floor and leaned forward to open the door to an enormous private bath, "I will wait outside the door in case you need me."

I nodded my head and closed the door behind

me. It was all I could do at the moment. Answers, I needed answers, yes, but first I needed a shower. I paused in front of the mirror, shocked to see the faint yellowish bruises that dotted my skin as I dropped the oversized robe to the tiled floor.

Shivering, I turned the water on as hot as it would go. I would never forget the feeling of being cold in that alley. Not as long as I lived. Thank goodness *he* found me. There was no way around it. Alek had saved me last night. I hated feeling indebted to anyone, but for some reason this was okay.

Maybe it was because deep down I recognized him. I don't know how or why. Maybe it was from another lifetime. I only knew my soul seemed happy when he was near.

What was it he said again? He was a member of the old *Sanguinem Council*? A secret Vampire group dedicated to helping normals. Somehow it felt made up. I didn't really know much about Vampires. Supernaturals had come out into the open, but they were still very secretive. Besides, I never had a reason to dig deeper. Until now.

The hot water felt good against my skin and while I appreciated the job he'd done cleaning me up, there was nothing like a good, hot shower.

Twenty-minutes later I emerged from the steaming bathroom with a fluffy white towel wrapped around my body to find a red shopping bag sitting on the bed with a note taped to a cell phone sitting beside it.

Please use this to call me when you are finished dressing. If you need anything in the meantime, let me know.

-Alek

I raised my eyebrows and took in the name of the very expensive boutique the shopping bag boasted. A quick peek inside the large bag told me he had thought of everything. Panties, a bra, even a box with shoes, socks, deodorant, moisturizer, and cosmetics.

Amazing! How was he able to get clothes delivered at this time of night? And so quickly. Still, I doubted they were the right- *Well, shit.* They were the right size. I was shocked to admit not many people understood women's figures, and I was a thick kinda gal.

Plenty of thighs and ass on my short frame, but I was in no way lazy. I worked out. Kickboxing and Tae Kwon Do. Not that it did any good against those fuckers who attacked me.

I shouldn't be surprised though. They weren't

human after all. Werewolves were touchy little puppies. Didn't like it at all when I called the taller one Fido. Oh well, I never was a crowd pleaser.

I blushed wildly as I lifted the tiny scrap of pink lace that was supposed to cover my privates and the matching demi-cup bra. Never in my life had I splurged on lingerie like that. Who would I wear it for? Besides looking at the price tags, that underwear cost more than my grocery bill for a week.

I bit my lip and shrugged. He'd already bought them and underwear was non refundable. I slid into them despite my blushes, sighing at the superb fit and the way the fabric felt soft as baby's breath against my skin.

Next came a pair of kickass faux-leather leggings that molded to my curves perfectly. Paired with a thin long-sleeved blouse, I was more than happy with the fit. Both items were black and not fussy in the least. I had to admit they were just my style. Not my price range, but still, I loved the outfit.

Regardless of whether this patronage thing worked out, I was so keeping the clothes. Especially the chunky-heeled, blood-red, steel-toed leather boots. I *floved* those bad boys and like everything else. They were just my size. When I was finished going through the make-up, I picked up the phone and sent a text.

Mascara? Yes. Blush? No. Lipstick? Maybe.

A second later, I opened the door, and there he was.

Gorgeous.

CHAPTER 3
ALEKSEI

Pacing up and down the hallway like some fucking lovesick puppy was not a good look for the new Knyaz of the Delov Clan. And yet, I couldn't stop.

Yes, I left her alone at first. Tried going to the library, then my office, to get a little work done. But it was impossible.

"Alek, everyone knows better than to enter your wing," Klaus reminded me.

My blood brother had stayed nearby to guard my Chosen, but that did nothing to soothe my anxiety. What if some young, *or old*, upstart thought to attack me in my quarters?

It had happened once after my ascension to the position of prince. Some did not care for my role as the new *Knyaz*, I would weed them all out and destroy them all. It was imperative now that I had someone to protect.

"Fuck, I can't be here," I snarled and used my ability of translocation to jump to the hallway in front of my bedroom where I'd left her.

Sprinting tended to leave me winded, but I was anxious to see her. Her caramel and cocoa butter scent drifted through the hair's breadth of space between the door and the polished hardwood floor.

I sucked it in, relishing it. That crazy sexy scent that was so absolutely perfect wrapped itself around my heart and my cock. Both were hers already, and I was royally fucked. How did I explain to a normal what it meant to be my blood song? Would she understand that I had spent lifetimes without any hope that I would ever find her? That I would spend the rest of my life worshipping her, if only she would let me.

I truly had no idea, and that was terrifying. The idea of losing her was unthinkable. The growl building in my chest deepened, and I cut off the sound before she heard it. Fuck. I was losing my grip on myself. But what could I do? It was a biological imperative. I had to have her.

Shit. Calm. Stay Calm. I repeated the phrase over

and over again in my head. This was beyond the experiences of even my vast lifetime.

I heard the knob twist and lifted my eyes in time to see my Chosen standing in the doorway. My breath left my lungs and for a moment my brain seemed to shut down. Desire, need, and a single moment of absolute serenity swept over me followed by a much stronger emotion I could hardly put a name to.

"Hi," she said but her smile soon left her face, "uh, thank you, for the clothes," she mumbled and looked down.

I realized why after a moment. I was growling at her like some rabid beast. Fuck. I cleared my throat and nodded.

"Yes, the outfit is very nice," I said inanely, but she was the true star.

Spectacular in all her curvy glory. Somehow I knew she would approve of the red boots and black ensemble. Holy hell, she looked good enough to eat and yes, I meant that quite literally.

"Fits great," she replied.

Cocoa butter and caramel wrapped around my senses completely and before I knew it I'd walked closer. The need to be near her was overpowering.

"I am glad you're pleased with them."

"I am, thanks."

"How do you feel?"

"Better. You were right though, I am a little hungry."

"Come, let's get some food and then we will talk."

I led her down the hall to one of the informal dining rooms on the estate. This one was often used by my guard and myself when I was home.

"Wow. This place is enormous."

"Yes," I nodded, "a man in my position has to make a statement," I held a chair for her and her shoulder brushed across my chest as she sat down.

The almost-touch had me trembling like a schoolboy, and I closed my eyes a second to regain my composure. At this rate, I'd spend the whole damn day waking up from the kind of erotic wet dreams that I haven't had since puberty.

Fucking hell. But it would be a sweet hell for certain.

I sent a command via telepathic communication to the servants to deliver food, and within seconds of entering the room, it was served. Platters of perfectly rare roast beef, asparagus in Hollandaise sauce, sauteed mushrooms, new potatoes with rosemary, and dozens of more small dishes arrived.

"This looks amazing," she lifted a slice of French bread, sighing as she took a bite.

I had never felt jealous of food before, and yet as she nibbled and moaned happily, I was positively green with envy.

You are behaving like a fucking idiot.

"What?" she stifled a laugh.

"Nothing," I had to work to stop myself from whispering into her mind with my thoughts.

A side effect of the bite I'd given her, and maybe something more as well. Staring at her was becoming something of a full-time affair, and she noticed too. Carina raised her eyebrows as if to say *and what?* I smiled, unbelievably attracted to the feisty human.

She was like a walking, talking real-life version of my deepest, most secret fantasies. All curves and valleys, her body was perfection itself. Soft to my hard, dark to my pale. Her bronzed skin was back to its healthy honey-glow and as I leaned forward I got a whiff of that sweet caramel and cocoa butter that seemed to surround her.

Fighting my impulse to kiss her silly right then and there, I continued with my forward bend. The breath caught in her throat and her pulse went wild as I drew closer. Good. She was not as unaffected by me as she would pretend.

"I won't hurt you."

For some reason I wanted her to know that. It was important. As important as the fact that I knew if I touched her, I would not be able to control what happened next. Neither of us was ready for our relationship to progress to that level. Not yet.

Carefully, I raised my napkin, waiting for her nod before wiping a crumb of butter from her lips. Then I backed away, exhaling as if I'd just run a fucking marathon.

"Oh, excuse me," she murmured and took the napkin from my hand, pressing it to her mouth.

The dusky color that tinted her cheeks was entirely too enticing. She looked good enough to eat, but I settled for the rare roast beef instead.

"So, Vampires can eat?"

"*I* can eat," I admitted, "we are all different, with unique abilities, talents, and preferences. Food cannot sustain us alone. Blood is required."

"How do you get blood?"

"Donors."

"Donors? Like people?"

"Yes. Believe it or not, there are many people who would lineup for the opportunity to feed a Vampire. Some establishments have been created for that sole purpose."

It was true, though personally I was not a fan of

the more popular trends. Seeing people treated like cattle was about as appetizing as most fast-food these days. Quality was rare in both cases.

"Really? People want to be bitten?"

"Yes. A Vampire's bite usually involves some intoxication and satisfaction, in other words humans can get a sort of high from it."

"I don't remember that," she said.

"I was not feeding from you," I explained, "I would not do that without permission."

"Really?"

"Of course. I only ever feed from willing donors, but typically, I drink from my stores."

"What do you mean?"

"I have a reserve on site. A mini blood bank of sorts."

"Isn't it better from the vein?"

Her innocent question echoed in my mind. Of course it was. But how could I impart that to her without rousing her fear? The last thing I wanted was Carina backing away from me.

"I will not lie to you, Carina. Feeding from the source is better in many ways."

"Then why don't you?" her eyes were at half-mast and the sweet scent of her filled the air.

Not fear. I was surprised that she was not afraid

and running screaming at this point. But she was curious, and I approved wholeheartedly of that. I welcomed her questions with relish.

There was nothing I wouldn't tell her. She was quickly becoming the focus of my world, and I knew I had to focus on appeasing Princess Ana and getting the artifact to her then I needed to exact revenge on Vladek, but the truth was nothing had ever interested me more than sitting there with her.

"I have not wanted to drink from anyone in a very long time."

That was about as honest as I dared be. Hell, if I told her I wanted to bend her back across the table, take her mouth with mine, sink deeply into her sex, and drink her blood, she might actually run screaming. And I didn't want that.

Mine. My stomach clenched at the possibility. It was all I could do not to reach out and grab her, pull her out of her chair and onto my lap. The female was emphatically dangerous to my self-control. A nerve twitched along my jaw, but I kept myself still.

"I see," she cleared her throat and pushed her near empty plate away, "Well, um, thank you for healing me, and cleaning me up, but I think I have to get back now."

It was unclear to me what she thought she saw,

but it seemed it was time for our discussion. How did I explain to her, to a normal, what it meant to be *moya krov' pesnya*? She had no concept of the important of her position in my life. Nothing to measure it by.

One thing was certain, I could not just let her leave. Her life was still in danger from Vladek and his fucking mutts. The thought brought me from content to furious rage in an instant. I barely managed to shove down my baser impulses and concentrated on her face.

"That's not possible now, little one."

"Am I your prisoner then?" she asked and her brown eyes flashed in her anger.

She was beautiful, especially when her eyes glowed with annoyance. Of course, I did not make the mistake of telling her that. One glance behind her and I saw Klaus had joined us,. He stood with his back towards us, as guard to the only entrance to the dining room.

"Carina, you agreed to accept my patronage," I began in a low voice trying for patience when all I wanted was to take her in my arms, drag her lips under my mouth, and have her in my bed.

"I wasn't in my right mind at the time, I was dying-"

"You knew enough to accept my offer to save your life," I smirked, liking the crease in her forehead as she glared at me.

"Look. This was great really. I like the clothes, I won't be giving them back. But you need to open the front door and step aside while I go finish the job I set out to do."

"Which was what exactly? Tell me what was a normal like you doing going after a Vampire anyway?"

"I didn't know he was a Vampire."

"Your recklessness concerns me, but that is beside the point. What is the job you set out to do, Carina?"

"I want to kill Vladek the Merciless."

"Why? What has he done?"

"He is responsible for murdering my parents."

CHAPTER 4
CARINA

I couldn't believe this was happening to me. It was impossible. Like some deep dark fantasy finally fulfilled. A thing I would never admit to in broad daylight. At least, not unless asked directly.

First of all, I'd spent the better part of the night in a mansion. Albeit, unconsciously, but still. I'd woken up in silken luxury the likes of which I'd never experienced.

Secondly, my host was a Vampire. Not the old, wrinkly dude with the long-ass braid and hella scary fingernails either. Nope. Aleksei Delov was a different kind of Vamp.

More Brad Pitt than Bela Lugosi. In other words, he was totally fucking hot, but he was also totally off the menu. All my pinkish, girly bits wanted to cry aloud at that decision, but it was what it was.

Just because I avoided supes, didn't mean I knew fuck all about them. The second I was old enough to understand what *they* were, I'd studied what I could.

The different species and factions were incredibly secretive, but after being backed into a corner by a couple of Shifters in foster care, I'd done my research.

I knew enough to understand that if I fed from Alek, if I accepted even one drop of his blood, I would begin the process of becoming a Vampire. Fae and Demons were born, but Vampires and Shifters could be turned with a bite or scratch. But only if I was predisposed to the change. Some people died during the process.

I felt my entire body tremble with longing at the prospect. Like some part of me wanted that forbidden truth to become my own. It frightened me, that strange, dark longing.

I closed my eyes and breathed in a slow, deep breath. The spicy scent was like plump juicy mangos laced with habanero peppers. It seemed to cling to Alek and whenever I was near him. It invaded my nostrils, soothing my irritability and filling me with security.

Laying my hand on the console that sat between us, my abilities seemed to reach out on their own, seeking, siphoning, and gathering information on the man who owned the vehicle. I was not always aware when my other senses would activate, but they'd never steered me wrong.

In all honesty, I was curious about him. I wanted to know more about my so-called patron. As I allowed the data to come flowing back to me, I became aware with absolute surety that this car was indeed Alek's. Not some Vampire minion's.

Then I concentrated on the man. He was an old soul. I saw him in centuries past, and he was powerful too. Important to his Clan. Good and just. His abilities were vast, and even more astonishing was his self-control.

No wonder he was able to risk giving me his bite and taking me back to his place. Alek was a leader. A noble. A Prince. I gasped with the knowledge. He didn't tell me he was fucking royalty!

"We are almost there," his voice intruded on my exploration and it took me a minute, but I pulled myself back together.

Vulnerability was one of the nasty side-effects of my psychic powers. I turned my head as if to stare out the window, but instead I was piecing the information I'd learned back together and storing it away for later study.

He was a prince. A real prince. Fuck. Why didn't he tell me he was the actual leader of his Clan?

"Are you alright?"

"What? Yeah, I'm fine."

But I wasn't fine. Inside, I was a whirlwind of thoughts and unreasonable emotions. Why should it matter to me what he was? Why should I feel so hopeless at the fact that he was royalty and I was nobody? I was not his. And more importantly, Alek was not mine.

"We are almost there."

Timeless Possessions was one of his businesses. His favorite if I wasn't mistaken. He'd insisted on this little field trip and we were on our way to the warehouse that housed many of the artifacts he'd collected over the years.

"How long?"

"Five minutes."

I nodded and tried to focus on what was going on around me. What was I even doing? I couldn't even begin to explain. Okay, maybe I could.

Daydreaming in a car with a dangerous predator, fantasizing about becoming a Vampire, that's what I was doing. Yeah, well it wasn't that strange. Every girl who grew up reading as many Young Adult books as I had, had that fantasy at one time or other. But I was just setting myself up for failure. He was a fucking prince and I was so not his type.

The day before I was lying in a gutter choking on my own blood. I must seem ridiculous to him, I thought, and wanted to smack myself on the forehead. My life was a series of mishaps. Orphaned as a baby with no relatives to speak of, I'd been alright in foster care until my abilities started to make an appearance.

That was when they decided I should be grouped with those *other* children. The Supernatural ones, only I wasn't like them. I was a *normal*. A boring, nerdy, and yes, chubby human girl who just happened to tap into the history of an item when I touched something every now and again.

Alek was Vampire royalty, and curvy orphans were not exactly in vogue as appropriate consorts. I knew all about snobbery. The way Ivan had looked at me, as if I was something he'd stepped on when he'd seen us eating together. Even now he thought of me as something marring his perfect Italian leather shoes. It only confirmed what I already knew.

I was definitely not the sort of woman seen on the arms of a guy who drove a quarter of a million dollar car, lived on an estate, and had actual servants at his beck and call. Speaking of which. The motherfucker in the backseat, the one doing all the glaring, was really starting to piss me off.

"Hey buddy, you mind sliding over?"

Alek turned to look in my direction, but I ignored the silent inquiry of his raised eyebrow. I could handle myself. It was important he knew that.

"Yeah," I said and looked down my nose at the creepy Vampire version of a butler, "you're kinda breathing on me and I'd rather not. Type O isn't exactly refreshing."

The man raised his lip, but before he could utter a sound, a loud, fierce growl erupted from Alek. Without any reply, the Vampire, *Ivan*, slid over to the other side of the car.

I glanced at Alek, his eyes were trained on the road, but the telltale signs of a smirk lingered at the corner of his mouth. I shivered and he touched a button on the impeccably clean dashboard. Instantly, my seat began to heat up. He seemed very much aware of every move I made, and there was something exciting and dangerous about that little fact.

"We're here."

Alek parked the car and was at my door faster than I could unbuckle my safety belt. I tried not to react, but I was only human. My heart thundered in my chest as I accepted his hand and stepped out of the vehicle. It was close to midnight.

His warehouse was on the outskirts of Elizabeth, between Harrison and Jersey City. It was an enormous building with a surprisingly modern security system that would rival the best museums in the world. But that only made sense, considering his inventory.

I watched as he placed his hand on a biometric scanner and waited for Ivan to use the retinal display before adding his own keyed in password. It took only moments, but seemed longer as I tried to take in everything all at once.

"Good evening, *moy Knyaz*," an enormous burly Vampire wearing a security uniform met us at the entrance.

His nametag read Boris K. I didn't know what the K was for or why it needed to be there. Were there multiple Borises in the warehouse? Were they all alphabetized to keep them straight?

Okay. I admit I might've been cracking up at this point. In terms of a nervous breakdown as opposed to the laughing out loud sort. Alek cocked his head and looked at me as if he was afraid I was going to break. Fuck that. I glared at him, then went back to my perusal of good old Boris.

There were two guns strapped to his massive thighs and another weapon across his back. This one resembled a katana, but the blade had a sharp, serrated edge instead of a smooth one. It was a wicked-looking thing, and I trembled at the sight of it.

Boris bowed deeply to Alek before acknowledging me with a slight flare of his nostrils. He ignored Ivan altogether, which immediately had me on his side. Ivan was a douche. Anyone who agreed with me on that was aces.

"Boris," Alek greeted the guard and walked down the corridor.

I noticed Ivan seemed surprised, and I wondered why, but was quickly distracted as we walked through the heart of the building. Row upon row of ancient artifacts sat behind glass encasements that were both temperature and light controlled. Priceless works of art, actual pieces of history, glinted at me as we headed to a pair of double doors.

"This is incredible," I whispered, and for the first time I felt that sense inside of me awaken without touching a single thing.

It was as if every artifact in the place was calling

to me. Like they wanted to be touched and read, wanted to share their stories. It was overwhelming and I could hardly remember how to breathe, except for the firm, warm hand that clasped mine and grounded me back on earth.

Alek, my mind whispered gratefully, and I exhaled. I didn't know if he knew how lost I was in that split second, but I was so damn happy he'd found me. This dependence I was starting to feel for him was worrisome, but he squeezed my hand in his and it didn't matter anymore. Nothing did. Only him.

"Come," Alek held the door for me, and I tugged gently, removing my hand from his grip and stepped inside what must have been his private offices.

"Ivan, go over the delivery schedule with Thalia. She is waiting for you at the loading dock," he instructed and closed the door, impervious to the shock and touch of indignation on the Vamp's face.

"I don't think he likes me," I said.

"Hm," he grunted, "Ivan doesn't much like anyone. But Ivan is not important in this matter."

Inside the confined space, I noticed his scent seemed stronger. Spicy and exotic, it wrapped around me like a warm lasso, pulling me towards him, pressing me closer. It took some effort, but I managed to sit down in a chair opposite his desk. Alek lifted a black file folder and handed it to me.

"This is the manifest from the shipment you'd arranged to have stolen from Vladek."

I stared at the paper for a moment and handed it back to him. There was no doubt he was telling the truth.

"And?"

"The truck was disguised as a bread delivery van and it was hijacked on route here for verification before it was sent to my clients."

"I didn't have it stolen from you," I said, not quite sure where he was going with this.

"I know that, but what I want to know is how you found it when Vladek had already taken it?"

I pursed my lips. My sources deserved to be protected, but I owed him. Clearly this artifact was important, but I'd been less concerned with the item and more intent on hurting Vladek at the time.

"First, I want to say I had no idea what was being transported, only that it was something Vladek seemed to want. Second, Elena is a friend of mine from my days in foster care. She runs a bakery during the day and hacks through the un-hackable at night."

"How did you know what truck to go after?"

"I didn't," I almost laughed, "for real, look, all I did was some basic reconnaissance. I mean, I followed Vlad's goons around town for a few weeks-"

"You tailed Werewolves?"

"I didn't realize what they were," I answered, embarrassed now by that lack of foresight.

Besides, I didn't see what he was so angry about. Then it hit me. He was concerned. The feeling warmed me to my core and once more I had to fight back my growing attraction to him. I licked my lips, watching as he tracked the movement with his laser-like stare.

"I, uh," clearing my throat, I continued, "I found out he was making a move on his enemy, *you*, but I didn't know it was *you*. I mean, I just met you! Anyway, Elena and I decided that would be the best time to strike since his guys would be intent on making sure yours didn't find him."

"That's brilliant."

I rolled my eyes at his apparent shock that I had a brain in my head. Why did all men think boobs equaled brainless?

"I did not mean to offend you, Carina," he grinned and his eyes settled on my chest for a moment before returning to my face, "I am well aware how intelligent you are. My surprise was simply because I never thought of being on guard for such a threat."

"Why have *Tiny* packing up in here then?"

"You mean Boris? I had Thalia, one of my oldest and most trusted employees, set up a security team the second we were hit."

"Why didn't Ivan know?"

I could tell that I'd surprised him again. Good. A powerful Vampire like him shouldn't grow complacent. For some reason, the idea of Alek being in any kind of harm made me very uneasy. But why should it? I'd only just met the Vamp. Why should he mean so much to me?

I didn't want to examine the answer closely or at all for that matter. Living alone was what I did. My revenge was my only purpose. Afterwards I could go live my life anywhere I wanted. I could get out of the Garden State. Travel, see things. I didn't know what exactly, but those were the dreams I'd had before I met Alek.

Were those still my dreams? I wondered and knew without a doubt something had changed in the last twenty-four hours. And I wasn't sure I was okay with that.

"I do not share everything with any one person," Alek explained.

"Sounds lonely."

His silver eyes glittered in the dim light of his office, and I was struck again by how remarkably handsome he was. Truly, he was beautiful. One-hundred percent masculine, and yet those stunning eyes, the sensual lips, his defined cheekbones, and that small cleft in his chin made him cover-model worthy. But that was part of his being a Vampire. A beautiful creature that needed to attract his food with his looks as much as his innate magnetic pull.

"It can be, but I never really noticed. Until now."

His response broke the silence that had fallen around us like a shroud. Time stood still as I stared into his eyes. They were glowing. Twin pools of starlight and I was hypnotized by them, by all of him, actually.

Someone knocked on the door, I turned towards it, but not him. Alek watched me instead. His eyes were branding me with their intensity, but honestly, I didn't mind the heat. Not one bit.

"They won't come in, unless I say so," his voice sounded from directly behind me.

How did he do that? I wondered, but I knew. He was a Vampire, not a man. He could move at super-speed, and even sprint through time and space, or so he'd explained. His hands closed around my shoulders and I felt his face nuzzle my neck as he took in a deep breath. My heart was pounding inside my chest. I knew without a doubt he could hear it, was right then listening to my own body's traitorous response to his nearness.

"Carina," he said my name and the warmth of his breath tickled my ear.

Instead of pushing him away, I found myself leaning back into his touch, wanting more of it for my own. I closed my eyes on a wave of arousal so strong it nearly swept me off my feet.

Alek's hands tightened on my shoulders. He lifted and turned me around so I was suddenly standing, facing him. He was so big and tall. His shoulders were wide, his body lean and hard, muscular like nothing I'd ever seen.

"We should-"

"I know."

He agreed with me, but still his hands stayed put and I sure as fuck did not move. I couldn't even if I wanted to. It was like my feet were glued to the damn floor.

My own breathing was shallow as I wrestled with myself. He'd offered me his patronage, nothing more. I was fooling myself if I thought my growing crush would ever mean anything to someone as important, ruthless, and rare as Aleksei Delov, Vampire, Prince, or what was it everyone called him, that's right, *Knyaz* of his Clan, owner of a global conglomerate, and total fucking hottie.

"We, we should go. I can call Elena on the way."

"As you wish."

CHAPTER 5
ALEKSEI

"**I** can't believe you quoted *The Princess Bride*."

"I'm sorry? Which princess?"

"The movie."

"What?"

"Nothing," she blew out a short breath, and I focused on the road ahead of me.

Her directions were brief, but I knew my way around this part of the Garden State. Hell, I'd lived there since before the roads were paved.

We turned onto Communipaw Avenue, then made a left on West Side. There it was. A little bakery and coffee shop with a carved wooden sign that read *Elena's Bread, Fine Food, & Pastry* over the top.

The rich aroma of fresh bread baking in old-fashioned brick ovens was mouthwatering, but not nearly as tempting as the luscious morsel sitting beside me. I'd almost lost it back at the warehouse. Had barely managed to control my urge to bend her over my desk and tear that damn outfit off her.

What was I thinking buying her that sexy little black number? I'd thought it professional and a little sassy, but I had no idea my Chosen's curves would fill it out quite that way. Hell, I'd almost killed Ivan and Boris on principle. No one should be able to see her luscious curves but me. Sit. Even I recognized when I sounded like an ass, but what could I say, my feelings about her were somewhat covetous.

Vampire females were oftentimes slender and angular creatures, though they were beautiful, as was the rest of the species. But I had never seen anyone like Carina before. She was curved like a racetrack and just as dangerous if you didn't know how to drive.

I was pretty damn confident in my abilities, and yet I'd stepped back. I let her move away from me. Because she was not just any conquest. Carina Martin was my blood song.

I needed her more than I needed air to breathe or blood to live. I had to win her heart before I claimed her body. Wanted her to love me as I already loved her. Was it greedy and selfish of me? Probably, but I would never want another. I was made for her surely as she was designed for me.

"Come on."

I followed behind Carina, mindful of our surroundings. We had about three hours till sunrise and I was eager to hear what her friend had to say on the matter of the artifact that had been stolen from me not once, but twice.

"Hey girl, we're here!" Carina called to the back of the quaint little coffee shop as I took in the front.

We were alone. The building was secure and even had a topnotch *Draco Fortis* alarm system installed. A moment later, a small woman with a mop of curls covered by a black hair net that held them away from her rounded face came rushing to the front. She squealed and embraced Carina, rocking her steadily before stepping back.

"Damn, 'Rina you look good!"

"Thanks. You got my text, right?"

"Yeah. This him?" she pointed at me and pursed her lips.

"Hello Elena, I am Aleksei Delov."

"I know all about you Mr. Vampire-Prince. Hmph."

I looked at Carina whose face was turning a

dusky shade of red. The woman, *Elena*, gave me the once over and crossed her arms.

"Girl, I know he cute, but he a Vampire. You best watch yourself."

"Elena!"

"Fine," she sighed, "look when I had your van picked off from Vlad's puppies, I had my driver bring me what was inside. I am telling you, I don't know what the fuss is all about," she wiped her hands on her apron and stalked to the back of the shop where a small print of Van Goh's *Sunflowers* hung against the otherwise unadorned brick.

Once she removed the painting, I saw the safe and waited while her biometrics scanner took her fingerprints. Impressive for a baker, but this woman was more than that. A hacker and a thief, and by all accounts a good one. I would have to remember that.

"This was the only thing in there. What is it anyway? Some kind of jewelry box?"

"Elena!" Carina gasped as the woman tossed the priceless artifact in the air like a baseball, but before she could catch it, I did.

Sprinting across the bakery took hardly any effort, but I could not risk the egg being broken by such careless display. Besides the anger of Princess

Ana, I could not bear to see history destroyed that way.

"This," I said using a silk handkerchief to handle the precious Russian artifact, "is called *Cherub with Chariot*. It was one of the fifty Imperial Easter eggs created by Peter Faberge for the then royal family of Russia. Alexander III, had this and many more made for his beloved wife, the Tzarina Maria Feodorovna."

I quickly looked over the incredible masterpiece before wrapping it in the silk kerchief and placing it in my inside coat pocket.

"Wow," my Chosen gasped as she stared at the place I placed the egg.

She then turned to her friend, "Thank you," Carina murmured and hugged Elena as I withdrew a thick envelope from my pocket and handed it to the human woman.

"What is this for?"

"That is a finder's fee," I nodded, "perhaps in the future I will have work for you."

"No doubt," she raised an eyebrow and eyed the stack of bills I'd given her before placing them in the safe, "Carina, you can call me later, I have to check on the baguettes."

They exchanged hugs, and I held the door for Carina. We strolled back to the car where I withdrew the egg and placed it in a small velvet-lined box I had prepared for it.

"Why did you pay her?"

"Because she earned it. She kept the egg safe."

"But she's my friend, she wasn't expecting anything."

"I know," I glanced over at Carina, her beauty was such that I nearly slammed us both into the car in front of us, "that is why I paid her."

"I don't understand."

"She is your friend, and I wanted to express my thanks. That is all."

"So, we have your property back. What happens now?"

What indeed?

A voice inside of me whispered that I claim my Chosen, drink her blood, give her my vein, and make her mine once and always. I cleared my throat and tapped the steering wheel.

What the fuck was wrong with me? Was I doomed to be an impatient fool driven by lust whenever she was around? Fucking hell.

"Now, we go home. We rest, then in the evening we have a party to attend."

"A party?"

"Yes, but first I thought you might take a look at

the egg?"

"I'd like that," she replied, and honest interest brightened her entire demeanor.

In fact, she practically glowed with it. *What I wouldn't give to see her glow for me*, I cleared my throat at the thought and squirmed in my seat. It was a prospect I found all too intoxicating. So many possibilities, but I had to stop myself from thinking about them. My pants were already too damned tight.

We arrived back at the estate and I nodded at Klaus while passing him by. I waited for Carina to enter my bedroom first, following her inside, and she turned and raised an eyebrow.

"Can I see it?"

"Yes," I replied, though I must admit my mind immediately went somewhere else.

"Really? Grow up," Carina snorted and held her hand out, "You're how old? Four? Five-hundred? A powerful Vampire. And yet, you still have the same impulses of a fourteen-year-old boy."

"Well, yeah, but in my defense, when I was fourteen women did not look and act like you."

"What do you mean?"

"I mean that you are perhaps the one person in the entire world who can throw me off balance. How's that for a confession?"

Her breath hitched and those warm butter-scotch-colored eyes raked over me like I was something entirely altogether tempting. For a moment, I lost my train of thought. This was dangerous, but I could control myself. I had to.

The symphony that was her blood flowing through her veins called to me. Her heart pounded out a rhythmic tattoo and filled my senses. Fuck, she was divine, and I wanted her more with every minute. I was aware of our growing connection.

This uncanny ability we had to pick up on one another's thoughts and though new to me, I welcomed it and her. Wanted a deeper connection with my Chosen. All Vampires had one ability or other, but mind-reading was not one of mine. At least it wasn't, until I met her.

"The egg?"

"Yes," I motioned to the small chaise that sat against the wall near the fireplace and waited.

Carina's hips swayed as she walked and sat down with all the elegance and grace of carriage of anyone I had ever met. She was perfect, and I craved her more and more with every second that passed.

I wondered if that seductive little twitch was on purpose, but I didn't think so. She seemed unaware of her beauty, which only made her even more tempting to my jaded eyes.

I had seen every manner of female, or so I'd thought, in my many years on this earth. But no one came close to her. The guidelines of the old Sanguinem Council were not exactly clear on how far we were permitted to take our patronage, but even if they were, I was not sure this was something I could stop.

Protective instincts I did not even know I was capable of welled up as she combed her hair with her fingers and rolled her shoulders before fixing her gaze on me. She was tired.

"We can do this after you've rested," I frowned, but she shook her head.

"No. I'm okay. I want to see it up close."

"Alright. If you are sure," I said, unable to deny her, "*The Cherub and Chariot.*"

I withdrew the priceless egg from the box where I'd left it for safekeeping. No one had seen the artifact in decades and I admit, I was sort of giddy with that knowledge. And the fact I could share it with her.

Carina's soft gasp seemed to echo in the silence of the room. She made no move to touch the egg, and I was content to hold it for her. The magnificent design left me speechless for a moment. So simple, and yet the craftsmanship was superb. A golden egg sat nestled in a two-wheeled wagon being pulled by a chubby child-like angel who looked back at his prize with a small smile on his face. Like he knew a secret that was hidden within and couldn't wait to deliver it.

It's opulence was evident in the heavy gold and silver ornaments, the glittering gems that studded the surface. Dozens of diamonds and a large sapphire adorned the trinket, but the real surprise lay on the inside. I turned the egg carefully and opened it, revealing an equally decadent golden clock.

"It's beautiful," Carina whispered.

"Yes. I have a special client who is quite the collector."

"Who?"

"She is a Vampire, Princess of her Clan. Ana de Medici. We are going to attend a party she is throwing tomorrow where I will present her with this, the real Fabergé egg she'd conscripted from me."

"I'm sorry if I in any way caused-"

"No. It was not your fault. You see, when Vladek stole my shipment, he'd already sent a fake in its stead. Ana sent two of her men with a message for me that day."

"What happened?"

Lying would have been so much easier, and yet, I couldn't bring myself to do that. This was as much a part of me as my fangs, as my need for blood to survive. I was the Knyaz of my Clan. I was a Vampire. I was also a businessman.

Carina needed to know all of me before I presented her with the truth. I braced myself for her reactions to what I was about to say. Would she be afraid? Disgusted? I guess I was about to find out.

"Her Vampires are strong in number. Ana's Clan is across the river, in Manhattan, but they have grown accustomed to modern life and were not expecting me, the Knyaz of a small Clan to defend myself as I had."

"You speak of her as if you're in a relationship with her."

"Are you asking mc if I am?" I studied her, waiting to see her response, but Carina was not about to give herself away.

I grinned. It was just something else for me to admire about the beautiful woman who had full command of my heart, even if she didn't know it.

"How did you defend yourself?" she asked, changing the subject.

I paused a moment. This was a moment of truth, like nothing else. She'd seen me as rescuer and as patron, now she would see me as ruthless. How would she react? There was only one way to find out, and I was not a coward in any sense of the word, though I was not sure how I would respond if she backed away from me in fear. Taking the plunge, I opened my mouth to explain.

"I had the misfortune to send one of her men back to her carrying the head of his coworker with a note that I would rectify the error."

"Were you hurt?"

The terror in her voice at the prospect of me coming to harm warmed me like nothing else could. She cared. It was there in her bright eyes and frantic heartbeat.

"No, I was not hurt, little one."

"Good," she closed her eyes a moment then held out her hand, "let me see what I can read from this fancy egg."

I smirked and shook my head. Her uncanny way of speaking was like a breath of fresh air, as was everything about her. So much effort was spent in trying not to be bored when you lived forever, but I could see I would never have that problem again with Carina in my life.

Handing over the egg was easy. Watching what it did to her was not. A bolt of some kind, like some unseen lightning or electrical short, seemed to rack her entire body before she went completely still.

Head back, wild mass of curls tumbling around her shoulders, I growled as an ethereal light began to cover her body. She was breathing far too quickly. Her heart was racing and movement beneath her eyelids told me her brain was working rapidly.

"Carina!" I yelled and tried to take the egg from her hands, but it was no good.

She was in some kind of trance, and I was powerless to help her. I heard Klaus' booted feet running down the hall before stopping at my door.

"*Moy Knyaz?*" he shouted.

"It's Carina," I said through gritted teeth, "she is caught in a vision."

I tried to touch her, but she was shrouded in magic. Afraid it was burning her with those little electric shocks, I crouched by her side. My eyes went to Klaus as he opened the door.

"I have seen this sort of thing before, there is nothing you can do, but wait," he said, "but do not fear the *Knyazhna* will be okay."

A snarl erupted from my lips, and I hardly noticed he'd referred to her as *princess*. Later I would thank him and offer her the title as well as my heart. Later. When she was well again.

Fucking hell. That was what this felt like. Like I was trapped in a deep dark hole and I couldn't get out. Helplessness was not a good look on me.

"You should rest. I can watch over her," Klaus said after the first hour, but I shook my head. I would not leave her. Not like this.

"You must feed, Alek, keep your strength up."

"No," I snarled at him, then turned back to my beloved, "Come back to me, *moya krov' pesnya*, wake up."

CHAPTER 6
CARINA

My body was aflame. That was the only intelligible thought I'd had since I touched the *Cherub and Chariot*. One of the incredible fifty Easter eggs made by Faberge for the royal family. Lost to the human world for decades. This piece of the imperial history of Russia was so much more than met the eye.

I wonder if Alek knew that. Probably not, seeing as how the Vampire's every move since meeting me had been to protect me. I didn't know why at the time, but even now as he called my name and knelt by my side with fear racing through his veins, I knew.

Mine. The word I'd been hearing since we met was not just in my head, it was in his. We were meant to be together. A single kiss, one small bite, that was all that had transpired between us, but in between was so much more. Ever since I met him, I'd felt a mystical pull of attraction to him.

Yes, I'd been denying it, but what was the point? Scrounging out a life, pulling myself up, brushing off the stigma of being an orphan, I knew all about hard work. Being with a Vampire, giving myself into his absolute power, was probably not going to be easy. But I swore to myself right then, if I got out of this alive, I sure as hell was going to find out.

Time waited for no one. My parents' time together had been cut short. I mourned them and wanted to avenge them, but I wanted Alek even more than that. I felt as if they would approve. Like my parents were watching me in that moment as time and space fell away and a secret history unfolded before my eyes.

The egg heated in my hands until it felt like it was branding me. Blinding lights destroyed my vision, and I could not hear a sound, except for the whisper of Alek calling me back to him.

Not yet. I sent the thought his way. I don't know why, but it was important that I finished what I set out to do. Images of people in fancy clothes from a history I had not lived but knew well. I was a fan of tales of Anastasia as a child. The only Romanov rumored to have survived the Bolsheviks during the Russian Revolution.

But these images were before that. Faberge was a master craftsman and a cunning artist. He'd created and hid secrets within secrets inside his jeweled eggs. This one was powerful. This secret was old.

I pursed my lips and felt the images get clearer, sharper. A bearded man with electric blue eyes stood in the background, swathed in a black-colored cloak. He seemed to blend into the night, one with the darkness, and I knew him then.

Vampire.

But unlike Alek, I felt no shiver of attraction for the stranger. Revulsion and fear rippled through me and I shuddered as his gaze seemed to fixate on where I stood. But that couldn't be. My abilities allowed me to track where things had been and to whom they'd belonged through time, but I was never seen or recognized when travelling through those visions.

But what did I know? I was just a *normal* with an unusual skill. And that black-cloaked man smiled at me, revealing his sharp, needle-like fangs. I shivered as the scene changed before my eyes. No more fancy dresses and happy music in the background. No more wine, or presents, or feasts. No more well-dressed children laughing.

Those images were replaced by the sounds of screams, terror, smoke, and gunfire in the background. The sharp stench of fear permeated the air and that terrible smell was only outdone by the next, and that one was much more horrible. The sickly-sweet decaying aroma that accompanied death filled my nostrils and made me drop to the floor.

The egg was witness to it all. The *Cherub and Chariot* was stowed away in a suitcase. Taken from the land, hidden from eyes, keeping inside of it a secret that I, with all my sight, still could not see. But it was important somehow, and to me of all people.

"Carina!"

Finally, I felt Alek's arms around me, and I trembled in them, allowing his heat to push the icy chill away from my skin. I clutched at his shoulders, pushing myself firmly against him.

"Is she alright?" a voice said.

"Leave us," Alek commanded, and I was never so grateful.

I didn't want anyone to see me like that. It was like I'd been ripped apart. Vulnerable and terrified in the aftermath of such brutality.

"Shhh," he whispered against my hair, turning to

press kisses to my forehead, my nose, my cheek, and finally my mouth.

"Alek," I whispered and opened my lips for him.

He breathed my name and accepted my invitation, invading and conquering me with that deep, dark, perfect kiss. This time when I trembled, it was with need. He was too good to be true. Tasting of habaneros and mangos, like some titillating, sinful concoction made only for me.

"Mine," he growled against my lips.

I pushed my tongue into his mouth, carefully tracing his fangs before deepening the kiss. His rough snarl was so fucking sexy. Moisture pooled between my legs and I whimpered as he stood, lifting me with him and dragging me to the bed.

"This is your room, isn't it?" I asked.

Suddenly realizing where I'd spent the last day, I understood now why it was so familiar, why I'd felt so safe. It was because of him, all because of Alek. He nodded and pressed his forehead to mine. I could see his struggle to control himself, but I wanted none of that.

"This is dangerous, Carina. I don't know if I can stop myself."

"Then don't. I want to be with you."

"I could hurt you."

"I don't believe that," I undulated my hips beneath him, pressing my core against the long bar of steel inside his pants.

He was so big, so hard, for me. And that gave me power over the Vampire. Lifting up, I slid the top over my head, noting with pleasure, the way his silver eyes burned as they ran over the scraps of pink lace covering my breasts.

"Your turn," I whispered and tugged on his lower lip with my teeth.

Alek ground his mouth into mine, claiming me possessively as he tore the shirt clean off his body. Fuck, that was hot. I trembled at the newness of it all.

I had to admit, I was closed off from the world in a lot of ways. My search for vengeance had blinded me to everything else, but for some reason I didn't regret the fact that this, here, now, would be my first time.

"What?" Alek's head shot up.

Dang it. I forgot he could read my thoughts. Or at least, that was my assumption.

"You're a virgin?"

"Technically," I confessed, "but I am hoping you could relieve me of that problem?"

"Fuck, Carina," he growled and flexed his hips,

pressing against me once more and kissing me with so much passion I damn near swooned from it.

"We have to stop," he said.

"No. Please don't stop."

"You don't understand. In my Clan, a Virgin's blood belongs to one man only," he shook his head but I was not about to let him go, "you have to be clearheaded about this, little one, your blood belongs to your mate-"

"You. My blood belongs to you."

The words left my mouth as if of their own accord. I wasn't even sure where they came from, only that they felt right. So right.

Reaching up, I licked a trail from his neck to his earlobe, sucking it into my mouth and using my teeth to nibble on his skin. Alek's groan was delightful and his weight pressed me down into the mattress.

I relished the heat and pressure that was all him. He was so powerful. He could break me like a twig, but I trusted him. I don't know why. It was eighty percent instinct, and twenty percent blind faith, but nothing could've made me want to walk away.

"You tempt me so, Carina, I don't think you understand what you mean to me and what this will mean between us."

"I trust you, Alek. I need you. Please, I was so cold in that vision. It was unlike any read I'd ever done before, and I need you to warm me, Alek, to make me feel again. Please," I begged.

"If I lay claim to you, sweet, I will never let you go."

"Don't," I said, and I meant that one single word more than I meant anything else in my entire lifetime, "Don't let me go."

No one had ever claimed me before. No one had ever wanted me.

"Then you will be mine tonight, *krov' moyey krovi.*"

His voice deepened and with blurred movements suddenly we were both naked and on his bed. Alek's hands roamed my body as his mouth sought my lips. The deep bass of his heartbeat pounded through his chest and into mine as he kissed me even more deeply than before.

I never wanted to let go of his lush, beautiful mouth, but he pulled away, grazing over my neck and chest. Suckling one plump nipple into his mouth, I felt need spike through my blood as he tugged on the hardened nub with his teeth.

Everywhere he touched he was branding my soul with his mark and how I wanted it. I longed for it, for him, wanted him to bite me, to mark me and make whatever this was between us permanent. Aleksei ran his hands over my face and neck, then down to my breasts while he slid the length of my body until his face nuzzled my weeping center.

I'd dreaded the day I would lose my virginity ever since I was a child. Fearing it after the countless tales told by the other kids in foster care about pain, hurt, and general embarrassment over the sex act. It was why I was still a virgin. But not for long.

Even more amazing was the fact I didn't fear those things now. Not with Alek in the driver's seat. It all seemed so primal, so urgent, and so very natural. Even as he spread my thighs with his long hands and licked a path from my forbidden hole to the tight little bud that held a million nerve endings, I trusted him.

He growled again, deepening his kiss and sucking me into his mouth as he slid one finger, then another into my wet heat. Pulling and stretching me, I groaned as his tongue flicked against my clit. The speedy movement had me trembling, whipping my head from side to side while he stroked my core with those long, skilled appendages.

Those precise little licks pushed me closer and closer to the edge of bliss, and all I wanted was to fall off. Hell, I wanted to dive straight into the silvery, dark oblivion of pleasure with him beside me.

Alek was whispering in Russian, words I did not understand, but it didn't matter as my orgasm hung right there in front of me, and then suddenly, it washed over me. Like an all-conquering tidal wave, a tsunami of bliss, and I was powerless to do anything but go with it. And why not? Alek was there, and I knew no harm would come to me. He wouldn't allow it.

"Mine," the word echoed in the room.

It spoke of possession, dominance, and proprietary rights that I would definitely be going over with him, but for right now, all it did was make me come again. And harder than the first time.

Alek slid up my body and placed the broad head of his thick cock at my entrance. Lips glistening with my juices he bent down for an openmouthed kiss as he pressed inside of my heat. I groaned as I tasted myself on his mouth.

It was raw and sexy and I wanted to fall off the edge into that river of bliss again and again with him. His silver eyes blazed with feeling too many emotions to name. They bore into mine as he broke the barrier of my virginity.

I moaned, but Alek soothed me with his hands,

his kisses, his beautiful body as he made love to me. His fangs descended, and I nodded as he built momentum.

Yes. I wanted this. Craved the connection. Needed to belong to him. As that now familiar tug began to build deep inside my core, I gasped and turned my head, pulling him closer.

I knew it was reckless, borderline insane, but it felt so fucking good. Something had happened when I touched the artifact. The lost Faberge egg was much more than an imperial decoration. It was a key of sorts.

The memories it had revealed to me had burned my very soul, brought me close to death, and now all I wanted was to feel alive. To seize the moment, to be one with Alek. Here. Now. Always.

He roared above me, but he did not bite. I frowned, but I couldn't do more than that as I was soon swept up in the tide of pleasure that had every inch of him stiffen above me. He cried out with his release and I raked my nails down his back, if he wasn't going to bite me then I would mark him in this way.

We would have to talk about. Later. Right then, I could hardly do more than breathe. I fell asleep with him still deep inside of me as he whispered in Russian and kissed my face.

Hours later, I couldn't really tell the time anymore as my days had somehow become nights and vice versa, we were seated in the back of a long limousine with Ivan behind the wheel. I didn't know when that asshole had turned back up, but he was here now.

"Have I told you, you look divine?" Alek said without glancing my way and I could not help the smile that spread across my face.

"You might have mentioned it once or twice."

After some debate, I went along with his suggestion of what to wear in terms of a gown. The short-sleeved black confection looked as good as he said it would when the boutique had sent it and a dozen other items over for my perusal.

It was modest from the front, though I had to admit it was so tight it outlined every curve of my body down to my ankles. And the back was another story entirely. By that, I meant there was no back, like at all, to the dress. It was a miracle it stayed on.

Okay, maybe not a miracle. More like a silver clasp behind my neck that held the top in place and a thin band of rubber that kept the skirt from sliding off my ass. But all in all I was bare all the way down to the small butterfly tattoo I'd gotten as a teenager that sat right above my right cheek.

The gown was designed so that I was forced to forego undergarments. A fact which seemed to make Alek grin wickedly while bringing out his increasingly hot, possessive side. The memory of the long, warm shower we'd taken together after waking up from our first round of lovemaking had me licking my lips in pleasure.

"Behave," he growled and nipped my earlobe, "I can scent your arousal."

"And?"

"And I love it, but if anyone else comes near you when you smell so delicious, I will kill them where they stand."

Okay. So that should not have made me wet, and yet it did. Holy sexy-pants. He took my hand and placed it on his elbow, eyes straight, and I couldn't help but think how good he looked in his tuxedo.

"I know you've been avoiding it, but we will discuss the whole biting and drinking thing, Alek," I whispered and he lifted my hand and kissed it before placing it back down on his arm.

He'd been close-lipped about the whole thing, but I heard him talking to Klaus. Not all humans survived the blood exchange. That was one reason there weren't millions of Vamps running around. I had something to tell him that would change his mind, but not yet. Nerves made my stomach clench, and I inhaled his spicy scent for strength.

This was not my scene, not my crowd, but for some reason, as we pulled up behind the other limos at the exceedingly gaudy estate of the Vampire Princess in the heart of Manhattan, I felt perfectly at ease.

My gown was couture, my shoes cost more than my rent, but that wasn't why I felt so good. It was because of him. Alek was generous in many ways. None of which could compete with how thoroughly giving he was when it came to sex.

I didn't want to think about how he became so knowledgeable, after all, I'd been a virgin. We'd exchanged everything but blood, and I was still as human as ever, but I felt different somehow. Changed evermore.

Everything I knew about Vampires said they were beautiful, powerful and well, I was just me. How could I compete with that? With Princess Ana and her minions?

"There is only you for me, Carina," he whispered in my ear and placed a kiss on the spot where he'd first bitten me after I was attacked by Vladek's men.

For some reason, that caress seemed to ease every doubt and calm every nerve. I believed him. He was not lying when he said he wanted me. That much was very true. The things he'd whispered to me when we made love were not the words of a man or Vampire who was afraid of commitment.

Yes, we had yet to discuss turning me, if such a thing could even be accomplished, but we would. It didn't matter right now. I knew I wanted to be with him more than anything. Even more than the revenge I craved for the crimes against my parents. Maybe I had to let go of the past in order to embrace my future. Only time would tell for certain.

Life was an adventure, a glorious journey for most. I never thought it would be that way for me. Never dreamed I would have a fairytale ending of my own, even if that fairytale was somewhat dark and twisted. Maybe I wouldn't get to keep him after all.

There was no way of knowing. I would have to learn to enjoy the life I was living. To be in the present. Glancing at the man beside me, I knew it wouldn't be difficult. He was mesmerizing. Almost too beautiful in his tailor-made tux with his thick hair combed away from his perfect face. And I meant perfect. The man had cheekbones most women would die for. That and those crazy silver eyes framed by thick lashes and dark eyebrows. And lastly, the carefully trimmed smattering of facial hair that drove me wild with need.

Guys like him never gave girls like me the time of day, and yet there I was. And I had never felt better.

"Are you ready, little one?" he asked.

I nodded though, to be honest, I wasn't sure. Was I ready? Who knew?

But one thing was certain, it sure as hell was time to find out.

CHAPTER 7
ALEKSEI

"*P*rincess *Ana de Medici* cordially invites you to her annual *Wolf Moon Court Ceremony*," Carina read the invitation I held in my hand.

The touch of her hand seemed to burn through the fabric of my jacket, scoring the skin beneath, and I growled softly. I would've given anything to be anywhere else.

Two exchanges. We'd had two exchanges of fluids, one through my healing bite, and one through sex. More was required to start the process that would alter her DNA to make her like me, but could I risk it?

Not everyone survived the turn. Of course, I hadn't planned on what had occurred between us earlier that night. Her near-death experience after her encounter with that damned egg left us both needing to reaffirm that she was still alive the moment she came out of the trance-like state.

Vampires don't typically do fear. And yet I had never been more afraid of anything in my life than I was of losing her. I was glad to be getting rid of the fucking vile artifact.

Still, I was curious about what had transpired. Carina was tightlipped, and I knew she needed time to process everything. But that might not be possible. Especially not now that I had a taste of the caramel and cocoa butter scented beauty.

The sound of her heart beating inside her chest was the only thing that calmed me as my Vampire instincts picked up on the predators lurking nearby. These damn moon ceremonies were always full of Vamps, but Ana, well, she enjoyed a wide variety of guests.

Members from the Royal Court of the Fae, the local Werewolf Alpha, and a few other Shifter Clans were represented here tonight. The sound of classical music swelled softly from the open doors as we walked up the marble staircase to the first security guard. I knew the Vampire well.

Charles accepted the invitation I passed him but did not move aside. Growling a bit louder when I discerned the reason why as his gaze settled on Carina with more than passing interest, I lifted my lip in an open snarl. Charles raised an eyebrow but this time he moved. Swiftly.

Maybe he was not as dumb as he looked. We walked past the double doors into the ballroom where the evening was to take place. Ana had, of course, outdone herself.

Black-clothed tables were decorated with gilded cups. Blood-red roses spilled from vases and candles floated in crystal bowls of water on every available surface. The wait staff passed flutes of champagne and tall glasses of a deep red liquid that smelled like A positive.

From where I was standing, I recognized another waiter pass with a very rare carafe of blood and smirked at Ana's decadent ways. She was truly incorrigible. The floor had been polished to gleam under the light of the actual full moon. The entire ceiling was made of retractable clear glass panels, and the sky was visible even in the center of midtown.

It was winter, so she'd kept them closed, but still, the moon looked magnificent. Along the walls were glass cases filled with treasures. Many of which I had curated for the Vampire Princess.

"Is *Timeless Possessions* responsible for all this?" Carina asked in a whisper of a voice that tickled my sensitive ears.

"Most of them, yes," I nodded, "but this is the only Faberge in the lot."

"What about that?" Carina raised her eyebrows and I saw in the center of the room on a pedestal a replica of *the Cherub and Chariot egg*. I was unsure what game Ana was playing, but there was definitely something going on.

As we made our way through the crowd, I found myself fighting the instinct to pick up my Chosen and flee to safety. But I was in no position to do so. To run would be to admit defeat and to keep Carina safe, I needed to be strong.

Instinctively, Carina pressed against my side, and I calmed, slightly. She did not look too closely at anyone. Smart. Very smart. But what did I expect? She was that and so much more.

"Aleksei, darling," Ana practically shouted my name, and I stilled immediately, "come. You are the guest of honor after all."

"Am I?" I smiled coolly and kept a slow pace as I ignored Ana's outstretched arm in favor of my Chosen.

It was ballsy, but I meant no insult. The fact was,

I could not bring myself to touch another. Carina was my all.

"Indeed, I see things are different now," she said and smiled widely at Carina showing off her sharp white teeth for too long a moment.

I hissed softly, and she raised her eyebrows. Ana was not as strong physically, but she was blood-thirsty in her own ways. And this was her territory. Despite the measures I had taken to ensure Carina's safety, I needed to keep my protective instincts to a dull roar.

"Everyone," Ana smiled and clapped, turning her back on me in a show of arrogance I silently applauded, "I have an announcement to make. The egg you have all been admiring is a fake! A fraudulent piece that came into my possession bearing Aleksei's seal."

"I told you, Ana, that was not of my design-"

But she did not let me finish, and I clenched my jaw in frustration. Out of the corner of my eye I saw Klaus, with him was Boris, Gregor, and Marcus. Ivan too had left the limo and was now taking up residence against the wall.

My Clan would not have their *Knyaz* vulnerable to attack. I was certainly strong enough to protect myself, but I had Carina to think about. And I thanked my guard through our Clan bonds.

"Yes, poor Aleksei was the victim of a little subterfuge by my other guest," she grinned and turned.

Then I saw him. Vladek the Merciless. Immediately, I hissed and placed myself slightly in front of the suddenly stiff female beside me. Carina's mouth hung open, but I did not ask myself why. I had to control my own emotions and her fear was driving them wild with the need to protect.

"What is this, Ana? Do you know what he has done?"

"Indeed, I do. Vladek, maybe you would like to explain while I observe the piece you have brought me, Aleksei."

I moved to hand over the egg, but Carina took the case from me and removed it herself.

"So, you're calling yourself Vladek now?"

My Chosen held the priceless egg over her head as if to throw it. Shocked, I raised my arm to stop the tide of Ana's clan from rushing over. Klaus and my men moved into position, surrounding us as Carina's eyes blazed with something like rage.

"That's mine!" spat Ana.

"That's funny cause I am the one holding it,"

Carina responded and she glared at her before turning to him.

I cursed under my breath. What the fuck was going on? I liked Ana, but if she even looked at Carina the wrong way I would rip her throat out with my fingers. Fucking hell. I would burn the entire world down for her. She was my reason. My blood song. The only thing in the world worth anything.

"Ana," I warned then turned to my lover, "Carina? Maybe you can explain?"

It took me centuries to find her, and now that I had. I was not letting go. Especially not for a fucking Easter egg.

"But that's just it, Alek. This is not the typical Faberge egg," she responded , picking up on my thoughts again, "Is it Vladek?"

"You think you know what you have there?" the crazed Vampire with the long beard grunted and began to close in on us.

I crouched low, taking up a defensive stance with my claws out and my fangs descended.

"I know exactly what this is," she held her head high, "This is why you killed my parents and made it look like drug dealers were responsible. This was why you attacked me. It was never about the egg, it was the secret inside."

Carina too had been keeping secrets from me. Quite astonishing since we'd been in and out of each other's minds and bodies for the past two days.

"You're just a filthy human, you have no idea what that is," Vlad hissed, and I growled with all the rage building inside of me.

"My name is Carina Martin. That's short for *Martynovna* and my bloodline can be traced back to the imperial house, but you know that don't you? Vladek, or should I just call you Rasputin?"

Heads turned and shocked gasps sounded as Carina identified the Vampire who'd been plaguing me for decades. Vladek the Merciless was Vladimir Rasputin. A fucking cockroach in the history of Russia. A madman and self-proclaimed mystic who'd left bodies upon bodies wherever he roamed.

"This egg holds the key to where you hid the rest of the Romanov treasures, doesn't it? I absorbed the information. I know where they are, and I know how to access them. This, this has no secrets now," Carina said.

"You stupid fool," Rasputin spat and to my surprise he sprinted the distance, blinking out of existence and back again directly in front of Carina with his hands around her neck.

I snarled and hit him hard, forcing him to let go. Carina didn't hesitate she tossed the egg to Ana who whipped it from the air. Those treasures were priceless, but to me she was the only thing worth anything. And I would kill anyone who dared touch what was mine.

Rasputin lunged forward, but I was faster. As Knyaz, I was trained since my childhood for combat. The blue-eyed Vampire was no match for me. Even so, he was strong. And killing him in Ana's territory would not be wise. But I didn't give a fuck. As I raised my clawed fingers to remove Rasputin's head, Carina's voice rang clearly in my brain.

"Wait," she said, and put her hand on my shoulder.

She was the only person who could've gotten away with touching me in a full on fury. I was hers to command. Stilling immediately, as our hostess stepped in.

"Seize him," Ana commanded, and for once I was grateful for her unusual taste in guests.

Only the combination of Fae, Shifter, Witch, and Vampire magics could safely imprison a mystic

Vampire such as Rasputin was claimed to be. Of course, no one had put the criminal Vladek together with the vile cretin who helped destroy the Romanovs.

"Are you okay?" I asked Carina moments later and ran my hands over her body to ensure she was whole.

"Yes, I am fine," she nodded, but I could see she was shaken.

Lifting her in my arms, my guard surrounded us as I walked to the exit, but we were stopped by Ana before we could get away.

"Alek," the Vampire Princess called out, "Bring your Chosen back after you've turned her. I can't have my guests being so vulnerable to attack, besides, I might want in on the treasures she can locate."

Carina sat up and gave Ana a sly wink before curling her arms around my neck. I nodded once and took off for the stairs.

"Ivan bring the limo around. I will meet you all back home."

I hardly ever sprinted from such a distance, but I needed Carina home. In my bed. Now.

The need to reaffirm her safety burned within me, and I used all my speed and strength as I pulled us through time and space until we were back in my bedroom.

"What happened when you touched that egg?" I asked as I sat her on the edge of the bed and knelt down to remove her shoes first.

"I saw the past, Alek. I know who I am not, who my parents were," she licked her lips, "My father's people were lower nobles, but related to the Romanov line. I saw Vladek, or Rasputin, and how he lied and connived, stole from the family. He made a deal with a Vampire to be turned so he could come back and find his treasures after the Bolsheviks destroyed the royal family. He," she frowned, "he knew they were going to kill the children, and he did nothing to stop it. That lowlife only wanted the treasure. Money and power."

"I am glad you were not hurt," I said and pulled her into my arms. Even kneeling on the floor while she sat on the mattress I was taller than her, but she felt so good in my arms. Where she belonged.

"But don't ever do that again," I murmured into her hair.

"Do what?"

"Put yourself in danger," I growled and kissed her hard on the lips.

"You know what to do to stop me from being vulnerable, Alek," she said.

Fear trickled up my spine even as my cock throbbed and my gums ached with my fangs. Yes, I wanted to claim her again, to drink her blood and to give her mine, but what if she didn't make it? I could not risk it.

"It's too dangerous," I said, "Not everyone survives."

"I can," she stated with absolute assurance.

"How can you know?"

"I saw it. My bloodline has been linked with yours for ages. The same way your Grandfather knew he could turn you and make you heir to the Clan. My family and yours, tied for centuries," she smiled and tears rolled down her cheeks.

"What? How can you?"

"It's why Ivan acts like he hates me," I laughed as someone knocked on the door.

"Come in," Carina said, while I would've refused entry.

"*Moy Knyaz i Knyazhna*, you are both safe," Klaus nodded at me, and shoved Ivan forward, "Tell him."

"She tells the truth, Aleksei. Carina Martynovna is my cousin, though a few centuries removed. She can be turned."

Carina stood up then and walked towards my blood brother and my oldest servant. Ivan backed up, but she was too fast, even for a normal. Still, I couldn't stop my hiss as she hugged her cousin briefly and wiped the tears from her eyes.

"I'm not an orphan now," she laughed and Ivan smiled too.

"This is great and all, but I think our Knyaz is holding on by a thread. Come on," Klaus nodded and pulled Ivan out the door before closing it.

And not a moment too soon. Carina turned to face me. The bittersweet joy that had shined in her eyes a moment ago was replaced by something else. A desperate need that was echoed deep within me.

EPILOGUE

ALEKSEI

"Carina," I whispered her name as my rising hunger for her grew to unbearable heights.

She stepped forward slowly. Too slowly. I sprinted across the remaining space. Overkill? Maybe, but fuck if I cared. We came together like waves crashing against the sand, and I never knew a more perfect feeling than that of having her in my arms.

Slow down! I cursed myself for my impatience, but I needed her. My body worked as if of its own free will and within seconds we were both naked and panting. She was my mate. My blood song. My Chosen. I never wanted anyone like I wanted her and I always would. That was my vow. My sacred promise to her.

Parting her slick sex with my fingers, I dipped inside, allowing her wet heat to coat them as I pushed inside her. Fuck, she was so hot, so tight. I needed to have her in my mouth. Falling to the floor, I didn't bother heading for the wall or bed. I needed her now. She clutched at my shoulders while I lifted one leg up and over and nuzzled her pussy with my lips.

Then with long, hard licks I lapped at her core. Tasting her cocoa butter caramel sweetness and swallowing her down. She fell apart with my name on her lips and I was there to catch her even as she lost control of her body and her legs buckled beneath her.

"Oh Alek," she moaned as I settled us both on the mattress.

"Need you, Carina" I grunted as I drove deeply inside her tight body.

"Yes," she nodded and pulled on my neck until our lips melded together in one of those inferno-hot kisses she loved to give me.

I'd never known anything like it, and I never would again. I locked my arms to hold most of my weight off her, but she was having none of that. She wrapped her legs around my waist and pulled me in deeper.

"No holding back," she said.

"*Moya krov' pesnya*," I growled against her lips.

Words were nothing compared to how I felt with her walls stretched tight around my sex. She gripped me perfectly. Lifted her hips and rocked against my thrusts in a rhythm as old as time itself. And yet it was new and different, a symphony of our own making, my blood song.

Fangs descended, I tried so hard to resist the need, but Carina grabbed my face. Every wiggle and move had me seeing stars, I wanted her so fucking much. I set the pace, controlled the act as much as I could with her matching me every step of the way. But didn't that just make it sweeter? She was wildly dominant and submissive at the same time. So fucking beautiful in her passion. Clawing my back and making my heart beat for her alone.

"Now, Alek, now. Now!" she tuned her head and I knew what she wanted, knew what was coming that I could not deny.

That burning, stinging thirst clawed at my throat even as bliss began to pulse, starting with my cock and racing throughout my body. This time would be different. This time when I pierced her skin she would feel only pleasure, not pain.

"Come for me, Carina, come now and I will give

you my bite, tying you to me for all eternity," I commanded, and she opened her mouth in a silent scream as waves of ecstasy washed over her.

Each ripple of her pussy caressed my cock, and I could not wait another second. Rearing back, I struck. My own orgasm held me as I took delicious pulls from her neck, and I felt her sex squeeze even tighter around mine as I rocketed into pure ecstasy while I drank from my Chosen.

"Drink from me, sweet. Be mine in every way," I growled and bit into my wrist, holding it to her lips.

The scent of spicy caramel filled my nostrils as she closed her mouth over the incisions I'd made. I felt her thirst building inside of her for the dark red, life-sustaining fluid that was my blood and it was incredible. Carina growled against my skin and our mind-sharing abilities seemed to increase. It was like I was feeling what she was experiencing. The changes were sharp and fast, and as I rocked into her sex, another orgasm exploded between us.

"Yes, drink, *krov' moyey krovi*," I growled and noticed my accent became thicker as my cock continued to pump deep inside of her slick heat, "Blood of my blood."

I bent my head and pressed my lips to her neck, sucking down the spicy sweet blood that was sweeter than wine and swallowing it deep inside of me. Doubling my efforts, moving with lightning speed, I took her harder, faster, driving deeper and deeper into her slick heat. It was like tasting heaven for the first time.

She sucked harder, needing more from me, and I gave it willingly. Lifting her hips so she could wrap her legs tightly around my waist. That angle allowed me to fill her even more completely. She suckled me like a babe, drinking my blood even as I still tasted her own sweet, spicy essence on my lips.

"I am yours, Carina, and you are mine. My blood song. My Chosen. Here, now, and forevermore."

"Yes," she repeated the vow, "I am yours, Aleksei Delov, and you are mine. Here, now, and forevermore."

"*Moya krov' pesnya,*" I nuzzled her cheek as tiny aftershocks of bliss raced through my body and hers.

Our bond, our connection pulsed around us in lights of dazzling blues and golds and I never felt so complete. Our future, whatever it would bring, would involve the two of us together.

Our bedroom echoed with the sounds of our hearts beating in time, and for the first time in forever contentment settled over me.

"*Moya krov' pesnya,*" she said, breaking the silence.

Carina kissed my lips hard. Her whiskey-colored eyes burned bright, and I knew in my heart the change would take. She was my heart, my life, the blood in my veins.

"I love you, Carina," I said and knew then that this woman owned me body, heart and soul, and even more astonishing, I was proud of that fact. Reveled in it.

"I love you too, Alek," she said, and my heart swelled with pleasure and pride.

"When did you know?"

"That night in the alley," she replied, "when you lied about the *Sanguinem Council.*"

"The ideology is real. Not all council members agree."

"Mmm hmm. Why don't you come back here, and I will show you something real?"

Carina smiled slyly and I was a goner. I always would be where she was concerned. Whatever my mate wanted, she would have. Thank fuck what she wanted was me.

"Show me," I growled before I crushed my mouth against hers.

Nothing compared to kissing Carina. It was a sentiment I would have often. I was sure. Then a word entered my mind, and I knew with a grin it had come from her. And how right she was.

Mine.

T*he end.*

L*iked this story? Discover Paranormal Romance Books by C.D. Gorri by visiting http://www.*cdgorri.com.

THE TIGER KING'S CHRISTMAS BRIDE

A MACCON CITY SHIFTERS ISLAND STRIPE PRIDE BOOK

BLURB

Will this scroogey Tiger find love where he least expects it?

He's the ruler of a Tiger Pride spending the holidays in his solitary cabin in the woods. She's a nail technician on her way to a client's house before her Christmas vacation.

When her car spins out of control on the icy road, and crashes into a tree, she is stranded with no help in sight until he happens upon her.

Saving the strange woman from certain death will put a damper in his plans to spend the holidays alone, but his Tiger is convinced she is more to him than meets the eye.

Can he convince the dark haired beauty to be his Christmas bride?

Find out in this classic holiday romance with a furry twist!

DESCRIPTION

Dean Romero is not your average Tiger Shifter. He is the king or the *Neta* of the Island Stripe Pride, operating out of Manhattan.

Wanting to avoid the hustle and bustle of the holiday season, this Neta elects to spend Christmas at his newly built cabin in a remote section of the Pine Barrens just outside of Maccon City, New Jersey. A town notorious among supernaturals for its Shifter ties.

Violet Martinez is a nail technician stuck working on the holidays. Asked to make a house call she has no choice but to drive to an important client's house on Christmas Eve.

She'd much rather be at home curled up with her favorite mug full of steaming spiked hot chocolate and a marathon of old black and white movies to keep her company.

Resigned to her fate, she heads out in the wintry weather which has made the drive nearly impossible. Halfway there, Violet's car spins out on a lonely stretch of road and she slams into a tree, hitting her head on the dashboard.

Passing out in the cold with a head injury was not on Violet's Christmas list, but good thing there's a Tiger king who just happens to be out for a run nearby.

When Dean gets a whiff of Violet's sugar cookie scent all bets are off. This Neta wants her for his own, but will the dark-haired beauty accept him and agree to be his bride this Christmas?

PROLOGUE

"Damn it, Dean, you're supposed to be there!" Alex raised his voice and slammed his hand down on the desk.

The man obviously forgot himself in the excitement of his discussion with his boss, but one growl from Dean and the feisty Tiger Shifter averted his gaze and bared his throat. After all, Dean Romero wasn't just his boss, he was also his *Neta*.

Alex Kensington was not the first who'd scoffed at Dean's announcement that he'd be spending the holidays alone in his new cabin in the Pine Barrens of South Jersey, but that was one of the perks of being in charge.

Dean Romero was the *Tiger King*, the Alpha, or as Bengal Tiger Shifters the world over preferred to call their leader, the *Neta*, of the Island Stripe Pride. His Pride was small, but fierce with a reputation for such. They operated primarily out of Manhattan but had footholds in several other major cities.

The Island Stripe Pride was also a large global conglomeration with interests from imports and exports, to farming, winemaking, shipping, and construction, and Dean was the CEO.

His Pride mates worked for him, learned from him, basked in his protection, and took care of one another as he instructed. Community, loyalty, and structure were important parts of living in the Shifter World, and Dean was very good in his roles as both Neta and CEO of the Island Stripe Pride and their corporation, *ISP Inc.*

"You will represent the Pride at this year's holiday celebration," Dean instructed.

"But-"

"Alex, as my Beta, you will do quite well filling in for me at the Christmas party," Dean told the younger man, who was still looking at the ground and baring his throat in submission.

Dean cursed inwardly and cut off the resounding growl that was still reverberating in his chest. His *Neta* powers were causing his Pride mate to basically grovel, and that was not the kind of man, not the kind of leader, he was. Dean had no interest in constantly proving his strength and control to others. He was the *Neta*.

Enough said.

"I'm tired, Alex," Dean finally admitted the truth aloud as he picked up one of the sugar cookies his administrative assistant had delivered him that morning.

The darned things were his favorite and he'd already scoffed down two dozen. Good thing Shifter's had an extremely fast metabolism or he'd worry. As it was, he could eat ten dozen and still be trim and fit for a man in his position.

"My Tiger is restless. Has been these past few months. The beast is hungry, but what he craves cannot be found in this city. I think the quiet space will help."

Dean gestured to the crowded streets below them, visible through the impressive floor to ceiling windows in his penthouse office of the ISP Building in lower Manhattan.

"Perhaps a woman? Who knows you might get lucky this Christmas with a little miracle of your own?" Alex suggested and Dean shook his head.

"There is no such thing. Besides, there is no one

in the Pride or among those close to us who sparks my interest. I just need a break."

"Ouch! Excuse me, *Scrooge*. Hey, you're not going rogue, are you, Neta?" Alex joked, but Dean could hear the sincerity behind the question.

His oldest friend feared for his beast's sanity. He wanted to laugh at the impossibility of it all, but Dean could only grunt at him in response. The idea had crossed his mind, but he pushed it back. A Shifter went rogue for many reasons, but Dean didn't have the luxury to give in to his own fancy.

No, he simply needed rest and some peace and quiet this Christmas. What was wrong with that? And Alex would do fine at the party. They'd known each other for years, having grown up with each other.

Alex had seen Dean rise to his position after his father had stepped down. He'd been a devoted part of Dean's inner circle ever since. There had been no one to challenge him when he ascended to Neta, and he'd heard of none since.

Dean had always tried to run the Pride with justice and fairness. The same way he ran ISP, with the keen expertise and intelligence his vast education and years working with his father had afforded him.

He was just tired, that was all. It was as simple as that. And if his inner beast was restless and anxious, that was nothing to worry about.

Just tired, he repeated to his animal who rested inside of his mind's eye.

"Maybe you need a woman?" Alex suggested.

As soon as his Beta posed the question, Dean's enormous Tiger pushed forward, his glowing teal eyes bright in his mind's eye, the beast thought a single word that made Dean recoil.

Mate.

Well, fuck. He didn't expect that. But even as the seconds passed into minutes, he knew it was the truth. The beast inside of him wanted his mate.

Lonely at the top was too cliché, but it fit. He needed a partner, someone to share his wins and losses with. It had been a long time since Dean felt something other than the urge to quench his carnal appetites with a woman.

Still, he wasn't sure he was ready to take a mate. Not yet. And besides, where would he find one? He already knew all the females in the Pride, and they were not for him.

"I could call one for you," Alex was still talking, but Dean had stopped listening.

"No. Absolutely not. In fact, it's just another

reason I'm leaving the city and going to the cabin for the holidays. There is just no way I am going to spend the entire Christmas party dodging the wily females of the Shifter community."

"Yeah, I hear that. Thanksgiving was no fun at all. That Hyena delegation kept trying to shove their Alpha fem's granddaughter at you. The one with the lazy eye," Alex said and shuddered.

Dean shook his head at the memory. That idea was not appealing in the slightest.

Nope. Dean wanted to give his Big Cat the opportunity to run and roam through the still untouched Pine Barrens without fear of being caught under the mistletoe by some desperate woman looking to catch him in a weak moment.

Last time he took a member of his Pride home with him for the night, she'd had their firstborn named before he even slipped the condom on. Blue balls were so not his thing.

Fuck it. He wanted no misunderstandings this Christmas. Dean would go far away where he was safe from all the women trying to earn themselves the coveted position of his mate and the Pride's *Nari*.

"The cabin will suit my holiday needs, Alex. My assistant has stocked my car with food and clothes for the weekend."

"But what if-"

"Alex I am the Neta. I will be fine. It'll be like my gift to myself. Far away from all the people and things demanding my attention. I can connect with my Tiger and recharge my batteries so to speak."

"If you're sure," his Beta muttered.

"I'm not going rogue, Alex, I just need some time alone. Now, I signed the bonus checks and had Carl send them out via hand delivered couriers to everyone in the company, as well as, to the all the Pride families."

"They do love your yearly bonuses," grinned Alex.

"Yes, and this year they will get them without having the opportunity to shove their single daughters in my face at the Christmas party."

"But Dean-"

"No buts about it, Alex, end of the day today I am out of here. No phones, no computers, no messages. Do not call me until after Christmas Day. That is an order," he growled and downed the two fingers of Mason Lane's newest artisan distilled whiskey, *Holiday Bite*, that the Werewolf had sent him as a gift.

Dean enjoyed quality spirits and poured himself the glass to toast the upcoming holiday with his Beta before he skipped town. *Holiday Bite* slid down his throat warming his chest and leaving behind a smooth, delightful hint of rosemary and cranberries.

The amber colored liquid was quite excellent and he made a mental note to drop Mason a line of thanks for the gift. He grabbed the bottle and nodded at Alex while heading out to his sleek blue *Aston Martin Valkyrie.*

The four-million dollar automobile was his other Christmas present to himself this year.

With his plans to avoid the holiday party, his new custom luxury automobile, not to mention the cabin in the woods and his bottle of Holiday *Bite,* this was already turning into the most excellent Christmas indeed.

Grrr, agreed his Tiger.

CHAPTER 1

Violet Martinez had just finished cleaning her work station at *Hair and There*, the beauty salon in Maccon City where she worked when her boss, Sherry Morgan McAllister interrupted her.

The woman had a wonderfully lilting accented voice that Violet wished she had. It made her seem so mysterious and alluring. That and the fact she was like crazy beautiful. Though Violet did not understand her crazy penchant for colored contact lenses or her multi-faceted locks. One minute her eyes were blue the next they were yellow or purple. Same with her reddish, goldish, pinkish, silverish hair.

LOL.

Violet didn't have the kind of looks that could carry such extravagance. She was just the average woman. Short, chubby, brown-haired, brown-eyed, and skin a permanent olive-tan color.

She was a nail technician who had aspirations for becoming a full-time author someday. As it was, she'd self-published a few short stories over the past year in between work and volunteering at the local senior center.

She'd sort of made a family for herself there by borrowing other people's often ignored and neglected grandparents. She'd been raised by her grandmother after her own parents had split and decided raising a kid wasn't in the cards for either of them. She'd have gone into foster care if her *abuela* hadn't stepped up and taken her in.

The old woman had been kindness itself, but when her Alzheimer's had advanced, Violet found she'd needed help. Placing her in the *Maccon City Senior Center* had been a lifesaver.

She missed her so much, especially this time of year. This was her second Christmas alone since her *abuela* had passed on. Violet still visited the other seniors at least once a month to give manicures and pedicures to the tenants who wanted them free of charge.

In fact, she was just there yesterday and had already treated the dozen or so seniors who'd wanted her services to a holiday palette of mani-pedi's. This was her night off and she couldn't wait.

Tonight was Christmas Eve, and all she wanted was to go home to some spiked hot chocolate and a marathon of old movies that she had already carefully picked out. The salon would be closed tomorrow, and since she had no family or close friends to share Christmas Day with, Violet planned on editing her current work in progress.

Unlike her other lighthearted comedies, this one was a romance. The only problem was the ending. Typical love stories were supposed to end happily, but how could someone who had her history with men even know what a happy ending was?

Sigh.

It was frustrating, but that was what it meant to be a writer, she supposed. Anyway, she could rest tonight and work on it tomorrow.

"Violet?" Sherry interrupted her train of thought.

"Sorry, Sherry, my brain went off on a tangent. What is it?" she asked.

"I am sorry to ask this of you, but I need you to go to the Leeds' Mansion for an emergency situation," she began and Violet's stomach dropped.

Oh no. Not tonight.

"Yes, I am sorry, it seems Margot, or Grandmother Leeds, you know how she prefers everyone to call her that, has come home unexpectedly and chipped two nails on her flight down from visiting her grandson in Canada. She will pay you in cash, and because it is Christmas Eve, you can keep it all, Violet. You see, I would go myself, but Seff would prefer I did not," she patted her burgeoning belly and Violet nodded.

She couldn't ask the heavily pregnant woman to drive all the way out to the Pine Barrens on Christmas Eve. Besides, Margot Leeds was a very important client. She and her granddaughter-in-law spent thousands of dollars a year on hair and nails at the salon, and they were good tippers.

Violet wasn't exactly thrilled about it, but there was also no way in hell she could afford to turn down that kind of money. She mustered up a smile for her worried looking boss and stood up nodding.

"Of course, I can do it. I am almost finished packing up for the day anyway. It's no problem."

"Are you sure?" asked Sherry.

"Of course, I am. Now, you go home to your husband and family and I will lock up tonight. I'll head straight over to the Leeds' Mansion when I am done."

"Oh, thank goodness," Sherry sighed and

hiccuped, covering her mouth while her cheeks turned bright pink which oddly enough seemed to match her colored contacts, even though Violet could've sworn they were brown a moment ago, "don't dawdle the weather might kick up a notch, but Mrs. Leeds said you were welcome to stay if anything happened."

She was still stuck on Sherry's eyes when the woman spoke, but it was probably a mistake. Violet was the one with boring brown eyes and brown hair. They went perfectly with her boring lifestyle she supposed. Sherry must've had the pink contacts on.

"What? Oh no, I'll be on my way home before the weather gets bad," she said.

Hours later.

"I want to thank you for coming out at such late notice," Margot Leeds, walked Violet to the door and smiled at the sounds of laughter coming from the South parlor.

"My granddaughter," she said and Violet smiled.

The older woman had definitely mellowed out, she thought with a tight smile. There was something odd about the Leeds' family though they were kindness itself. Stephanie, her grandson's wife, had been so happy to see her, she'd even given her a gift in the form of a red cashmere scarf.

It was so luxurious and soft, Violet had put it on over her ugly Christmas sweater that was the theme of the day at the salon.

"Are you sure you won't stay?" Mrs. Leeds asked, but Violet shook her head.

The sounds of the older woman's family from inside were tempting, but this wasn't her place. Violet couldn't bear the thought of intruding and having everyone feel sorry for her.

She had accepted the fact that she might spend her whole life alone, however hard that might be. Of course, she hoped that someday she would have her own family, but as the years went by the likelihood grew less and less.

Sigh.

"I appreciate it, Mrs. Leeds, but I must get back to my apartment. I have a manuscript waiting for me," she smiled.

"Ah, yes. I enjoyed your last two stories, my dear, and I am looking forward to this one. Thank you again and have a wonderful holiday," Mrs. Leeds smiled as she watched Violet walk out to her small car.

"Thank you. Merry Christmas!" she waved back.

Violet shook off her morose train of thought. Not everyone was cut out for a family, she told herself. She had her work after all. And maybe this time she would get noticed, having queried half a dozen agents and another half dozen publishing houses with her new and unpublished manuscript.

The full-length novel was a sci-fi fantasy romance that took place on another planet. It was her real baby. The short stories were a means to get her words out there faster, but the book, well, that was everything.

Someday, she'd make it, but for now it was nails and paying the bills on time that mattered. The extra hundred dollar tip Mrs. Leeds had given her on top of the regular fee for the repair done to her nails, plus a little manicure for her granddaughter, would definitely be helpful.

"Oh, darn it," she shivered inside her fleece-lined jacket and opened the trunk to place her manicurists' tools inside. The dented, faded gray Toyota Camry was old but reliable. Even so, she hated driving in the snow and thick, fat flakes had just begun to fall from the sky.

It was just her luck that it would begin now as she headed out for the minimum thirty-minute drive back home. The Leeds' Mansion was deep in the Pine Barrens and far away from civilization.

She'd never understood why anyone would build

a place like that out in the middle of nowhere, but maybe it was for that reason alone. After all, it was plenty quiet up there. Perfect for writing, she thought and put the car in drive.

Damn it. She tried getting her GPS app to start, but her phone was dying and the cell reception was crap. She tugged on her belt to make sure it was firmly in place, and drove down the long, winding road that crept through the forest. She only hoped she could get back home before things got bad.

"It'll be fine," she talked to herself as she tuned in to a staticky station that played Christmas carols.

With her wipers going full speed, Violet's car drove through the dark road until she could hardly see more than a few feet in front of her.

Everything was either black or whited out by the snow, and to her consternation, it had already begun to accumulate on the ground.

"Really? Just my damn luck," she sighed again, trying her best not to curse as she hurried along the path, hoping to make it home before it got too bad.

If she got stuck out here, well, she could sleep in her car for a little bit. At least it would be someplace warm. Of course, even as she thought it the heat stopped blowing and Violet tapped dials of the car's faulty temperature control button.

"Not now," she groaned.

The old Toyota was the last thing she had of her grandmother's. It had been a reliable little car, but the thing was older than she was, and Violet couldn't keep up with the repairs.

Soon, it would have to be junked, and she'd need to start taking public transportation again. Something she was so not looking forward to.

"Oh!" she screamed as something furry and dark ran out past the car and back into the woods before she could see what it was clearly.

Violet gripped the steering wheel painfully and closed her eyes as the vehicle began spinning out of control down the slick road. Her stomach lurched and icy cold fear zipped up her spine as the world blurred before her eyes.

Suddenly, the car hit something and Violet was thrust forward, slamming her head against the hard dashboard. The sound the wreck made was loud, but to her it felt distant, as if she was removed from it all.

The car made another sound or was that the tree? It was like something snapping a twig, or in this case, the trunk of the tree she was looking at through the cracked windshield. Her whole body seemed to be tilting forward and the sounds of rushing water filled her throbbing head.

Violet blinked, but she couldn't focus. Somewhere in the back of her mind she recalled a creek running through the woods out there, but she couldn't be sure where it was.

Black smoke billowed up from the hood. At least if the car caught fire it was soon going to fall into the creek.

Good, she didn't relish the idea of burning to a crisp. Not that drowning sounded like much fun either.

If only she'd known this was going to be her last Christmas maybe she would've done things differently, opened her heart and mind to new possibilities. She'd been hiding behind her own fear and loneliness for too long.

If only she'd taken the chance and put herself out there, maybe she could've found her soulmate. Someone to love and be loved by. Maybe she could've had a family of her own.

Too late now, she thought sadly just before her vision began to darken, and the blackness took her.

CHAPTER 2

The cabin had been built to his exact specifications Dean thought as he looked around the luxurious space.

He had spent months consulting with the architects before hiring the right construction crews to get the job done. Dean was a man used to getting his way, and this was not unlike most projects he undertook.

The tract of land he'd purchased had once housed a large hunting cabin. It was listed for sale over a year ago and he'd bought it on a whim while scanning one of the several real estate digests he subscribed to.

A man could never have too much land. It was one of his dad's favorite sayings. Another was, no man succeeds without a good woman, and fuck, if Dean wasn't feeling the need for a woman in his life right about now.

His discussion with Alex had replayed over and over again in his head the entire way down to the South Jersey Pine Barrens. His Tiger had grumbled the entire way too. As if he'd wanted him to hurry.

Maybe the beast was right. The cabin was awesome. Having had a place on the property before only made it easier to have it knocked down and his own cabin rebuilt in its stead.

Of course, he'd done a major plumbing and electrical upgrade. But that wasn't why his beast had been so excited upon arrival. It was the sheer majesty of the woods.

Cooped up in the city, his Tiger had to make do with rooftop gardens and the occasional run through Central Park, but that was always very dangerous. Being spotted often led to all kinds of cleanup and he didn't want to have to worry about that right then.

No, out here, he was alone. Nothing but man, *Tiger*, and nature. There was even a stream nearby, and not a single neighbor for twenty miles on any given side. The snow covered trees and grounds, the glacial blue sky, and the golden glow of the fireplace made the whole thing take on a Rockwellian aspect.

Perfect.

He'd loved the idea of a rustic hunting lodge, but because of his lifestyle, Dean had required a bit more than the average cabin offered. In the end, it had been better to simply tear down the old structure and build a new one, though he had re-purposed a lot of the old, seasoned wood inside his new extreme log cabin.

Extreme in the sense that it was powered by a large, environmentally safe generator, solar panels, and even a small wind turbine. He'd wanted plenty of light and had floor to ceiling one-way windows installed throughout, as well as skylights. There was a huge wraparound porch which housed a hot tub and outdoor entertainment area and fire pit.

While inside, there was an enormous fireplace in the living room, a gourmet's dream of a kitchen, a master bedroom in the loft with an enormous Alaskan king bed, and a luxurious bathroom with a sunken tub and separate shower stall.

There was an enormous ninety-inch television flatscreen, and plenty of movies saved to a hard drive, a sound system, and a large bookshelf that housed some of his favorites, including some classics, various biographies, thrillers, and a few mysteries.

Dean exhaled as he wandered from room to room. It smelled clean and perfect, the company his assistant hired to care for the property had obviously done a superb job. But even better than anything else was the one simple fact that this cabin was *his*.

This place was not for the Pride. Not like his penthouse in the city, which was often overrun with Tigers as was customary in most Shifter groups. There was no open door policy here.

This space was *his* alone. And he looked forward to his time there.

Mate, his Tiger pushed the thought at him, but Dean grumbled and swatted the word away. He wouldn't be finding his mate this holiday. Not alone in the woods. Maybe when he got back to the city he would call his mother and arrange for some meetings. Shifters in his position often employed something along the lines of a trusted matchmaker to help locate suitable mates. He hoped the idea would settle his Tiger and allow him to enjoy his first Christmas off in a long, long while.

After unpacking the car and stocking the fridge with the delectable goodies he'd arranged for himself, Dean opened the sliding door to the patio and sucked in a deep breath of refreshing forest air.

It was cold and snow had begun to fall heavily, but he found the clean air refreshing. His inner beast scratched at his skin, begging to be let out and he hesitated one moment before he began to disrobe.

In fact, his Big Cat had been pining for a run the second he'd seen the glorious white snowflakes falling from the skies. You just couldn't get snow like that in the city, not without a blizzard, and it was Christmas Eve after all. Why shouldn't he indulge his Tiger?

Dean stripped off his suit and tie, tossing his very expensive, tailor made silk shirt and gold cufflinks carelessly on the table as he stepped onto the deck, fully nude, and called upon his magnificent beast.

Fuck yeah, his Tiger growled inside of him. True, he was king of his Pride and while Lions might claim themselves King of the Jungle, there was no doubt in his mind, that Dean Romero was the Tiger King of New York City.

He was much larger than his wild cousins, over a thousand pounds of pure muscle, speed, and agility. His coat was thick and shiny, his fangs sharper than the sharpest knives, and his claws cruel when they came in contact with his prey.

He was a hunter, a master, the *Neta* of the Island Stripe Pride, and his beast was more than aware of his prowess. He lived and breathed duty and took his position very seriously. He was fair and just, and he commanded obedience and loyalty.

Dean's skin hummed as little electrical bolts of energy danced along its surface. The familiar magic that accompanied his change pulsed and caressed his limbs, while at the same time urging his bones to snap and muscles to tear, re-knitting and shaping themselves into his beast.

He and his Tiger shared a soul, and yes, he was still very much in charge when in his fur, but his instincts were purer and the animal was louder when he wore his stripes.

Dean tossed his great, feline head back and opened his mouth tasting the air around him before taking off in a single leap with which he cleared the fence that closed off his porch to the elements and wild animals that roamed the land.

He could already scent the deer, black bears, and occasional coyote that had crossed his domain. Not to mention the faint odors of the other Shifters in the area.

None had dared come too close to the Tiger King's property, and he growled in acknowledgement of the respect they'd paid him in absentia. Decorum would dictate they seek permission first, and he appreciated it even more as he understood he was the guest here.

The true boss of the Pine Barrens was a mystical creature, something of a local legend that was known as the Jersey Devil. Of course, he was seen as a myth, but he was as real as Dean was. A fun guy, truth be told, even though he recently mated.

His Tiger chuffed and stretched, slightly jealous perhaps of his boyhood school chum finding his mate. But Dean pushed that envy away. He rolled his big shoulders before pouncing over the next drift of snow.

It felt wonderful, racing around with no destination or time limit on his fun. He climbed trees, went for a swim in the near frozen water of the stream and ran until ice glistened on his fur.

How his mother would've scolded him in his youth for such a trick! He chuffed again and rolled in a pile of snow just because he could, racing a branch as it floated downstream in the water, and loving his sudden, brief freedom before the sound of something loud reached his sensitive ears and brought his head up.

Screeeeeeeech! It sounded as if someone's car had

lost control, and that was of course, followed by a loud crash.

What the hell was that? His rational mind had guessed the cause of the noise, and his Tiger snarled. The beast was annoyed for a moment that his fun would have to stop.

Grrr.

There was no way around it. He was alone out there for miles and miles and the snow was falling even harder now. Dean would have to check to see if anyone was hurt, even if the idea was not tempting in the least.

He used his supernaturally enhanced senses as he raced through the frozen wonderland to where he'd initially heard the crash. There was something wrong, he thought as he listened for the sounds of humans exiting their vehicle and calling for help.

It was oddly quiet, *too quiet,* and that didn't bode well for the people in the accident. Probably a family on their way to some relative's home for the holiday, he thought and growled softly. Should've known better than to drive in this.

In New York, the snow would've melted as it hit the pavement. There was so much going on under-ground it hardly ever stuck in his experience, but out in the woods there were no underground grids and subways to melt the heavy, frozen white stuff. Driving in it was far too dangerous.

Once he found the man responsible and ascertained that he and his family were all right, Dean was going to tear the normal a new one. How dare he risk his family by driving in this weather!

That was the problem with humans, his animal thought back to him, *they had no Neta to lead them.*

He chuffed and ran harder. Closer now, he thought as the scent of burnt rubber and fuel reached his nostrils.

Shit. That smell was bad. It meant the car was burning. Dean hauled ass. He bounded over frozen tree roots and snow covered shrubs until he reached the wreckage.

All at once, two things became clear to him. As Dean's Tiger leapt onto the trunk of the burning vehicle he saw that it wasn't a family inside, and not a man driving.

A female. Yes, it was a woman. She was slumped over in the driver's seat, injured he knew by the coppery scent of blood coming from her. As he breathed in the delicate fragrance, the other thing that became clear almost stunned him into immobility.

Mine. The stranger was not just a woman, she

was his fated mate. Thunder roared in his head and his heart damn near squeezed him to death, but the sparks and black smoke rising from the vehicle spurted him into action.

Mine, growled his beast again as Dean swapped fur for skin so as to pull her from the wreck.

Sure, he was naked and it was cold as fuck, but he paid little attention to the weather. His mate was his only concern as he used all his might and strength to pull the crushed metal door off its hinges so he could free her from the burning car before the tree cracked completely and plunged them both into the water.

Dark eyes blinked open as he wrapped his arms around her to free her from the confines of the hunk of twisted metal. He could tell from her pupils that she was more than likely concussed.

"What happened?" she moaned as he lifted her in his arms.

"You're okay," he whispered offering her what comfort he could.

Fuck, she smelled even better up close. Like sugar cookies and warmth.

Like home, he thought and bent his head to breathe deeply of her.

"Hurts," she moaned.

"You'll be fine," he answered, "I got you."

"S-sorry," she whimpered, and he looked down to see she'd passed out.

Damn. That was not good. He tightened his hold and hauled ass back to the cabin, moving inhumanly quick. Dean ran as fast as he could, holding her tiny frame carefully, bearing her weight easily as he hurried over the frozen forest, uncaring of the rocks and twigs that cut into the soles of his feet.

Finally, he made it back, and once there, he laid the dangerously pale woman out on the sofa. Chest heaving, Dean was hardly able to manage a breath. He did not know what to do first so he removed her shoes and coat.

Because of the crack in the windshield and being exposed to the elements, she was frozen to the touch. Fear reared its ugly head and the Tiger inside of him roared. He was not letting her die! He removed as much of her soaking wet clothing as he could, cursing the snow for chilling her delicate skin. More worrisome was the blood still seeping from her wound.

Head injuries were dangerous and Dean swallowed down another wave of fear. Unused to such emotions, he exhaled deeply to get his cat under control, hissing as he examined the deep gash on her scalp.

He knew the basics of emergency care and checked her pupils to see if they were dilated. He did not like his findings, and his worry grew as she remained unresponsive to his gentle probing. She was breathing evenly, but she was so, so pale.

He needed to stop the bleeding. That was the first thing he should see to. Decided now on what to do first, Dean ran to the bathroom and grabbed his first aid kit.

Shifters didn't have much use for things like that, as they tended to heal rapidly from injury. Panic began to set in as he cleaned the deep gash. Blood continued to ooze and her pulse began to slow down.

Fuck no! Dean could not afford to lose her. Not when he'd only just found her. Already his heart squeezed with an unnamable emotion for this stranger.

"No, no, no. Come on. Stay with me," he murmured and pressed his ear to her chest, listening to her heart beat.

Dean roared aloud, frowning harder as she seemed to be worse off now than before. Her heart rate was dropping dangerously slow even for a normal.

No. No. NO! He paced and shook his head. What

the fuck had he been thinking no phones this trip? Not that it would matter. No one could get there in time.

Dean dropped to his knees as tears threatened to spill. Why did this have to happen? How could he save her?

Then suddenly he knew. His Tiger pushed the answer into his mind. It was unheard of, unthinkable, and yet, it might work. Fuck it, he had to try.

There was no way Dean could explain this to a normal without the possibility of her hating him in the end, but he had no choice. There was only one way he could save her. One thing he could do that might make all the difference.

He had to give her his mating bite.

"I am so sorry to do this to you without your consent, little one, but I have no choice. If I don't give you my bite, you will die, and I will not allow that to happen," he spoke softly as he lifted her in his arms and tilted her face.

The beautiful, sweet smelling stranger blinked up at him and he stilled. Warm, brown eyes met his before drifting shut once more. She looked pale beneath her naturally bronzed skin, and for the first time in his life Dean understood true fear.

He didn't know anything about her. Not her

name or her age. Not her favorite color or what kind of TV shows she watched. But he knew one thing with every fiber of his being. She was his mate.

The human woman belonged to him, and he was going to save her. Emotions he'd never thought to feel swelled within him as he moved her soft curls back from her face and neck. Her sugar cookie scent invaded his nostrils and the beast within him growled in appreciation.

"I am sorry, this will hurt, but it is the only thing I can do to heal you," he whispered and kissed her lips briefly before his fangs descended.

Dean lifted her close, holding her gently while he tilted her head to give him better access. Next, he did the only thing he could to save his mate's life.

He bit her.

Mine!

His Tiger's roar thundered in his head as he swallowed down his mate's sugar cookie tinged life's force. Her heated blood slid down his throat even as he injected his own Shifter DNA into her bloodstream through the mating mark.

His heart hammered and his cock hardened to the point of pain, but he ignored the appendage. Sex was not the issue at this moment, but it was simply a large part of Shifter biology.

The mating bite was typically given during sex. His body's natural response was in anticipation of that. Easily ignored in deference to her condition and unique situation. He could only hope his bite was going to heal her for the time being.

Everything else could wait until the moment she opened those gorgeous brown eyes of hers.

"Come back to me, little one, wake up," he whispered and knelt by her side.

Minutes turned into hours, but he did not budge. He kept his vigil in silence, holding her hand and praying to the gods, Fates, and anyone else listening that she would wake.

It would take a miracle, but it was Christmas and what better time for miracles, he thought and his Tiger roared inside of his mind's eye echoing the sentiment.

"Please," he begged, "wake up."

CHAPTER 3

"What the?" Violet screamed in silence as pain unlike any she'd ever felt exploded from her neck and pulsed throughout her body.

She heard the strange man whispering and telling her each step of what he was doing, but she couldn't speak, couldn't move.

She felt bruised and damaged and different all at once. And yet, she felt safe too. As if being there, with him, was exactly where she should be.

Slowly, as the pain receded, Violet blinked her eyes until they opened. When they did, she came face to face with the most handsome man she had ever seen.

"Who are you?" she whispered and her voice sounded unbearably hoarse to her own ears.

Wincing, she tried to sit up, but big, warm, strong hands held her still.

"You're awake. Thank the gods! Easy now, slowly," he said and helped her to sit up.

The deep, gravelly voice was comforting and something inside of her warmed at the tone. She tried to focus on the gorgeous stranger, but it was difficult.

His dark head bent and she felt him take her hand, dropping a hard, quick kiss on it before bending his head to the crux of her neck as he helped her sit up. She was too weak, not to mention stunned, to move on her own.

But still, Violet had to admit she probably should have said something. After all she didn't go around hugging strange men. Then again, truth be told, she didn't exactly mind his gentle embrace as he pulled her into the warmth of his body.

His very naked body, she realized as his arms contracted around her. She patted him with her hands, not sure of how to respond. A yelp sounded from her lips as his nose pressed against her earlobe.

Wait. What was he doing? Was he licking her? She shivered as his mouth closed around her neck in a kiss she hadn't been expecting, and if she were being honest, she didn't exactly mind. Tiny little electrical impulses seemed to dance along her skin from the brief touch of his mouth on her neck. It sizzled through her veins and headed straight to her core.

"Um. Who are you?" she asked and pushed against his enormous, and *holy cow,* completely ripped chest, needing distance to regain her composure and figure out what the heck she was doing with this stranger.

"It's been over two hours. I was so worried," he said and she could practically feel his relief as if it were her own.

Strange, but even stranger was her desire to soothe and comfort him. Violet shook her head and tucked her hair behind her ear, trying to make sense of everything she was feeling. He must have felt her confusion because he moved back and gave her some space which she should've appreciated but much to her consternation, Violet found herself missing his nearness.

She moved to stand too quickly and sat back down heavily on the sofa.

"Whoa, easy, little one," he said and she could almost see his frown despite her closed eyes.

She felt as if the whole room was spinning around her and yet, *and yet,* she felt surprisingly good. Like *better-than-ever* good.

"Here, hold on to me," he murmured with that same concern lacing his hypnotic voice, "that's it give yourself a moment."

She felt herself gripping his forearms and for some reason the contact steadied her. His deep voice penetrated the haze that was clouding her mind, and slowly, ever so slowly she felt herself relaxing. Blinking deliberately, she looked up to find herself pinned by his compelling teal colored gaze.

They were not quite green and not quite blue, more like caught somewhere in between. Like pictures of the Mediterranean Sea that she'd seen once upon a time on the internet. Even more fascinating was the way his strange seafoam eyes seemed to glow in the dimness of the room.

Like magic, she thought and had to stop herself from reaching out a hand to trace a line from his thick, perfectly arched eyebrows down his chiseled face to the hint of shadow that graced his chin. Violet shook off the impulse and looked down at her disheveled clothing.

"There was an accident," she said, suddenly recalling the wreck even if what happened afterwards was still a bit fuzzy.

Oh no! She must've totaled her poor car. Violet expelled a breath and touched her forehead gingerly.

She recalled hitting her head against the dashboard and the enormous pine tree her car had smashed into.

"Do you remember what happened?"

"I think I swerved to avoid hitting an animal. It was small and dark, a bear cub, I think, I am not sure," she answered.

"I see."

"I must have hit my head harder than I thought because I swear I saw a tiger afterwards in my rearview mirror. Crazy right?" she laughed, but he didn't seem to think it was funny.

No duh. Probably thought she was nuts. She cleared her throat, but he interrupted her before she could speak.

"You are okay now. That is all that matters," he said and for some reason it seemed more like a command than a statement, as if he could will her to health with just his words.

Violet frowned at the level of intensity she felt radiating off him. She looked down, covering her eyes with her hands as her gaze fell right to that part of him that was currently resting against his thigh in what she could only refer to as a semi-flaccid state.

It was long and thick, perfectly veined and the longer she looked, the harder he got. He growled and she jumped, her cheeks burning in her embarrassment.

"Um, sorry, were you bathing, or, uh, that is, why are you naked?"

"No," he growled, "I was not bathing," he finished the statement and licked his lips, eyes riveted to her face.

She could only imagine how she looked. Caught staring at his nudity, Violet tried to explain but it came out a sputtering snort, and her face burned even brighter with her next faux pas.

Sigh.

"Look, I am so sorry, that is none of my business. What are you a naturist or something?" she asked, and tried to pretend it was totally normal that Mr. Sexy-Naked-Buff-Man-With-Teal-Eyes-That-Glow was actually growling at her.

Did she mention he was like totally butt ass naked?

"Um, where are your clothes?" she asked trying her hardest to keep her eyes on level with his.

"What?" he asked, and she was shocked to see he seemed almost unwilling to break eye contact, but then, he looked down at his body and finally, it seemed to dawn on him that he should be clothed.

"My apologies, little one," he grinned and leaned over to grab a throw blanket from a basket underneath the coffee table, "you see, I was indisposed when I heard the crash and came running without thinking. Afterwards, you were bleeding and I was tending your wounds," he explained.

"Really? Thank you so much. I'm so sorry to be a bother-"

"Are you seriously apologizing for being in an accident?" he laughed and draped the crocheted afghan over his lap with a knowing smile on his face, as if he could tell she was very interested in his sublime physique, "You must be the nicest person in the world."

"Hardly," she returned and felt her cheeks heat up at the compliment.

Okay, you caught me, she thought to herself, *I'm injured, not dead.*

Violet was still a bit embarrassed, but she was only human. He probably had women throwing themselves at him by the boatload. Never before had she seen such a superb specimen of man.

"Anyway, I am sorry to have inconvenienced you and on, oh no, I mean it's Christmas Eve and, uh, your family-" she said remembering her manners, and licked her lips, wincing as she did.

"I am here alone. I don't have a wife or girlfriend in case you were wondering."

"Oh, I, um, that is none of my business."

"On the contrary," he murmured.

Violet felt her body heat at the way he said that and a little voice inside her told her it was very much her business. Why should she feel all proprietary about the man? It was a mystery to her. Maybe she'd hit her head harder than she'd thought.

"The car?"

"I'm afraid there was no saving the car. After you hit the tree it began to burn and then, after I pulled you out, the tree gave way. It is stuck in the creek for now, but when the roads clear I'll send someone out," he said.

"I can't believe it," she whispered and covered her mouth with her hands.

Violet figured the car was totaled, but she hadn't realized just how bad the accident was until her rescuer explained it.

"It's a miracle I'm even alive," she whispered, meeting his concerned stare, "thank you."

"I would never let anything bad happen to you," he said and for some reason she believed the statement even as he broke eye contact, closing his eyes for a moment.

While he seemed to need a second, she took the time to do a personal inventory. Her entire body felt sore and tired. She knew she must be bruised and maybe even badly hurt, but for some reason she just felt achy and out of sorts.

All she wanted was to sleep, but that probably wasn't a good idea. She had hit her head after all.

Ooh and eat, whispered her inner voice. What was up with that thing anyway, she wondered? When had she become so vocal? Oh great, maybe she hit her head and now she was nuts. Perfect. Either way, crazy-inner-voice Violet was correct, she was hungry, but figured she should start small.

"Do you think I could have some water?"

"Sure, of course," he jumped up flashing his very fine gluteus maximus her way before securing the blanket around his hips in kilt-like fashion.

CHAPTER 4

Violet stared at her rescuer while he moved about what she now realized was a log cabin of sorts, though truth be told, it was the height of luxury from what she could see. There were marble accents to go with the highly polished wood walls and floors, expensive throw rugs, and the furniture was all richly masculine in varying tones of brown, beige, and forest green.

It was all very modern and yet rustic, impeccably clean and light with enormous floor to ceiling windows, whole walls of them in fact, and the roof was half made up of what she guessed were retractable skylights that showcased the surrounding Pine Barrens in a way that was flattering and inviting.

This place would impress anyone, she guessed, but her favorite was the enormous fireplace. The burning wood cast off the perfect golden glow and gave just enough warmth to not be overbearing.

She sank back into the couch where she'd been lying down minutes before. It was butter soft to the touch and large enough to fit at least eight people. Turning her head carefully, she saw bookshelves that intrigued her, and of course, a state of the art entertainment center.

The lights were dimmed down probably in deference to her head injury, but she could see everything with remarkable clarity. She was curious about her rescuer and what kind of books and movies he preferred. What kind of things he liked to do.

"This place is incredible," she called out and snapped her mouth closed when her stomach growled audibly just as the strange man returned with a tray in his hand.

"Thanks, I am glad you like it. I thought you might be feeling a bit peckish," he grinned approvingly and placed the tray on the coffee table in front of her.

He sat down next to her making his mock-kilt ride up slightly and Violet felt her cheeks heat up at the familiar and yet careless way he seemed to ignore his nudity.

The body is perfectly natural, she thought and decided to shrug off her own puritanical closed-mindedness. With this kind of place the man had obviously been brought up with a different kind of background than she, and besides, he was her host. The least she could be was gracious.

His bare thigh rubbed against hers as he moved the table closer to them. The touch was somehow comforting as it was arousing, but she was much too hungry to pay it any mind. Actually, more like starving, and that was surprising considering she'd had tea and cookies with the Leeds family before she'd left.

At any rate, she was too hungry to notice the careful way he was watching her. Violet closed her eyes and inhaled a deep breath, practically salivating at the delicious aromas from the antipasto plates he'd put together.

"This looks great," she said.

"I am glad you approve," he said and his voice seemed deeper than before.

Violet was practically drooling at the delightful assortment he'd put together in record time, she could hardly keep from gorging herself on all the goodies.

There was a plate filled with delicate little rolled up cold cuts, a bowl of calamari salad, an array of cheeses with plump grapes and strawberries, and a basket of crackers and breadsticks.

It looked positively divine. Before she could stop herself, Violet had piled the small dish he'd handed her with three slices of perfectly rare roast beef, a couple of cubes of sharp cheddar cheese, some sesame crackers, and a scoop of calamari.

"Try this," he said handing her a breadstick dipped in some kind of spicy mustard and she took it happily opening her mouth for the crunchy sesame goodness.

The second she tasted the delicious goodies, Violet hummed happily. Hell, she was practically purring aloud. She'd always been a fan of eating, as her thick thighs and rounded ass could attest to, but even so, she felt her face blush in embarrassment.

"Oh my, um, excuse me please, I must be hungrier than I thought," she mumbled and grabbed a napkin, mortified by her behavior.

"Please do not apologize. There is nothing sexier than watching a beautiful, confident woman enjoy herself."

"Beautiful and confident? Who me?" she practically snorted and shook her head.

"Yes. You," he returned matter-of-factly, "I like watching you eat, little one. I think you're refreshing, delightful, extraordinary in truth," he said and tucked a stray curl behind her ear.

For some reason, she believed him. The voice inside her had gone quiet, but Violet felt approval hum throughout her body. As if she should not only accept his praise but bask in it as her due.

What the heck? I'm not entitled to anything he, uh, darn it, what is his name? She could not believe she hadn't asked her rescuer's name. Wiping her mouth she sipped her water and decided it was now or never.

"So, uh, I'm Violet, Violet Martinez," she said and offered her hand.

"That's a beautiful name," he grinned and closed his hand around hers, engulfing it completely and pressing his thumb against her palm.

The touch was innocent, and yet she felt it sizzle through her, all the way down to her toes. Next, he lifted the cold cut dish out to her and nodded approvingly while she perused the selections and took a slice of prosciutto this time.

"I'm Dean Romero, and I am very pleased to make your acquaintance, Violet Martinez."

He smiled at her and his teal eyes reflected the glow coming from the fireplace. He was absolutely gorgeous, she noted once more. Certainly, the handsomest man she'd seen in her lifetime. Not that that was saying much. Her last boyfriend was a sous chef at *Chez Jaqueline* in Maccon City and thought her too provincial for him.

Sigh. This man was completely out of her league. And yet she couldn't help but stare at the abundance of honeyed skin on display. He was huge, with a near seven-foot tall frame that was heavily corded with muscles that seemed to be naturally acquired as opposed to gym-made.

He made her mouth water. She knew she shouldn't be staring, but she couldn't help herself. Suddenly she felt warm, warmer still as she took in his sculpted torso and bulging arms in one long, sweeping glance.

A rumbling sort of noise escaped his lips and her eyes flashed back to his. His features appeared sharper, more distinguished than before, and she had to hand it to him, the man could've been a model with those chiseled good looks.

Her pulse started to race and the heady masculine scent of him invaded her nostrils at the same time. He smelled like pine trees and clean, fresh snow. She didn't know how she recognized it, she just knew she liked it.

Dean parted his lips and that slow rumble became more pronounced, a sexy growl of a noise that made something inside of her stand up and take notice. Desire flared to life between them, she knew for certain that he was interested and that only served to fan the flame of her own yearnings.

Kiss him. Touch him. Claim him. She shook her head, not understanding that last bit of advice from her inner voice. What the heck did that mean anyway?

It was as if her need was a sentient thing, she scoffed at the thought, and shook her head to clear it. This whole thing was truly bizarre, but her awareness of him seemed to grow by the second.

She stilled, watching him intently. In that one, drawn out moment, Violet felt as if the entire universe had stopped. Every inch of her seemed to be aware of him and only him. Down to the tiniest little molecule, she stifled her moan and looked down.

Violet licked her lips, fighting her increasing need with everything inside of her. No longer hungry for the imported ham and cheese, she wiped her hands on one of the small festive napkins he'd provided and tried to ignore the naughty little voice inside of her head.

She didn't want food, she wanted something else. Something warm and alive. She wanted him. She wanted to climb that mountain of a body and take him deep inside of her.

To mark him with her scent. Give him her bite. Stake her claim. What? Holy shit!

"Are you okay, little one?" his voice interrupted her inner monologue and she blinked away the voice inside of her.

"Sorry, uh, yeah, I'm fine. I guess I ate too fast."

"Here, have some more water," he said and held her bottle to her lips.

His eyes held hers for a moment and it was as if some strange, wonderful understanding passed between them. She felt safe there, with him. More than safe, she felt cared for, and wasn't that wonderful?

Is this what they meant by love at first sight? His eyes flashed at hers and she decided then and there to accept whatever happened.

Violet leaned forward and pressed her lips to the

opening. It felt cold and wonderful as she sipped from the glass bottle.

She moved to take it from his fingers, but Dean shook his head and grinned.

"I got it," he said and actually insisted on holding it for her, so Violet gave in and drank her fill.

Swallowing down a long sip of the icy cold liquid, Violet moaned in gratitude at how good it felt sliding down her throat. It was a noise Dean seemed to follow quite closely, licking his lips as he watched her.

CHAPTER 5

ine, a strange yet familiar voice whispered inside of her, and Violet almost choked.

What was happening to her? She backed up and Dean removed the bottle from her mouth, placing it on the table with a low click. Violet had to distance herself before she really did something embarrassing she thought and set her feet on the smooth wood floor.

She stood up and ignored his outstretched hand. Touching him now would be a mistake. Looking down she realized that someone, *him,* must have taken her shoes off she thought idly as she tried to get her emotions under control.

She felt hot and restless. Like something inside of her was itching to get out and take over. Her heart squeezed inside of her chest, her stomach flip-flopped, and she was having trouble breathing. She tried to suck in a deep breath but was too close to panicking to succeed.

"Easy. Slow breaths."

Oh my, she thought as more of his incredible scent filled her nostrils. Pine trees and cool, clean snow.

She loved the way it tickled her senses and made her want to bury her nose close to its source. She wanted to strip off her clothes and rub herself all over him, to absorb his scent into her skin.

Wait. What? Since when did she want to roll around with a complete and total stranger?

Not stranger. Mate.

"What is that?"

She whimpered, and clutched her head while her heart hammered rapidly inside her chest.

"Are you okay?"

"No, I'm not. Uh, I think I might be sick. Thank you for taking care of me, but I need a doctor, an ambulance, something. Did you call someone?"

Okay, she was getting hysterical but Dean just held his hands up in a calming gesture.

"Easy, little one. It's okay. I am sorry but I specifically did not bring a phone this trip because I wanted to get away for the holiday and I didn't want anyone to find me."

"Oh, I am so sorry, I ruined your vacation."

"Not at all. You have made it completely worthwhile. The snow is really starting to come down and even if I did have a phone, you're not going to be able to get anyone out here now," he continued reasonably.

"I, uh, maybe I can walk?" she said and knew from the expression on his face that it was a bad idea.

"Sweetheart, we are twenty miles outside of town, in the woods, and in the middle of a bad winter storm on Christmas Eve. The roads are all closed already, I saw State Troopers closing them when I arrived here and that was about six hours ago," he pointed to the windows and she could see the snow falling and wind howling outside.

It was a veritable blizzard. Shit. That meant Violet was stuck indoors with a *sexier-than-any-one-man-should-be-allowed-to-be* stranger and a weird, possessive, sex-crazed voice talking to her from inside her head.

OMG! Maybe she was nuts or dying? Maybe she'd banged her head harder than either of them knew?

"Look, I don't mean to sound crazy, but I, I'm hearing voices, I really think I need to go to the hospital."

"If you just calm down, I will explain, okay?" he said and looked very concerned about her well-being.

Of course he does, I'm a raving lunatic, and this is his house. Shit. Shit. SHIT!

"It's so weird because I feel fine, I mean I know I should be hurt or aching, I mean look at my shirt," she pulled the ugly Christmas sweater she'd worn to work that day and looked at the blood-splattered thing in horror.

"Easy, it's okay, love. Look there is a bathroom at the end of the hall. In the cabinet you will find a bathrobe and slippers and some brand new pajamas still in the package. Please, help yourself to all of it. I will grab some of my own clothes from the bedroom, and meet you back here when you are finished and we will talk this all through, okay?"

Oddly enough, Violet nodded at him, suddenly calm though she had been close to hysterics mere moments ago. For some reason, the big man with his deep voice and glittering seafoam eyes had the strangest effect on her.

She wanted to climb him like a tree, there was no

denying that, but she also seemed to trust him. Wasn't that weird? She didn't know him from Adam!

Mate. The voice inside her head whispered the strange word again, and she closed her eyes, counting to three before she stepped inside the large bathroom.

She could hardly believe the luxurious space she was in. Golden-accents and marble tiles covered every bit of counter and floor space. There was an enormous sunken bathtub that sat in the middle of the huge bathroom, though it was more like a bath-suite really, and she sighed in anticipation.

"This is bigger than my apartment," she muttered as she glanced longingly at the tub before turning her head to see an equally decadent, glass-walled shower on the opposite end of the room.

If she was going to be stuck there a while, she could probably explore the bathtub later. Right then, she needed a shower. She only hoped the water pressure was hard enough to ease her aching limbs and wash out the strange vibes.

Violet stopped in front of the floor length mirror and gasped as she took in her reflection. She was a mess. Her hair had escaped its pony tail and was sticking up in some places and matted to her head in others. Clothes dirty and torn, there was dried blood in her hair and on her sweater, though it was clear someone had wiped her face clean.

Dean, her thoughts warmed as they settled on her rescuer. He'd been nothing but courteous and polite, even if he was oddly naked when she'd woken up from her accident.

Maybe she'd imagined the whole licking her neck thing? Maybe it was some weird custom where he was from?

Yeah. Right. He comes from an alien tribe of throat lickers. Ha!

Well, whatever it was, truth be told, she felt better now than she had before the accident. Physically at least. Mentally and emotionally, she wasn't quite ready to make any bold statements yet.

Violet's thoughts wandered as she stripped out of her damp and stained clothing. She had some glass in her hair and sweater but managed to toss all the bits into the garbage so they didn't hurt anyone.

Finally, she entered the shower. As the warm spray from the six separate shower heads massaged her skin from every direction, she moaned audibly and rolled her neck and shoulders at the delicious onslaught. Pouring some shower gel onto a loofah, Violet lathered and scrubbed her body until she was clean of all traces of her accident.

Her skin never felt so good as she rinsed the sudsy layer of bubbles off. Next, she washed her hair with the delicately scented orange blossom shampoo, relieved when she saw he had the matching conditioner on hand as well.

Her thick, tight curls required massive amounts of conditioner to keep it from looking like a giant frizz ball. Normally she'd forego washing it without the special treatment her boss concocted for her, but there was no helping it. She had to get the blood out.

Speaking of blood, she felt along her scalp looking for traces of cuts or bumps and came up empty. There was a very small, very thin scratch, but it was already scabbed over and could hardly be the cause of all the blood and her loss of consciousness.

But she couldn't seem to find another bruise like it. It was all very odd. She shut off the water and stepped out onto the soft rug, sighing once more as an overhead heating fan came on, drying her skin while she patted it with a thick, fluffy towel.

All her towels had holes and were mismatched, she thought with a grimace. Crazy how when she was in her twenties, she'd dreamed of finding love and hitting it big, but now in her thirties she dreamt of matching towels that were big enough to wrap around her chubby little body.

Sigh. How our priorities change!

Okay fine. Maybe she would add daydreams of sexy, teal-eyed men who walked around rescuing damsels from car wrecks in the buff!

LOL. Yes, she could definitely admit she'd be dreaming about Dean. Probably that very night. It was Christmas Eve after all. Maybe if she was really good, Santa would get her one very tall, very hunk man as a present.

As if.

Violet shook her head and walked over to a large built in closet that was against the far wall. She found lotions and hair brushes, nail clippers, etc., as well as a pair of gorgeous bathrobes.

Of course. No girlfriend, huh? Yeah. Right.

Grrrr, the voice inside her head was angry at the thought, and Violet squeaked out loud.

She shook her head, choosing to ignore this latest bit of weirdness, rifling through the shelves until she found a pair of white silk men's pajamas. She had to admit if there was a woman in his life she wasn't there very often because everything was tailored for a man's needs as opposed to a woman's, in other words, not one tampon in the place. Not that she needed one. And no, she wasn't snooping! Well, not really.

He'd told her to help herself after all. She sighed as she touched the incredibly soft pj's. There was no doubt they'd be big enough to fit her slightly over-weight, *er, fluffy* body. The man was enormous after all. The only thing was, Violet was short at five-foot three-inches, and Dean was nearly seven-feet tall.

That could lead to some issues, she thought and frowned at the bottoms. No way could she put those on and walk around without falling on her face.

What to do?

She shrugged. Well, the good news was the top came down to mid-thigh and with the bathrobe over it, she was covered to her knees. Maybe she could ask him for a pair of sweatpants or something where the bottoms were tapered, she thought as she walked down the hall with her ruined clothes in her hands.

"Here let me take those," Dean said startling her from behind.

"Oh," she gasped as his fingers brushed hers while he took the clothes and placed them inside a woven laundry basket.

"I will just put these in the wash," he whispered and nodded his head towards the sofa, "please sit. I made you some cocoa."

"Thanks," she said and smiled at the mug of hot chocolate.

He'd topped it with whipped cream and chocolate shavings and, *sniff*, he'd added a drop of something alcoholic.

She wondered how he knew that was how she liked it, but decided it was too good to pass up.

"I hope you don't mind, I spiked it. I figured we could both use something to take the edge off," he grinned as he walked back into the living room.

He was wearing a pair of jeans and a black tee, and damn, but he looked good enough to eat. Moisture pooled between her thighs and she closed her eyes tight to stem the need that was rising inside of her.

Yowza. Since when was she as hormonal as a teenager? Violet had had sex before, but her experience had been nothing to brag about. So, why was she so hot and bothered over him? And that was putting it mildly.

Easy girl. She didn't know anything about him other than his name. Violet was not in the habit of bedding people she did not know and the man was a total and complete stranger.

Mine, growled the strange voice inside of her.

It was more insistent this time and when she closed her eyes, she swore she saw a pair of glowing golden eyes hovering around in her brain.

Oh shit.

"What is happening to me," she whispered, putting the cup of cocoa back down on the coffee table.

"Hey, hey, it's alright. Look at me. You are okay, little one, you are safe with me," he was kneeling in front of her with his big, warm hands wrapped around hers and before she could stop herself, Violet vaulted forward and crashed her mouth to his.

She couldn't control herself. She wanted to rub her entire body along his. To feel every inch of his heavily muscled frame under her fingernails, her mouth, her sex.

Yes, yes, yes! Violet wanted him with something akin to violence.

She wanted to devour him with her mouth, like she was currently doing. Sucking on his tongue only made her long for that big, hard cock she knew he possessed between his thick, muscular thighs.

That deliciously hard appendage pulsed and throbbed beneath her and she pressed herself more fully against him, damning the jeans that separated them. Fucking hell, she was grinding herself on him like a cat in heat, but he didn't seem to mind, in fact, he seemed to like it.

His python-like arms held her tightly as he angled her head to have better access to her mouth.

Fucking hell, he kissed like a god. Of course, he did, he looked like one for Pete's sake! Their tongues twisted and tangled together. Every moan, grunt, and growl propelled her further into passion and she pulled on his hair, demanding more, wanting all of him.

Violet tasted every sweet nuance of his own personal flavors during their shared kiss and not just the hint of chocolate and rum from the cocoa he'd obviously sipped. No, she tasted him down to his pine scented, snow fresh core. That essence that was so uniquely his, and so perfectly suited to her.

Mine, growled the voice again and Violet moaned, pushing against his chest in horror as she realized she'd just jumped the guy.

"What the hell is going on?" she yelled, slapping a hand over her mouth and backing off of him until her ass hit the floor and her back leaned against the bottom of the sofa.

"There is something growling around in my head and so help me, I want to rip your clothes off and have sex with you right on this floor, but that is so not me. Now, did you spike the food? Did you roofie me? Please tell me what the hell is happening?" she demanded.

"Okay, okay. Easy, we can talk," he said sitting up and looking deliciously rumpled.

No, bad girl! She scolded herself and raised a hand when he moved to get closer to her.

"You're fine right there, buddy. Not one inch closer. Now talk!" she growled.

"Come on, Violet, easy now. You know me," he said trying to get that scared look off her lovely face.

"But I don't know you, Dean. Not enough for this," she said and gestured between them, "I don't usually jump guys who rescue me from car wrecks!"

"It's alright. Look at me. You are okay, little one, you are safe with me," Dean said, trying his best to calm his mate down.

Shit. He shouldn't have kissed her back. But how was he supposed to react when she'd jumped on him?

His cock throbbed inside his pants at the image of her slamming him down onto the area rug with that gorgeous, half-dressed body of hers.

Holy fuck.

Dean had growled lustfully when he found himself sprawled out with his arms full of his luscious mate. Her soft, sugar cookie flavored lips devoured him upon contact. Tongues tangled, teeth nipped, Dean growled and wrapped his arms around her, crushing her full breasts against his chest.

For a first kiss, it was hot, smolderingly so, and he was hard pressed not to flip her over and tear the robe from her incredible body.

Good idea, his Tiger had growled inside his mind's eye.

Patience, he'd returned and slowed the kiss, even as she'd straddled his hips and pressed her hot core over his rock-hard cock.

Fuck, it was a trigger reaction, he knew this, but it was the best he'd felt in forever.

"What the hell is going on?" she ended the kiss abruptly and scooted off of him, slapping her hand over her mouth.

He scented her embarrassment and fear, and his Tiger didn't like that. Not one bit. His mate should be comfortable around him, and never ever should she be embarrassed of her natural attraction to him.

She was dynamite, a firecracker and he was going to hold onto her no matter what. One thing Dean knew for sure, he was not letting Violet Martinez go anywhere but with him.

After she'd basically told him to back the fuck off, Dean found himself sitting crisscross applesauce on the area rug like a fucking toddler at story time.

Whatever. That was all fine with him. As long as he could be near her, he was perfectly happy. So was his Tiger, who right about now, was acting more like a lovesick tomcat, belly up and purring softly in his throat vying for her attention.

For fuck's sake, have some pride!

He scolded the animal gently, but it was no good. He was already head over heels for her, and if that wasn't love, he didn't know what was. Had there ever been a more beautiful woman on the entire planet?

With the glow from the firelight dancing across her warm bronzed skin and the stark white snow falling outside, she looked beyond beautiful. And she was his, *er*, well, she would be. As soon as he told her the truth.

"Okay, let's talk," he began, "First, you can kiss me whenever you want. Second, you are not going crazy-"

"Well, something is wrong," she interrupted and he could see tears glisten in her dark brown eyes and it made his heart constrict, "I don't usually do things like that," she tried to explain but he could only imagine how confused she felt and that was all his fault.

Shit. Time to pay the piper.

"Listen, Violet, I have to tell you something but I don't want you to get upset," he began.

"Well, don't start like that," she mumbled.

"What?"

"You can't tell me not to get upset, I mean it's like a red flag just went off now and of course I'm going to be upset," she quipped back.

"Oh, um, well then I guess I should apologize," he said and ran a hand through his hair, "You know, I run a global conglomerate, and I would prefer walking into a boardroom full of those corporate bastards than having to tell you this, but here I go," he couldn't believe how difficult this was.

He was the Island Stripe Pride Neta for fuck's sake and he couldn't tell this woman that she was his mate and he'd given her his bite to save her life, which in turn had started the *Puspa*.

The magical process literally meant "change" and was seen as a blessing by Tiger Shifters. It was granted by the Fates to those couples whose hearts and souls were so perfectly aligned that they would only benefit from the gift of becoming a Shifter.

"You run a global conglomerate?" she interrupted his thoughts, which was good, because Dean, Pride Neta and President of the huge international corporation, was about to have a panic attack.

"Uh, yea," he said, "ever hear of ISP? Island Stripe Pride Inc?"

"ISP? I think I've seen that stamped on some of the boxes my employer gets shipped to her warehouse. She manufactures organic beauty creams, shampoos and stuff and a lot of her ingredients are imported from all over the world."

"Who is your employer?" he asked distractedly.

"Sherry Morgan-McAllister," she replied, "she has a few salons in New Jersey and New York, I think, but I work for the one in town. I'm a nail technician. Well," she blushed and tucked her hair behind her ears and he found himself fascinated by her story, "I'm a writer, aspiring anyway, but doing nails pays the bills."

"I see," he grinned, "I'd love to read something you've written sometime."

"Oh no, I'm sure you wouldn't," she blushed a dark shade of pink that he found ridiculously charming.

"I am serious," he said, "what do you write about?"

"Oh, well, actually I write some romance and fantasy. I have a few short stories that I self-published, but I am trying to get some eyes on a longer book I finished recently."

"And?" he said enjoying the conversation immensely.

"Well, it's about an alien planet where the majority of the population is made up of supernatural creatures, Shifters to be exact, and they come to Earth and perform abductions. They use humans for sport, to be hunted and experimented on until the main character is kidnapped by an alien scientist who happens to fall in love with her, then of course together they bring about peace and equality for all species," she cleared her throat and looked away, but he tilted her face back to him.

"That sounds amazing," he said and meant it, "in fact, it might make what I am about to say a little easier."

"How so?" she

"Well, love, you see, I'm a Tiger Shifter and when I found you in that car crash, it was bad. You'd hit your head and lost consciousness almost immediately. I brought you back here, but I knew you had a concussion and with head injuries, well, it was touch and go. I did the only thing I could think of to save you," his voice grew quiet as he watched her.

She was oddly still. Just listening as he told her incredible things, fantastical things that no normal would ever believe, but maybe, maybe she would?

Dean could not be sure, he simply knew he had to take the chance. Everything rested on her acceptance of his claim. Without her, his Tiger would surely die, as is what happened with most rejected mates, but he refused to believe that his Violet did not want him.

He'd felt her need, her desire, tasted it, smelled it. She was aroused by him, and if his words could not woo her, his body could. It was a dirty trick, but he'd do anything to secure her as his mate.

Sigh. Not true. If she wanted to go you would let her, his Tiger growled sadly.

Maybe, he told his beast, *but not until I tried to make it work.*

He already loved the woman. That much he knew. Maybe, just maybe, she would fall in love with him too if he was patient enough. For now, she deserved to hear the truth.

But would she believe him? Encouraged by her continued silence, Dean continued.

"You see, Violet, I knew the moment I found you that you are my fated mate. I gave you my *mating bite* to save you, knowing that our *matebond* would allow you to borrow from my supernatural abilities and you would be able to heal. But something happened that I never anticipated," he couldn't stop a grin from splitting his face as he spoke, "the *Puspa*."

"The what now?"

"The *Puspa*, the *change* happened. That voice inside of your head that has been whispering to you and telling you things is real. It is still *you*, Violet, it's just a new side to you. You see, little one, with my bite I gave you an incredible gift, you are a Shifter now too."

CHAPTER 7

"*Y*ou *are a Shifter now too.*"

His last statement echoed in the otherwise cozy living room and Violet blinked slowly. Of course, this would happen.

Naturally, the hottest guy in the universe who happened to rescue her on Christmas Eve, *like her own personal Hallmark movie,* was too good to be true. In other words, the man was batshit crazy.

Dang it.

Still, all her volunteering at the senior home had allowed for her to see the violent episodes that could accompany *dementia,* even early onset as he was clearly exhibiting. Its evil alter ego *Alzheimer's Disease* was just as bad, but Violet knew better than to rouse his emotions.

She nodded and got to her feet while he watched her from his perch on the floor. Odd how catlike his movements seemed to her now that he mentioned being a Tiger Shifter.

His entire body was so lithe and graceful, and the way he was sprawled on the floor very much reminded her of cats she'd seen sprawled in the sun.

Violet closed her mouth and pulled the borrowed robe around her waist, securing it more tightly and turned to give him another small, tight lipped smile. There was nothing to be done for him now. Maybe when she escaped she could call for help. The kind that brought sedatives and white jackets.

"Excuse me, a moment," she said and headed for the bathroom.

"Violet? I am not crazy," he said and from the sound of it, he was following her.

"Oh, I didn't say you were crazy," she returned and hurried.

"Violet! Please, turn around," he said in a voice that brokered no denial.

She stopped and closed her eyes, hating that she was stuck indoors with a man she wanted to jump on, but who happened to think he could turn into a big cat.

Of all the stupid luck, she growled and stopped

abruptly when the sound turned into an actual growl.

What the fucking fuck was going on?

"Violet, I am going to change into my Tiger now, but I want you to understand that I would never hurt you. Don't be afraid, okay?"

By the time she turned to face him, Dean was gloriously naked once more. Violet's mouth went dry as she eyed him slowly from the top of his dark head down his impressive chest, ridiculously defined eight pack, to that part of him that was currently standing to full attention.

"Never mind that now, little one, it's my Tiger that wants to meet you," he said in a voice that was even deeper than before.

She continued to stare a beat longer, then her gaze dropped and she could hardly stop herself from looking her fill. Her eyes travelled down his thick muscular thighs to his calves, and even his feet.

She was sick, she told herself, even as her insides warmed at the sight. Oh well. It was true though, he had nice feet, she thought, and as a nail tech she truly appreciated that in a person.

"Dean, look, I know what I write doesn't appeal to everyone, but you don't need to poke fun," she decided to call this what it was, a joke at her expense.

Wouldn't be the first time, after all, but still, she hadn't pegged him as cruel. This was why she used a pseudonym in her writing. Not everyone was mature enough or had a wide enough imagination to handle the content that went hand in hand with paranormal romance.

"Look at me," he commanded and she did, unable to stop herself from obeying when he used that strange tone of voice.

It was like something inside of her recognized his power and strength. She wasn't forced to watch, it was nothing like that. More of a compulsion, a deep seated interest in seeing this thing through.

"Dean, look, I get it. I should be grateful to you and I am for saving me, but I understand if I made you uncomfortable with that kiss. I was out of line-"

Grrr.

"Holy shit," Violet gasped as the man she'd been trying to apologize to stopped being a man.

One second Dean was standing there, the next second, an enormous orange and black striped Tiger was prowling towards her in the suddenly very small hallway. Violet backed up, one step after another until she hit the wall.

"Okay, I admit it. You were right. Big kitty, nice

kitty. Please don't eat me," she muttered and closed her eyes as the great, striped beast advanced on her.

He was so much bigger than the Tigers she'd seen at the zoo. So much prettier too, something inside her whispered.

Her poor frazzled brain could hardly put together the facts. Dean Romero was a Tiger Shifter. A real, live Shifter. Like the ones she wrote about. Only better because, well, because he was real.

She winced as she felt his beast's hot breath on her face, anticipating his next move with all the bravery of a B-Horror movie *TSTL*, that is too-stupid-to-live female main character.

Sigh. Okay, this was so not her proudest moment, but at least she didn't scream when his hot, sandpapery tongue swiped her from chin to forehead.

"Ooh," she gasped and giggled instead as the Dean-cat proceeded to lick and sniff at her face.

"Okay," she said when his massive paw reached out and pressed against her cheek as he licked and licked, "okay, that's enough. Bad kitty!"

His Tiger chuffed loudly, but the beast allowed her to push him away from her face, choosing to bump her belly with his nose next. His head was enormous, and as he laid down, she realized she could probably ride him like a pony. Not that she would try.

Now it made sense, the size of the cabin. The extra wide hallways and huge couch and skylights. He probably did like to lie in the sunshine, like a big overgrown tabby.

Violet grinned, fascinated with the creature as she reached out a cautious hand to stroke his thick, rich fur. She'd always loved Tigers. Who didn't? She thought as she proceeded to scratch him behind the ears and pet his gloriously thick coat.

"Such a big, boy. Such a pretty boy," she murmured and laughed when he sniffed indignantly, "sorry I mean, what a handsome man."

His Tiger seemed to preen at that, and the beast pressed closer to her, knocking her off her feet and purring loudly as he dipped his head to sniff the apex of her thighs.

"No, no! Naughty kitty!" she said and tapped him on the nose, "No sniffing my girly bits!" she scolded when he attempted to do so again.

She watched in awe as the air around his fur began to shimmer and glow as he swapped fur for skin, then suddenly, Violet found herself wrapped in the arms of a very handsome, very naked Dean Romero.

Sigh.

"Believe me now, mate?" he growled, his voice still thick with his Tiger as he dipped his head to inhale the skin at the base of her neck.

Shivers of anticipation raced through her at his nearness. She felt drunk with wanting him, her need spurred on by the possessive hold and the feeling of his long, hard thickness pressed against her soft belly.

At some point the robe had opened and she was wearing only the thin, silk pajama top. Moisture pooled between her legs and Violet knew without a doubt she was going to give in to this man, to this Tiger Shifter, before the night was through.

So, why wait? A voice inside her asked. *Take what is already ours.*

"Mine," she said the word aloud and Dean's hold tightened.

His teal eyes glowed with what she recognized was his beast and his nostrils flared as he breathed in deep and growled as if tasting her arousal in the air.

"*Yes, yoursss,*" he hissed the word with a little more of his Tiger showing in the sharpening of his features.

For some reason, that alone was ridiculously hot. She felt the rumbling growl that was building inside his chest through the thin silk and her own body like he was her own, personal vibrator and wasn't that an interesting thought.

"Um, Dean?"

"What is it, little one?" he said and adjusted his hold, dropping hot, open mouthed kisses to her shoulder and neck.

"Fuck, that feels good," she moaned.

"I can make it feel better," he said, and met her wide eyed stare with his smoldering seafoam gaze.

She saw the promise in them as clear as day and for once in her life, Violet was ready to take the plunge, to do something completely out of character,

"Then do it," she raised her head and dropped the challenge, gasping when he lifted her off the floor and proceeded to carry her up the spiral staircase to the second floor loft that served as his bedroom.

CHAPTER 8

Dean placed his mate carefully down on the thick quilt that covered the custom built Alaskan King bed inside his cabin.

Maybe the Fates had lent him some insight when he'd designed the thing. It was extravagant for one person, but for two, it was perfect. Like her.

She looked divine with her curls billowing out like a dark sail across the white bedding. He straddled her hips, grasping the edges of the pajama top she wore and meeting her eyes before tearing it clear off her body.

She gasped aloud, but her lust-filled gaze told him she was more than willing to go forward. Her own Tigress recognized him as her mate, and though his sweet Nari did not quite understand what that meant, her instincts told her to trust him and that was good enough for now.

Dean slid alongside of her, using his arms as purchase on the soft mattress, he looked into her eyes, seeking permission before capturing her lips with his own.

Violet arched her body off the bed, teasing him with her smooth, silky skin. Her hardened nipples bit into his chest and he growled at the thought of capturing them with his mouth and between his teeth.

Oh yes, she was a veritable feast. A banquet for his senses and he wanted every last morsel for himself. Even better, his sweet mate was no whimpering damsel, she was fierce and strong. Their tongues continued to war and dance together, battling for dominance as their exchange grew heated and more intense.

Dean stroked his hands down her face and neck, caressing her shoulders, and ribcage, those wide, perfect hips, to her plump, shapely thighs. She opened her legs for him instinctively and his hands found the skin there to be even smoother, softer than he'd ever imagined.

"Oh god," she moaned and he caught the sound, sipping it from her lips.

Traveling down her chin, to her neck, and clavicle, then down to her berry-tipped breasts, Dean paid homage to her body the way a priest did to the gods.

Sucking on one perfectly rounded nubbin, then the other, he rolled her nipples between his teeth gently tugging the sensitive flesh until she was writhing beneath him.

His Violet was perfect in every way, and when she tried to shield herself, wrapping an arm around her middle, Dean simply tugged her hand away and kissed the soft flesh there, locking his gaze onto hers.

Society could go fuck itself for all he cared. He had no desire to make love with a stick figure and couldn't fathom why the media chose to emulate one particular body type over all the others. To each his own, that was his motto, and he never wanted anyone like he wanted her.

Humans and supernaturals came in all shapes and sizes. Unfortunately, the world didn't seem to celebrate all of them. Well, he would show her just how stunning she was to him, even if it took all night.

"Never hide from me, little one," he growled, dipping his tongue into her belly button as he did so.

"I'm, uh, I'm overweight. My stomach is too flabby and I have cellulite on my thighs," she confessed as if it were something bad, and he hissed at her shaking his head.

"No, you are just right. The perfect size and shape, exactly as a woman should be, and I never want to hear you talk badly about your body, *my body*, again, okay?"

"I, oh, *oh*, I, yes, uh huh," she moaned as his fingers slid up her thighs and stroked the soft curls that hid her most secret flesh from his gaze.

Fuck, she was soaked. Her cream coated his fingers and he couldn't wait to lick them clean one at a time.

Grrrr. Mine.

"You're perfect, little one. Beautiful and soft, built to cradle my hard body with your sweet, soft flesh. To carry my young and keep them safe. I am gonna fill you, love, but first," he bent and used his shoulders to spread her legs even wider, "I need to taste you, sweet. Have to see if that sugar cookie scent goes as deep as I intend to."

"Dean!" she yelled as he pierced her with his tongue, strumming her throbbing clitoris with his fingers.

He buried his face between her legs and feasted

on her sex, suckling that plump little nubbin and sliding two, then three thick digits into her tight sheath until she was bucking wildly against him.

She tasted like manna from the heavens. Pure sex and sugar cookie sweetness all the way down to her core. And she was all his.

Possessive much? Fuck yes. Dean was the Neta, and he did not share. Violet was all his and he was going to satisfy every single one of her desires if it took him the rest of his life.

Dean teased her nether lips, slowing his pace and licking her slowly from asshole to clit with the flat of his tongue. Violet moaned and moved with him, attempting to get him to go faster, but he would not be rushed.

Loving her was never something to rush. He intended to show her how much she meant to him with every kiss and caress. She deserved every bit of attention he intended to lavish on her.

And she would like it too. That much he could guarantee. He growled, allowing the vibration to flow from him through to her, swallowing down her sweet cream greedily as her sex clenched around his fingers.

Fuck, she was perfect and he would never get tired of that or of her. He knew that even as his heart raced and the strength of his arousal spiked a fever through his blood.

She was his mate, his perfect match in every way, and he thanked the Fates and all the gods that had delivered her to him this Christmas Eve. His perfect present. The only one he would ever want.

"S'good, Nari," he whispered approvingly.

In the throes of passion, his shy little mate was fierce as a Nari should be. She gripped his hair until she had him right where she wanted him, fucking his face with every buck and thrust of her hips. And when she came apart, it was a thing of pure beauty.

Dean almost spilled his seed on the bedspread like some green cub from the mere sight of her. Eyes at half mast, mouth open, her orgasm seemed to pulse through her entire being before she fell back to earth with him.

He couldn't wait to do it again. To make her come even harder than the last time. He doubled his efforts. Kissing, stroking, caressing every inch of her.

It was all he could do to gain control before she'd turned the tables and had him flat on his back. Her newly found Shifter strength served her well, though she probably was unaware of it as of yet. He was too turned on to explain, couldn't wait to seal their bond.

That would only happen when he came deep within her, marking her with his cum and his scent. And yeah, he was probably going to bite her again. Cause that was just the kind of possessive asshole he was. He wanted everyone to know she was his.

Mine, growled his Tiger as Violet straddled his thighs looking for all she was worth like a warrior queen as she sank down onto his thick shaft.

"Fuck," he growled, gripping her thighs tightly as she rocked her hips, sliding along his cock in a rhythm as old as time itself.

Dean sat up, capturing her breasts in his mouth before kissing his way to her lips. Never before had sex been so soul-crushingly sweet.

Dean was thoroughly captivated by every twitch of muscle, every sigh and moan, and every minuscule movement that brought him and his mate closer to that ultimate pinnacle. She was everything he'd ever wanted in a woman, a partner.

She was earthy and real, and at the same time, like a gift from the heavens themselves. Dean's Tiger clawed at him from the inside. He begged to be freed, to join in the union, and take his rightful place beside his Nari.

"Want to bite you again, mate, to claim you," he said trying to explain this time, to wait for her ascent.

"Yes," she nodded, "mine," her Tigress showed behind her glowing eyes and Dean recognized the she-Cat's need for affirmation as well.

"Yes, yours, and you are mine," he growled.

Even as his fangs descended, Dean felt his sweet mate go rigid above him. She was so close to the edge, so near to ecstasy, and he would deliver her all the way there. Fuck yes, he would.

"Now, now, now!" she yelled as he thrust upwards with his hips and closed his jaws over that same place where he'd bitten her earlier.

Need drove him now, pure mating instinct. He needed to reaffirm his claim, with her every bit a part of their union as she was unconscious before. His Tiger knew she was his one true and fated mate, her soul called out to his, and he could not wait until the time when she would claim him back.

"Dean!" she called his name and the scent of her ecstasy rose.

"Mate," he growled back as the combination of her walls tightening around his cock and the slide of her sugar cookie scented essence down his throat had Dean soon following her into oblivion.

"Fuck," he snarled the word as a sharp, stinging pain started in his left shoulder, increasing his pleasure tenfold and he looked down to see her dark head bent as she staked her own claim on his flesh.

White hot bliss pulsated around Dean as they clung to one another, sealing their *matebond* in the most basic and yet, entirely profound way that only two beings who were fated could ever do.

Mine, his Tiger roared the word this time, announcing it to all who existed on that metaphysical realm where Shifters' beasts dwelled until called.

He sent the message through his Pride bonds and knew in the resounding joy that his Pride had felt his call. He was a single Neta no more.

He had his Nari now.

Mine!

CHAPTER 9

Hearing a man that looked as good as Dean did telling her she was beautiful was better than any gift she could've ever wished for.

Having him make love to her, well, that was something no words could describe, but she certainly tried with a lot of *hell yeah's, fuck yes, harder, faster, now, now, NOW's*. So maybe Violet had found a couple that worked.

Being bitten by him during their heated exchange, and then biting him in return, well, it was beyond her scope of experience. But as Violet clung to her mate, yes her *mate*, the animal she had yet to meet inside of her assured her this was the correct word, was as close to heaven as she'd ever been.

Mine! She heard his beast's roared announcement

inside her mind's eye and could not stop the joy the single syllable induced from bubbling out of her lips in the form of a soft laugh.

But how had she heard him? His mouth was closed as he wrapped her up in his solid embrace.

He is our mate, was the only answer her Tigress had. But she had so many more questions.

"Mmm," Dean tucked her into his side and covered them both with the blanket.

"That was," she began, and sighed heavily.

There were really no words. Wonderful, amazing, fantastic! Those all seemed to fall flat when she thought about how she felt.

"Extraordinary," he supplied for her and she smiled liking the word immensely.

Was it possible for her to love him already?

Yes, answered the animal inside of her, but it was too soon for such declarations.

"Are you hungry?" Dean interrupted her thoughts and kissed her on the temple.

Oddly enough she was hungry. In fact, she was starving. Violet nodded and smiled as he brought his head down to nibble at her lips.

Kissing him was like magic, she thought and threw herself fully into it like she never had before. This entire thing was like some fantasy, something she would write about she thought and giggled ending the kiss.

"What? Did I do something funny?" he asked and looked hurt before she realized it was just his way of throwing her off balance.

"No, no tickling," she laughed and yes, snorted, while his fingers bit into her ribcage, but she got him back.

It seemed, her big strong Tiger was ticklish himself.

"Okay, I give, I give," he gasped for air and smiled as she pinned him to the bed. "In fact, I'll give you anything you want if you stay right there," he growled and nipped her lip.

This time, when they joined, it was a slow, slippery slide of limbs. The urgency of their first coming together sated, now it was more like a symphony of sensation.

She faced him on her side as he lifted one leg up and over his, grinding his pubis into her core, while his magnificent thickness filled her to maximum capacity.

She'd never felt anything like it. Her eyes locked onto his, and she saw his Tiger staring behind the teal-colored glow as they made love, slowly, deliberately, completely while snow fell over them, making the skylight above them completely white by the time they were breathless and gasping with pure elation.

He was her heart's own desire. The one man in the world she had ever felt this magnetic pull towards. Violet had always been a dreamer. Her hopes and imagination are what caused her to want to be a writer, but with him she felt as if she really could achieve those dreams.

She felt loved and safe for the first time ever. Through the wondrous new power of her *matebond* with him, she felt emotions she had only ever read about.

He was incredible, sinfully handsome, a natural born leader, powerful and charismatic, and yet she felt truly comfortable with him. Like she could be herself and he would always accept her.

Violet knew it was impossible, a fantasy for sure, but she also knew it was as real as the snow falling outside. Her body hummed with delight as he touched her in places no man ever had.

"Beautiful," Dean cupped her face between his hands and rolled over on top of her, changing angles his cock sunk deeper inside of her.

Stroking that perfect spot that only he had ever reached and soon she was struggling for breath as he swiveled his hips, rocking his body with such tender care into hers and bringing her more pleasure than she had ever felt.

He swallowed her cries as her orgasm overwhelmed her senses, until he joined her in that sweet oblivion. Eons later, he ended the kiss with dozens of smaller, tender touches of his lips to hers.

Words could hardly express what she was feeling, but one did. One word said it all.

"Mate," she exhaled and pressed her forehead to his, sucking in the fresh pine scent that was all him and cradled him in her arms.

Pure joy and elation filled her and she realized it was coming from him too. Something inside of her recognized the rare beauty and profound power of their special bond. It was humbling and awesome in ways she had never experienced, but looked forward to, with him.

After she scrounged around for some clothes that would fit her, Violet joined Dean in the surprisingly large kitchen.

"You know this cabin is insane," she said and laughed as she accepted the glass of white wine he held out to her.

"Really? What do you mean?"

He was cutting some lemons and adding them to

a beautiful cut of fish, which had her salivating. That was weird she didn't usually like fish, but she was almost ready to eat the thing raw.

"What is that?"

"Pacific Cod, I had Alex, the ISP Vice President and Beta of my Pride, arrange for the cabin to be stocked when I arrived and I always have fish on Christmas Eve," he shrugged.

"Yeah? That is an Italian thing, isn't it?"

"Yes, my mother is Italian. She is going to love you," he grinned and Violet's stomach flipped.

It had been a long time since she had any family of her own. The idea warmed her even as it had her nerves standing on edge.

"Hey," he said and her eyes met his across the marble counter, "I mean it. She and my father retired years ago, but I can call and have the jet fueled up at a moment's notice. We can visit them in Florida maybe after the holidays. Do you like Florida?"

"Uh, I don't know. I've never been," she answered and suddenly felt as if the walls were closing in on her.

Here she was in this fancy cabin that to him was nothing more than a blip on his radar. How could she fit into his world? She was just a nail technician.

"Hey, little one. It's okay, look at me now," he was

suddenly in front of her and his big warm, hands were on her face, tilting it up towards him, "We don't have to do anything you don't want to. If I am moving too fast, it is just because I am so happy. You did that, you know."

"I did?"

"Yes, you make me happier than I ever thought was possible, but I get it if you don't want to meet the family right away. My parents can be a bit over-bearing," he frowned.

"No, it's not that," she laughed and to her horror a tear rolled down her cheek.

"Hey, no crying, please," he bent and kissed away all traces of her tears from her cheeks.

"I just, well, it's been a long time since I belonged to anyone," she tried explaining and he wrapped his arms around her, tucking her head against his chest.

"I got you now, little one, and you belong right here with me," he whispered against her hair.

She felt safe and warm, and most of all loved wrapped up in the security of his embrace. Violet released the breath she'd been holding and with it expelled all her frazzled nerves.

"Tell me about the Pride," she said recalling his mentioning a Beta, which from her writing meant there was probably an Alpha too, "who is in charge?"

"Uh," he stepped back and wiped his hands on a dishtowel before picking up the broiler pan with the seasoned fish and placing it under the fire to cook, "I am."

"You're what?"

"In charge," he answered and turned to face her, "I am the Neta of the Island Stripe Pride and you, mate, are our *Nari*, that is what we call our Alpha fem."

"But I, I don't know anything about being a Tiger," she said and he could sense her growing anxiety.

"Let me feed you, little one, then I will teach you everything you need to know."

Dinner was phenomenal and Violet had to admit she was now a fan of fish. He'd seasoned the flakey perfection lightly with sea salt, crushed red pepper, olive oil, parsley, and lemon slices, and she'd practically purred while digging in.

Paired with some almond tossed string beans, dinner was absolutely divine. She couldn't wait for dessert and nearly snarled aloud when he told her it was for later, but she remembered herself in time.

"Won't I be cold?" she asked as Dean took her hand and led her to the snow-covered deck.

"Not really. We need to do this now, more snow

is coming in an hour or so," he said as he watched the darkening sky.

"But I don't know what to do," she whined as she began to strip, mimicking his actions.

Nerves had her acting a little bratty, but she could hardly blame herself. The last few hours felt like some kind of crazy dream.

"Love, you will be fine," he rubbed her shoulders and she leaned into him longing to feel his weight atop her once more, "I promise, I will do anything and everything you want me to, but right now it is time you meet your Tigress."

She growled impatiently and huffed as he turned her around to face out towards the frozen Pine Barrens.

"It's cold."

"Forget the cold, sweet, close your eyes. Look deep within yourself. She is there. Waiting for you, love, let her out, let her know what you want. Remember she has a voice and a mind, but you share the same soul," his voice was hypnotic as he whispered into her ear.

Violet's rational mind wanted to scoff at the ridiculousness of it all, but there was something else inside of her. And that something was very interested in what Dean had to say in that deep, rumbling timbre that was both soothing and arousing at the same time.

Violet decided to follow her instincts. She closed her mind off to the doubt and her pesky rationale. She didn't need that anymore, not here, and not with him.

Instinct, nature, fate, *hell*, maybe even her boss or just the universe at large had all convened to bring her to this exact moment in her life. It was time she stepped up and away from the drudgery that was her previous existence.

In these last few hours with Dean, Violet had felt more and done more than she had in the entirety of her thirty years on Earth. She trusted him. Crazy as that sounded, she did. With her body, her mind, and yes, even her heart. There was something so refreshingly honest about him.

"Just breathe, love," he whispered and she felt her limbs go soft and heavy as her trust in him allowed her to relax fully.

Expelling a breath, she finally saw her, a beautiful sleek Tigress with shining golden-orange fur and inky black stripes. Her beast was magnificent. Beautiful and graceful as she stepped forward inside her mind's eye.

Let me in, her Tigress pushed the thought into her

head and suddenly she was propelled forwards, slumping on her bare knees in the cold snow that had fallen on the deck.

"That's it, mate. You can do it. Don't fight her. She is you, let her in, accept the change," Dean talked her through the worst of it, and finally, when her skin ached and the sounds of her muscles tearing and her bones breaking and reknitting no longer echoed in her mind, Violet stood.

The world was slightly askew when she opened her Tigress' eyes. It was sharper, like switching from regular old television to high definition, she guessed and chuffed at her wayward thought.

"You are beautiful, my Nari, as I knew you would be," Dean knelt before her, waiting until she bumped his shoulder with her big head to touch her.

He pressed a kiss to her head and stood up in his nudity. She recognized the hum of magic now, saw it even as it worked to transform him from man to beast in the blink of an eye.

Violet grunted at that. Her own change had been painful and much longer. Not at all easy like his looked.

It will get easier with time, little one.

Violet snarled and stopped in her tracks. To hear his voice so clearly in her head felt strange, though not unwelcome. She narrowed her eyes and flicked snow in his direction with her long tail.

You could've warned me about that.

About what?

That you can read my mind when I'm like this, I mean what if I was thinking about how hot you are, or what if I was thinking about another guy.

At that, Dean roared loudly.

No other. Mine!

Okay, easy there, buddy, I was just kidding.

Sorry. I am afraid my Tiger is very possessive of you, Violet. Joking about other men is probably not a good idea.

Really? Well, how about this? Is this a good idea?

She used her massive paw to toss a huge wave of snow at Dean's Tiger's face before vaulting over the fence and out into the woods.

The air on her fur felt divine as did racing over the mounds of snow and tangled roots and limbs. She smelled everything, like everything, from field mouse droppings to larger animals like deer and bears that had passed along the way. Mostly though, she scented her mate, and her Tigress approved wholeheartedly of him.

Her Tigress chuffed and teased him, loving the strength and energy of her other self. She frolicked happily in the woods, chasing and being chased by Dean for what seemed like hours but couldn't have been too long before he led the way back to his cabin.

We want to be back in time for Santa, don't we?

She snorted at him but was happy to be headed back. Truth was, being a Shifter was exhausting.

Don't forget dessert, she thought at him and got the distinct impression her mate had been thinking the very same thing.

Grrr.

CHAPTER 10

Dean wandered up to the loft where he'd left his exhausted mate sprawled out on the bed with a ridiculously satisfied gleam in her eye.

It was well past midnight, and still he was starving for her. Always would be, he thought with a grin and sent another prayer of thanks to the universe for blessing him with his Violet.

Fated mates were rare and cherished among his kind, now their kind, he corrected himself, and he would never forget how blessed he truly was to have her.

"Shit," he grunted, almost losing his grip on the plate of dessert he'd promised her earlier that evening.

"Mm, do I smell watermelon and chocolate?"

"You do and some other bits of goodness here and there. Sit up, love," he gestured to the headboard and Violet gave him a saucy growl before rolling over, to crawl up the enormous bed giving him one hell of a spectacular view, even if she was somewhat hidden by the silky sheet.

He sat down next to her scooching her over with his hip and held the plate just out of reach when she went to snag a bit of chocolate sauce.

"Un uh, you get dessert, but I get to feed it to you," he said and loved the way she faux pouted at him.

"Okay, but you better gimme some chocolate before I hurt you," she teased.

Dean took a slice of strawberry and dipped the tip into the bowl of melted dark chocolate, blowing on it before holding the treat to her kiss-swollen lips.

"Mmm," she moaned and took it in her mouth causing him to have all sorts of naughty thoughts regarding other things he'd love to see slip between her lips.

Next was a thin slice of watermelon that he rubbed with a slice of lemon then coated with ultra-fine sugar before feeding it to her.

"*Ohmygawd*," she moaned around the mouthful

and once more he found himself hard pressed to ignore the almost torturous level of arousal she evoked.

Next was a cherry he'd pitted himself, covered in melted white chocolate, followed by a peach slice dipped in lemon and sugar, and a plump raspberry delicately dredged through the melted milk chocolate and sprinkled with Himalayan pink salt.

All the while she moaned and licked at his fingertips. Every scrumptious morsel was nothing compared to the act of watching her enjoy each bite.

By the time she patted her tummy, Dean didn't think he could stand up straight. He placed the near empty dish on the floor, save for the small bowl sugar and a slice of lemon.

"What are you doing with that?" she bit her lip.

"It's my turn for dessert. I like chocolate, but straight up sugar is more my speed," he tugged on the sheet until it fell away from her breasts loving the way she arched her back proudly as he gazed lovingly at her spectacular shape.

She was full-figured in all the best places with generous tip-tilted breasts that more than filled his extra-large hands. Dean took the lemon wedge and rubbed it lightly over one plump berry of a nipple then dipped his finger in the bowl and put a dusting of the fine powder-like sugar on one then the other.

Violet's eyes heated as he leaned down and lavished attention on first one, then the other. The sugar and lemon combination only served to bring out her natural scent and when all was said and done that was what he wanted the most.

"Finally," she said as he nibbled his way to her mouth, "this has really turned out to be some Christmas," she smiled and he wanted to beat his chest and holler to the whole world that he was the man who'd done that.

Dean Romero put that look on her face, and he planned to do it often and again, for as long as the two of them walked the planet.

Suddenly it hit him. She was his own Christmas miracle and he just had to tell her. Why wait?

"I love you, Violet," he whispered eyes wide as the truth of his words wrapped around his heart and soul like a vise, he never wanted to be free of.

"Dean, I-"

"No, you don't have to say it back. You've been through so much today, I can only imagine how you feel."

"I don't know if you can. This is all like some fantasy, a dream come true. I mean not the accident, but if that is what it took to meet you then yes, that too," she sat up and took his face in her hands in earnest, "Maybe I'm a silly romantic, but I've always believed in love at first sight. You saved my life, gave me a wonderful gift, and now my Tigress is growling in my head constantly that she knows you're my mate. So don't tell me to shush when I tell you that I love you too."

"You do?" he said, and fuck it, yes, he might have teared up at her confession.

"Yes, I do."

"Thank fuck," he pulled her close and hugged her tight to him as they both laughed and whispered those three little words over and over again.

Of course, the sound of something landing on the roof had them both jumping apart and looking up at the skylight, where truth be told, the sight Dean saw left him absolutely speechless.

"Was that?"

"Uh-"

"Is he real?" Violet stage whispered and Dean was too awestruck to answer.

"I mean, I've heard rumors, but I have never found any evidence either way."

Violet bit her lip again and her warm brown eyes glowed with mischief as she tugged on his hand,

"Come on! Let's see if he left us anything," she giggled and sped down the stairs wearing nothing but the sheet she'd pulled from the bed.

Dean was still wearing the pajama bottoms he'd donned earlier to make the dessert plate. His Tiger pushed at him to hurry up so as not to leave his mate unattended for any amount of time and that was something he could totally understand.

"Hang on, let me go first," he said and gently pulled her behind him as they walked to the softly glowing embers of the fireplace in the living room where a very small, very red package waited.

Curiosity got the best of Dean and Violet and together they knelt in front of the small prettily wrapped gift.

"You open it," he grinned when he saw her expression.

"You sure?"

"Yes, I already got my gift."

That little statement earned him a kiss, which caused him to think silently that he got two presents now. He liked watching her enthusiasm rise as she tore the paper carefully.

A familiar blue box sat in the palm of her hand, and Violet bit her lip while Dean picked up the tiny card that had fallen out with the paper.

"What's it say?" she asked wondrously.

"It says 'don't be an ass, ask her already,'" he laughed, and took the box from her hand, opening it towards her while assuming the proper position.

On bended knee, heart on his sleeve, Dean looked up at his mate with heat and love in his worshipful gaze, "Violet Martinez, the last twenty-four hours have been the most amazing of my entire life and I want you to know that it is because of you. I'm kneeling before you now asking you to take me, Dean Romero, Neta of the Island Stripe Tiger Pride, as your husband and mate until eternity. I promise to respect, love, honor, cherish, and worship you for the rest of my life. Will you marry me?"

EPILOGUE

"Are you freaking kidding me?" Alex blinked against the bright light, his head still pounded from the Christmas party and he had no idea what to make of what his Neta was saying.

"I said, I found her, my mate. We were married this morning and will be returning to the penthouse this afternoon. Have it cleaned and make sure everyone is ready to meet their new Nari," Dean commanded from the satellite phone Alex had snuck into the trunk of his Valkyrie.

"Yes, *Neta*," Alex wasn't too hungover from the night before to not recognize that tone of voice.

"Is she hot?" he asked and pulled the phone away from his ear as his Neta roared ferociously into the phone.

"Mine!" growled Dean.

"Holy hell! She is your fated mate! All will be made ready, Neta," Alex said and grinned from ear to ear.

Once he hung up on his Beta, Dean turned to his beautiful Christmas bride. She was smiling happily, resplendent in a white gown they'd picked up from her boss, Sherry McAllister, who happened to be a Witch married to a Werewolf, on their way to be wed.

After the small, intimate ceremony, which was performed by a Wolf Shifter who lived near Atlantic City, Dean and his new bride decided to head back to his penthouse.

"Are you sure you don't want to take a few days to get used to this?" he'd asked, but his mate shook her head.

"I don't want to wait another moment to start my life with you."

"This has turned out to be the most incredible Christmas," he brought their entwined hands to his lips and kissed her wrist, loving the shiver that travelled through her at the contact.

He would enjoy spending the rest of his life finding those special places that made her purr and tremble with desire. After explaining to her what it meant to be his Nari and offering to step down as Neta if she was uncomfortable because her happiness was tantamount to everything else, his mate had narrowed her eyes and demanded he take her to meet his Pride immediately.

"You are the rightful Neta, and I am your Nari, I would never ask you to step down, Dean. I am proud to be at your side," she'd said.

"I love you, Violet Romero, you are truly the most extraordinary woman I have ever met, and you are the best damned Christmas present I have ever gotten," he grinned and yes, the Tiger inside of him liked that she chose to take his name very much.

"I love you too, Dean, but I think you're wrong. I am the one who was given a gift and that's you," she returned.

"I love you," he growled and Violet leaned over to take his lips with hers.

"Get us home so you can show me how much," his Nari commanded and Dean didn't need to be told twice to put the pedal to the metal.

The scenery flew by and his mate laughed as he sped along to their penthouse in Manhattan. It was truly a wonder that she had come into his life so suddenly and perfectly, even he had to admit. Violet had irrevocably changed his solitary ways.

For the better though, always for the better, he thought with a grin splitting his face.

Yes, he just had to introduce his mate to his Pride, but first, he would show her just what it meant to be his one and true fated mate. She was the single most important person in his entire world and she deserved to hear that from his lips, to taste the truth behind his vows in his kiss.

Indeed, growled his beast in agreement. This was going to be a Christmas his sweet, sugar cookie scented Nari would never forget. Dean would make damn sure of that.

Mine, growled his Tiger.

Mine, echoed his Tigress.

He heard her husky growl whispering in his mind through their *matebond* and fuck if that wasn't the most incredible thing.

That ethereal link pulsed and glowed in that metaphysical plane where it resided, allowing them both the gift of knowing how the other felt. He basked in the knowledge that his mate was as crazy about him as he was about her.

How had he gotten so lucky, he wondered that for some length as he drove.

Dean held Violet's hand the entire way back home. As he neared the penthouse he recalled his conversation with his Beta before he'd left for the cabin. What a fool he'd been! So arrogant and sure.

Well, his adventure proved one thing for certain, Christmas miracles really did exist and he'd been blessed to have his own sitting right there next to him.

"Are you nervous?" he asked as they pulled into the private lot of the ISP Building on the Upper West Side.

"A little," she confessed, "but really I'm excited."

"Oh yeah?"

"Yes," she bit her lower lip in a way that made him ache to soothe the abused skin, "I can't wait to start my life with you."

"Me too," he agreed, and it was true.

He'd never expected to have a whirlwind romance when he'd left earlier the day before, but here he was, the Tiger King of Manhattan with his own Christmas Bride!

"Merry Christmas," he said and captured her lips one more time before leading the way to his private elevator.

It would be some time before they were alone, so Dean pushed the stop button and showed her just how delightful small spaces and city life could really be.

"Love you, mate."

"I love you," she sighed into his embrace, and Dean forgot everything but her.

Right then, she was the only thing in the world that mattered to him.

As it should be, thought his Tiger approvingly.

T*he end.*

D*id you like this story? Look for more Island Stripe Pride Tales here* http://www.cdgorri.com/series/island-stripe-pride/.

GRIZZLY LOVER

A PURELY PARANORMAL ROMANCE BOOK

BLURB

Teresa broke Oliver's heart once before, but now she needs his help. Can her Grizzly lover put the past behind them?

Oliver Pax is one of the most prolific composers of all time. He is the award-winning writer of such Broadway hits as The Beast of Brooklyn Heights and its upcoming conclusion Where Beauty Lives. A loner known for his grumpy and secretive nature, the reclusive Grizzly Bear Shifter is in for the shock of his life when a blast from his past washes up on his doorstep after a terrible accident.

Teresa Witherspoon has been on the run for the past two years. She's traveled across the country and back again fearing the day her father and his henchmen find her and her son. Caring for Thomas has kept her going this far, but when an accident leaves her hospitalized, she has no choice but to call the one person she swore to stay away from.

Will the Grizzly Bear Shifter she'd once loved help her in her time of need?

PROLOGUE

"Resa," Oliver fisted the note he'd found tucked under the secondhand keyboard he'd just finished paying off.

The instrument sat against one wall of the cramped room, right beside the only window in the small Brooklyn Heights apartment he'd been renting the past six months since he came to the city.

For a Grizzly Bear Shifter used to the wilds of the woods as his backyard, it was quite the change, but he just had to try to see if he could make a go of his music. Oliver had always been gifted with a good ear, but even as a cub, his mother had encouraged him to go and seek his destiny.

Brooklyn Heights was as close to Manhattan as he could afford with his meager savings, but what did money matter anyway? Especially when there was music to be written. The window faced the south brick wall of another small apartment complex identical to his.

It didn't matter what it looked like outside, as long as he was able to breathe some fresh air. At least on the fifth floor, it was somewhat fresher than the heavily congested streets below.

She was gone. His mind registered that fact as he took in the empty room. She'd left.

"No," he growled, and aimed his fist at the tiled counter top, cracking a few of the old ceramic squares in the process. Mrs. Goldstein, the landlady, would be pissed when she saw that.

Oliver's Bear roared inside of him and his heart contracted painfully in his chest. It was worse than being sucker punched by Thor his idiot cousin, who was as big and strong as his namesake. Why would Teresa say such cruel things? He couldn't believe it, couldn't fathom his sweet Resa saying such foul callous words about their relationship. He read the hated missive one more time.

Oliver,

It was fun while it lasted, but even you can't be so naïve as to think I could find true love with a nobody. I just wanted to get back at my father. Don't bother looking for me or calling, I will have already changed my number.

Teresa

Yes, it was her handwriting. He closed his eyes on the wave of anguish that washed over him. Gasping, he sunk to his knees while the beast inside of him roared and stomped his massive claws in fury.

Mate, his Bear cried out, but Oliver refused to answer his other half.

How could she just leave him like this? He'd been so sure of her, of them. He was positive that she loved him too. Being with her was everything to him. She was his fated mate. It was the first time he had ever tasted happiness. A taste that was bitter now that he knew it was all one-sided.

The first time he'd seen the golden-haired beauty, Oliver's Grizzly Bear had stood up and taken notice. The second he'd breathed in her peaches and cream scent, his animal had roared one single word in his mind's eye that would change Oliver's life forever.

Mate.

Following his heart, he'd approached the soft spoken, elegantly dressed Teresa Witherspoon after spying her at the park day after day. She'd sit on one of the cleaner benches and read from a book of seventeenth century cavalier poets.

"You like Lovelace? Looking at you I pictured a Donne fan," Oliver said when he'd finally found the nerve to approach her.

"Spiritualist poetry doesn't appeal as much to me I guess. I like Lovelace and Suckling. They're fun and witty."

"But they're just trying to get in a girl's pants with their poetry. You approve?" he grinned.

"It's not so much the seduction that appeals to me, it's the living in the moment. Carpe diem and all that," she shrugged.

There was something so tragically sad about her that his heart had squeezed in his chest with longing. He'd wanted to make her smile. Heck, he even pretended to stumble in the grass, laid himself flat just to get her to walk over and touch him. And she had, put her soft, long hands right on him to see if he was alright. He'd stolen a kiss and had never looked back. Until now. The dream was over. She'd left him.

Oliver's Bear roared in his grief. That last night they were together, he'd told her the truth about what he was. The fact that there were more things in the world than she had ever imagined.

Oliver Pax had committed a most grievous sin against his Clan. He'd confessed to a normal, a human woman, that he was a Grizzly Bear Shifter.

It was allowed under certain circumstances, like when the woman in question was your fated mate. He'd thought she'd taken it well, after all, they'd made wild, passionate love immediately after. Hell, he'd been so caught up in the moment, he'd marked her with his bite, tying himself to her irrevocably, but now she was gone.

What would become of him? Would he go mad like so many other Shifters who'd lost their mates? He had heard the stories. The tales of broken matings and rogue Shifters who needed to be put down.

Oliver tipped the bottle of whiskey back emptying its fiery contents down his throat. Then he threw the hated thing across the room. Something about the muted violence of the act satisfied his animal's need for savagery. The Bear inside of him wanted to tear the whole world down, but maybe work would be a better outlet, he thought.

Oliver sat down at his banged up keyboard and began to play. He poured out his bruised heart. Wrote lyrics and tied them together with a fairy tale as old as they come. The Beast of Brooklyn Heights was born that day. And the rest, as they say, was history.

CHAPTER 1

A couple of years later...

Cameras flashed as reporters shoved their equipment in his face despite the pouring rain. Oliver Pax did his best to get through them as he attempted to leave the *Madoc Grand Theatre*. The beast in him wanted to snarl and snap his teeth, but these were *normals* and he had to keep the secret of the supernatural world.

It was his duty, and he'd already transgressed on that once before. No, he pushed the thought of her out of his mind. She would not haunt him here. Not tonight.

The buzzards seemed immune to the thunderstorm that was brewing around them, but not Oliver. The scent of ozone had the hair on the back of his neck standing straight up. It was bound to be a nasty one.

He blinked under the bright marquee and grinned despite himself. Chance Madoc had bought and refurbished the old rundown eyesore of a theatre and had turned it into something grand and useful. It was, Oliver had to admit, an amazing old place. The acoustics were simply sublime.

Of course, he'd come straight to Oliver asking him to allow the "golden boy of Broadway" first dibs on producing his latest at the new site. *Surviving On Breadcrumbs*, was a smash hit.

Oliver's newest musical was a retelling of the classic fairytale featuring Hansel and Gretel. In this version, the infamous twins were actually a pair of bounty hunters looking for witches and supernatural creatures in order to hunt them down and kill them. The pair meets out death and violence wherever they go, until Gretel falls in love with a Werewolf, and has a consequential change of heart.

It was a silly thing really, a secret hidden wish of his own, but Oliver would never reveal something so personal. So, he covered it up, with dark humor, and an appropriate amount of blood and gore. Add to it a fantastic musical score that he was told would translate well to film, and bam, a hit was born.

Or so his agent had said once the deal from Hollywood came in just that morning to the little man's unending delight. Whatever. Money, fame, they did not matter. His work was an outlet for his pain and sorrow. Feelings that could lead to much worse if his Bear ever tipped the scales from barely hanging on to his sanity to going rogue.

Oliver worked night and day to make sure that never happened. It was the only way to appease the beast, and to keep his fragile hold on his stability. Thunder cracked and a flash of lightning brightened the crowded walkway that led to the theatre doors. He ignored the gasp of the crowd and stood still like a deer in headlights. For one solitary moment, Oliver thought he'd seen a ghost.

"Smile Pax, you've got another hit on your hand," Chance Madoc slapped him on the back jovially, jogging him from his fancy.

Good thing too, he supposed. Visions like that were dangerous to his health, and to others. Chance nodded at the paparazzi who were trying desperately to get Oliver's attention at that very same moment.

"You know I hate this circus," he snarled at the half-Demon who was also one of his closest friends.

Not that he had very many of those to boast

about. Still, Chance was a fair man. He believed in Oliver when he was new and unknown. Hell, he'd given him a leg up and Oliver never forgot it. A couple of years might be a flash in the pan to most Shifters, but it was a long time in the fickle eyes of fame.

"Why aren't you waiting for your wife?" Oliver asked the man curtly.

Leandra Katrell-Madoc was Chance's mate and wife, not to mention the star of Oliver's first mega hit, *The Beast of Brooklyn Heights.* She was a lovely woman, a supremely talented songstress, and besides that, Oliver liked her. She was spunky and more than fair.

She didn't complain the way most stars did about his notes or direction. Even when he'd asked her to play the Witch in this new show, as opposed to the younger starring role of Gretel. Yes, he liked her. Leandra had integrity. Something far too many people lacked in his not-so-humble opinion.

"She'll be along in a moment. So, where are you with, *Where Beauty Lives*? The pages are late, Pax, that's not like you."

Oliver had been waiting for the question. Chance had been patient, but the half-Demon never failed to mention the fact that Oliver was late with his promised sequel to his retelling of the classic Beauty & the Beast story.

He hadn't meant for it to end so cruelly in *The Beast of Brooklyn Heights*, but his heart had been broken at the time. After reviewers and audiences, the world over had clamored for a sequel, Oliver had finally announced that it was in the works.

That had been a year ago. He figured he owed it to them, and to his characters. They deserved better than how he'd left them. The problem was simple, Oliver was stuck.

Writer's block, that galling game-stopper, that vexatious variable, had hit him hard. Oliver was simply unable to find the perfect end for the tale. He growled softly, careful of the non-supernaturals, the *normals* in the crowd.

He straightened his shoulders. He was no longer the sad young Bear, orphaned in his teens who'd remained solitary and penniless until he finally hit it big. But that was only after he'd arrived in the city to fulfill the destiny his mother had described to him when he was a young cub. After he'd met her and had his whole life turned upside down and inside out.

Oliver had left a part of him behind in Brooklyn Heights. In the wake of the worst heartbreak of his life. Even worse than having to grow up far too soon. He'd spent most of his adult life alone. Away from the Clan of his birth, and with no family of his own. What did he have now?

He had money. He had fame. And he clung to both desperately. Jaw clenched he straightened his shoulders. The tailored suit he wore was like armor to him. The absolute best money could buy, and he had tons of that these days. The vultures circling him could not harm him as long as he remained aloof and in control.

Being a successful composer, playwright, and screenwriter had its perks. He'd worked feverishly the past couple of years and had sold more stories than he'd been expecting. Hollywood loved him and wanted his input on several of their fantasy fairytale retellings. He was Broadway's baby as far as Chance was concerned, not that he enjoyed the moniker one bit.

Still, it allowed him some freedom, he admitted. Oliver could now afford the finer things in life and that included his privacy. He could have anything money could buy.

Unfortunately, it was true what they said. Money could not buy happiness. Neither his human side nor his beast would ever feel that again. The Bear inside him chuffed at the thought. But Oliver would not relent. He could make such a statement with absolute certainty these days.

"You'll have the pages, Chance. I just need some time. I'm going away to my cabin for a few weeks to finish it. Should be ready before the Easter holidays."

"Perfect. And I get it, Pax, sometimes a man needs a little quiet. Say, did you want to do a late dinner with Leandra and me?"

"Uh, no, I-" Oliver was having a hard time concentrating on Chance's words as reporters clamored for his attention.

"Okay, people, enough," Chance waved them away.

"It's fine," he growled.

A few of the crowd moved away from his snarling, but one form did not sway. Oliver blinked slowly. It couldn't be, he shook his head. Great. He was hallucinating.

The vultures were everywhere. Usually, he brought a woman with him to opening night as a sort of armor, but just lately his Grizzly was having a difficult time being around members of the opposite sex. His beast would tolerate no one getting close to him.

The last time he went out with a woman, his date

had mistaken gratitude for an invitation. Oliver had to work way too hard to stop the animal from rising within him and flinging the forward female away. It simply wasn't worth the risk to himself or anyone else.

He looked at the throng and frowned hard. Had his eyes deceived him again? He could have sworn he saw, but no, it was impossible. She couldn't be there. That was twice now, he growled at himself.

"Damn it, do these people have no regard at all for privacy?"

"Come on Oliver, it's part of the job. You know that. Just look at them for a sec and wave, let them get their picture and be done with it," Chance nodded and smiled, and finally, Oliver turned his head to do the same.

They could snap their pictures, but the hell with smiling. It never ceased to amaze him how these fiends all looked the same with their ill-fitting rumpled clothes from hiding in corners and behind bushes to get photos for whatever rags would buy them.

Still, if it sold tickets, he owed that to Madoc, the stars, and the dozens of employees at the theatre. Shows ran for however long they were popular, and newspapers and bloggers helped spread the word.

"Look this way Mr. Pax!"

"Can we get a smile Pax?"

"Ollie?"

His head snapped in the direction of the softly whispered nickname that only one person in the world had ever had the gumption to call him.

"Teresa," he whispered.

Mate, his Bear roared.

"Ollie," she stood over a dozen feet away, but he heard her loud and clear among the shouting crowd.

Oliver's whole body tensed. Feelings he'd worked hard to suppress over the past two years threatened to erupt inside of him like a volcano. His Bear pushed to be let out, to do the things his human side wouldn't, like go to her side.

He watched as her jade green eyes filled with tears. It couldn't be her. Why here? Why now? Anger and hurt welled inside of him.

"Please, Ollie?"

"Pax, who is that woman?" Chance asked him, but Oliver couldn't answer.

"No one," Oliver said hardening his heart to her beauty and his beast's natural impulse to go to her.

The sound of her gasp was heart-wrenching, but he ignored it and her. Painful as it was, Oliver turned his back on the one woman the universe had created just for him. The only woman he'd ever loved and who'd thrown his love back in his face.

Yes, he turned his back on her, but not before he saw her reach out her hand as if to touch him. She retreated as if burnt and brought that very same appendage back to her lips in some vain attempt to try and hold in the sob that had already escaped.

"Pax?"

He shook his head at Chance. There were some things he simply would not discuss. Teresa Witherspoon was one of them. His breathing came deep and heavy as he tried to get control of his internally rampaging Grizzly Bear. He hardly noticed Chance lunge forward.

"Holy shit. Stop! Wait!" Chance yelled, but it was too late a warning.

Oliver turned in time to see the woman who'd broken his heart run from his cruel rejection and straight into oncoming traffic.

The sound of tires squealing on the wet asphalt and the grinding of brakes were nothing compared to the crunch of Teresa Witherspoon hitting the windshield of a yellow cab right outside the theatre.

"No!" he roared as he ran over to her broken and blood-soaked body.

"Ollie," she whispered before closing her eyes.

"No. No. NOOOOOO!"

"Someone call 911," Leandra's voice reached him, but he couldn't look at her or anyone else. His eyes were riveted to the pale face of the woman he held to his chest.

Blood soaked through his ten-thousand-dollar suit, but Oliver couldn't have cared less. The sounds of sirens reached him through the roaring inside his head.

He let go of her reluctantly so the EMT's could do their job, ready to walk away and follow when her hand reached out and grabbed his.

"Get in the back," yelled one EMT above the thunder.

"Go ahead, Oliver, Leandra and I will follow you there," said Chance.

"Yes," Oliver nodded.

The EMTs worked together feverishly hooking her up to all sorts of machinery and some kind of IV drip. Oliver had to fight to stop his Bear from snarling at the men. They were only doing their jobs.

He looked down at the pale hand gripping his so tightly before it suddenly went lax. That moment was the single most terrifying in his life. He felt as though he were in a trance, as if he wasn't really there.

"What is happening?" he asked trying hard not to let despair take him.

"We're losing her," one of them said, "is she your mate?" he added almost imperceptibly. Oliver gave a single nod in response.

"Then you might say something, anything to help bring her back while we work on her, alright?" The soft glow of that one EMT's eyes told Oliver all he needed to know.

The man was a Shifter, like him. He understood the pain and the agony that came with losing a mate, but what he couldn't know was that Oliver had been dealing with that pain for a couple of years now. He'd thought himself immune to her, but he'd been a fool.

It was true, Oliver was the biggest damn fool in the world to think this woman did not matter to him anymore. His Bear roared inside of him and he felt his heart constrict in his chest as the men brought out the defibrillator.

That precious pale hand was so small in his, he wondered how he ever let her go. Her blood pressure dropped, the machine monitoring her heart let out a long single note, and then Oliver knew real pain.

"No! I can't lose her now! Do something!"

"We are. Clear!" yelled one of the strangers.

Oliver watched helplessly as the EMT's worked frantically to get her back. She couldn't turn up again in his life simply to die now. He wouldn't allow it. No, she had to wake up and answer for what she'd done. He needed an explanation. He deserved one.

To hell with all that, his Bear snarled. *Mate!*

"Teresa, come back, come back to me dammit, I won't watch you die!" he yelled, and felt wet tears streaming down his face without embarrassment.

Two years might have passed, but he remembered every single moment of their time together. The way she laughed at his jokes and clung to him during their lovemaking.

She'd been new to passion. A virgin when he'd met her. That precious gift she'd given to him and how he had savored it and her. Dammit! He couldn't watch her die. Not now.

So many nights he'd dreamt about her. The ghost of her had kept him awake for months on end. He'd written scores about it. Musicals and movies describing his longing and his hurt.

The critics called his unrequited love stories angsty and unfinished. He supposed they were. Just like him.

"Come on, Resa! Wake up, dammit! Fight, you fight and you tell me why you've come back now! Wake up!" he roared.

"We have a pulse," the Shifter EMT smiled and nodded his head.

"Thank God," Oliver breathed and pressed his forehead to hers.

Mate, chuffed his Bear.

CHAPTER 2

Teresa's entire body felt as if she were on fire. Like that burning sensation of pins and needles in your back when you cough too hard or hold your breath for too long.

What happened? Where was she?

She opened her eyes and blinked against the harsh fluorescent lights. The acrid smells of cleaning detergent and disinfectant made her want to gag, but there was something in her mouth preventing her from doing so.

"Easy, don't fight the tube, it is helping you breathe," said a deep, rumbly voice next to her head.

It was familiar, and so welcomed she wanted to cry and smile at the same time. Her thoughts were hazy, even she recognized that. Teresa tried to move to see the owner of that voice, but she couldn't.

What the heck? A deep throbbing ache pulsed from her ribs and her shoulders. An accident of some kind? She recalled the sounds of wheels spinning on asphalt and the crunch of broken glass.

Crap. She blinked slowly, willing herself to calm. Then *he* came into view, and her heart started pounding once more inside her chest as panic took hold.

Ollie.

Deep brown eyes so dark they sometimes looked black stared at her from a face so handsome and familiar, so loved and missed that she could hardly breathe. His hair was shorter and his beard longer now, but she would know him anywhere.

He'd gotten older, more cynical, but she was probably to blame for that. It didn't matter, he was still handsomer than any other man in the universe as far as she was concerned.

Oliver Pax. His name lit up inside her brain like a neon sign. It all came pouring back to her in a storm of memories overwhelming every other thought. She couldn't stop the echoes of the past from filling the space between her ears.

Two long years since she'd last seen him, lying asleep in the bed where they'd made the sweetest love and created a life he didn't know about.

Thomas! Her son. Their son. Teresa had to get back to him. She tried sitting up, but Oliver pressed her back into the bed with a firm, yet gentle hand on her shoulder.

"You can't move yet, Resa. You're hooked up to a million machines here. Calm down, okay? I'll call a nurse," he went to move but she grabbed his hand.

Just then a strange man and woman came into the room. Panic rose and once more she struggled to sit up, he quirked an eyebrow at her. His expression hard and curious. She couldn't blame him. Not after what she'd done.

"Oliver?" the woman said his name and ran to him.

She embraced him in a quick little hug that made the darkness inside of Teresa rise up in jealousy. No, she told the thing and furiously beat it back to the cell where she'd trapped it. She visualized the hard iron bars until the dark thing inside of her quieted once more.

"Pax, is she okay?" the man said.

He was handsome, she supposed, with neatly

combed hair and an easy smile, but he had nothing on her Ollie. Except, he wasn't her Ollie anymore.

Yes, she could have had a life with him once, but she'd given that up in order to protect him. Not that he knew about any of that. It didn't matter now. Only Thomas did.

"She is awake," the woman had a nice face, and a pleasing smile, "we were so worried. I'm Leandra and this is my husband Chance. We work with Oliver. I found your purse in the street and brought it with me," she said, and held up the tattered canvas tote Teresa had been using as a pocketbook for some time now.

To think she'd once donned the latest in fashion trends. She'd had her choice of haute couture hanging in her closets and the shoes and accessories to match. Nowadays, it was thrift stores and garage sales for Teresa.

She didn't mind as long as that meant she had more for Thomas. Her sweet boy was growing like a weed these days. His solid little toddler body seemed to need new clothes and shoes every few weeks.

Thomas. Her boy needed her. It was why she'd sought out Oliver to begin with. She hated herself for the secret she'd kept for so long, but now she knew there was something wrong with her.

Something had finally risen after she'd escaped from her father's and Witherspoon Tech's strange experiments. She needed help protecting Thomas and who better than his father?

"I see our patient is awake," a man in a white coat came in and she looked hard to see if she recognized him from her father's labs.

She couldn't be sure, so she waited seemingly complacent. The so-called doctor smiled and asked everyone to leave the room to which she violently shook her head.

"Oh, I think we'll stay," said the woman, Leandra, with a smile that didn't quite reach her eyes.

Teresa decided right then and there to like her. Oliver stood closer to her bed, and the man, Chance, mimicked his position on the other side of her. She watched the doctor and saw anger in his eyes before he placed a fake smile on his face once more.

"Alright then I will be right back with some medicine," he ducked out of the room.

The second he was gone, Teresa sat up and yanked the tube out of her mouth despite the cries of the three in her room. She coughed and held her throat. It would stop in a moment, another side effect of her father's madness. Teresa was a fast healer. Like magically fast.

"Teresa?" Oliver wore his concern on his sleeve and for that her heart swelled with a long since felt emotion.

"Ollie," she gasped, her voice rough from the tube, "we have to go now. That man is not a doctor. Have to leave."

"What?"

"I'm in trouble. Please," her eyes pleaded with him to believe her.

To her surprise he nodded his head and looked from her to his friend. Chance and Leandra nodded and the woman smiled at Teresa.

"Go, take her with you, Oliver. Get her to safety and then let us know where you are," Leandra said and started removing her coat. She handed it over to Teresa along with her jeans and a pair of white sneakers.

"I'll wear Chance's coat. You just put these on, here Chance give her your tie, she'll need it as a belt."

The slightly curvier woman giggled and helped Teresa don her haphazard outfit. It was perfect. She impulsively hugged the woman before leaving.

"Thank you," Teresa said.

"He's coming back, let's go the other way," Oliver grabbed her hand and pulled her along down the corridor.

Once outside, he flagged down a cab and closed the door.

"Where to?" the cabbie asked.

"High Falls Towers-"

"No, we have to go to 201-B Allen Street, please," she sat up and gave the cabbie the directions to the apartment she'd been sharing with a young would-be actress.

"Why there?"

"Ollie, there is a lot you don't know-"

"Oliver. My name is Oliver," he corrected her and her stomach flipped.

"Okay, Oliver then. Look, I have a lot to tell you. I don't expect you to just forgive and forget but believe me when I say I need your help," her voice cracked at the end and she bit the inside of her mouth to stop from crying.

She didn't expect pity, hell, she didn't even deserve it. But this was bigger than her. It was bigger than them both.

"Can you wait?" she asked the cab driver who nodded his head.

"Teresa, where are we going?"

"I have to get something first, then can you get me out of town?"

"Yes," he nodded. Just like that.

"How are you feeling?" Oliver squinted at her as she took the stairs to the second floor two at a time.

"I'm fine," she shrugged.

"You have five broken ribs and a fractured clavicle," he said.

"They must've been mistaken," she said.

"I saw the scans, Teresa," he said and grabbed her arm.

"I will explain, but we have to move fast. Please," she insisted.

She hated keeping it from him, but she needed to get to her son first. It wasn't fair to keep it a secret, the darkness inside her, even as it healed her quickly, was something that was growing and would soon take over. She couldn't risk hurting her son.

Oliver had to keep him safe. Besides, like father like son. Teresa knew Thomas was a Shifter like his dad. The boy already showed signs. Oliver could teach their boy how to control his own Bear.

Oliver had told her everything back when they were together. He'd confided his wondrous secret of being a Shifter when they were carefree and in love. Back before she'd known the truth about her father and his nefarious deeds.

"You seem *different,*" he said and followed her down the hall.

"I know and I will explain, but first I think you need to prepare yourself," she started.

"For what?"

"Ollie, I have a-"

Before she could finish her sentence the door to the apartment burst open and the almost two-year old whirlwind also known as Thomas Pax came crashing into her legs, nearly toppling her to the ground.

"Mommy!!!" her boy shouted and rained a dozen sloppy precious little kisses on her cheeks when she'd scooped him up.

"Hello, sweet boy," she rubbed her nose against his and winced a little as his very-big-for-his-age forty-pound body wriggled in her arms hitting any one of the bruises she had left from the accident.

"Mommy's late! Nancy sleepin'."

"She is? How did you know I was here?"

"Sniffed ya, Mommy," he giggled.

"You did, huh?" she smiled at her curly-haired son and breathed a sigh of relief that he was with her and safe.

"Teresa?" Oliver's near black eyes met hers and she knew he'd scented the truth without words.

"Mommy, who's the man?" Thomas whispered loudly as most children his age tended to do.

"Thomas, this is Oliver Pax."

"My name Pax. Thomas Pax!"

"Yes, it is, sweet boy. Oliver, this is Thomas. He's our son."

CHAPTER 3

Oliver's chest squeezed painfully around that useless organ that dwelt inside. A son? He had a son.

Too many emotions to count raged through him as he took in the dark haired little boy who had the same brown eyes and stubborn chin as him. This was his boy, his son.

Our cub, corrected his Grizzly Bear, and all he needed was one sniff to scent the truth in both words.

He smelled the familiar deep pine forest scent that was his own with a bit of peaches and some sunshine thrown in. Oliver smiled. The small cub was his and he was a Shifter too.

He could scent the fur beneath the skin and even

that was strange. Most Shifters did not have their first transformation until after puberty, but this young cub's seemed much closer than that.

"I need to get our bags from the closet, can you stay here with your Daddy?"

"Uh huh, hi Daddy," said Thomas.

He looked up at Oliver curiously. Fear and apprehension were both absent, which immediately had Oliver's previously unknown paternal pride soaring to ridiculous heights. The boy was brave. So fragile and new, his paternal instincts came rushing forward and regardless of what had happened in the past he knew he would do anything for his son.

"Hello, Thomas," he greeted his cub.

Not the bells and whistles, triumphant introduction of a prolific composer to his long-lost progeny, but what else could he say. A few minutes ago he hadn't even known the child existed.

"The bad men comin'?" the boy, *his son* asked.

His inner Grizzly snarled at the words. What bad men dared threaten his young? That could wait though.

Oliver crouched in front of his cub. He wanted the toddler to be able to look at the strange man who was his father, to see him eye to eye so that he could gauge the truth himself.

"Thomas, I promise no more bad men. I will protect you. Always."

"Mommy too?"

Oliver looked up and saw Teresa standing there, holding her breath. She placed the two suitcases she was holding on the floor and bent to scoop Thomas up before he had a chance to answer the boy.

"That's enough questions, buddy, come on," she said, and smiled brightly at the child despite the tears in her eyes.

"I'll get those," Oliver said and reached for the two small suitcases before Teresa could try to lift them.

Despite what she said about being fine, he saw her wince when she lifted their son. He stopped and swallowed. It was a momentous occasion after all. Those two small words were now suddenly a part of his vocabulary.

My son, he thought with wonder as he preceded the mother and cub down the hall.

Even though she would not let him answer Thomas's question, Oliver would always protect her and their cub with everything he had inside of him. That meant with all the strength of his Grizzly Bear.

The beast inside of him chuffed and grumbled at the idea that the two most important beings in the world to him, that his precious and newfound family, were in danger. He didn't know what they were running from, but that wasn't important. He would see them safe, then he would get answers.

Grrr.

After they'd reached his apartment, Oliver directed them to the parking garage and to his fully equipped black Range Rover. He was already packed for the trip up to his cabin deep in the woods behind Indian Lake in upstate New York.

"We're not going upstairs?" inquired Teresa, and Oliver just shook his head.

"It's a long ride, you might want this," he handed her a small travel pillow and blanket that he had in the trunk from the last time he'd driven up there with Terrence and Daisy.

Terrence was an exceptionally talented Broadway director, and one of Oliver's only friends along with Chance. He was also a Vampire and had recently mated a human woman by the name of Daisy who had a penchant for growing things. She'd been thrilled to come up to the cabin to explore the native flora, but in her delicate condition had required naps along the four-hour drive.

"Sleepy," mumbled Thomas who was already close to dozing in his mother's arms.

"Does he need a car seat?" Oliver stopped in his tracks.

"It's fine. This model has a built-in booster," she smiled.

It wasn't a coincidence that Oliver had bought Teresa's favorite car. It was one of those things he'd almost forgotten in their many silly little conversations they'd had about everything and nothing.

"He's big enough to sit in the booster with the seat belt on," she said softly.

Oliver held the door to the back of the SUV open while Teresa leaned down to open the booster then placed the precious cub on the plush leather interior. He watched as she competently buckled him in and checked to make sure he was secure before propping the pillow on the backpack he'd brought with him filled with his toys and things only a child would find important.

Teresa tucked a lock of thick glossy brown hair behind the child's ear and rubbed the lobe. He was so small and innocent. Clearly, she cared for him a great deal. He could see it in the way she touched his forehead and dropped a kiss on his plump cheek, then covered him with the fluffy fleece blanket Daisy had left behind. He was grateful now that she had.

Teresa moved to climb in next to Thomas, but

Oliver stopped her with a hand on her elbow. Even that simple platonic touch was enough to make his Bear growl and his heart thump heavily inside his chest.

He wanted her, he realized, and accepted it for the fact it was. She was his one true and fated mate. Desire was a byproduct. He'd known it the second he'd spied her reading in the park the very first time. Fresh as a spring flower just ready to bloom, she'd stolen his heart, then she ran away with it. The cut of her betrayal was still raw despite the passage of time and he tightened his hold momentarily before releasing her.

"Sit in the front," he muttered the gruff order before turning his back on her.

Surprisingly, Teresa obeyed him. She took the long way around and eased into the passenger seat, wincing gingerly when she fastened her seatbelt over her ribs. They must still be bruised. The truth of her rather quick recovery bothered him as did the odd hint of something *other* in her natural peaches and cream fragrance.

"You want answers, I'm sure," she said in a quiet voice without any emotional inflection apparent.

How can she be so calm when my heart is beating like

a thousand drums and my brain feels like it's about to explode?

He shook his head and started the vehicle. The tank was full and a small cooler with sandwiches and drinks was packed. It sat on the floor at her feet.

"Pass me a water, please," he pointed at the cooler and watched her fulfill his request slowly.

Shit. He'd forgotten her injury already.

"Sorry, I shouldn't have asked you to get that."

"No, it's fine," she handed him the bottle and he gestured for her to take one for herself, which she did.

She drank thirstily, finishing the entire thing before she pulled it from her plump pink lips. He'd been hypnotized by that bee-stung mouth of hers from the first. He knew from experience just how soft and warm those lips were. How they tasted like her scent, fresh peaches with sweet cream to be savored under a warm spring sun.

Oliver swallowed his water along with the bitterness of his memories. Whatever was going on, Teresa definitely owed him more than she'd said so far. He glanced in the rearview mirror at his sleeping son and his beast rumbled.

Mine.

Whether he meant the cub or the woman beside

him, Oliver wasn't sure. He had the feeling his animal was laying claim to both. Unfortunately, he didn't know if he had it in him to be rejected again. He might not survive it this time around.

"He is my son."

It was a statement. Oliver waited a beat before looking at the woman who'd turned his world upside down then tore it to shreds when she'd left him with a single callously scrawled note.

"Yes. He is our son."

"When?"

"I think he was conceived the last time we," she swallowed, "uh, it was just after Christmas. Anyway, he was born early, the second of May."

"Shifter pregnancies are usually a few months less than normal ones. Did you have any difficulty?"

"At first, you see I didn't know I was pregnant, and my father, well," she was grasping her hands tightly together.

The scent of her anxiety was making his own beast want to hunt something down and kill it, whatever it was that had made her so afraid. That sounded fine to his Bear. Hunt, kill, protect.

"What? I knew so little about your home life. Other than the fact you're the heiress to the great man Mathias Witherspoon himself-"

"My father is not a great man," she said angrily, "my father is a madman who experimented on his own child. He injected me with something, I don't know what it was, but it's bad, Oliver."

"What? Teresa what are you saying?" he gripped the steering wheel tightly in his hands.

"Witherspoon Tech isn't just making applications for medical research and development. They have a research facility, a secret one. And I don't know how, but my father knows about your kind."

"What do you mean? Did you tell him?"

"No," she gasped, "I would never betray you like that."

"Oh no? You left me, Teresa, I can't think of any worse betrayal than that," he sneered before he could stop himself.

"I know. I don't expect you to believe me , but he threatened to put you in a cage. I couldn't allow that, Oliver. And no, I didn't tell him, he had video of you in the woods."

"What?"

"Our one camping trip we took out of the city. He had me followed. Look, he knows and he did something to me after I left you, I let him do it. I wanted to protect you, but I am so scared now. Whatever he did, it was bad, Ollie, I mean Oliver," her frightened words reached his ears over the hum of the engine.

"What are you saying exactly?"

"I have something bad inside of me, Ollie," she whimpered and cleared her throat, "I have it locked down right now, and yes, I know I sound like a crazy person, but I am telling you the truth. I'm scared, Oliver, for Thomas' sake. I don't know if I can keep it under control much longer," she whispered that last bit.

Oliver turned his head briefly to look at her as they made their way towards the bridge that would take them out of Manhattan. Her ashen face was like a knife to his heart, as was the stoic way she swallowed her tears. She looked at him with her head held high. She always was brave when he'd expected her to cower. Like the first time he'd shown her his Bear in an effort to stop her from seeing him.

Oliver thought he was doing the noble thing, but she'd walked right up to his thousand-pound animal and petted him like a dog. Stupid Bear went belly up for her. Even now, she still was brave, despite the fact he didn't have a clue what she was talking about.

She faced him like a stowaway about to walk the plank, he thought as he watched resignation leak into her gaze. She clenched her jaw, eyes darting to the cub who sat sleeping in the rear seat before returning to him again.

"I won't bother to explain why I did what I did. It's enough that you trust me so far as to take us out of the city and away from Witherspoon Tech. Some of my father's men spotted me this week and I can't be sure but that ER doc didn't seem legit," she shrugged.

"There was something off about him," Oliver muttered and turned his head to the street in front of him.

It was nearing on two o'clock in the morning, but he was wide awake. She'd given him a lot of food for thought, and there was his Bear to deal with the animal couldn't understand his reticence. All the beast knew was that he had his mate within reach and he wanted to hold on tightly to her.

He tried to refocus on the reasons he should stay away, to keep his heart distant, but it was a losing battle. Even a Grizzly couldn't take on the Fates. Oliver inhaled a deep breath, allowing the subtle sweetness of her scent to invade his senses.

He knew the exact moment Teresa succumbed to sleep in the quiet interior of the vehicle. All tension left her bruised body, and she slumped away from him, her head resting on the cool window. She looked so small and tired.

Oliver frowned, but he made no move to touch her. Still, he didn't want her uncomfortable. Concern got the best of him, and he took off his suit jacket and draped it over her, keeping one hand on the wheel at all times. After all, he was hauling precious cargo.

The fact that he was a father astounded him. Pride, love, sadness, and anger warred within him for dominance. He was sad that he'd missed even a second of his sweet little cub's life. He was angry that Teresa had run from him, but he wasn't quite sure if that anger was directed at her or the monsters, real or imaginary, that she was still running from.

He decided to settle on the love he felt for Thomas. His heart swelled with the irrational feeling, almost impossibly so. He felt like the Grinch at the end of the story, when his heart grew so large it burst through the measuring slide. How could he love someone so much that he just met?

Easy, his Bear answered, *ours.*

His feelings toward the cub's mother were a bit more complicated. Teresa was his fated mate, there was no denying that, but it was impossible to just forget the hurt and pain she'd caused him. Was he big enough to let all that go? He supposed he would have to wait and see what the rest of her explanation was when they got to the cabin, and what her plans for the future were.

Mate, said his Grizzly Bear.

The animal inside of him didn't seem to care about the past, only that she was with him now, and his furry beastie had no intentions of letting her go a second time around.

Mine.

CHAPTER 4

Oliver stopped at the last gas station and minimart before they reached the mountain and his log cabin. It was just after five o'clock in the morning and the air was nippy but typical for early spring.

"Resa," he called her by the nickname he'd given her back when they were together, and watched in fascination as she slowly blinked those creamy jade green eyes up at him with a small smile on her face.

That soft expression lasted all of a few seconds before the hard mask fell once more and she shot up too fast. He felt guilty when she winced against the pain such a fast movement had surely sent through her healing bones.

"Are we there yet?" she asked.

"No, I just wanted to ask if you needed anything? I am stopping for some perishables before we head up to my cabin."

"A cabin? Oh, um, I have some money," she started rummaging through her jeans, and shame welled up inside of him.

"I have money," he said, "just tell me what you need."

"Thomas likes orange juice and milk, um, eggs, bacon, sausage, and wheat bread. Peanut butter and honey with bananas," she whispered.

"That's my favorite," Oliver said and watched in amazement at the pink blush that spread across her face.

Still lovely after everything that had happened, he thought. Without meaning to, Oliver reached out with his hand and touched her wan cheek. His heart pounded with feeling as she pressed her soft, warm skin against his palm. He narrowed his eyes at her and, as if he'd been burned, he took his hand away.

"I'll get everything," he said and cleared his throat, "lock the doors till I get back," he left the car running just outside the entrance to the minimart.

It was still early and no one else was there, but he wanted Teresa and their son in his line of vision at all times. Oliver entered the tiny, but adequate store and waved hello to Mr. Barad, the owner and proprietor of both the station and the small mini-mart. He walked down the store's four aisles gathering supplies, stopping suddenly at a small stand displaying a variety of cheap but cute children's toys.

He pursed his lips before grabbing a couple of plastic play cars and some coloring books and crayons. He added two gallons of milk, three cartons of fresh squeezed orange juice, and as many packages of butter, eggs, bacon, and sausage that he could fit in his basket. He also grabbed some bags of salad, broccoli, carrots, onions, potatoes, tomatoes, and peppers. A boy needed his veggies.

Oliver had plenty of peanut butter and honey at the cabin already. Along with other non-perishables he used for cooking. At the checkout counter, he added four loaves of sliced wheat bread to finalize his order.

"Will that be all?" Mr. Barad asked as he started ringing up the items.

Oliver nodded and took out some cash, for some reason a little voice inside of him told him to forego paying with his credit card. Whatever. He grabbed his bags and walked to the back of his Range Rover waiting for the telltale click of the lock.

He settled the bags safely inside the spacious

trunk, snug against their luggage and the cardboard box containing his work. He'd forgotten he was heading out to the cabin to finish the score for *Where Beauty Lives*.

"How much longer is it to your place?" Teresa asked.

"About forty minutes. My cabin is just behind the lake."

"Are there lots of people around?"

"Hmm? No. I like my privacy. There's a woman who lives up there year-round. Her home is about a fifteen-minute walk through the woods from my place. Everything else would take over half an hour by foot and longer by car."

"I'm sorry we're intruding on your privacy, Oliver."

"I have a son, Teresa, he is no intrusion. I want to get to know him."

"I see. Well, thank you, it means a lot."

"We will figure something out. I have a lawyer who handles my contracts and I am sure he can recommend a family lawyer to come up with some kind of custody agreement-"

A sob tore from her throat, and he looked up in shock to see her face buried in her hands. Noise from the backseat had his eyes glance to see Thomas stirring. Teresa must have heard it too because she covered her mouth tighter and slowed down her gasping.

"Mommy?"

"Yes, honey?" she answered the cub with false brightness, but Oliver still gave her points for trying.

Damn. He was a callous ass for bringing up custody. Especially when that wasn't what his Bear wanted him to say at all.

"You sad, Mommy?"

"No, honey boy, of course not. Look outside, see all the trees," she distracted their sweet cub who *ooohed* and *aaahed* for the next few minutes while playing *I Spy* with his mother.

The bags under her eyes and frown lines around her mouth, though taking nothing from her beauty, they also did nothing to appease his guilt. Oliver felt like an even bigger douchebag now for bringing up lawyers. His Bear grunted angrily inside him.

This was new territory for him, but he supposed it was for her as well. He made a mental note to apologize once they were settled and turned his attention to the narrow road that led to his cabin.

He'd purposely had it built into the landscape to discourage random stalkers, and yes, he did have some, from trying to find him. The address was unlisted, buried beneath several aliases and corporations so as to be untraceable to Oliver.

What could he say? He was a Bear who appreciated solitude. The air was nippy for spring, but it was to be expected at this altitude. Still, he hoped Teresa had packed appropriately.

Hell. It was thoughts like that one there that was going to wreak havoc in his life. When was the last time he'd cared about someone other than himself?

Oliver growled, ignoring her questioning stare, and turned into the semi-circle driveway. There were still patches of snow on the rocky ground. Combined with the buds on the trees, it looked as if mother nature had yet to make up her mind on what season it was. Typical for the Northeast, he supposed.

He'd worked with the architect on the design for the log cabin so that it would be inconspicuous and yet maintain the standard of luxury he was newly accustomed to. What could he say? Even Grizzlies liked their creature comforts.

"Wow," Teresa gasped as she took in the rustic looking two-story structure.

"I need to unlock the door, then I'll get the bags," he said and exited the vehicle.

Oliver had the latest state-of-the-art tech in security systems. *Draco Fortis* made the best. The company was owned and operated by a rare Dragon Shifter with exceptional skills and powers that he infused into all of his designs. The Falk brothers also happened to be fans of Oliver's work and the youngest, Nikolai, had installed the system himself just to get a chance to meet him. It was flattering and he welcomed the opportunity to visit with the unique and rare Dragon.

Oliver opened the sleek security pad that was hidden under a cut-out piece of log like the rest of the entire exterior, and he pressed his thumb to the reader before entering a secret passcode. After that, he used a standard key to unlock the massive wood door. Once inside, he activated the smart cabin using the touchscreen that was recessed into the wall.

Immediately, his generator started and electricity began to hum throughout the building. He was proud to say he'd also utilized wind and solar panels that stored energy into backup batteries to give power to the cabin. Oliver quickly pressed commands to start the central heat and he lit the fireplace, while switching the lights on. He swallowed nervously.

A woman, not any woman, *Teresa Witherspoon*, his runaway mate was about to enter his home away from home and oddly enough, he wanted her to like it. He straightened his shoulders and shook his head. What the hell was wrong with him? He walked back to the SUV, nodding at her to go in and went to the back to begin unloading the bags.

He tried not to notice the curve of her shapely body as she bent and took Thomas out of his seat. He was definitely sick for taking pleasure in her rounded bottom in her condition. His chest rumbled and he shushed his inner Bear.

"Mommy, forest!" the cub laughed and pointed at the tall pine trees and a single red cardinal that peeked out at him from one of the limbs.

"Yes, baby," she said and held his hand while he navigated the three steps to the open front door, slowly and carefully, "Thomas, easy does it," she said when he tried to run.

"Hungry," he said and rubbed his tummy.

"Alright, now let's sit at the table and I'll get you something to eat," Teresa spoke to him gently and he approved.

Oliver listened to the cue and grabbed the grocery bags first. He walked into the kitchen and almost tripped at what he saw there. Teresa settling Thomas on one of the tall counter chairs and licking her thumb to wipe a smudge from his nose. He snorted.

"What?" she asked mid-swipe.

"Nothing," he smirked, "it's just such a mom thing to do."

"Oh," she grinned back, "sorry."

"This Mommy," Thomas said and tilted his cherubic face to the side as if questioning Oliver's sanity.

"Yes, Thomas that is your Mommy. Do you know who I am?"

"Daddy," he bit his lip and waited, uncertain of Oliver's response.

"That's right," he said and crouched down to eye level with the boy, "I am your father."

Oliver watched as the boy cocked his head to the other side and his brown eyes deepened to near black. Oliver heard the chuff and whine of the child's young Bear and his own animal rose to respond to his cub for a brief poignant second. But how could that be?

His eyes darted to Teresa's and he saw her biting her lower lip. She was scared, that was obvious, and he wanted to snarl and roar once again to protect her.

"*Grisle* Bear likes you," Thomas said in a whisper.

"Grizzly, Thomas, it's Grizzly Bear, and that's good cause I like him too," Oliver said patiently.

"Hungry, Mommy, want dippy eggs," he blinked up at his mother, his Bear momentarily pushed aside.

"Me too," Oliver winked and stood, turning to Teresa who had started unpacking the groceries.

"Is it alright if I put these away and make something?"

"Of course, make yourself at home. I'll get the rest of the things."

Oliver vaguely registered the background noise of Teresa cooking in his kitchen. That was a marvel in and of itself, but he was distracted by another obvious and unusual truth.

Thomas, his cub, was a Shifter like him. Now, typically Shifters did not experience their first transformation until puberty. The child couldn't be more than two-years old, though age was difficult to tell in a Shifter baby since they grew more rapidly than normal children. Still, his Bear was very near to the surface. The boy could possibly have his first change a lot sooner than was usual.

He needed to call Jennifer. The Owl Shifter woman was the oldest creature he knew at over six-hundred years, though she didn't look a day over thirty. She lived in the forest near his cabin year-round and he knew her to be connected to some secret Shifter agencies that worked with keeping their secret from being outed to the rest of society.

Jennifer would know just how rare a thing it was for a young cub to be so close to his Bear, and she could possibly tell Oliver what to do. Besides, he could use other advice as well. Like on what he should do with Teresa. Plus, he'd brought the supplies she'd asked him for so that was a good excuse to call her for a visit. Maybe they could all go. Thomas would like to walk through the woods, he was sure.

The image the thought conjured up made his chest swell. Oliver had been alone so long, but now he had something he'd only ever dreamed of. A family.

That is, he had a son for certain, but whether or not Teresa would want to stick around was an unknown. Could he trust her even if she said she would stay?

Mate, his Bear once more supplied the answer, but Oliver was still unsure.

CHAPTER 5

"I finished washing the dishes and pans from breakfast, and Thomas is taking a nap in the bedroom you suggested. I thought, maybe now we could talk?" Teresa had spent an extra fifteen minutes washing the dishes just to build her courage to approach him.

Gosh, he was so handsome. More so now than he'd been back when she had first known him. Oliver Pax, the man himself, was as tall and wide as ever. Big as a house with taut muscles cording his enormous frame, smooth skin, usually bronzed from his time outdoors, was still a little on the pale side from the long, harsh winter they'd experienced.

He wore his beard close-cropped but thicker and longer than before, and his dark hair was shorter. He used to keep it a bit more shaggy, but she supposed that was more from it not mattering to him at the time. He looked more polished now.

His teeth were white and straight, and his chiseled features more emphasized by the expensive new hair-do. It was obvious he had become a success, even if she hadn't read all about him in every article and blog she could get her hands on over the past two years.

But his eyes are still the same, she thought as she inhaled the deep woodsy scent that she'd always attributed to him. Those rich brown orbs resembled freshly ground coffee beans with a dash of magical sparkle thrown in. Whenever his Bear was close to the surface they darkened impossibly so, to near black but they were not cold like the word implied. They were rich and warm, like molten dark chocolate.

Sigh. Teresa had given up her virginity staring into those bottomless velvet brown pools. She'd always known he was different, special somehow. Just like she'd always known she would love him until the day she died.

Oh, Oliver, her heart squeezed painfully in her chest. Looking into his now cold eyes, she couldn't help but remember how it used to be. How they'd once glittered in the darkness full of passion and love for her. She'd felt so safe, so cared for when she was in his arms. When he told her his secret she'd cried tears of joy. Just knowing real magic existed in this sometimes cruel world had given her so much hope.

Hope that she could end the nightmare that was her homelife. Her father had gone from distant and cold to intrusive and cruel once she'd started dating Oliver. She tried, oh how she tried, to keep it from him, but the man had her followed on more than once occasion.

She had to tell Oliver the truth now. All of it. She had no other choice. Thomas's life depended on it. Swallowing back her fears, she took one last look at the closely guarded expression on his gorgeous face. How many nights had she gone to bed sobbing into her pillow, tears in her eyes and pictures of him floating around in her head? It didn't matter now. Only Thomas mattered.

"Well?" he looked up from the sheet music in his hands.

The sight of Oliver writing music was nothing new. He seemed to always be working back in Brooklyn Heights and she used to love watching him. Amazed that he'd tolerated her presence while he captured the beautiful music in his brain on paper and recordings. There was none of that forbearance in him now. She shivered at the sharp note in his voice.

His eyes flashed behind her, concern on his face, and she warmed to him once more. It was obvious he was worried about their son, obvious he cared for their sweet baby as she'd always known he would.

Wow. She'd never expected to be able to even think those words much less say them. She inhaled a deep breath allowing the familiar forest scent of him to fill her nostrils. She opened her mouth slowly, taking the chance to utter those words aloud. Finally.

"Our son is special, Oliver, he's growing very fast, much more advanced than any human children," she watched him swallow down that fact, "he is bright and strong, and so very precious to me. You have to know I would do anything, hell, I would die to protect him."

"Teresa," he started, but she didn't allow him to finish the thought, she used the moment to take the chair across from him.

"I know this is not easy for you, Oliver. Believe it or not, it isn't easy for me either, but I need to say it. What I am about to tell you is going to sound mad, and you may not want to believe it, but I swear on my life it's the truth," she closed her eyes for a moment, the thing inside of her was riding her hard, and she had to work even harder to shut it down.

"I heard some of your story, Teresa, and I suppose it is only fair to warn you before you go down this road that Shifters like me can pick up on certain things with our supernaturally enhanced senses, like emotions, heightened pulse, even a rise in blood pressure," he quirked one eyebrow as he spoke, and Teresa couldn't help but think he was cute when he was being all arrogant.

Sigh. She'd been talked down to most of her life by one man or another. It was one reason she'd fallen so hard so fast for Oliver. He didn't treat her like an idiot. Until now.

"In other words," she looked right into his deep chocolate-colored eyes, "I shouldn't bother lying, is that it?"

"That's right," he said in a gravelly voice.

God, how she missed that about him. Oliver had the deepest, sexiest voice she'd ever heard. Especially when his Bear was pushing him as his majestic beast surely was now. She could only imagine why. The animal probably hated her for her abandonment.

The very thought brought a stab of pain straight through her heart.

"I didn't know it then, but back when we were seeing each other my father was having me followed."

"You said that, but why would he do that?"

"A million reasons I suppose, but mainly to control me," she swallowed.

It was difficult to reveal this side of her life to him. Back then, she'd brushed aside all his inquiries about her home life, choosing to remain firmly in the comfort of his presence. It was so much better than thinking about her father and his maniacal attempt to control every aspect of her life.

"He found out, Ollie," she slipped, calling him by the nickname she'd given him back when he used to smile at her, before she left him thinking their relationship had been some trifle when in reality it had meant the world to her. Ollie she wanted to still be able to call him that. Her Ollie. But he'd corrected her that morning. He wasn't her Ollie anymore. He was Oliver.

The flare of his nostrils and slight widening of his eyes made her own breath catch in her throat, but by the time she blinked that look was gone. Maybe she'd imagined it.

Teresa would give anything for him to look at her the way he used to even if just for a moment. She closed her eyes and shook away the silly wish. She needed to remain focused on what she had to say.

Lord knew, she wouldn't get through this if she started thinking about all her regrets and longings. There were just too many and too much time had passed for that. She had Thomas to consider now. With that in mind, Teresa took a fortifying breath and moved on.

"Witherspoon Tech has been working in collaboration with some secret organization, I don't know what they are called, but I found messages signed or not signed exactly, but stamped with the image of a beetle on the bottom."

"What are you talking about?"

She huffed out a breath in frustration. The truth was she didn't have enough information on all the nefarious deeds of her father, but she knew it was bad. The fact that he had never stopped hunting her and her son, that he wanted to put sweet Thomas in a cage, frightened her more than anything else in the world.

"My father is into something truly evil, Oliver. He wants to study Shifters, and not for anything good. After the last night I spent with you, his men grabbed me just outside your apartment when I'd gone to catch a taxi. They brought me to him and he was horrible. He threatened you," her voice cracked as she lost herself in the memory.

Her father's steel eyes glittered at her wildly in the confines of his home office. Unfamiliar in his rage and revulsion, Teresa recoiled each time he raised his hand. He slapped her hard across her face and she tasted blood inside her mouth. She'd bitten the inside of her cheek with that last hit. Teresa begged him to stop, cowering on the floor in confusion at his apparent hatred of his only child.

"You little slut! How could you bed an animal! Just like your mother. You're no Witherspoon!"

"Father, please!"

She'd cried and begged. He did stop hitting her, but then he did something much worse. Nodding at someone behind her, Teresa found herself soon bound to a chair and forced to write a note to Oliver callously ending their relationship.

Afterwards, he had her taken to a secret lab where his henchmen took her blood and gave her a series of injections. Once she discovered her pregnancy, she was able to bribe one of the guards to release her. All she had to do was give the man the numbers to one of her father's bank accounts. After that, she ran.

"I couldn't go back to you, he would have been

watching. I had to protect you and the life growing inside of me," Teresa blinked at the paper towel that was thrust in front of her face.

She'd been so lost in the memory that she didn't even realize she'd been crying. Oliver was kneeling beside her. His concerned expression made the tears fall harder, and she bit back a sob.

"Teresa, I don't know what to say," he began, and she nodded covering her face.

"I know you don't believe me, but I swear, he made me write the letter, he told me he would kill you otherwise. He had pictures, Ollie, of you and your Bear, he was going to blackmail you and expose you," she cried harder, "then when I knew I was pregnant I had to get away from him. I don't know what he did to me, but there is something inside me now. Something bad. I can't let it out. If something happens to me and my father gets his hands on our baby who knows what he will do. He wants Thomas. He's tried to take him before, but I can't let that happen. You have to help, please, even if you don't believe me. You have to protect our son," she begged, foregoing all pride in her fight to save her son.

"Easy, easy, I believe you," he looked at her hard for a moment then tugged her into the familiar warmth of his powerful embrace, "I got you, Resa," he murmured and she clung to him.

"Thomas?"

"I have you both. He's my son, I will protect him. I have money now, power, connections, I'm a Grizzly Bear for fuck's sake and if anyone tries to mess with my son or his mother, that person will die," he vowed.

"Ollie," she breathed as relief and something else inside her began to take flight.

The feeling took off and lit up like fireworks. It felt good, right, being in his arms. Safe and protected. She breathed in his scent and clung to his strong capable shoulders. Teresa was finally home.

CHAPTER 6

"Resa," Oliver squeezed her tight in his arms and nuzzled her cheek.

He turned slightly so that they were facing each other. They were so close that he could see the tear drops that clung to her dark blond lashes and his reflection in her creamy jade eyes. Oliver pressed her even closer still.

She was so beautiful. Even more so now that she'd matured. Her lovely lithe body had filled out in wondrous ways that both animal and man were dying to explore.

Shit. If he went down that road, he'd never find his way back. But right then, Oliver and his Bear did not give a damn. He wanted her. Wanted to feel her soft submission under his searching lips. Wanted to taste her peaches and cream scent on his tongue and swallow it down.

"Ollie," she said his name unconsciously swaying closer.

The scent of her sweet arousal reached him and he growled softly in response. She was hypnotizing him all over again, and right then he didn't care, wouldn't fight it. He wanted it and her, that sweet oblivion only she could give him. Oliver's heart thudded inside his chest.

Mine, growled his Bear.

He cupped her face in his hands, wondering at the way she turned into his touch, and the soft rumbling sigh that escaped her plump pink lips. Need flowed through him, an unstoppable tide. Why should he fight it?

Oliver made up his mind. He wouldn't go into this blindly this time, but now he had something else to fight for. His son. The child they had made out of love, yes love, he realized and believed it with every-thing in him.

This woman ripped out his heart once, but here she was begging him for help. It hurt to see her humbled and frightened. He wanted her strong and safe, and with him, always. Fate had given them another chance, and Oliver was going to take it and hold it with both hands.

He dipped his head, ready to take the first step. Teresa's eyes flashed and he growled in response to the desire he saw there. Their noses bumped, and he smiled, it had been playfully awkward the first time too.

Memories of how good it was tried to force their way into his mind, but he pushed them back. He didn't want to think about the past anymore. He only wanted to concentrate on the now.

"Resa," he said her name once more and carefully lifted her face to his, then he kissed her.

His temperature went from normal to boiling in that instant. Shifters tended to run a little hotter than *normals*, but even he felt the sizzle. She was right there with him, her skin was on fire under his searching hands and lips.

So hot. So good.

Her peaches and cream flavor burst on his taste buds, sending ripples of desire zipping up and down his spine, straight to his groin. She moaned and wrapped her arms around his back, pressing her soft breasts firmly against his chest. He could feel the bite of her pebbled nipples through their combined shirts and the animal grunted, wanting a closer touch.

This was a not just lust, it was mating fever. Oliver recognized it, reveled in it, and deepened their shared kiss. He delved into the hot cavern of her mouth with his tongue until he found hers. He sucked on it briefly, wanting to swallow down every single drop of her sweet flavor.

"Ollie," she moaned and slid off the chair.

She practically leapt off the chair with her legs wrapped tightly around him. Grunting, he caught her and held her to him, using minimal strength to stand. He lifted her up, cupping the firm globes of her ass, and walked them over to one of the sturdy log walls.

Oliver pressed into her core, allowing her to feel just how much he wanted her. Cock throbbing, pulse racing he kissed her deeper and ran his hands over her curvaceous form. She was so damned sumptuous. Every nuance and angle seemed to fit him like a glove.

"Mm, I'm bigger than I was," she whispered almost apologetically, and his Bear roared.

"You're perfect for me," he grunted, cupping her ripe breasts which were in fact larger than he remembered.

A result of having gone through childbirth, he supposed and his heart ached for the loss of time between them, but he didn't want to think about that just then. Oliver wanted to live in the moment like the cavalier poets she'd once relished. He wanted to stop time and dive right into the depths fully and completely with her.

"Bed," he said, and she nodded. That was all the consent he needed.

Oliver took the stairs to his master bedroom and dropped her gently on the bed. He was stunned for a moment. How many times had he dreamed of this moment? Of having her in his bed? Sure, he'd thought about exacting his revenge on this woman who had broken his heart and threatened to drive his Bear insane, but those thoughts were quickly fleeting. Mostly, he just dreamt of having her back.

And here she was, but this was no dream. This was real. Teresa was here in his bed, and revenge was the last thing on his mind. She bit her lip and looked at him, then, as if she'd come to some firm decision. Teresa sat up, eyes heavy-lidded with lust, she tore her shirt off, then her pants revealing every glorious inch of her lush body to his greedy eyes.

Oliver's dick throbbed as he took in her mouth-watering curves in the simple flower printed bra and panties she wore. Following suit, he stripped himself quickly.

He tumbled into the bed with her, growling softly as their lips met. A few maneuvers had them both fully naked and Oliver settled his body between her two soft thighs.

"Ollie," she whimpered, another wave of her arousal filled his nostrils.

His Grizzly Bear rose up inside of him and Oliver took one long look at her face before he pressed the head of his cock into her hot, slick entrance. Oh yes, she was more than ready for him, just as snug and tight as he remembered.

"Oh God, Ollie," she moaned and clung to his shoulders.

Oliver flexed his hips, trying hard not to lose it right then and there. So damn tight, so good. Perfect.

"Relax for me, sweet," he murmured kissing her again until he felt her muscles loosen their hold.

He was a big man, a big Bear. Even though they had done this before, it had clearly been a long time for her. Oliver had to go slowly, carefully. He would never willingly hurt her. He knew her body could take him, she just had to relax, and accept all of him into her hot, slick, velvety channel.

"S'good," she moaned, and he could feel her rising desire as it matched his own.

He looked down at her heavy-lidded eyes and dipped his head to capture her mouth. He thrust his tongue deep, mimicking the movement of his hips. Slow, steady at first, then faster and harder. Oliver's body was slick with sweat, his heart raced as he quickened the pace. This was crazy. They should have talked, but what did Shifters need with words when he could say it all with his body?

Mate, his Bear pushed him to mark her.

No, he shushed the beast.

This was not for the Bear. Not yet. This was for them. For him and Teresa. They needed this release, this closeness. Their relationship was too complicated for another rushed mating bite.

Still, even without the ritual biting, he could feel their *matebond* renew between them. He recognized the subtle difference, the new changes in her, and even though he didn't quite understand them, it did not matter. Oliver knew she had told him the truth earlier. He trusted her, in spite of their past. And he wanted her. Then. Now. Always.

"Ollie!" Teresa groaned his name and dragged her nails down his back.

He hissed in a sharp breath, the sting of her

scratching hurt so good. His animal loved it. Her walls tightened around him, and her pussy rippled as she groaned her pleasure. She gripped his cock like a vise as she abandoned herself to the ecstasy only he could give her. He was her mate, there would be no other who could touch her this way.

The knowledge made it all the sweeter as he pumped harder and faster, chasing his own orgasm until he felt it erupt from him like a volcano. Arrogant, maybe, but he had right to be. Teresa was his.

"Mine," he couldn't stop the possessive word from spilling from his lips, just as he spilled his seed deep into her womb.

The idea that even then they could have created a life made his Bear chuff in approval. He wanted family. Wanted Thomas and all of their future cubs. Wanted Teresa now more than he ever had before.

Her eyes were still closed, mouth open as she tried to catch her breath. Oliver simply stared for a moment. With her blonde hair spread out over the gray comforter like a halo, she looked ethereal. He'd always thought there was something angelic about her appearance, so sweet and precious. Unearthly, and almost unattainable, but not for him. She'd let him have her.

"It's only ever been you," she said as if answering his unspoken question.

"I know," he kissed her softly and slid from her heat, missing the warmth immediately.

The sound of little footsteps had both of them jumping up, and Oliver had his pants back on before the little cub could wander into their room.

"Mommy," Thomas was still rubbing his eyes so he missed the look between the two adults as she donned one of Oliver's t-shirts and stood up to walk to him.

"Hey, baby," she dropped to her knees and hugged their son.

Thankfully, the shirt fell past her thighs though at his tender age he would hardly notice his mother's nudity. Besides, Shifters were not prudes about things like that. Being naked was natural and made transforming from one skin to another easier and less messy.

He watched mother and cub kneeling together and Oliver's heart threatened to burst at the picture they made. Were they really both his? He listened to the pleasant conversation the two were having and watched as she drew the cub along with her out into the hall with a wave for him to follow. Oliver did with wonder in his heart.

Teresa brought the boy to the large guest bathroom on the first floor and started the water. The bathtub was massive but not too large for so young a Bear. It was done in natural creams and blues, but suddenly Oliver wished he'd had something fun painted on the walls. He'd made a mental note to have an artist come and do the bathroom and guest room over as Thomas' private rooms. Perhaps he had a favorite character or movie they could use as models. So much he didn't know about his cub.

"What's wrong?" Teresa broke his reverie and he looked into her worried eyes.

"Nothing, I was just wondering if he had a favorite book or TV show?"

"Oh, no favorites yet, but he does like it when I sing to him. Mostly show tunes or movie theme songs," she shrugged and began humming one of the numbers he'd written for a big cartoon movie that had released last year.

Thomas clapped and splashed in the water and Teresa winked at Oliver. He felt his Bear rumble happily inside of him. She was teasing him, but there was truth to her statement. Also, that meant she'd been keeping tabs on him.

"Toys, Mommy?" Thomas asked.

"Oh, buddy, I'm sorry I forgot the bath toys," she frowned, but Oliver interrupted.

"Actually, I have something young master Thomas might like," he said and went to retrieve the toy cars he'd bought at the minimart.

"Vroom!" Thomas squealed with delight when he saw the tiny plastic cars things and Oliver looked at Teresa for approval.

"That was nice of Daddy," she smiled, "now, settle down you don't want to slip," she chided the cub who immediately started racing the two cars through the bubbles on the side of the bath.

"He likes them," Oliver grinned and Teresa walked over to stand by him.

He immediately tucked her into his side as they stood together and simply watched their son play. Nothing could describe the happiness that welled inside of him at seeing his heathy, mischievous lad splashing water over the side of the bath and giggling wildly at his mother's faux chiding.

"Thank you," she whispered to Oliver.

"They're just little things," he shrugged.

"To you maybe, but to him it's a lot. We haven't had much, but I did my best for him, Oliver," he caught the hitch in her words and he frowned.

"Hey, I know you did, I would never say otherwise. It's going to be alright now, I got you both."

Looking to make sure Thomas was safe for the moment, Teresa tugged him out into the hallway. She turned to face him and he could tell by the way she squared her shoulders she'd made up her mind about something.

"So, I just want to make sure you will take care of Thomas?"

"What? Of course, I know he's my son-"

"Cause I've decided to turn myself in to my father and Witherspoon Tech in exchange for them leaving you and Thomas alone."

"What?" he whispered barely holding on to his rage.

"It's the only way," she pleaded, but he wasn't hearing it.

"No, Teresa. Just no. I let you go once. I won't do it again."

"But-"

"You came to me this time, Teresa."

"For him. So you can keep him safe," she said.

"It's not enough. I love him so much, but I need you too, now do you trust me?"

"Of course, I do," she said and he could tell from the misery rolling off her that she only wanted to protect them both. It touched him, but it made him crazy all the same.

"I got this, Resa," he said.

"Alright," she answered and leaned in, just a breath away from his lips.

"Mommy!" Thomas called, and the two adults jumped apart and raced back to the bathroom just in time to get splashed.

"Welcome to fatherhood," she laughed as Oliver spit out a mouthful of bubbles.

CHAPTER 7

After his bath, Teresa and Oliver took Thomas outdoors to play for a while. Her, no, *their* son had oodles of energy and needed to expel them in positive ways.

It wasn't easy to be creative with them always living in the city, but here in this lovely forest, though still a bit chilly, Thomas was in heaven. They'd stopped by the water to fish for a little bit. Thomas was still young, but he played and splashed while Ollie did all the work of hooking the fish. He'd caught quite a few after just a little while.

"How did you do that?" She asked eyeing his catch with wonder. He dropped them into the small cooler packed with ice and grinned.

"An old Grizzly secret, I'd tell you, but then I'd have to, you know what," he grinned.

"What if I tickle it out of you? After all I happen to have myself a big, strong Grizzly lover," she said naughtily and loved his growly response.

"Mommy lookee me!" Thomas ran and climbed on some big rocks.

He giggled as Oliver swung him up onto his shoulders. They picked berries and skipped stones on the lake for what seemed like minutes but was really hours. Her heart beat heavily, filled to the brim with emotions she never dared to dream she'd ever feel again. But here she was, and she did, as if those lovely feelings had never gone away or been put on hold.

Love. She gulped audibly. Teresa still loved Oliver Pax. As truly and deeply, and possibly even more than she had two years ago when she'd been a green girl with no knowledge of the very real cruelty that existed in the world.

He hadn't said anything about love, but she was certain she'd felt it in his careful touch. Her eyes rolled back into her head as she thought about the pleasure he'd brought her mere hours ago. The physical side of their relationship had always been explosive.

There was nothing on the planet that could compare to Oliver's lovemaking. Not that she had any experience otherwise. He was her one and only. Surely, he knew that, but if he didn't she could certainly find ways to show him.

Thinking about that made her stomach clench and her needy clit throb with anticipation. Her panties moistened, her breath caught, the need to go to him now, to strip her clothes off and ride him into oblivion coursed through her. Like she was just an empty shell waiting for him to fill her. It was scary, it was heady, hell, she didn't know what to think about this sudden carnal urge to strip them both and indulge in his magnificent body once again.

She coughed to cover up the moan that escaped her lips. Her entire body felt as though it was on fire. Teresa shook with the strength of it. She looked up to find Oliver had stopped chasing Thomas. He stood between the still bare trees, nostrils flaring, his pupils dilated as he watched her like the predator he was.

Eyes bled to black, a great rumbly growl echoed from his chest as he sucked in a great deep breath. The growl grew as he took in her scent. His eyes flashed as he recognized her desire, and damn, but she found it hard to breathe.

He looked so good. Utterly masculine and tempting in his jeans and cotton shirt. Something inside her rumbled in awareness as even more moisture seeped between her thighs. Her sex clenched on air, breasts swelled, and nipples hardened.

Oliver sucked in another deep breath and licked his full lips. That was nearly her undoing. She wanted those lips, craved them on her own, and further down still. She wanted his hands, his mouth on her breasts and belly, and finally, between her thighs.

"Mommy, thirsty!" Thomas ran through the few feet of space that stood between her and Oliver, and she dropped down to capture him in a hug immediately, breaking their strange intense stare.

"Here have some water," she smiled and offered one of the three refillable bottles she'd packed in the small rucksack she'd found in the closet along with some snacks, wipes, tissues, and band-aids for her sweet, but adventurous boy.

Teresa stood and wiped her sweaty hands on her pants before reaching in the bag and offering another bottle to Oliver. He stepped forward crowding her a little, and her heart beat double time.

"Thanks," Oliver winked.

He was still a little breathless after engaging in a

game of tickle tag monster with Thomas, or maybe it was from that tempestuous look they'd shared. She couldn't be sure. That gaze had been filled with promises of impending delightful seduction. Maybe if she was lucky, she'd find out just how delightful later.

Their boy gulped down his water greedily and he watched his parents with a twinkle in his bright eyes. The fresh air was good for him. Guilt and shame washed over her as she thought about all the time hiding and on the run. Living in motels and eating ramen noodles out of cheap cartons.

"It's alright now," Oliver said, seeming to read her mind and she offered him a small smile in turn.

"Here, Mommy," Thomas handed her back the water then tucked his hand shyly into Oliver's.

Tears pricked her eyes as she watched the only man who'd ever touched her heart accept the child's hand as if it were the most natural thing in the world. Perhaps it was for Shifters. She wasn't quite sure how the biological dynamic worked in so far as familial relationships between supernaturals.

And yes, there were more things out there than Shifters. Her time in a cell at Witherspoon Tech had shown her that. She shuddered in revulsion, maybe fear, and something inside her rumbled. Teresa stopped moving, her panic rising, threatening to take over.

It was back. That strange sensation of the *other* inside of her. Her body burned and her stomach cramped. Something was scratching at her from the inside out.

A darkness. A demon. What had her father called her? Oh yeah, an evil, cheap, vile bitch. A whore, like her mother, and that she didn't understand at all.

The thing inside her growled at the memory. It's anger obvious, and Teresa almost laughed. At least whatever the darkness was, it seemed to like her at times and it definitely hated her father as much as she did. It pushed again, and her fear increased. She closed her eyes, straining to keep it leashed.

No. She would not give in to darkness now. She pushed that *other thing* deep down inside of her and focused on her two boys. They were her whole heart, she realized quite suddenly. Regret filled her as she saw the hard lines in his face. The untrusting glint that had never been in his eyes before. Damn, she had caused that.

She was responsible for the sorrow lines that creased his brow. But no more. They were together and she would do her best to smooth them all out, if only he'd let her.

Yes, something inside of her spoke.

Teresa ignored that other voice and focused on him. After all this time, she would never love another. Just him. Her Ollie. Like it had always been, but different, better, stronger now for everything they had both experienced.

"Hey, what's wrong?" he said quietly.

"Nothing," she returned, "I just, I feel strange."

"It's okay," he soothed and went to touch her shoulder, but stopped suddenly.

The sound of twigs snapping had all three heads turning to look. Oliver moved in front of both her and Thomas, shielding them with his big body. Teresa felt every muscle inside of her clench and strain. Prepared for something, though she hardly knew what. The need to protect her son was paramount in that moment.

It only let up the moment Oliver relaxed his own stance. Trusting him implicitly, she waited for him to explain. Of course, patience was never one of her virtues. Curiosity got the better of her, so she peeked around him.

It was a woman, she soon realized. A lovely woman. And, much to Teresa's rising anger, she was not a stranger to Oliver. She watched as he smiled warmly at the stranger with her long straight hair.

Locks that Teresa had always envied for her own unruly waves were certainly a bitch to tame at times.

The stranger had big amber eyes behind rather stylish glasses, and they too, smiled up at her Ollie behind thick lashes. She was tall and lean, more slender than Teresa at any rate, but it was her easy grace and confidence that she belonged there, *with him*, that stuck in her craw.

Jealousy surged, irrational and misplaced, maybe, but she couldn't help it. In fact, she seemed to not be fully in control of her emotions at all.

"Mommy? You're rumbly like my *grisle*!" Thomas said.

She looked at her cub and panic had her hyperventilating. A deep, gnawing rumble started in her chest, and Oliver whipped his head around to catch her in his curious stare. He lifted Thomas out of her arms when she thrust him towards his father.

"Thomas," she said the boy's name and dropped down.

Her body tensed, a flash of pain shot through her stomach, like a cramp, but much more direct and acute. The pain seemed to grow as quickly as it had come on, but she hardly noticed it in the face of the raw jealousy that had threatened to consume her.

Teresa was scared for her son, but something

inside of her told her she would never harm the child. No, not the child, *their child*, their *cub*. Whatever was happening, it was happening now. Every inch of her burned with hurt.

"Resa?" Oliver's eyes went wide.

He motioned for Thomas to move behind him, which thankfully the cub did.

"I'll take him," the strange woman said, and that really pissed off the thing inside Teresa.

She snarled and snapped at her. Burning, itching, gnawing pain shot through every cell inside of her. She felt as if she were being torn into pieces. Loud snapping, tearing, cracking noises echoed in her ears along with the sound of her blood thundering in her ears.

"It's okay, Thomas, go sit by Jennifer," he said and Teresa snapped her jaws around teeth that weren't hers, "Teresa? Look at me, don't fight it, baby, it's okay," Oliver dropped to his knees in front of her.

Poor man. He looked as though he were the one in pain, being torn apart but it was her. She was being eaten, consumed, ravaged by whatever monstrous demon her father had injected her with.

"Thomas," she growled around her misshaped mouth, worried for the safety of her son despite the thing's insistence he was safe.

"He's fine. I'm worried about you, love. Listen to me, you have to stop fighting. Trust me, it is not what you think," he said, and she saw the Bear bleed into his eyes.

That beautiful, strong, dominant Grizzly of his was staring at her. Suddenly, Teresa stilled and quieted. She did as he asked and stopped fighting. Then, the most marvelous thing happened.

Mate, she heard a voice inside her head.

Her whole body though wracked with pain, seemed to heed that distant whisper. It was as if the sound was reaching for her through some sort of thick, hazy fog.

She turned to Oliver for help, only he didn't look like himself. His facial features contorted under her watchful gaze as more of his Bear leaked through. Something inside of her responded to it almost violently. No, not violence. A rapid succession of emotions filtered through to her. The most urgent were need, desire, and most of all *love,* she realized.

Mate, the voice repeated more clear than last time.

It wasn't scary this time. It felt right. Teresa relaxed her body and embraced the fire inside. In doing so, she felt as if her skin was being touched and stroked by the softest of hands. An electric hum seemed to fill her ears and the fire grew in intensity for the briefest of moments.

Magic, the voice whispered, *let me in.*

Teresa felt as though she were being ripped in two. She had only one choice and she chose to trust in Oliver. She acknowledged the power flowing through her and prayed to God and whoever else was listening to keep the ones she loved safe during whatever was happening to her.

"That's it, Resa, let her in," Oliver coaxed and she heard the wonder in his voice and relished the scent of faith and love that all seemed to come from him.

Finally, she willed herself to relax. She closed her eyes and groaned, commanding the muscles in her body to unclench and loosen. Only it wasn't her body. Not her usual one anyway.

Teresa stood on shaky, powerful, fur-covered legs, four of them to be exact. What the ever-loving hell just happened to her?

A roar erupted from her mouth, and she opened her eyes to see that the world looked different to her somehow, it was sharper more acute. She blinked rapidly to see Oliver standing in front of her with his arms wide as he directed her focus to him.

"Look at me, look at me, Resa," he commanded and she did, reluctantly.

She did not want to obey her mate. She wanted to run, to play, to hunt, maybe even fish. Oh yes, Bears loved to fish!

Bears? Me? A Bear?

Rawr! Her answer flowed from her maw and Teresa fell backwards onto her big furry butt.

"You're so beautiful, baby," Oliver grinned wickedly and took a cautious step forward,

Damn right he should be careful. She was a Bear! Not just any bear, but a full grown Grizzly Sow!

"You're a Shifter," he said once more with awe in his voice.

"Mommy's a *grisle*," Thomas said.

Teresa turned to see the strange woman holding her son and she saw red.

Grrr.

CHAPTER 8

Teresa chuffed and snorted angrily. She pawed the ground, but Oliver stepped between her and the stranger who dared touch her cub.

"Easy, baby, she's a friend."

Easy? Oh no, he didn't. She tried to yell at him to tell him she wanted that slut away from her baby. A few other choice curses filled her head, but she couldn't talk. She tried again and heard more growling and snarling.

"Don't panic, use your mind not your mouth to speak to me," he instructed.

Oliver! She screamed his name in panic inside her mind's eye.

"I hear you, baby," he answered and shook his ear.

Oops. So, she yelled a little bit too loudly. But she

needed answers. She dropped to all fours and stomped her feet.

"Easy, love," he approached cautiously, "may I?"

Hands raised in her direction, Teresa nodded at him.

Mate, that inner voice chuffed happily and Teresa found herself rumbling pleasantly as Oliver stroked his big, strong hands through her fur.

Fur?

Yes, answered the voice, *we have magnificent fur.*

"Sweet mate, you do have a lovely coat," he said and brought his forehead to hers.

"You've been cooped up a long time, haven't you?"

A deep, mournful growl sounded from her Bear's lips and Teresa felt shame fill her. But how could she have known? Her mother had died in childbirth and her father was a *normal.*

Not our father, her she-Bear growled.

Suddenly, she knew the truth. Teresa was not the daughter of Mathias Witherspoon. He didn't have the right scent. But why had he claimed she was his daughter?

"We will find the answers, love, but for now, want to run with me?"

Her Bear's happy rumble cut short when she snorted in the direction of their cub.

"We won't go far. Jennifer is a friend. I swear to you. She would never harm our son. Jennifer?"

"We will walk back to your cabin and wait there for you, alright?" the woman, no, the Owl Shifter, said, and Teresa watched her go with a warning growl.

"Come on," Oliver removed his clothing and within seconds he stood before her a magnificent Grizzly Bear, much larger than her own.

Together they ran through the woods, over the budding shrubs and patches of snow, down to the rocky shore on that side of the lake just behind the cabin. She took a moment to admire her handsome Grizzly before he shimmered back to a man before her eyes.

"Will you change back now, beautiful? Let me have my, mate," he told her.

Wow. Teresa caught sight of her reflection in the water. She had fur, and claws, and huge teeth.

Gulp. Okay. She could live with that. But that wasn't what had her reluctant to change back. No, it was the fact that he had just called her mate. That word alone meant everything to her.

"That's it, sweet, your cub and your mate need you to change back," Oliver cajoled.

Be with our mate now, her Bear suggested and she closed her eyes and willed her human body forward.

"Wow," she said as Oliver waited a beat before putting his arms around her.

They stood in three feet of freezing lake water, and suddenly she felt a tad conspicuous out in the open with nothing at all covering her body.

"You're lovely, Resa," he said and claimed her mouth in a searching kiss that she was desperate to explore.

After some time, however long, she was unsure, Teresa opened her eyes. Oliver had lifted her shivering body out of the cold water and held her against his warmth while plundering her mouth. Her inner Sow reveled in his possession. Patches of snow still littered the rocky shore so he carried her to a large tree and used it for leverage while covering the bark with his hands.

"Need you," he grunted, but waited for her hands to travel between them.

She gripped his heavy cock in her hands and placed him at her slick entrance. The tree was rough under her bare ass, but she did not care. All she wanted was him.

"That's actually kind of funny," Oliver said as he allowed just the tip of his dick to pierce her slick heat.

"Why funny?" She asked.

"Because love, a moment ago you actually had a Bear ass," he grinned and instead of fear or disgust she saw utter joy in his gaze.

"Please," she rolled her eyes and begged him, ignoring her accidental pun.

She needed him now, desperately, and she wasn't too proud to show him just how much. Her body throbbed and ached in places she'd neglected for far too long it would seem. Being with him again sparked her senses, ignited her heart, and fanned the flame of desire she'd thought extinguished.

Mine, her Bear whispered inside her mind and she welcomed the thought.

"Mate," he grunted as if in response and all traces of humor fled his gaze.

Oliver needed no more coaxing after that. She clung to his shoulders as he made love to her beneath the setting sun. The cold went unnoticed as her magnificently muscled mate moved fiercely, passionately over her, giving her pleasure that only he could deliver.

Oliver mashed his lips to hers. He didn't stop

kissing her, not even when stars exploded behind her eyes and the whole world spiraled out of focus.

"Ollie," she gasped his name, trying to catch her breath as tiny little aftershocks continued to tremble between them from the place where his body still possessed hers all the way to that muscle that was pounding furiously inside her chest.

When they were both finally sated, Oliver kissed her gently. He carried her princess style up the steps he must've had carved into the stone, leading to his back porch.

"I'm too heavy," she started.

"You're light as a feather," he snorted.

"They'll see us," she sat up when she heard Thomas inside the cabin giggling brightly.

"No worries, love, you go shower and I'll bring up a tray."

A while later, Teresa wandered back downstairs to where Oliver was chatting with Jennifer while he prepared dinner.

"Hi," his eyes found her and she smiled at him a little shy since she her new senses told her this woman was a Shifter and she would know what they had been up to in the woods just behind the cabin.

"Well, I think proper introductions are in order," the stranger said brightly.

Teresa's eyes snapped to the woman's oval shaped face. It was strange now, but she felt her Bear deep within her assessing the situation. The animal inside of her might've been in a rage of jealousy earlier, or maybe her Bear saw this person as some sort of proprietorial challenger, but not now. Now, she was the woman who had taken care of Teresa's cub and for that she was grateful.

"Thomas? Why don't you come over here and let your mom see you're alright," the stranger spoke up.

It was a good idea. Yes. Teresa wanted her cub. She scooped up her son and felt Thomas cling to her. Immediately, the animal within stopped her grumbling. Scaring her cub was not on her list of things to do that day.

"Mommy," Thomas squealed when he ran to her, pumping his chubby little legs as he did.

He'd been playing on a plush throw rug in the center of the large living room that was visible from where she stood. She could make out the box of crayons he'd upended everywhere, a few coloring books, his new cars, and a few of the dolls he had brought with him. The place was a mess, but the good kind, she thought fondly.

"Hello, my sweet boy," she dropped a dozen quick

kiss on his forehead, nose, and cheeks all while cuddling him close.

Thomas liked it when she did that and he laughed out loud. He smelled like forest and sunshine, and yes, just beneath that, a hint of fur. Her little whirlwind squirmed after a moment or two, and she released him. He was a happy and healthy cub, anxious to get back to his toys.

"So, Teresa," a voice interrupted her musings and she turned back to the two adults, "I'm Jennifer."

"Hello," she answered.

Oliver walked over to her wiping his hands on a dish towel before he reached for her, tugging her close to his big, hard body. She loved the sheer size and strength of him, leaning into his touch she inhaled his scent and savored it before releasing her breath.

He brushed her lips with a soft hello kiss and pressed his forehead to hers with one hand on the back of her neck. The touch was welcomed, cherished in fact by woman and Sow. It was quite something for her to admit these things, to feel them so fully now that she had embraced her true self.

"You okay?" he asked.

"Yeah, I'm adjusting quickly actually, but I guess I'm sort of confused."

"I can only imagine," his concern shone through his dark eyes as he brushed a curl behind her ear, "What did that bastard father of yours do to you?" He growled.

"Yes, I'd be curious as well," Jennifer interrupted from her perch on one of the sturdy chairs in the dining room.

Teresa's eyes flicked to the woman, but before she could respond Thomas ran straight to *Jennifer* from the living room. She watched in shock as he climbed on the woman's lap and whispered something in her ear. Jennifer laughed brightly before letting him down again. Teresa watched the harmless byplay, but she was unable to fully control the growl that built up inside her.

"Easy, she-Bear, I have not harmed your cub," Jennifer said and nodded in Thomas' direction, "he is safe and well, see?"

"I swear to you, Teresa," Oliver interjected, "I wouldn't have left him with her if I didn't trust her. She's a friend."

That only made the growl grow that much louder. Uh oh. She shook her head to try and regain some control.

"Well, this the whole family then?" Jennifer

nodded in Teresa's direction and she found herself smiling at the other woman.

Okay, it was more snarl than smile, and Teresa immediately stilled. What the hell was wrong with her?

"I see," Jennifer laughed, "well, would it help you to know that I am not interested in Oliver that way," she cocked her head and stared at Teresa with piercing predatory eyes before warming them.

Her birdlike gaze darted to young Thomas, who was watching them with a concerned expression on his cherubic face.

"Maybe we can be properly introduced now that Mommy isn't going to fight her Bear anymore?"

"Mommy's grisle!" Thomas said from the other room.

"Yes, Thomas that's right Mommy's a Grizzly, just like your Daddy, and you. Teresa, allow me to welcome you officially to the world of Shifters," Jennifer gave a little bow.

CHAPTER 9

Teresa might have been under the influence of a certain green-eyed monster a few hours ago, but looking at the warm smile on Jennifer's face, she and her Bear came to a decision. If Oliver trusted this woman, then so would she.

"Why don't we all sit and have a chat?" she suggested.

Thomas was still in sight, and she supposed she needed some answers too. Being a Bear was new, so was being with Oliver again. Still, she didn't fuss when her Grizzly lover tugged her onto his lap.

He was a very physical person, always wanting to touch her, hold her. She remembered that from before, and to be truthful, it was one of the things she'd loved best.

Her father, no, that was wrong, *Mathias Wither-spoon* was not the hugging kind. She'd had little in the way of hugs and kisses growing up. That came with being raised by nannies and attending private schools her whole life. She was practically starved for any little crumb of physical affection by the time she'd met Ollie, and he'd given her so much more than that.

His head was cocked to the side and she saw his intelligent brown eyes searching hers for answers. Unfortunately, she didn't have any for either of them.

"First, I want you to know Teresa that I've known Jennifer for a long time. She is just a friend. There is no reason for you to be jealous of her or anyone, I swear," he told her.

"I'm sorry, I don't know what came over me," she said.

It was the truth. She didn't know exactly why she'd had such a strong reaction only that she was a Bear now. Or, she always had been, but now she was finally in contact with her animal side. Perhaps there was something about the nature of Shifters that made them jealous of their significant others? The fact that he seemed amused under his worry made her feel slightly foolish.

"No, I don't mean to tease," he said, reading her mind again, "it's just you remind me of me."

"How so?"

"Hell, Resa, don't you remember how I used to get those rare times we left my apartment and went to eat or wander through the park?"

"Yeah," she laughed at the memory, "you always got so growly, but I thought that was because of your Bear."

"It was. It is. A dominant Shifter like me wants to keep his mate to himself, especially since at the time you were unmarked."

"Mate? Unmarked?"

"Shit, I suppose I should explain."

"That might be good," Jennifer said amusedly, but Teresa was too focused on Oliver to pay attention to the woman.

"Remember that last night," he started and memories began to flood her mind, of course she remembered it. So much pleasure followed by the most intense heartbreak of her young life.

"I mean specifically, the sex.," he said without embarrassment, though she felt her cheeks burn.

"Ollie," she whispered.

"Sex is very natural, Teresa, I assure you I know all about the birds and the bees," the woman grinned at her remark.

"Sorry, love, I have no wish to embarrass you," he reassured her.

"I know. To answer, yes, I remember," she whispered back trying to wrap her head around everything that had just happened.

"So, when I shifted were you expecting that?"

"No, love. But I am happy you did. You are the most beautiful she-Bear I have ever seen."

Something inside of her, *her Bear* she supposed, chuffed happily at his praise. Okay. So her Bear was a slut for a compliment. At that thought, the Bear snarled, and Teresa shushed the beast. She was entitled to a little freak out wasn't she?

Sheesh!

"Anyway, I bit you that night. Do you remember?" he added.

She nodded her head. Of course, she recalled the passionate love bite he'd given her. In his enthusiasm, he'd broken skin, and left a small scar just below her left ear. She still had that scar. Had traced it over and over again during their years apart, whenever missing him had seemed almost impossibly painful. It gave her peace and she'd felt connected to him whenever she touched it.

"That wasn't an ordinary bite, Resa. I never got to explain it then, but please, allow me to now."

"Alright," she waited and Oliver lifted her hair over her shoulder and found the scar with his fingertips.

She shivered at the slight brush of his hands and more so when his lips touched it in a small, simple kiss.

"This is my mating mark, Teresa," he looked at her with glittering black eyes.

She knew it was his Bear pressing forward, and she felt no fear. Only wonder and love. In fact, the beast residing inside of her rose to meet that gaze. Ollie blinked and growled in his throat. A possessive comforting sound, she somehow understood.

"You see, a mating mark is a bite from a Shifter to his fated mate signaling to all and the universe itself that they belong together. This bite means you are mine, sweet. Claimed by me, for eternity."

Teresa swallowed and almost slipped off his lap. She would have if he hadn't been holding her so securely. She tried to comprehend what he was saying. His fated mate.

Could it be true? She'd heard some stories in her wanderings, but that would mean that he loved her. Could he? Even after what she'd done to him.

"Ollie?" she glanced at Thomas, their son was happily playing away.

"Resa?"

Teresa refocused on Oliver. She had so many questions, so many stimuli hitting her at once. She raised her hands to his shoulders to steady herself. The world seemed off its axis. Everything was askew, except for him. Ollie was just so big and strong, so constant, and dependable. Like an oak. God, she loved him.

"DO you understand what I am saying? You're it for me, Teresa. My one and only. When you left, I thought I would die, but you're back now. I swear to do everything I can to keep you and Thomas safe, just say you will stay. Please."

"You're saying you still l-love me?" tears pricked her eyes.

"Always, mate," his arms contracted around her, "I love you, want you, need you, more with each passing minute. You are my fated mate. There is nothing on this earth or any other more important to me."

"Oh, Oliver," she wrapped him tightly in her arms, heart soaring at his words, "I love you too."

His chest rumbled pleasantly, and she recognized it as his Grizzly Bear. Her own Sow rose up inside of her, and for the first time she saw in her mind's eye the complete image of her Grizzly Bear.

"Oh my God. I can't believe I'm a Shifter!"

CHAPTER 10

Oliver smiled at Thomas while he cut up vegetables for lunch. After last night's discussion, Jennifer had gone home with the promise to return today for a longer chat. That gave him the night with his family.

Thomas was such a sweet cub. He was so proud of Teresa for the incredible job she'd done bearing and raising him under impossible circumstances. Of course, he was angry he could not be there for them then, but he would be now.

They'd spent the rest of the night in each other's arms, talking about the long years apart. He understood she'd been afraid of Mathias and Witherspoon Tech, and even worse, she'd been made to feel scared of her own Bear.

The very thought enraged his beast. No Shifter should ever be forced apart from his or her own animal. It was blasphemy! He wanted to hunt down the bastards who'd drugged and experimented on her and tear them to shreds. It was his right as her mate.

Already, he'd set the wheels rolling and had alerted the proper Shifter agencies, including the High Council. If Witherspoon wasn't on their watchlist before, the bastard was now.

The wind whipped through the open window and he looked to see more flurries falling from the skies. Spring was late in coming, but he didn't mind it. Not when he had a mate and cub to snuggle with. Thomas liked the fireplace last night, a little too much and he'd quickly made a mental note to babyproof the cabin and his other homes.

They hadn't really discussed the future, but there was no way he was letting either of them go. Not now. Not ever. Still, they had some things to discuss, one thing Oliver understood now was the importance of total honesty with his mate.

For that, they needed to finish talking about her so-called father. Then he could tell her what plans were being made to protect both her and their cub.

Cooking gave him time to gather his thoughts

and as he prepped the side dishes, Jennifer sat sipping tea with Teresa at the table. From what he could gather, the two women were getting along, which was an immense relief to him.

The idea that Teresa thought him capable of wanting another made his Bear snarl and stomp inside of him. The animal wanted to console her, to take her over his shoulder, bring her upstairs, and fuck her until she understood he wanted no one else.

Of course, that kind of thing would have to wait until they were back home in a soundproofed room. He already had people working on that. Oh, he would still make love to her while they were here.

He wanted her to know how much he loved and adored her in every single way possible. Then maybe he could broach the subject of claiming her once more with her full consent and knowledge.

Once little Thomas had gone to sleep, Oliver had made sure Teresa had an idea of just how much he wanted her. Three times last night alone. He just couldn't help himself, and why should he try? Fuck proprieties and all the rest. She was his mate. The mother of his cub.

He grinned as he thought of his sweet boy. His cub was smart and funny, a fast learner too. In one afternoon, he'd taught him how to pick the sweetest berries and recite the names of almost all the trees around them. He even watched the tyke get six skips across the lake with a small stone.

He was a proud papa. Couldn't wait to show him off to Terence, Chance, and the others. Over the years, Oliver had become friends with a small, tight group of supernaturals and their mates. One of those couples had recently had a child. Maybe Avail's babe could prove a good playmate for his own cub. The Leeds Mansion was quite the estate and the new father was already readying the grounds for a custom playground that could withstand anything his Devilish offspring could throw at it.

Hmm. That was something to think about too. Oliver had a great apartment in the city, but surely his family would prefer a real house. A home in the suburbs maybe, or down by the ocean with a nice forest backdrop. Maccon City was well-known amongst supernaturals as a great place to raise a family. *A safe place,* which was the most important thing to him.

"Daddy! Want nummies," Thomas ran into his knees, and Oliver was shocked by the fact he'd almost been toppled by a toddler.

The cub was stronger than even the average Shifter, and he'd been off balance trying to reach a baking dish he'd put on the top cabinet for some foolish reason or other.

"Easy, buddy," he said, and handed the cub a carrot, "here snack on this until it's ready."

"Nummies!"

"Yes, nummies, next I am grilling some of that fish we caught in the lake yesterday. Like fish?" he teased the cub.

"Fishies," he giggled.

"That's right, Daddy's making fishies, with extra butter and lemon on top," he winked as the tyke scampered off back to the living room where he'd been systematically marking his territory with toys. Little cutie.

Oliver frowned as he shook the box of rice. It had only been a couple of days, and already they were halfway through his food supply. He'd have to go back in a day or so. His sensitive ears picked up bits of conversation coming from the women and his heart squeezed in his chest as he heard Teresa recite some of the horrors of her past. He looked down to see he'd crushed the stainless-steel serving spoon in his hand at her words.

"My father, no I guess I can't call him that anymore. Okay, so Witherspoon Tech had me locked in a cell for about three months, but in that short time they ran all sorts of tests. They took my blood, monitored my heart, my sleep, and they gave me injections. I think they drugged my food too. The man I thought was my father had always been crazy strict about my diet most of my life. He'd insisted on a solid vitamin regime too. I took pills blindly from the time I hit puberty until I ran away."

"I see," Jennifer said, "did those vitamins come in a bottle?"

"Oh no, just a plastic cup. They were already separated for me, but I always hated taking them I just never fought him."

"Did you ever stop taking them that is?" Jennifer asked.

"Yeah, actually, for those months when I was with Oliver. I went off the vitamins or whatever they were because they made me feel sick all the time," she shrugged, "In fact, that was why I spent so much time in the park to begin with. That was where we met. The sunlight and fresh air made me feel better."

"Teresa, did you ever see anything with an inscription on it like a bug or beetle at Witherspoon Tech?"

"Yes, I did. Oliver?" she called him, and he went to her side immediately, "Remember when I told you about the beetle?"

"Yes," he nodded and looked at Jennifer, "she mentioned this the first night after the hospital."

Jennifer leaned forward and pursed her lips. Oliver knew the Owl Shifter had a past she didn't like to speak of, but he sometimes wondered about it. There were many hidden organizations in the Shifter world, many societies and councils tasked with one important job, to keep their secret. He knew Jennifer had once worked for one of them.

"I can hear your mind whirring, Oliver Pax, and no, I can't answer your questions. Suffice it to say the group I suspect of being involved in your mate's abduction and imprisonment uses the scarab as a signature of sorts. They have been on our radar for an awfully long time, but we did not know Witherspoon Tech was involved. This information is extremely useful."

"There were others," Teresa said, and looked at him first, then at Jennifer with tears pricking her jade eyes, "others in cells. I couldn't help them. Once I found out I was pregnant, I ran. He said he'd kill you, Oliver, he would hunt you down like an animal, and I couldn't risk it, not then. I had to keep you safe and Thomas too. Then when I thought, that is, when I suspected that whatever they had injected me with was taking over, I came to you for help. I didn't know it was my

Bear, and I'm glad I didn't, because it brought me back to you," she sniffed and wiped her face.

"I know, love, I would never want you hurt, but I am so glad you are here now," he kissed her on her head and pulled her close, "but I'm, glad you know your Bear isn't evil. She is part of you, always was and that bastard did something to her. Trust your Bear's instincts to protect you and Thomas both. They don't use the term mama bear lightly you know."

"I've been running for so long. I only just came back to New York after seeing one of Witherspoon Tech's henchmen in Pennsylvania."

"You were that close?"

"Yeah. I couldn't stand being so far as it was. I tried California once, but it made me physically sick, I didn't understand it then."

"That was a result of you stretching your tentative *matebond*," Jennifer supplied, "Oliver marked you, and being away from him would've caused significant physical distress. Shifters are not built to be separated from their one and true mates for very long or for great distances. I imagine you are right and those so-called vitamins were Shifter gene suppressors of some sort."

"So, how is it that I am a Shifter?" she turned in his arms and looked at Jennifer.

"I imagine your natural parents, one or both were Shifters. Perhaps even a grandparent. It has been known to skip a generation. Whatever he did to you, it doesn't seem to have done permanent damage. Your she-Bear was strong yesterday when I saw her. Also, I suspect it is why your son's Bear is showing signs early."

"What do you mean?" Oliver injected.

He felt Teresa's rising fear as if it were his own. Maybe it was. Parenthood did strange things to a man.

"Is Thomas okay?" she asked.

"Yes, he is fine," Jennifer laughed, "though I suspect he will experience his first shift sooner rather than later. It won't hurt him, his Bear couldn't. It is just exceedingly rare for one so young, but with you as his parents I believe Thomas will adjust beautifully."

"Thank you. I sensed his Bear was remarkably close to the surface when I first saw him," Oliver admitted.

He rubbed his hands up and down his mate's spine to soothe her agitation and worry.

"But he will be fine?" his mate asked again looking for reassurance.

"Like I said, it is rare for a cub to shift so early, but there is really no such thing as normal in the supernatural world. When you live as long as I have, you've pretty much seen it all," Jennifer lifted her tea and sipped.

"Thank you, it means a lot to have my questions answered," Teresa sagged against him.

"Just how old are you, Jennifer?" Oliver grinned to lighten the mood.

"And you know better than that," she glared.

"Ollie! Never ask a lady how old she is," Teresa laughed and pinched him on the stomach.

"Ouch!" he laughed, his mood lightening with her own contagious happiness.

The woman was truly a wonder. An idea sprang into his head just then. He kissed her nose and turned to the mysterious Owl Shifter.

"Stay for supper, Jennifer?"

"Yes, please do!" Teresa seconded.

"Jenny!" his cub yelled and came running, "color me!"

"Okay, sweet cub, we can color," Jennifer smiled at Thomas then nodded at Oliver.

With the cub occupied, Oliver and Teresa worked

side by side prepping the rest of the meal, but he nudged her away when it came time to set the table and carry the dishes out. It was his privilege to serve dinner to his family and friend on the patio. They laughed and ate the delicious fish with herbed rice and veggies that they had prepared. It all tasted better to him somehow, richer, and sweeter. Oliver insisted on cleaning the dishes and put everything away.

"You'll make her a handy mate," Jennifer walked into the kitchen and placed her cup on the counter.

Darn woman always knew when he was brooding. He supposed he should just give in and tell her already.

"You know, I got the supplies you asked for. I forgot to give them to you. They are in the hall closet, but I was wondering if you wouldn't mind staying and babysitting for us?"

"Oh, big plans?"

"Look, my mate just found out what she is. I think maybe she needs some comforting. It's a big change for her," he shrugged.

"And you want to reaffirm your mating. Ugh, just please don't stay within range of my hearing Bear, or I swear you will never see another jar of my boysenberry jam!"

"I swear," he grinned.

Was he blushing? Shit. He shook his head and filled the kettle.

"Where is Teresa?"

"She's giving Thomas his bath. He slid on a bit of snow right into a muddy pile of leaves after you brought the dishes inside. The little scamp," she laughed.

Her amber eyes glowed with her Owl and Oliver stopped what he was doing. He understood the animal inside her was sizing him up.

"You will do fine by her, Oliver, don't worry. I'll watch your cub."

"Thank you, Jennifer."

"Thomas is in his room," Teresa walked into the kitchen and straight by his side.

He loved that part of her that recognized that he was where she belonged. So much so, he took advantage of it, wrapping her in his arms and nuzzling her neck. Her peaches and cream scent filled his nostrils and he felt his pulse race just being near her.

"He's asking for you Jennifer, would you mind?"

It amazed him how quickly she'd changed her opinion on Jennifer. Some of it was his word that he trusted the Owl Shifter, the rest, he suspected, was her own Bear giving the woman the thumbs up.

"Actually, I was just telling Oliver he should take you for a little twilight stroll while I mind the cub," Jennifer smiled.

The blasted woman stole his idea! Oliver rolled his eyes at her then squeezed his mate. She was looking at him curiously.

"Want to go for a walk with me, love?" he asked.

"Sure, but you don't mind Jennifer?" Teresa asked.

"It would be my pleasure."

"Great. Thank you," Oliver said to Jennifer, then turned to his sweetly blushing mate, "give me a sec, love, then we can go."

CHAPTER 11

Teresa spent the last day and a half marveling at the fact that she was not a monster. That the man she thought was her father had not injected her with some sort of demon like she'd suspected. She was in fact, a Shifter.

"Actually," Oliver interrupted her thoughts, "demons are like Shifters too. A friend of mine, my producer, you met him at the hospital in fact. Anyway, Chance is the son of a luck Demon."

"Did you just read my mind?" she asked in surprise.

"Uh, no love, you were talking out loud," he looked at her strangely, and she closed her eyes in embarrassment.

That was a quirk of hers from years ago, thinking out loud. She'd only ever done it when she was with him. Would she ever not act the fool around this man?

Sigh.

"You're not a fool, and you speak your mind because you know you can trust me. It's an honor, sweet, one that I cherish," he squeezed her hand as they neared the path that led to the cabin.

With Thomas back at the cabin safe and secure with the state of the art system Oliver had installed and with Jennifer with him, Teresa could relax and just enjoy being with him. Jennifer was actually quite nice, Teresa admitted reluctantly.

"Yeah," Oliver agreed, "you got to know each other a little, right?" he asked.

"Yes. She is nice and I feel like we can trust her," she said and allowed her Bear to rise up a bit to measure the truth in her words.

There was no doubt, only trust. Good, she sighed with relief. She had the oddest sensation of completion whenever she allowed her, she-Bear to come out even just a little.

That is because we are one, two sides of one person, the voice she'd feared for so long spoke inside of her mind, and instead of being scared, Teresa felt only joy.

"I know, it can be overwhelming meeting your animal spirit for the first time," Jennifer had said kindly earlier that afternoon. She'd handed Teresa a mug of herbal tea and a napkin.

Hell, Teresa hadn't even been aware that she'd been crying. She blotted her cheeks and eyes and smiled at the woman whom she now thought of as a friend. The Sow inside of her grumbled gently and she knew she did right in trusting Jennifer. The following snort was one she recognized as her Bear expressing happiness.

"Shall we chat? Get to know each other and your circumstances a bit?" Jennifer had offered over tea, "you know I have only ever been a friend to Oliver. He's gotten quite the reputation as a grumpy old Bear in your absence," the woman laughed.

"Now, don't growl," Jennifer mock scolded and Teresa cut off the sound.

"Sorry," she said, "this is all so new, and yet it feels perfect. Like I have been missing something my whole life, some piece of myself, and I guess that make sense, because I have."

"Yes, and now you have your Bear, your cub, and

your mate in one place. She is going to push you to mark him, you know."

"Yes, my, uh, hormones seem to already be a little out of control when it comes to my Ollie," she felt her cheeks burn with embarrassment at her familiar use of the nickname she'd called him years ago.

"Ollie, huh? Well, don't be shy now, dear. We are, all of us here, dual-natured spirits with primordial instincts, supernatural powers, and real actual animals living inside of us. Mating is serious business, and an unclaimed fated mate is fiercely coveted by his or her significant other or others."

"Others?"

"Why, yes, some Shifters have multiple partners in a mating. It is accepted as tradition and sometimes expected in Packs or Clans where a Triad rules."

"Really?" she'd giggled at the scandalous thought, but then her Bear assured her it was quite natural.

"Oh my, you are positively delightful, the Fates and Oliver have chosen well for him. You will be good together," Jennifer, the wise Owl Shifter and Teresa's newest friend, had stated matter-of-factly.

"Thanks, let's just hope Ollie means it when he says he wants me for keeps. I don't think I can let him go now," she said and felt the truth in her words in her Bear's grumbling response.

"You definitely don't need to worry about that," Jennifer reassured her.

The two had talked some more while Oliver finished preparing supper. He was handy in the kitchen she noted with glee as cooking was one of her most hated chores. She'd rather fold towels to be honest. Plus, he was good at it. The food was absolutely delicious. She never realized she loved fish so much.

"Bears like fish," he smiled and winked at her which led her to believe she'd blurted some of her thoughts while they'd been walking along the woods aloud.

"Only a few, love," he answered, "about the food though, my rather superior grilling skills aside, Bears do like a good fish."

"Yes well, Thomas certainly had," she giggled.

"Yes," Oliver smiled, "I love him, you know. Something inside of me just lights up when I see him."

"I can tell," she said and meant it.

There was something about the usually serious and dignified Oliver Pax crawling around on all fours making silly faces at his barely two-year-old cub, that simply melted her heart. She enjoyed watching them as they chased each other and played together, getting to know one another over the past few days.

"You know Jennifer teased me about you being a keeper and all since you cook and clean too."

"Oh yeah?"

"You're not bad looking either," Teresa shrugged.

"Is that so?" he snorted and she kept her face even while she pretended to look him up and down with a critical eye.

"You'll do," she bit back her grin.

"I see," Oliver straightened to his full height and faced her.

Love swelled inside of her until she thought she would burst with it, but she kept her expression simple, except for the twitch at the corner of her mouth. The man was quick to spot it and he gave her a smoldering look that made her want to jump his bones.

Everything she had ever wanted her whole life was finally within her grasp. She just had to take it. Was she brave enough to grab onto happiness with both hands and never let go?

Teresa inhaled deeply, biting back tears. It was as if all her emotions were simply too much for her, they threatened to spill over and bubble out like those same tears that pricked her eyes.

She thought about the past two years and leaving Oliver. It had been the most difficult thing she'd ever had to do. Running to protect their son was a no brainer. Thank God it was all over now and the hard life she and Thomas had been living, was truly behind them now. Thomas would have a real home with parents who loved him.

Mate, her Bear pushed the thought at her and this time, she readily welcomed it.

Thomas had already accepted Oliver with that wonderful perseverance, flexibility, and endurance all children had and adults could only dream of. Before they'd left, she'd kissed his head and said she'd loved him to which he'd answered back that he loved Mommy *and* Daddy.

She'd seen the way the matter of fact statement had touched Oliver. The big Grizzly had nearly teared up. She could still hear the echoes of Thomas' laughter and the car sounds he made while racing the red toy car against the blue one, his parents temporarily forgotten as he played with Jennifer. It had made both of them smile all the way down the lane and into the woods.

Their cub was a good boy. He deserved this

chance to have a real family. She'd moved him around so much in his young life. She had no idea how good it would feel to be back here for the both of them. To be home with Oliver. Her mate and Thomas' father.

She cursed her own stupidity for believing her lying, scheming, violent pretend father. The idea that Witherspoon Tech was out there and still searching for her scared the crap out of Teresa. But, and it was a big but, she finally understood why Mathias Witherspoon wanted to keep her away from the man she loved. Pure and simple malice.

He wanted to keep you from your true inner strength. To keep you apart from me. I am your strength, I am the other half to your soul. We are one, her Bear spoke to her, supplying answers to questions she hadn't even asked. Rage like she never felt before towards her parent filled her hard and fast.

Grrr.

Teresa closed her eyes and pushed the beast back down. She didn't want to be filled with hate. Not now, not ever. Thomas deserved better than that from her, so did Oliver.

Mate. Claim. Mine, her Bear chuffed.

She opened her eyes and walked alongside her mate. Perhaps with a little luck and some patience, she would find out what being mates really meant for them both. She had no doubts in her mind that together they would be stronger, better, happier than she'd ever been alone.

Together, they would be a family.

Yes, agreed her Bear, *good plan.*

CHAPTER 12

Using the rucksack Teresa had found in the back of his closet the day before, Oliver had stuffed an oversized throw blanket inside, a couple of stainless-steel tumblers, and a vintage bottle of red wine he'd been saving for a special occasion.

He had thought to celebrate the finished version of *Where Beauty Lives* alone with this bottle, but this was so much better. It might not be the most planned out evening, but it would be perfect.

Mate, Oliver's Bear grumbled inside of him, anxious and impatient to get started. If all went well, he would re-claim his sweet Teresa under the stars this very night. Nerves danced along his spine and butterflies turned into fighter jets inside his stomach.

He was as nervous as a green cub. His Bear chuffed and snorted, laughing at his human side. Then he got serious, the Grizzly inside of him demanded that he do everything in his power to not fuck this up.

Oliver was full on board with that plan. Teresa was his now and forever. He just needed to prove to them both that he was a worthy mate, his beast a perfect match for the breathtaking beauty.

"What's in the bag?" she asked as they wandered through the cooling evening air.

"A little surprise. Come on, I want to show you someplace special."

"Oh," she lifted her jade green eyes to his and smiled coyly.

Her stunning beauty always seemed to take him by surprise, leaving him dumfounded and void of all reason. Not that it should've. He had spent countless hours studying the angles and curves that made up his ever-lovelier mate.

Oliver had written music and lyrics in award-winning shows based solely on the color of her soulful eyes and the tempting way her top lip jutted out, only slightly larger than the lower. Peaches and cream wasn't just her scent, it was her coloring too.

Glorious golden haired with pale skin that pinked up in various shades depending on what she was feeling.

When in the throes of passion, that blush travelled down her cheeks to her sweet, supple breast, all the way to her inner thighs. He licked his lips at the memory. She was in a word, superb.

And now he knew what he'd been missing the past two years. He understood why his work never seemed to satisfy him. Oliver had been missing his muse. He'd been missing Teresa.

"What?" she asked and he realized he'd stopped walking.

"Nothing. Well, not nothing. You're beautiful, you know," he stated.

"Ollie," she rolled her eyes, and he took lead.

Taking her hand he tugged her gently along and she followed him through the thicket of low standing trees. Just a few more feet, and he would be at his favorite spot in all of Indian Lake.

Way up high, a few dozen feet on the flat top of an enormous bolder that jutted out over the edge of the water was Oliver Pax's special place. He stood for a moment with her hand in his and just looked. This place was unique. It was close to his heart and he had never brought another living soul there before.

The air was crisp and cool as night softly fell all around them. The water glittered as tiny ripples made by fish and other animals stopping to drink broke the otherwise still waters. Those tiny breaks reflected the silvery moonlight. Like bits of broken silver, he thought.

It was breathtaking, beautiful, but it was nothing compared to her. Oliver removed the blanket from the rucksack and laid it across the hard stone. He took her hand and helped her to sit watching with interest as the long skirt slid up, revealing her long shapely legs.

She'd changed into a loose flowing dress that reached her ankles. It had short ruffles for sleeves the left her arms bare. Looking down he noted with approval a pair of flat sandals that slid easily off her dainty feet.

Tiny yellow flowers danced across the navy fabric of the dress. It draped across her splendid curves, molding to each dip and swell perfectly. It made his mouth water with wanting her, and his beast grunted in agreement.

"It's so quiet here. Still and perfect," Teresa murmured and laid her cheek across her knee as she watched the moon slowly climb higher in the near black skies.

Night fell quickly and Oliver had never felt so in tune with the elements as he did just then. Stars sparkled in the dark, velvety blanket that was the sky. They seemed to weave magic into the air as they looked down on Oliver and his mate from the heavens. He popped the cork on the bottle of Merlot he'd brought, and watched Teresa turn and gasp in delight.

"You brought wine?"

"Yes," he grinned at her surprise and he poured the dark red liquid into two metal tumblers.

He'd received a dozen of the polished gifts from Terrence to keep him and the rest of their circle of friends from constantly breaking glasses with their supernatural strength. As it was, they'd managed to dent only three of the set so far. He'd left those back at the cabin. He handed one unblemished cup to Teresa and his Bear growled lowly as their fingers brushed.

Mine. The animal inside of him longed to reconnect with her. Despite the fact they'd made love several times already, his beast wanted to re-claim his once lost beauty. For good this time.

Soon, he told his Bear.

"This is wonderful," she sighed, and sipped the fragrant liquid, "I love red wine."

"I remember," he slid behind her, opening his legs so that she could lean back against his chest.

"I used to only be able to buy the cheap stuff though," he shrugged.

"It was perfect then, and it is now," she said and he felt her heart beating rapidly right alongside his, "because of you, Oliver."

She set her cup down and turned in his arms. Kneeling between his legs, she reached up and pulled him to her. Oliver went without a fight. For her, he would do anything. Submit, give in, relinquish all control over his ordered life.

He would give her everything if he could just keep her. The best thing was, she asked for nothing except his love in return. That he would give her without hesitation.

"Need you, Ollie," she moaned into his mouth, and he readily allowed her entrance.

Her tongue twined with his, stirring up passion and long lost memories of nights spent entwined in his arms back in his tiny apartment in Brooklyn Heights. How he'd loved this woman!

Yes, he'd cursed her for leaving him, even as he'd yearned for her on those long lonely nights when he'd had no one to share the successes of his career, no one to simply hold in the coldness, to ward off the dark, and make his beast calm. But now, she was here, with him, and he and his Bear were positively elated to have her once more in his life.

Their kiss grew deeper and more urgent as Teresa tugged his sweatshirt over his head. He hissed as she raked her nails down his chest, kissing away the hurt with those maddening bee stung lips.

"Resa," he growled her name and changed position.

Laying her out on the blanket, he lifted her head and placed his sweatshirt beneath it as a makeshift pillow. Oliver leaned over her, inhaling her peaches and cream scent, swallowing it down as he soon would the very essence of that particular flavor from its sweetest core.

"Mine," he kissed her pretty mouth, undoing the buttons of her soft flowy dress one at a time.

He punctuated each tiny button's release with a thrust of his tongue, loving the way she submitted to his ministrations readily and with such unrehearsed enthusiasm. The night air cooled his sizzling skin as he shucked off every last article of clothing from his tall, muscular frame.

Oliver felt his Bear's power flickering just underneath his human skin. The beast wanted to join in on the claiming, and he saw no reason to object. She belonged to all of him. Both he and his Bear held claim to both sides of her. It was the way of fated mates, he supposed.

"Need you," she writhed on the blanket, sighing as he parted the dress and helped her remove it from her arms.

She wore only a small pair of pink panties over her heavenly sex. They were darker just at the center, evidence of her need. His Bear rode him harder in that moment of realization. His gums ached and fingertips burned with the need to loosen claw and fang.

Not yet, he told his beast.

"Gonna give you everything you need, mate," he licked his lips.

He was actually drooling. Oliver Pax, renowned composer, and writer, was not only speechless in the face of such beauty as was his mate and lover, the mother of his cubs, lying naked in the moonlight, but he was motherfucking salivating as well.

She was all swells and valleys, dips and curves, acres of pale smooth skin for him to explore and cherish. He traced her pink tipped breasts with his fingers first, then his mouth, relishing her gasp as she arched off the floor and fitted herself more fully to him. She was fuller there now, rounded, and plump. So fucking beautiful, it made him want to curse and cry, growl, and roar, all at the same time.

"Yes, Ollie, oh yes," she praised as he slid down the slight swell of her soft belly to that scrap of pink that hid her treasures from him.

"Mine," he grunted the word and took the elastic band in his mouth looking up to capture her green gaze with his own.

"Yours," she echoed.

The sound of fabric tearing was loud in the quiet forest, but it only made them both that much more excited. He could practically feel her anticipation as if it was his own. Maybe it was.

Her Bear brushed against his mind and Oliver welcomed the Sow with open arms. She was his now. His to claim, his to love, and his to protect. Always.

Inhaling her heady musk, he parted her nether lips with his hands, gently brushing over the dark blonde curls that she thankfully kept natural, though neat he noted dutifully. She was gorgeous, sublime.

"Mine," he growled his new favorite word.

Oliver's eyes were glued to her face as he licked her with the flat of his tongue, parting her cheeks, he started at the top of her crevice down to her forbidden hole, all the way to that tiny, needy little bundle of nerves that held all her secrets and legions of untold pleasures.

Pleasures he intended to ring out until she had barely any breath left in her body. Yes. Tonight there was no holding back. Under the heavens he would worship her on this altar made of rock and earth, he would claim his mate and bind her to him for all time.

"Ollie!" she yelled, tugging on his hair, trying to pull him up, but he'd only just begun.

He used his strength to hold her carefully where he wanted her. Spread out before him, a sacrifice to his need. He continued to feast on his woman. Never before had he treated her to such thorough oral gratification, but this was the way of Shifter mates, and she was soon bucking her hips in time to his tongue's movements.

"Mate," he grunted, and added two digits to the mix, thrusting his fingers into her tight heat, and stretching her sex to better prepare her for him.

Tonight he was insatiable for her. He deserved to be, after all two years was a long time, and Oliver was a Shifter with a bear-sized appetite. He treated her to several more long swipes of his tongue before he settled on her clit.

His Bear surged forth and the rumbling growl added that little bit of extra to his ministration, causing his talented Bear's lips and tongue to vibrate against that needy little nub. Spreading her pussy lips, he worked his fingers in and out of her molten heat, all the while suckling that tiny nubbin.

Teresa yelled his name and arched her back. Good. He wanted her like that. Wild, desperate, and a little out of control.

Fuck, he grunted. He should've watched what he wished for as her claw tipped hands found his shoulders.

His beast growled with pleasure, taking her scratches as a sign she was marking him. Yes, why not? That was the way of creatures such as they. They scratched and bit, signs of love and ways of forging eternal bonds between couples. He wanted it all, and more. He doubled his efforts and soon she was crying out as her first orgasm swept through her.

Oliver held her through it, lapping at her pussy like the lovesick Bear he was until she could not even cry out. He looked up to find her eyes glowing beautifully with her Bear as she reached for him.

"My turn," she said and flipped them both in a move so strong and quick, he'd been completely unprepared for it.

His mind blanked and Oliver embraced the primitive thoughts of his Bear as he rose to meet her in a crashing embrace that made them both groan aloud. His cock grew even harder at the contact and she straddled him, lowering her slick heat down ever so slowly. Inch by inch she slid down his shaft until he was buried deep within her tight channel.

"Resa," he grunted her name.

A prayer, a chant, whatever have you, all he knew was he kept saying it as she began to move. Rocking her hips and taking him to paradise with every flex, ripple, and thrust.

"Ollie, mine, my mate," she mumbled and moved faster and harder, impaling herself over and over again on his cock.

He brought one hand up to cup her face and lower her to him, grunting with the effort it took to keep his passion in check. She felt so damn good, plunging into her silken depths was the ultimate for him, and fuck, he wanted to come so badly, but not yet.

Tension started deep in his gut as she milked his cock with her weeping pussy. Teresa's mouth opened in a silent scream as her moves became erratic. Yes, she was close and he knew just what to do to bring her over the edge.

"Mine," he growled the word and struck, re-marking his mate right on the scar from where he'd first laid claim to her.

"Oliver!" she yelled and her walls contracted with the force of her orgasm.

He sucked on her neck, swallowing her life's force, and solidifying the *matebond* that had grown so pale over the past couple of years apart. Snarling he released her flesh and pain exploded on his own left shoulder.

"Fuck," he grunted watching as she bit and claimed him with her own set of Shifter fangs.

His dick pulsed and cum filled her womb as plea-sure unfurled and washed over him. The two of them clung to each other, trying to catch their breaths as ecstasy reigned supreme. It seemed to explode over the entire universe far as he was concerned. Never before had he ever felt such powerful joy and pleasure.

"Mine," she said and rocked her hips once more, and fuck him, if he didn't come even harder.

"Yours," he grunted, "mate."

After they'd packed up their makeshift picnic,

Oliver helped Teresa back into her dress. She was a little wobbly on her feet, and he was the same, he grinned wickedly.

"What?" She asked.

"I was just thinking if we keep this up we'll both need walkers," he joked.

"Ha ha," she said and walked right up to him, twirling her arms around his neck brushing the already healing bite she'd given him delicately with her fingertips.

"This means you're mine now, right?"

"I've always been yours," he returned and kissed her quickly.

The entire world could change in the blink of an eye, but Oliver knew one thing to be true among all others. He would never stop wanting to kiss this woman.

The sound of multiple cars driving nearby had him turning around. He used his Bear's ears and nose to try and gain their scent and position.

"Strangers are nearing the cabin, let's get back."

Teresa's panicked expression met his and he understood real fear for the first time in his life. Thomas was back at the cabin.

"I'm going to shift," he explained and dropped the rucksack.

"I don't know if I can," she started.

"Don't worry. It's still new to you. Just climb on my back and I'll get us there quickly."

She did as he asked and together, they raced through the woods. The sight that greeted him was as unwelcomed as it was unwanted.

Men in suits got out of two black SUVs. Two of them had long rifles in their hands. He discerned they were human with a whiff, but those goons weren't the ones he worried about. It was the sneering bastard who thought to come here himself.

"Teresa? Come out now, and I won't harm your *lover*," snarled Mathias Witherspoon.

Oliver growled low in his chest. Teresa slid off his back. He tried reaching her with his mind, wincing at his own shouted message.

No! Don't you dare. I got this.

She turned around and looked him in the eye, her posture exuded determination and he knew regardless of what he said, she would do as she needed. He saw that, respected it, understood it, and still, he feared for her safety.

"Let me talk to him, draw him away from the cabin and Thomas. If need be, you come in roaring."

"Teresa! You're only making it harder on yourself," Mathias' snide voice reached him easily.

It made his Bear want to rip the guy's head off, but he waited in the shadows of the trees, as his mate asked him to. He could scent her nervousness and fear, but even greater than those was her resolve.

"Hello, Mathias," she said startling all six men as she exited the woods and stood just to the side of his cabin.

"You do mean Father, don't you?" Mathias lied.

"No. I know you're not my father."

"Ah, well, good then we are past this charade. Come with me now. Bring your little animal bastard, and I won't expose Pax for the monster he is."

"I don't think so, Mathias, you see I finally understand that he is not the monster, neither am I for that matter."

"Is that so? Humans fornicating with animals. It's revolting," he spat the words at her and Oliver growled.

Teresa's head tilted towards him, a subtle sign that she was not ready for him to intervene yet. Except the men with guns were now trained on her. Oliver knew what to do.

"Your mother lied to me. I always wanted to marry her, but she was a filthy beast. And when I caught up with her it was too late, she wouldn't let me cure her. She'd already copulated with another and had you!"

"So you stole me from my mother?"

"Stole you? No, I saved you!"

"You're a bastard," she whispered as tears fell from her eyes.

"You are the bastard, and from the reports I got looks like the cycle has started again."

"My mother was a woman, a Shifter, and you killed her."

"Yes, she was an animal, and she wouldn't see reason. She didn't appreciate my cure for her ailment. Of course, I had to put her down."

"You are not curing anything," she screamed.

"So many doubters. I had to prove myself to others and now they see, you are proof my pills work!" he smiled evilly.

"No, you didn't cure me. You hurt me, kept me in a prison, lied to me, and look, *father*, I am still me," her anger was tangible.

She growled and snarled, embracing her Bear so quickly and savagely that Oliver couldn't help but feel pride in her quick transformation. She was learning to live with her Bear, but she was too far gone to see Mathias' signal to his men.

"That's too bad Teresa, I guess I will end you

now, and experiment on your *cub*," he raised his hand and both men with the rifles took aim.

Teresa stood on her back legs and loosed a roar that shook the very earth while Oliver sped from the trees and with a mighty swipe of his paw took down both gunmen. After that, Teresa joined and together they subdued the rest of the men.

EPILOGUE

Teresa sat down on the couch with Thomas reading a storybook while Oliver cleared up the details of the clean-up with Jennifer.

Fortunately, no normals had happened upon the two enormous Grizzly Shifters protecting their cub and each other from Witherspoon Tech's president and his henchmen.

The two gunmen were lost causes, but Mathias Witherspoon and the others had survived with a few broken limbs and scratches.

They'd been taken away by whatever secret organization Jennifer worked for, and Teresa couldn't be sure, but she thought she saw a group of Draconian bi-peds land earlier.

She had asked Oliver if it was alright for her to

stay in with Thomas since he'd been getting fussy and he'd readily agreed.

Good mate, her Bear chuffed.

Teresa agreed. She cuddled her son and finished the story. After a few minutes, his breathing evened out and she realized he fell asleep.

"Love?" Ollie walked into the room with a smile and a couple of familiar faces.

"Hello again," Leandra said softly.

Teresa nodded and pursed her lips, she placed Thomas securely surrounded by pillows on the low settee and stood up.

"Hi, wow, you look better," Chance said and Oliver whacked him in the side, "What? Last time I saw her she was hooked up to a zillion machines," the half-Demon rubbed his arm and winked at her.

"Oh Chance," Leandra rolled her eyes.

"So, what the hell happened here? Why is the head of the Wyvern Protection Unit outside?" he whispered to Oliver who growled at him.

"Oh that," Teresa smiled, "long story. How about Oliver cooks us up some food, then we can discuss it?"

"Sounds good," Jennifer entered the room and nodded at the newcomers, "the guys have finished cleaning up outside and I am famished."

"Okay," Oliver cocked his head at her and raised an eyebrow, "if my mate can help me for a minute in the kitchen?"

She nodded and followed him down the hall while the other adults took seats in the dining room promising to keep an eye out for little Thomas.

"Are you alright?" he asked and gathered her close to him.

"I have never been better. I know who I am and where I belong for the first time in my life," she said simply.

"I love you, Teresa, I almost died when I saw those guns trained on you," he whispered and dropped his head to kiss her.

"I wasn't scared because you were there. I knew my Grizzly Bear mate would never let anything bad happen to me," she smiled against his mouth feeling the pride her words encouraged to soar through him.

"Mine," he said.

"Yeah, yeah, she's yours, whatever, but when am I gonna see my pages, Pax?" interrupted Chance from the doorway.

Teresa's eyes shot to the half-Demon and her Sow rose up to greet him with a snarl. She did not like being interrupted while she was with her mate.

"Okay, we can discuss it later, no biggie," the smart man shrugged and backed out of the kitchen.

Teresa heard the thwack of his mate's slap and smiled. She had to remember to thank Leandra later.

"Now. where were we?" she asked and kissed her mate hard on the lips.

"There is good," Oliver grunted.

"I am yours," she echoed his earlier statement, "but you're mine too," she pulled him down for a harder, longer kiss.

The strength of their *matebond* pulsed through her and Teresa felt closer than ever to Oliver. Everything seemed to multiply in intensity now that she'd embraced her inner beast.

Oh yes, she thought, she was going to like being a Bear.

"After all this time, I have a Grizzly lover of my own, sweet mate," Oliver stole her breath with another meeting of lips, this one the sweetest kiss of them all.

"Wait till later," he winked, "we'll compose symphonies together in the dark," he promised and she bit her lips to keep from groaning.

Side by side, the couple set about preparing food for their family and their guests and Teresa's heart swelled with love.

Tomorrow looked brighter already, she thought as she took in the brilliant sun blinking overhead. Now that her family was together all the tomorrows were going to be stunning.

THE END.

Liked this story? Read More Purely Paranormal Romance Books by C.D. Gorri by visiting http://www.cdgorri.com/series/purely-paranormal-pleasures/.

OTHER TITLES BY C.D. GORRI

Other Titles by C.D. Gorri

Paranormal Romance Books:

Macconwood Pack Novel Series:

Charley's Christmas Wolf: A Macconwood Pack Novel 1

Cat's Howl: A Macconwood Pack Novel 2

Code Wolf: A Macconwood Pack Novel 3

The Witch and The Werewolf: A Macconwood Pack Novel 4

To Claim a Wolf: A Macconwood Pack Novel 5

Conall's Mate: A Macconwood Pack Novel 6

Her Solstice Wolf: A Macconwood Pack Novel 7

Werewolf Fever: A Macconwood Pack Novel 8

Also available in 2 boxed sets:

The Macconwood Pack Volume 1

The Macconwood Pack Volume 2

Macconwood Pack Tales Series:

Wolf Bride: The Story of Ailis and Eoghan A

Macconwood Pack Tale 1

Summer Bite: A Macconwood Pack Tale 2

His Winter Mate: A Macconwood Pack Tale 3

Snow Angel: A Macconwood Pack Tale 4

Charley's Baby Surprise: A Macconwood Pack Tale 5

Home for the Howlidays: A Macconwood Pack Tale 6

A Silver Wedding: A Macconwood Pack Tale 7

Mine Furever: A Macconwood Pack Tale 8

A Furry Little Christmas: A Macconwood Pack Tale 9

Also available in two boxed sets:

The Macconwood Pack Tales Volume 1

Shifters Furever: The Macconwood Pack Tales Volume 2

The Falk Clan Tales:

The Dragon's Valentine: A Falk Clan Novel 1

The Dragon's Christmas Gift: A Falk Clan Novel 2

The Dragon's Heart: A Falk Clan Novel 3

The Dragon's Secret: A Falk Clan Novel 4

The Dragon's Treasure: A Falk Clan Novel 5

The Dragon's Surprise: A Falk Clan Novel 6

The Dragon's Dream: A Falk Clan Novel 7

Dragon Mates: The Falk Clan Series Boxed Set Books 1-4

The Bear Claw Tales:

Bearly Breathing: A Bear Claw Tale 1

Bearly There: A Bear Claw Tale 2

Bearly Tamed: A Bear Claw Tale 3

Bearly Mated: A Bear Claw Tale 4

Also available in a boxed set:

The Complete Bear Claw Tales (Books 1-4)

The Barvale Clan Tales:

Polar Opposites: The Barvale Clan Tales 1

Polar Outbreak: The Barvale Clan Tales 2

Polar Compound: A Barvale Clan Tale 3

Polar Curve: A Barvale Clan Tale 4

Also available in a boxed set:

The Barvale Clan Tales (Books 1-4)

Barvale Holiday Tales:

A Bear For Christmas

Hers To Bear

Thank You Beary Much

Bearing Gifts

Also available in a boxed set:

The Barvale Holiday Tales (Books 1-3)

Purely Paranormal Romance Books:

Marked by the Devil: Purely Paranormal Romance Books

Mated to the Dragon King: Purely Paranormal Romance
Books

Claimed by the Demon: Purely Paranormal Romance
Books

Christmas with a Devil, a Dragon King, & a Demon:
Purely Paranormal Romance Books

Vampire Lover: Purely Paranormal Romance Books

Grizzly Lover: Purely Paranormal Romance Books

Christmas With Her Chupacabra: Purely Paranormal
Romance Books

Purely Paranormal Romance Books Anthology

The Wardens of Terra:

Bound by Air: The Wardens of Terra Book 1

Star Kissed: A Wardens of Terra Short

Waterlocked: The Wardens of Terra Book 2

Moon Kissed: A Wardens of Terra Short

*Now in a boxed set and in audio!

The Maverick Pride Tales:

Purrfectly Mated

Purrfectly Kissed

Purrfectly Trapped

Purrfectly Caught

Purrfectly Naughty

Purrfectly Bound

<u>Dire Wolf Mates:</u>

Shake That Sass

<u>Wyvern Protection Unit:</u>

Gift Wrapped Protector: WPU 1

<u>Standalones:</u>

The Enforcer

Blood Song: A Sanguinem Council Book

Spring Fling (co-written with P. Mattern)

<u>EveL Worlds:</u>

Chinchilla and the Devil: A FUCN'A Book

Sammi and the Jersey Bull: A FUCN'A Book

Mouse and the Ball: A FUCN'A Book

<u>The Guardians of Chaos:</u>

Wolf Shield: Guardians of Chaos Book 1

Dragon Shield: Guardians of Chaos Book 2

Stallion Shield: Guardians of Chaos Book 3

Panther Shield: Guardians of Chaos 4

Witch Shield: Guardians of Chaos 5

Vampire Shield: Guardians of Chaos 6

<u>Howl's Romance</u>

Mated to the Werewolf Next Door: A Howl's Romance

The Tiger King's Christmas Bride

Claiming His Virgin Mate: Howls Romance

Twice Mated Tales

Doubly Claimed

Doubly Bound

Doubly Tied

Hearts of Stone Series

Shifter Mountain: Hearts of Stone 1

Shifter City: Hearts of Stone 2

Shifter Village: Hearts of Stone 3

Accidentally Undead Series

Fangs For Nothin'

Moongate Island Tales

Moongate Island Mate

Moongate Island Christmas Claim

Mated in Hope Falls

Mated by Moonlight

Speed Dating with the Denizens of the Underworld

Ash: Speed Dating with the Denizens of Underworld

Arachne: Speed Dating with the Denizens of Underworld

Hungry Fur Love

Hungry Like Her Wolf: Magic and Mayhem Universe

Hungry For Her Bear: Magic and Mayhem Universe

<u>Shifters Unleashed Boxed Sets</u>

Check out these amazing anthologies where you can find some of my books and the works of other awesome authors!

<u>Island Stripe Pride</u>

Tiger Claimed

Tiger Denied

<u>NYC Shifter Tales</u>

Cuff Linked

Sealed Fate

<u>A Howlin' Good Fairytale Retelling</u>

Sweet As Candy (as seen in Once Upon An Ever After)

<u>Coming Soon:</u>

Asterion

Tiger Rejected

For Fangs Sake

Hungry As Her Python: Magic and Mayhem Universe

If The Shoe Fits: A Howlin' Good Fairytale Retelling

Chickee and the Paparazzi: FUCN'A

The Wolf's Winter Wish: A Macconwood Pack Tale

The Hybrid Assassin

Tempted By Her Protector: WPU 2

Alien Protector: WPU 3

Elvish Protector: WPU 4

Thrilled By Her Protector: WPU 5

Breaking Sass

Pinch of Sass

Kickin' Sass

<u>Young Adult Urban Fantasy Books:</u>

Wolf Moon: A Grazi Kelly Novel Book 1

Hunter Moon: A Grazi Kelly Novel Book 2

Rebel Moon: A Grazi Kelly Novel Book 3

Winter Moon: A Grazi Kelly Novel Book 4

Chasing The Moon: A Grazi Kelly Short 5

Blood Moon: A Grazi Kelly Novel 6

*Get all 6 books NOW AVAILABLE IN A BOXED SET:

The Complete Grazi Kelly Novel Series

Casting Magic: The Angela Tanner Files 1

Keeping Magic: The Angela Tanner Files 2

<u>G'Witches Magical Mysteries Series</u>

Co-written with P. Mattern

G'Witches

G'Witches 2: The Harpy Harbinger

G'Witches 3: Summoning Secrets

HAVE YOU MET THE BARVALE CLAN BEARS?

Looking for a Paranormal Romance series that is loads of growly fun?

Meet the Barvale Clan first in the Bear Claw Tales! A complete shifter romance series about 4 brothers who discover and need to win their fated mates!

Titles are:

Bearly Breathing

Bearly There

Bearly Tamed

Bearly Mated

Followed by two more spin off series, the Barvale Clan Tales, featuring:

Polar Opposites

Polar Outbreak
Polar Compound
Polar Curve

and, of course, the Barvale Holiday Tales:
A Bear For Christmas
Hers to Bear
Thank You Beary Much
Bearing Gifts

Look for more of these sexy, heartwarming holiday inspired tales soon!

No cliffhangers. Steamy PNR fun.
Go and read your next happily ever after today!

BEWARE... HERE BE DRAGONS!

The Falk Clan Tales are my stories surrounding four Dragon Shifter brothers and how they find their one true mates!

Each brother's chest is marked with his rose, the magical link to his heart and his magic. They each have a matching gemstone to go with it.

In *The Dragon's Valentine* we meet the eldest Falk brother, Callius. He is on a mission to find a Castle and his one true mate, one he can trust with his diamond rose....

She's given up on love, but he's just begun...

In *The Dragon's Christmas Gift* our attention shifts to Alexsander, the youngest brother of the four. He has resigned himself to a life alone, until he meets *her…*

His heart is frozen. Can she change his mind about love?

The Dragon's Heart is the story of Edric Falk who has vowed never to love again, but that changes when he meets his feisty mate, Joselyn Curacao.

Some wounds run deep. Can a Dragon's heart be unbroken?

Meet Nikolai Falk in the last Falk Clan Tale, *The Dragon's Secret.*

She just wants a little fun, he's looking for a lifetime.

*These first four books are now available in one convenient set. Look for Dragon Mates today. Now available in Paperback & Hardcover.

Meet another long lost Falk brother in *The Dragon's Treasure.* Castor Falk breaks free from his prison in search of his kin, he finds his mate instead.

She doesn't believe in fairytales, until a Dragon comes knocking on her door.

The Dragon's Surprise features a new Dragon, Devine Graystone, and a female Werewolf who makes him think twice about his lonely state of being…

Nothing can surprise this six hundred-year-old Dragon, except maybe her.

Lastly, in *The Dragon's Dream* we meet a spunky she-Wolf who gives Nicholas Graystone a run for his money when it comes to romance. Can a Dragon really have it all?

He's a hardcore realist until she dares him to dream.

EXCERPT FROM PURRFECTLY MATED

How the fuck did I wind up here?

It was all Elissa could do not to slam her face down on the table as she pondered that question for the umpteenth time since leaving her cozy Hoboken apartment to go on this so called date.

"So, babe," the over-stuffed, heavily-cologned, and downright fugly man said.

Her date of the evening looked like something out of a bad sitcom as he tried to lean over the stained tablecloth of the rundown hotel buffet room, he'd driven two hours to get to. Waggling his caterpillar-like eyebrows, he gave her the once over and Elissa's skin crawled.

Oh, hell no.

"I got a room upstairs, you know, for *after*," he told her, nodding his head, and biting his lower lip in a manner she assumed he thought was provocative.

At best, it was nauseating.

FML.

How was this guy Elissa's date for the evening? What had she done to deserve this?

Little Gianni. Yup, that was how he'd introduced himself. And here she was. On a blind date with a guy who had the word 'little' in front of his name.

Well, what did she expect? Roses and champagne? In this economy? She didn't know where Cinder-fucking-ella got her prince, but it sure as fuck wasn't in Jersey.

Elissa could only blame herself for agreeing to go on this blind date. Initially, the whole Little Gianni fiasco had been intended for her roommate.

Wait a second. Scratch that thought.

It *was* all Gretchen's fault. That ungrateful cow!

She tried to play it off like she was some sweet little homegrown maiden. Oh, just wait till Elissa got home. Gretchen was never going to hear the end of it.

She owed Elissa. Big time. Like a whole month of

washing the dishes big time. The rat trap they shared in her hometown of Hoboken was all the two women could afford, and for the most part, they got along just fine.

In fact, they'd grown to be close friends over the three years they'd lived together. It was the only reason she'd ever agreed to this date from Hell.

Elissa sighed and looked over at Little Gianni. Maybe he wasn't all that bad?

"*BEEEELLLLLLLLCHHH!* 'Scuse me, doll. Better out, am I right?"

Gianni winked and Elissa wished for a black hole to open up and swallow her up right through the floor.

OMFG.

The man just burped out loud like he was in a frat boy belting contest, only those days passed him up about thirty years ago.

For fuck's sake. Gretchen, you so owe me.

Elissa cursed her roommate and tried not to groan. But Little Gianni wasn't quite done. The grown ass man lifted his leg and let one rip.

Right. Fucking. There.

Elissa was going to die before the end of the night.

Literally.

This is what you get when you do a friend a favor without asking for details! Idiota!

The voice of her Italian grandmother sounded in her brain. She tried to ignore it, willing herself not to wince at the man while he sucked air, and who knows what else, noisily through his coffee-stained teeth.

Ew. So gross.

That was the perfect word to describe it. The only word, in fact. The entire date was just so fucking gross. She still couldn't believe her sweet little roommate from Iowa, *Gretchen Kaepernick*, she of the wispy hair and baby blues, had set her up with this guy!

What the actual fuck was up with that?

Little Gianni was a slob. Actually, he looked just like her Uncle Nico, and that was not a good thing. Seriously, not good at all.

He wore his hair slicked back in a too tight pony-tail that emphasized his rapidly receding hairline. As if that wasn't enough to put her off, he was sporting an enormous paunch. Now, being a curvy girl, Elissa appreciated food and was in no way against men showing the same appreciation.

She liked bigger men. Always had. But bigger did not mean you had to be sloppy. Little Gianni's stomach was literally hanging out from under a tight tan golf shirt that had definitely seen better days.

The man didn't even look like he had ever played a sport of any kind. With it, he wore brown polyester pants that were three inches above his ankles and unbuttoned at the waist.

He didn't look like he tried at all for this date. What kind of guy did that? His shirt collar was bent and wrinkled, and all three buttons were open to his chest, revealing a mat of oily, dark hair and pimples.

Somehow, he'd managed to tuck the back of the shirt in, but the front simply would not hold in that stomach. What worried her more were the tight brown pants.

As he sat back and stretched, she wondered if she should take cover. They looked like they were one bite from exploding off his body. Elissa shuddered at the image.

Please God, if You have an ounce of mercy, don't let that happen, she prayed.

"Hang on, doll, I gotta take this," he said, and turned to answer his cell phone.

It was ringing to the tune of '70s disco music she

hadn't heard since the last family reunion. Her eyes kept going to the huge stain on the front of his shirt. It was a little game she liked to call *what the hell is that*.

Coffee, she guessed.

"Up your ass, Bruno. I gotta have it by Monday," he cursed into the receiver.

Elissa winced at the spectacle he was making of them both. There were only a handful of people there, but still.

Deep breaths.

Ew. Maybe not.

She coughed as the strong body spray, that he'd obviously used a ton of in lieu of a shower, bad move in her opinion, invaded her lungs.

Oh, this was so bad.

Elissa was, by no means, a snob. But this guy looked like he'd stepped out of a bad 1980s mafia spoof film. What's worse, he kept smacking his lips together as he hung up the phone and looked her over from head to chest.

Thank fuck for the table, she thought, wishing she could hide her bosoms from his view.

"Ssssss," he hissed, like it was sexy or something.

She just grimaced. Elissa might be able to forgive a lot of quirks, but she hated mouth noises. Really hated them. It was a super pet peeve of hers. Never mind his totally inappropriate and unwelcomed leer.

She started counting the minutes, willing the date to be over already. Plenty of people would tell her she shouldn't be so choosy, but really? She was not this desperate.

Not yet anyway.

So, she was curvy and a little mouthy too. But was it wrong to want a man with good table manners? Even if men were thin on the ground for someone like her.

As a chef, she'd worked in a lot of restaurants and even as a personal cook for professional couples. She'd seen her fair share of unhappy couples and downright uncomfortable marriages. But as far as she was concerned, all relationships went downhill when good table manners were dismissed.

Good manners were merely a sign that a person was thoughtful and respectful. At least, that was what Nonna had told her. Gianni here had clearly missed that lesson as a child. Elissa had to work not to groan in disgust as he slurped a raw clam down his gullet.

Shudder.

Was there no end to his feeding? That's what it reminded her of. Feeding time at the zoo.

OMG. That was rude, she scolded herself. But it wasn't like she said it out loud.

All she wanted to do was go home. At least she was comfortable. *She'd* worn her softest pair of black leggings for this disaster date, paired with one of her favorite tunics on top.

It was dark green with tiny black buttons down the front and showed just the right amount of cleavage. She'd gone for neat and tidy as opposed to downright sexy.

Good call, in her opinion. Elissa looked perfectly fine for a nice *getting to know you* dinner, which is what she thought she was getting when her roommate asked her to step in for her on a blind date that one of her best client's had set up for her.

Elissa shuddered now, thinking how good old Gianni here would've reacted to the red dress and heels she'd contemplated before checking the weather report.

Gulp.

The lewd man was already salivating, and she was so not having it. Fending off his unwanted advances was not how she wanted to finish the night.

Ew again.

Elissa shivered, slightly chilled despite the fact

they were indoors. It was a cold, gloomy evening, and the forecast called for even more rain later that night. Not at all unusual for this time of year in the Garden State.

November was always chilly in the evenings, rainy too. Elissa tended to run warm, but she was glad she'd brought a jacket with her. Especially since her date refused to turn the heat on in the car.

When she'd asked, he'd looked offended and told her it wasted gas.

Um. Okay.

She checked her phone. It was only seven o'clock, but the two hour drive was still ahead of them. Maybe they could make it home before ten if they left soon.

Ugh. Did he just blow his nose?

"Allergies, doll. Say, you gonna eat that?" he asked before scooping a fry from her dish and swallowing it down.

Elissa was gonna kill her roomie. Gretchen was a hair and nail stylist. A lot of her clients were elderly, and they just loved her. They were always offering to set her up on blind dates with their nephews and grandsons.

Mostly, the sweet old ladies were kind. They swore they could find her curvy roommate the right man, assuming she was single because she was new to town. Well, when Elissa got home tonight, she was going to tell Gretchen she needed to fire the old lady who set this date up from being her client.

Like *ASAP*.

No one who liked Gretchen would've sent her out with this guy. Gianni reached over and touched her hand and Elissa pulled back, reaching for the napkin.

Gross.

"I sure hope you ain't a cold one, doll," he said, shaking his head.

"What?"

"Ain't gonna matter. I know just what you need, doll."

She was still wiping the greasy residue he'd transferred to her skin from the food he ate sans utensils. This was too much. Elissa was beyond uncomfortable with all the leering and bad attempts at innuendo.

Plus, she was starving. One look at the dump he'd taken her to, and she knew she could never eat there. The chef in her wouldn't allow it.

To think they drove two hours for this! She'd practically frozen to death in his maroon Cadillac, listening to a CD of the Rat Pack, while Gianni crooned loudly, and off key, to the music.

Normally, she was a fan of the famous group of legendary singers. Having grown up in Hoboken, she couldn't not be a Sinatra fan. Though, to be honest, Dean Martin had always been her favorite.

Still, Elissa was a firm believer that there were just some people you did not try to imitate. Especially not if you were Little Gianni. While he was belting his heart out, he'd been trying to get his right hand on her thigh. She'd asked him politely to stop.

Twice.

Then she'd been forced to try something a little more drastic. Like spilling her hot tea on the offending hand the third time he'd tried it. Finally, he'd removed his hand from her leg. Not making a fourth attempt, which she was grateful for.

Elissa should've taken that behavior as a sign and gotten out of the car. But no. She'd wanted to do Gretchen a solid. So, against her better judgement, she gave the creep another chance.

Idiota, her grandmother's voice echoed in her brain again.

The old woman had loved her. Elissa knew that without a doubt. She'd raised her after her own parents had passed on in a tragic automobile accident when Elissa was just twelve.

Her grandmother was a no-nonsense kind of lady who dished out priceless wisdom with brutally honest insights. It was the same way she dished out huge bowls of pasta with her amazing meatballs and homemade sauce. Not to mention a side order of back-breaking hugs that Elissa still missed.

Nonna cooked like that all the time. She made a huge pot of sauce every weekend, and she was happy to serve it to Elissa and her teammates and friends, especially after games and tournaments.

Soccer had been her sport of choice, and cooking had soon become her favorite hobby. Her grandmother had encouraged her in both pursuits. Guiding her in one and cheering her on in the other. Elissa still missed her terribly.

"Hey babe, ain't you gonna eat nothin'? You know they charge twenty dollars just to sit down," Little Gianni interrupted her train of thought.

Elissa was forced to turn her mind back to the present, which unfortunately included watching, *and hearing,* him as he sucked on his teeth and stuffed another breaded shrimp down his throat.

"I'm fine," she answered with a polite smile plastered on her face.

Just get home, Lissa. Just get him to take you home.

Elissa closed her eyes when he looked back down at his dish. Thank God for small favors, she mused. At least he was more interested in eating at the moment.

He'd taken her to the rattiest looking hotel and casino she'd ever seen in her life. And the buffet room?

Ew.

Seriously, the place had to be violating at least a dozen health codes. When Gianni had said Atlantic City, she'd thought at least the atmosphere would be exciting. But they were so far from the real glitz and entertainment, they might as well be anywhere else.

She sighed, looking at the plate she'd made for herself. Elissa couldn't even fake an interest in the food. As a chef, it was hard enough to dine out.

She was always judging the food, the service, the ingredients. How could she not? It was her business. And that was when the food was good!

This was not good. Not at all.

She'd been to hospitals that served better food. Old yellow lights buzzed and blinked around the buffet, giving it an abandoned kind of feel. The menu was made up of mostly frozen then fried or baked cuisine.

Reheated actually. It was like a giant TV dinner buffet where every item was previously frozen when already cooked and warmed up in an oven.

It was the kind of food sold cheap at restaurant supply stores in bulk. Yeah, this was much worse than hospital food, in her opinion.

There was a worn carpet on the floor, a handful of scattered tables in the dining room, elevator music on in the background, and the entire place smelled like canned soup.

Not to mention not one of the five people there besides them was under sixty years old.

"Gianni," she said, leaning forward so as not to hurt his feelings.

"I thought you mentioned something about seeing a show tonight. Is it here?"

Please don't be here.

If he was taking her somewhere else, she could beg off and hire a cab to take her home. There was no way she was sitting through anything else with this man. Not now. Not ever.

"Ah, I see, babe, you want some entertainment first, I get it," he snickered loudly, and she blanched.

Whatever he thought was going to happen wasn't. She needed to disabuse him of the notion, and fast.

"Alright, alright. Lemme finish this, babe. Then we'll go up to the room I got for us," he said.

Before she could make sense of the ludicrous statement, he slurped another fried shrimp, don't ask how. Then he grabbed her arm and yanked her from the seat before she could even react.

Elissa tugged on his hold, but the man was immovable. Tossing a five-dollar bill on the table, Little Gianni snatched a toothpick from the hostess stand before dragging her outside.

Great, he was a cheap tipper, too.

All she wanted was to go home. Figuring the best way to do that would probably be to get him to the car, she let him lead the way.

Once inside, she would ask him to drive back to Hoboken so she could wring Gretchen's neck. Fuming, she pulled her arm out of his hand and walked behind him.

The rain was really pouring, and the cheap bastard had refused valet. Elissa ducked her head so she wouldn't get so wet. Of course, the jacket she'd brought was light and had no hood.

Gianni had an umbrella, but he didn't offer to hold it for her, and honestly, she did not relish the idea of getting any closer to him than necessary.

Seriously, not happening.

Now all she had to do was break the news. She had no intention of watching a show or returning to the hotel with him.

What could go wrong?

GRAB PURRFECTLY MATED TODAY.

EXCERPT FROM WOLF SHIELD

"Why are we traipsing through the fucking swamp to meet your so-called contact, Fur?" Hudson Stormwolfe, or Storm as he was known, growled at his friend and fellow Guardian, "a goddamn coffee shop wouldn't do?"

The Horse Shifter snorted as Storm stepped in a hole cursing quietly as a trickle of slimy sludge slipped inside his once clean steel tocd boots.

"Oh, you are going to scrape these clean," he shot at Furio.

"Dude, just watch your step," Furio retorted making a show of how easily his long legs ate up the muddy landscape.

Fuck him, snarled Storm's Wolf. Trudging through the muck was not his animal's idea of a good time. Give him a dense, clean forest any day. Storm only agreed to accompany Furio because Kingston told him to go.

Their leader could be a hard ass at times, but no one fucked with the Dragon Shifter just lately. Not because they were afraid, but for other reasons. Losing one's mate could really fuck a guy up inside. Besides, Storm had liked Neela, may she rest in peace for eternity.

Damn the Loyalists. Those bastards were nothing more than terrorists and fanatics attacking supernatural creatures and hoarding magic for their own nefarious purposes. They wanted to control and siphon out the one thing every supernatural needed to live with their leaders as the gatekeepers. That thing was of course magic itself.

Loyalists believed that common folk had no business accessing magic. They wanted to keep it for the elite, the wealthy, and basically anyone who did what they said. They were nothing more than pirates and madmen as far as Storm was concerned.

They had been around for nearly as long as the Guardians of Chaos. Storm was proud to call himself a Guardian. He was more than able and willing to do his part to ensure freedom for all supernatural-kind.

Even after all this time, those bastards still failed to gain the momentum necessary to achieve their goals. Their terroristic acts were the stuff of nightmares. Especially this latest attack on the Guardians' leader. The heinous crime was without precedent.

It still left a bad taste in Storm's mouth. He gritted his teeth as his mind still tried to take in the fact she was gone. Neela Baldric, the beloved mate of their once fearless leader, was brutally attacked while on her way to the supermarket.

The gentlewoman was a rare and precious creature and was mated to his superior, Kingston Baldric, for many years. She'd only just succumbed to her wounds a few months ago, leaving all of them bereft of her company, but none so much as Kingston.

"We all miss her, bro," Furio said, and Storm realized he'd been projecting.

Fuck. He hated it when he did that. Though truthfully, it wouldn't have mattered. Furio felt her loss as well. Everyone in Kingston's group of Guardians felt the loss keenly.

These kinds of terroristic acts were the new tool the Loyalists used to persuade mainstream paranormal society to their way of thinking. Blackmail, bribery, murder, mayhem, all elements of destruction that this so-called law-abiding organization stooped to in order to fulfill their aims.

Not on his watch, Storm vowed to himself. It was his job and that of all the Guardians to stop those bastards and ensure freedom for their kind.

"Sorry," Storm muttered, "still, we had to meet in a fucking swamp, Furio?"

"What swamp, bro? We're in Secaucus," Furio opened his arms wide and gestured to the thick, musty smelling wetland they were currently stalking through.

It was just a little past ten o'clock at night, but summer in the Garden State meant hot and sticky. Especially in that small portion of undeveloped marshlands. Storm growled when his foot sank yet again, ankle-deep, into another muddy hole.

Goddamn it, he grimaced, and slapped his friend in the back of the head. Then he counted to three like he'd been told to do by another of their own, Egros, a male Witch who thought the Wolf Shifter would have better control if he could simply manage his anger.

Yeah. Right. The hell with counting. He was going to kick Furio's ass when they were done here.

"Half the fucking state is a swamp," Storm

growled, shaking the muck off his foot, "I thought you were born here?"

"I was. Born and bred in Hoboken, *cumpy.*"

"What?"

"Nothin' man, just some local slang from when I was a kid. Anyway, you're shittin' me right, New Jersey isn't a swamp," snorted the Stallion Shifter.

Storm rolled his eyes and blew out a breath. What was he going to do with this guy? Thirty years as a Guardian, and Furio was still a rookie to Storm, who'd spoke his vows over a hundred years ago this past April.

As a Wolf Shifter, he had a longer than average life expectancy, which had only increased when he'd pledged his allegiance to serve all the supernatural creatures living on this planet as a Guardian. He'd fought too many battles to count, but the work was meaningful. Protecting freedom always was.

It had been the same for his grandfather, who'd raised him just outside the boundaries of the Pack where his father still ruled as Alpha. His older brother was the heir which usually meant younger brothers were ousted or had to challenge for positions in the Pack. Rather than stay and fight for his dominance in the place of his birth, he'd left.

Storm respected tradition, but he had had a

higher calling to serve. The Guardians of Chaos were an elite order of supernaturals. The higher ups did not want it said they were showing favoritism to any specific Pack, Clan, Coven or what have you, so they composed each unit of a mix of *supes*. It took years to build the kind of team Storm was a part of.

Furio might be considered new, but he was still one of them. So fine, maybe Storm wouldn't kick his ass outright, but he could best him in training. That would satisfy both his Wolf and human sides.

"Did you hear Kingston has a meeting with the Assembly next week to discuss Neela's passing?" Furio spoke in a low voice, but with his supernaturally enhanced senses, Storm heard him just fine.

"I did. The Assembly, are all former Guardians, they will understand Kingston's loss and will likely support his call to mount a hunt for the Loyalist who'd ordered the hit," Storm responded.

"We're not Enforcers, Storm. Their job is to police the paranormal peoples of the earth, not ours. Guardians of Chaos don't promote actual chaos, right?" asked Furio, and he was right to a point.

"Look, we are called Guardians of Chaos, because from chaos, aka freedom, comes creativity. If we lose that, we perish. A Guardian is the ultimate protector of free thought, and therefore, the champion of creation itself. Neela was a cherished female and Kingston's to protect and to avenge. We might not understand what it is like to be mated, Furio, but he has rights and this did happen because of our war," Storm responded.

"All for magic? Neela was killed so the Loyalists could control magic? How would that even happen?"

"No, she was killed to break us. Without our leader, the Loyalists hope to win whatever scheme they are hatching and believe me, they are always plotting something. Whoever controls magic, controls us all," he grunted.

The way Storm understood it, magic was a finite thing, like ore, it was distributed organically, used, and recycled by each supernatural group as needed. The ancient ones, gods, goddesses, or what have you created magic out of chaos for each paranormal species to grow and take shape.

"What would they do, if they had it all?" Furio asked.

"What's with all the fucking questions?" growled Storm.

It was not for any one of them to control the others' usage of this gift. It went against their very nature as magical creatures.

Storm understood this. It was why he'd never

looked back after leaving the Black Moon Pack to follow in his grandfather's footsteps. With his father still ruling and his brother as heir, his life there would have been difficult to say the least.

He was too dominant. More so than his old man, yet the tradition dictated that the second son could not be Alpha.

Leaving was his only option, and his grandfather had ensured that he had all the knowledge he needed before his time came. Storm had joined the crusade against those who sought to rule over the entire supernatural world before he was old enough to vote. He knew his duty was no longer to Pack, but to his band of Guardians.

Which was why he was wading through the last thick patch of swampland left undeveloped in Secaucus, New Jersey, home of the best outlet shopping this side of the Hudson River for which he was named, at the behest of one of his own.

Fucking Furio.

"Sorry, *cump,* talking helps pass the time. Anyway, my CI prefers to be away from prying eyes, you know he's part Goblin, and more than a little skittish."

"Yeah, well, what news does he have, anyway?"

"He thinks he found the Loyalists' new headquarters. It was too good a tip to pass up. He's supposed to have the GPS coordinates for me tonight."

"Shit. That is important. But he couldn't have texted them?"

"Nah," Furio shook his head, causing his long hair, which was bound in a leather thong to sway side to side, mimicking that of his shifted form.

He stopped to touch one of the long overgrown cattails they'd passed, and Storm stilled in his tracks, wondering if he heard something. Like a woman breathing or humming or something. But how could that be? They were in the middle of nowhere. Furio dropped the cattail and turned toward the soft, and admittedly pleasant, vocals.

"Hey, you hear that?" Furio asked.

Storm raised his hand to quiet the other man. His Wolf was at full attention. A warm breeze blew in their direction, and he breathed it in deep siphoning through the various layers, hoping to identify whatever made that sound.

Along with the heavy scent of the dense and decaying vegetation, came another, lighter, much more pleasant fragrance. It sifted through Storm's highly acute olfactory system, teasing and tempting his senses. Whatever it was, Storm wanted more.

His Wolf's ears worked to zero in on the source

of both the sounds and the tantalizing fragrance that seemed too soft, too fine for the misty marshlands of Secaucus, New Jersey.

"It's like brown sugar and marzipan," he murmured as the sweet fragrance danced across his senses, like something out of a dream.

"What?" laughed Furio, but he ignored the Stallion.

He knew better than to go traipsing off after a phantom scent, but there was something about it. Something all too tempting and familiar. Storm's Wolf perked up. He growled low and deep as he took in another breath.

That scent, that crazy good scent, was like a shock to the system, but not necessarily unpleasant. More like an awakening. Storm noticed the Stallion Shifter walking through the thicket towards that divine fragrance, and the Wolf inside of him snarled.

"What the fuck, *cump*?" Furio asked.

Storm shook his head. What the fuck was wrong with him? Furio was his friend and fellow Guardian.

It didn't matter. It upset the Wolf. Storm shook his head and tried to silence the beast, but his animal was insistent. He needed to beat his friend to the source of that heavenly scent.

"Shit," he growled.

He hurried past the Stallion, using his superior height to gain the advantage, despite Furio's better speed. The Stallion couldn't beat him there. Storm would not allow it. He leapt over fallen trees and shrubs, avoiding the holes that had gotten him twice already in the deceptively soft, wet earth, until he reached the edge of what seemed to be a parking lot.

The heavy breathing coming from behind him told the Wolf that Furio had managed to keep pace, but the Stallion needed to hit the gym more if he was out of breath. It was shameful for a Guardian to be so easily exhausted. Then again, when had he ever beaten the Horse Shifter in a race?

"Damn, Storm, I never saw you run so fast," he huffed and Storm blinked in surprise, "shit, if I'd have known this lot was so close, I wouldn't have made us park behind the stadium and walk," the Stallion sucked in air greedily.

"Shhh," Storm held up his hand for silence.

His Wolf's enhanced vision allowed him to make out the details of the scene before him. They were just outside the fenced in parking lot of some kind of building. There was a municipal sign hanging up not too far away.

It was late at night, so it wasn't the courthouse, and there were no cop cars parked outside, so it wasn't a police station either. He looked around for any other indication of what the older cement building was. Ah, another dented sign.

"It's a library," Furio whispered.

"I see that," Storm growled.

He was angry and on edge, and he had no fucking idea why. His entire body vibrated with energy. He was not nervous, just impatient, he realized. That was odd, too.

What could he possibly be waiting for here? His Wolf dripped saliva from his fangs as he waited in that metaphysical plane where he rested until Storm called to him. He tried to consider what led him there, but all coherent thought fled his brain the second *she* came into view.

The strange woman was all the way on the other end of the tiny parking lot. A tall security fence and a good fifty feet of black asphalt stood between the female and the place where the two Guardians lurked, but Storm could still make out every detail of the stunning creature.

"She's a little round, but I always did like a girl with some cushion for the pushin'," Furio elbowed him jokingly, but his words enraged Storm.

The Wolf inside of him snarled and growled and before he could stop himself, he had Furio by the collar of his shirt. He'd lifted the Stallion a good foot off the ground before shock had him dropping his friend.

"The fuck?" Furio choked and rubbed his bruised neck.

Storm ignored him, eyes glued to the woman in the ankle-length skirt and short-sleeved blouse. She wore shiny red shoes with high spindle-like heels. *Stilettos*, he thought, and for the first time he understood why they were called that.

They might not be good for running, but the long, skinny heels could pierce a man's heart just like the stealthy blade someone named them after. As it was, he more than appreciated the way the shiny red heels lengthened her legs and caused her hips to sway seductively in the yellowish glow of the streetlights.

Her hair was pulled back in a loose bun. She'd obviously tried to tame her fiery red locks, but curls still fell around her lovely face. Storm observed the subtle highlights and lowlights in her hair color even in the diminished light, noting with pleasure her eyelashes held the same coppery tinge.

So, she was a natural redhead. Good. He did not like artificial things. Unlike most redheads who leaned towards fair-skinned, this beautiful woman had a healthy bronze glow to her. Her whiskey brown eyes were large and bright in the darkness.

He appreciated her plump pink lips, straight nose, and stubborn little chin. She was a knockout. The most gorgeous creature he'd ever laid eyes on.

Storm was thunderstruck. He watched her innocently sashay across the otherwise deserted parking lot to a beat up looking pick-up truck.

Hmm. Odd car choice, he thought.

That was all he had time to think as three men crept out of the shadows and circled the tiny female. Blood rushed through his being and he couldn't make out what was being said.

Whatever it was, didn't matter. One of them dared grab her arm and tossed her purse aside. Storm's fangs lengthened and claws popped free of his nails. The sound of her scream woke something furious inside of him. His entire body trembled with the strength of his fury. He needed to get to her. Now. There was no time to lose.

"Uh, what is that?" Furio tapped his shoulder and Storm turned and snarled.

His friend pointed down. Storm looked and took a step back in surprise. His palms were glowing. Small blue lights were circling both hands. His feet and legs were covered in what looked like shadowy black smoke billowing skywards. It was magic. He knew that much. It didn't hurt, but he'd never felt it before.

"Holy shit, Storm! Do you know what this means?"

Then it hit him. The reason for all the sudden changes. He turned to Furio and growled one word.

"Mine."

His female shrieked and hit the ground, and the Wolf inside him howled in fury.

Protect, the Wolf demanded.

He barely blinked his eyes, then he was directly in front of the female. It was like he'd moved through time and space. Storm appeared in front of her, shielding her from the soon-to-be-dead men who dared touch what was his.

He lifted his lip and snarled at the three assholes. It was nothing more than legend, he'd always thought. A fairy tale to keep younger *supes* from leaving the order. But he might have to change his mind.

He lifted his fists, still glowing with blue magic, and slammed it into the face of the first one of the three to launch an attack against him. Sparks flew, as did the assailant's teeth.

"What are you waiting for," Storm said to the other two.

He smiled wickedly. Looked like even Shifter fairy tales were true sometimes. It was rumored that the Guardians were blessed by the Fates that upon finding their true mates they would receive certain magical benefits to promote honoring their vows till death.

Stronger together, those were the words etched inside the doorway of the Keep. Now Storm finally understood their meaning.

"Mine," he looked down into startled butter-scotch eyes.

He knew without doubt; the woman was his mate, and he would shield her from harm.

Always.

GRAB WOLF SHIELD TODAY.

EXCERPT FROM BEARING GIFTS

"Thanks for coming tonight, Charity," Abigail Jensen, a nurse who worked at the Barvale Senior Center spoke softly as Charity hung her coat and hat on the rack near the desk.

It was already snowing, and she only had a few minutes, but Abigail never called her if it wasn't an emergency. Charity just had a way with people, and she enjoyed spending her time helping put others at ease if she could. True, she had about fifteen minutes before she needed to leave on time, otherwise she would be late for her shift, and tonight was important.

"No worries. You know I enjoy spending time with the residents, Abigail."

"I know, but normally you come on the weekends. Mr. K is a special case, and we have tried everything to make him feel at ease. His wife had to have emergency hip replacement surgery, and he is only here while she recovers, but he's been despondent without her."

"Wow, he must really love her," Charity whispered. She shuffled the box that held a single bear claw inside and followed Abby down the hall. Seated in a wheelchair in the middle of his room was an elderly man with white hair and a beard. He had a hand-knitted red scarf draped around his neck, and his hands were clasped together.

"Good evening, Mr. K. I brought you a visitor," Abigail announced, and Charity walked in.

"Hello, I'm Charity—"

"I don't need any charity, I need my Elaine," he muttered grumpily.

"I understand. If I had a wife or husband, I would miss her too, but the center isn't all bad, you know. I usually come by on weekends and bring treats like this and crafts or movies. Sometimes, we play card games and once we had a talent show."

"A talent show? And what can you do, my dear?" he asked, engaging already, and Charity smiled at the win.

"Well, Mr. K, not to brag, but I am a terrible dancer, and I can't carry a tune," she confided.

"I will leave you two to it," Abigail said and turned to leave.

For the next fifteen minutes, Charity chatted with the exceedingly kind Mr. K, answering questions, and getting the older gentleman to open up about his wife. Her recovery was slow going, but he talked to her every single day. That kind of devotion was really touching, and Charity's heart swelled hoping someday, she would have that kind of love for herself.

"So, do you still believe in Santa?" he asked.

"Oh, I don't know. When I was little, I used to stay up and wait to hear him, but I never did. I think that would be amazing—"

"Even now that you are a grownup? I am surprised."

"Why? Adults need magic too," she told him.

"That is true, my dear. This was so lovely, Charity. Thank you for visiting me," Mr. K said, taking her hand as she stood to leave.

"It was my pleasure."

"You know, Christmas is in just a few days. I hope you sent your letter to Santa already," he whispered conspiratorially, and she laughed.

"I sure did," she replied, and kissed his weathered cheek.

"Oh, how nice! I am going to tell my Elaine she must get well faster, a younger woman has her sights on me," he teased.

"You do that, and I bet she will be better in no time. You are quite the catch, Mr. K!" Charity chuckled.

"Seriously, my child, I want to thank you, very much so. I do not know many young women who would stop by to chat with a grumpy old stranger."

"You're not grumpy, Mr. K, just sad, and it is understandable. I bet you're worried something awful about your wife, and I want you to know I will be praying for her speedy recovery. I am sorry to cut our talk short, though, but I have to go."

"I see. Hot date?" he asked.

"Ha! No, I have to go to work."

"And after, is that when you will meet your boyfriend?"

"Actually, I am single—"

"I can see from the look in your eyes that is not exactly a choice, is it, Charity?"

"Well, I have a crush on someone, and tonight I am going to tell him. I'm kinda nervous," she confessed.

"My dear, if he has even one brain cell still functioning in his head, he will scoop you up and run away with you. I know quality when I see it, and you have it, child. Yes, indeed," he said and patted her hand. "You be a good girl now."

"Yes, sir. Thank you, Mr. K. I hope I will get to see you before your stay is over. Merry Christmas," she said, and waved goodbye as she raced to her car.

She did not hear the elderly man whisper his reply softly as he watched her go with sparkling blue eyes, "I'll be watching you, Charity Smith."

He knows if you've been bad or good...

GRAB YOUR COPY OF BEARING GIFTS TODAY.

ABOUT THE AUTHOR

C.D. Gorri is a USA Today Bestselling author of steamy paranormal romance and urban fantasy. She is the creator of the Grazi Kelly Universe.

Join her mailing list here: https://www.cdgorri.com/newsletter

An avid reader with a profound love for books and literature, when she is not writing or taking care of her family, she can usually be found with a book or tablet in hand. C.D. lives in her home state of New Jersey where many of her characters or stories are based. Her tales are fast paced yet detailed with satisfying conclusions.

If you enjoy powerful heroines and loyal heroes who face relatable problems in supernatural settings, journey into the Grazi Kelly Universe today. You will find sassy, curvy heroines and sexy, love-driven heroes who find their HEAs between the pages. Werewolves, Bears, Dragons, Tigers, Witches, Romani, Lynxes, Foxes, Thunderbirds, Vampires, and many more Shifters and supernatural creatures dwell within her worlds. The most important thing is every mate in this universe is fated, loyal, and true lovers always get their happily ever afters.

Want to know how it all began? Enter the Grazi Kelly Universe with Wolf Moon: A Grazi Kelly Novel or pick up Charley's Christmas Wolf and dive into the Macconwood Pack Novel Series today.

For a complete list of C.D. Gorri's books visit her website here:

https://www.cdgorri.com/complete-book-list/

Thank you and happy reading!

del mare alla stella,
   C.D. Gorri

Follow C.D. Gorri here:
   http://www.cdgorri.com
   https://lwww.facebook.com/Cdgorribooks

https://www.bookbub.com/authors/c-d-gorri
https://twitter.com/cgor22
https://instagram.com/cdgorri/
https://www.goodreads.com/cdgorri
https://www.tiktok.com/@cdgorriauthor